Praise for Anitra Lynn McLeod's
The Fringe series

"A most excellent read...Ms. McLeod did not disappoint. I literally couldn't put this book down, and when I did I had to go right back to it."
~ *Wicked Readings by Tawania*

"An exciting space adventure! If you are a PNR reader that likes futuristic, I totally recommend this book. Top Bite Award for Futuristic Romance 2010."
~ *Bitten by Paranormal Romance*

"A fun space-western futuristic romance...Good pacing and tight action speeds the story along with a believable plot and several adversaries...If you strap yourself in, you'll be in for a fun ride with plenty of action and laughs along the way. NOMINEE: BEST ROMANTIC SCIENCE FICTION/FANTASY IN 2010."
~ *The Romance Reviews*

"An entertaining space-western with a super-seductive hero and a tough, no holds barred heroine, who will alternately make you laugh and then tug at your heart-strings...The story shines with its fast pace, many surprises and tight action scenes."
~ *TwoLips Reviews*

"An interesting futuristic romance that twists considerably the traditional gender roles."
~ *Mrs. Giggles*

Look for these titles by
Anitra Lynn McLeod

Now Available:

Far Too Human

The Fringe
Thief
Overlord

Onic Emprire
Wicked Empress
Dark Empress

Thief

The Fringe, Book One

Anitra Lynn McLeod

SAMHAIN
PUBLISHING

Samhain Publishing, Ltd.
11821 Mason Montgomery Road, 4B
Cincinnati, OH 45249
www.samhainpublishing.com

Thief

Print ISBN: 978-1-60928-295-0
Digital ISBN: 978-1-60928-238-7

Editing by Linda Ingmanson
Cover by Kanaxa

This book is a work of fiction. The names, characters, places, and incidents are products of the writer's imagination or have been used fictitiously and are not to be construed as real. Any resemblance to persons, living or dead, actual events, locale or organizations is entirely coincidental.

First Samhain Publishing, Ltd. electronic publication: November 2010
First Samhain Publishing, Ltd. print publication: October 2011

Dedication

This one is for Marina, the best chef I know, and all the foodies in the world. Even the worst day can be made better by a good meal. ☺ Also, for Linda. Sometimes the greatest gift a writer can ever receive is finding someone who believes. Thank you.

Chapter One

"Life is a dance with daggers drawn."

Deep space, Majestic Quadrant, 2476

Everything felt wrong the instant Captain Jace Lawless boarded the derelict ship. His gut told him to skedaddle, but his empty wallet forced him to stick around.

"Ain't right." Garrett gripped his gun with one hand as his flashlight pierced the dark, abandoned shuttle bay. "An intact Basic, just sitting here, waiting for us? Smells worse than that crap we had for dinner, Captain."

Leave it to Garrett, his second-in-command, to translate his churning gut into words. "On account of our meager bank account, we'd best continue. Right?"

"Right," Garrett agreed with a reluctant sigh.

Heller fingered every weapon strapped to his massive frame and darted his suspicious gaze around. "Berserkers?"

"Don't look like," Jace reassured. "The wall coms are still in place." He pointed out the audio and visual communication panels. "Those vicious pirates would have stripped the ship."

Jace kept his gun drawn nonetheless. His flashlight bobbed as he led his crew from the inky shuttle bay to the upper hall.

"Berserkers would have left the bodies too," Garrett said.

Having thought of that himself, Jace said, "Since we're all on the same page, Garrett, shut up." Jace crept down the hallway. "We get in, get the goods, and get out."

"Simple," Garrett said, following behind.

"Yeah, right," Heller grunted, bringing up the rear. "We ain't ever done a damn thing that's simple."

"Like your mouth? Give it a rest." With silent steps, Jace led his crew through oppressive gloom. The ship thrummed with life-support, but not life itself. Room by room, Jace found a disconcertingly normal ship.

"It's like our ship, *Mutiny*," Heller said.

"If we vanished off it all of the sudden."

"Garrett," Jace said sharply. "Shut up. This is—"

"Creepy." Heller toed an open-faced, battered paperback abandoned beside a rumpled bunk. His flashlight swept the darkened crew quarters. "No bodies."

"So far," Garrett pointed out, scooping up the paperback. "Oo, a western." He slipped it to his waistband.

Agitated enough without Garrett's alternately sinister and sardonic comments, Jace glared at him with all the loathing he could muster.

"Ponder the weirdness wonder of it all," Garrett said defensively. "Not one sign of a struggle. No bodies. On a ship that has power, air and, supposedly, an intact, treasure-rich hull. I don't know about you, but I'm getting a strong whiff of way-too-good-to-be-true."

Jace gripped his gun, cast his flashlight forward and continued. He swallowed hard. Woefully gaunt, his light hardly pierced the looming black. He smelled sweat, not old and stale, but fresh. A familiar lingering scent of recently prepared freeze-dried food made the short hairs on his neck stiffen. What the hell had happened on this ship?

As they cleared each room, Jace locked it down. The crashing of metal on metal reverberated through the ship like Thor's mythical hammer.

"I could do without that." Garrett gulped. "One more jolt, Captain, and my old heart will shoot from my chest." He ducked behind Heller. "This is getting nothing but more peculiar."

"Freak-show," Heller agreed. "Where's the fucking crew?"

"Don't swear," Jace reminded.

Heller rolled his eyes, but shut his mouth.

"Shuttles are gone. They had to be in them, right?" Garrett asked hopefully.

"Right," Jace said, as if by agreeing he could make it true.

"Or at least two of them to pilot the shuttles." Garrett considered. "That'd leave about thirty on board, Captain."

"There's nobody here." Jace turned, exasperated. "Bailey's been tapped into the com for twenty minutes. He didn't hear a peep. Thirty people can't be that quiet for that long."

"Yeah." Heller snorted. "If they had what we had for dinner, one of 'em would've farted by now."

Garrett chuckled. "Keep your bodily comments about supper to yourself. Especially since I'm behind you."

"Would you two give it a rest?" Short hairs bristled on his neck while his crew made fart jokes. Nerves stretched tight as barbed wire, Jace feared he might spin and shoot if one of them actually blasted gas. Forcing down a tense laugh, he took a calming breath and then focused on leading his crew safely through this job. Bizarre or not, they needed the haul to survive.

"Okay," Garrett whispered. "It's empty. Want to take a grasp at *why* these folks left a perfectly intact ship?"

"Who the hell knows?" Heller asked. "If the cache is intact, who the hell cares?"

Both Heller and Garrett offered excellent points, but steadfast and true, Jace calmly said, "There's nothing around but that IWOG mothership. And that's an hour off at best. If we go slow and careful, we got ourselves a cakewalk." He doubted the fascist freaks of the InnerWorld Government would bother with a derelict Basic ship, no matter what its cargo. But he couldn't be sure.

Step by wary step, he led his crew to the room atop the curved belly of the ship. At the far end of the rounded, U-shaped room, he saw the huge circular cover in the floor that secured the cache. "Looks intact."

"Simple," Garrett said.

"Again, we ain't ever done a damn thing—"

"There's a first time for everything." Jace scanned the room. The only way in was from the dark hallway they all hesitated in.

"Give you a thousand to one this isn't it." Garrett peeked around Heller's bulk and stepped forward cautiously.

Irritated as much by Garrett's lack of confidence as he was by his comments, Jace turned a blistering glare on him.

Garrett retreated. "Hell, Jace, I'm a betting man, but I wouldn't bet on this being the first easy job." Garrett shrugged his narrow shoulders. "It's just too damn strange." Goggle-eyed, Garrett assessed the room. "Ponder the weirdness wonder of *why* this is the only room on this whole ship that's fully lit?"

"Good point," Jace said. "Heller, train your gun and flashlight back down the hall while I unpack this."

After due consideration, Jace said, "If it looks too good to be true," he looked into the empty, fully illuminated room, "it is." At the far end was the only way into the hold. "We locked the ship down on the way in. Right?"

"Right," Garrett said conversationally.

Trying to convince himself and Garrett, Jace said, "If anyone were around, the crashing doors would have called them out. Right?"

Garrett didn't answer. He hung close to Heller's bulk.

"If anyone is waiting around to jump us, they're gonna have to come through this hallway. Right?" Jace didn't wait for an answer. "Heller, you cover the hallway from here. Garrett, you cross cover from there."

Obeying his orders, they trained their weapons and flashlights on the dark hallway.

Jace holstered his gear then struggled to open the cover on the hold. No matter how much shoulder he threw into it, the damn thing wouldn't budge.

"Thief."

The word rolled from a whisper behind him.

He turned his head. A tall woman dressed head to toe in black dropped a gleaming silver blade to his neck smooth as butter-slicked bread.

"Tell your crew to stand down."

Jace shot a quick glance to Garrett and Heller. With startled eyes, they riveted their guns on the mystery woman.

Looking for a trapdoor in the ceiling, Jace found nothing and wondered if she'd teleported herself behind him. Baffled, he considered pulling his gun. Jace looked right into her fathomless black eyes as he inched his fingers toward his hip.

"You might want to rethink that, Captain Lawless." She pulled her sword back. "Look real close. I'm not holding a supper knife to your pretty neck."

Supper knife? No. She held a good three feet of double-edged razor blade. And how the hell did she know his name? For that matter, how in the blazes had she gotten right behind him without Garrett or Heller seeing her? He'd done everything by the book, took every precaution, and *still* nothing went right.

"No medic in the Void could reattach your head, let alone mine."

Her words startled him. When her gaze left him, he felt advantage until he followed her intense stare.

She looked right at Heller, who held his Gatewin Gusher about a foot from her face. If Heller pulled the trigger, he'd kill her all right—and blow a hole in the side of the ship.

"Your man points a cannon into a fish bowl."

Jace looked up her blade as she looked down the barrel of Heller's gigantic gun. Jace flicked his gaze and saw two slender barrels pointed at Heller and Garrett from the dark hallway.

Stalemate.

Jace uttered a longsuffering sigh. One wrong move and he'd be responsible for killing everyone on the derelict Basic.

"Seems to me, Captain Lawless, we've got a mutual problem with an obvious solution." Her gaze never wavered from Heller's gun. "It would be best, at this moment, if we all kept our heads."

He couldn't unpack how she got right behind him, or how she knew his name, and it didn't really matter at the moment. "Don't recollect ever having my neck called pretty."

The mystery woman smiled—slow and lazy and sexy. With a voice dripping raw honey, she said, "First time for everything, I suppose." Her riveted gaze never wavered from the wide barrel of Heller's gun, nor did her blade waver from Jace's neck.

"Guess so." Jace tried to stand. Before he could get more than a few inches up, she tapped his neck with her blade without even looking at him.

Garrett and Heller flinched.

Jace slapped a hand to his neck. He pulled it away to find her lightning tap drew a thin line of blood.

"You're awful pretty, Captain Lawless." She darted him a quick glance. "I'd hate to muss your hair, let alone your neck."

Her focus jumped back to Heller's gun.

"But hack your head off I will, even if I lose mine." Her whisper voice rolled strong and compelling. "I go down, we all go down. You tell your crew to stand down."

Trapped, Jace said, "Do it."

Garrett and Heller slowly lowered their weapons.

She shook her head. "Not good enough." With a low whisper, she demanded, "Make it official."

Blade to his neck, guns pointed at both Garrett and Heller from the dark hallway, he had no choice. "This is Captain Jace Lawless ordering the crew of *Mutiny* to stand down."

Garrett dropped his gun and thrust up his hands.

Heller clutched his gun, apparently considering the wisdom of following Jace's order. It seemed to take forever, but eventually, Heller realized he'd kill them all if he didn't stand down. Swearing a streak of blue, Heller flung off the many weapons strapped to his gigantic body.

Kneel-bound, Jace looked up into fathomless black eyes. Nothing ever came easy, but why did *everything* have to be so difficult?

"Just once," he mumbled, shaking his head. "Just one damn time things could have gone easy."

His imposing captor stepped close, tilted his face up with the point of her silver blade and considered him.

Leaning close enough to give him an enticing hint of musky perfume, she whispered, "Nothing worth having comes easy."

Chapter Two

"Now that's a rare thing." Kraft used her blade to bring her captive off his knees. When he put his big hands a bit too close to his guns, she said, "Hands up."

With an annoyed sigh, Jace Lawless lifted his hands, palm out, to his wide shoulders. A sudden flash made her picture him in the same posture horizontal. She'd pin his hands to her bed and rock like a wild woman possessed—

"What's a rare thing, Captain Kraft?" Tan kept her gun trained on Garrett while Bavin tied him up.

Pulled away from her wicked thoughts, Kraft pondered her captive. "I found a smart man."

Captain Jace Lawless struck her as nothing short of a fancy wrapped gift—not just his perfect face, but the whole of him. Tall, with curly handfuls of black hair and soft green eyes, he wore a battered green shirt, unbuttoned one button from the top. His trousers were a simple cut of raw flax, his hips crossed by a worn leather double-holster, slung low. His wide feet were clad with dusty, square-toed brown boots.

Jace looked like the quintessential gunslinger from every banned western novel she'd ever read. She wanted to start at the edge of him and rip her way to the center. Ride him hard. Put him away wet. Several times.

Kraft tilted her head curiously. Did Jace think the Wild West was alive and well on the Fringe? He must, dressed like that, with two ancient Sod Busters strapped to his hips.

Kraft noted that Garrett didn't fight at all as the women of her crew secured him. A tall, thin drink of water, Garrett had a deeply lined face, a prominent horse-bite, and he had to be forty-five if a day. He didn't look pleased, but he didn't fight.

The wisdom that came with age, she imagined.

Kraft didn't bother to check how Danna managed Heller. From where she stood, she could hear him grunting and swearing while Danna trussed him up. What a beast of a man. Seven feet tall and a good four feet wide. Heller reminded her of a backwards Minotaur; body of a bull with the head of a man—and the brain of a mushroom. Only an idiot would carry a Gatewin Gusher and threaten to use it in confined quarters. If he'd pulled the trigger, everyone on the derelict Basic would have tasted Void. Including him.

Gaze riveted to her tempting captive, Kraft let her powerful voice become that of every outlaw she'd ever read. Fluent in a multitude of languages, she pitched herself to the Western twang of Universal. "A man like you is most unsettling."

He kept his hands up.

"Lord on high, what a tantalizing man you are, Captain Lawless." His face, sweet and deceptively young, balanced his eyes, which were wise and old. He had a rugged body worn in all the right places... She shook off the distraction.

"Lock it down, Shar."

A booming crash shook the derelict ship like a dog with a chew toy. Jace and his crew jumped as every door and hatch in the whole ship sealed off all at once.

"Open the hold, Shar."

The circular cover twisted. Tan and Bavin rushed forward and pulled it away.

"Clear?" Kraft kept her gaze pinned to Jace.

"Clear," Shar said over the derelict ship's com.

"Time?"

"Forty."

Her captive stood, hands up, shaking his head and glaring at her, mumbling how just once a job could have gone easy. She felt for him. She knew exactly the fit of his boots. His crew, his ship, his life—she could take it all.

And they both knew it.

Chapter Three

"I hate to be so forward, Captain Lawless, but I insist you be bare." Kraft nodded to his hips.

"Of what?" Jace asked. A thousand thoughts ran through his mind of what this woman could do to him. Not all of them wholly unpleasant.

"Weapons. Not clothes." She considered. "Unless you'd like to take them off." She dropped him a saucy wink. "I'm a bit short of time at the moment, but I wouldn't mind a quick dance in your trousers."

Gritting his teeth, he dropped his pistols, a dagger, and put his hands back to level with his shoulders. If she had taken an interest in him, perhaps he could distract her long enough— Kraft dropped her blade tip to his heart.

"You have a chance to live to fight another day, Captain Lawless." Her voice rolled soft and seductive. "Foolish to spoil it now."

Could she read his damn mind? He looked at the blade to his heart, and then up to his captured crew. "Let them go."

Fathomless black eyes pinned him. "You'd give me the hold and yourself in exchange for your crew?"

"If you'd honor such a trade," Jace said.

"They say there is no honor among thieves."

"Is that what they say?"

She considered him, her gaze seeming to delve right into his soul. "Let us suppose there is honor among thieves. What would that make you? Honorable, or a thief?"

"Both?" He shrugged.

Her eyes lit up. "An honorable thief?" She pondered the

idea. "Tell me, Captain Lawless, would your crew hold to your word when you are in mind not to?"

"They stood down," Jace pointed out. "What more do you want?"

"You itch to grab my blade and turn it on me." Her dark eyes stripped him.

"There's an idea," Heller snarled.

Jace wished Heller would shut the hell up for once.

The gigantic armor-clad woman behind Heller gave his bonds a yank, and he yelped like a pup.

"Don't hurt him, Danna. Not yet." Kraft considered Jace with a speculative gaze that disturbed and aroused him all at once. She flipped three feet of black, linen-bound hair over her shoulder with a toss of her head.

"Can't we just kill 'em?" Danna asked.

"Wouldn't be neighborly," Kraft said. "They haven't given us a reason to. Isn't likely they will. I think I found more than a smart man. I think I found an honorable one."

The women of her crew laughed, but Kraft seemed genuinely perplexed. She examined him like one would an exotic pet of dubious origin. As she did, Jace studied her face. High, sharp cheekbones set off a wide, sensuous mouth. No make-up, but her highly creamed, coffee-colored skin didn't need enhancement. He'd never seen such stark, powerful beauty in his life.

Heller struggled against Danna, who edged a blade out of her hip holster. Still looking directly at Jace, Kraft said with soft menace, "Move your blade another inch, Danna, and this time I won't let any doctor reattach what I hack off."

After a momentary consideration of her right arm, Danna shoved the blade back into her hip holster.

"Got eyes in the back of your head?" Jace asked Kraft. How did she know what he was thinking and what her crew was doing?

"Could be." Kraft nodded. "Or maybe I just know my crew."

"Maybe her crew would be happier on our side," Heller said.

"Fetch!" Danna tightened the rope around Heller's hands a notch, and when he grunted she smiled, obviously enjoying her work, maybe a little too much.

"Don't waste your breath," Kraft said to Heller as she kept

her attention on Jace. "Danna hates men. She likes to carve them up like pumpkins."

"I take it you don't feel the same." Jace delved into the blackest eyes he'd ever seen. Huge and dark, but wide and open, staring into her eyes was like looking into the Void and discovering light.

"I got all manner of use for a man like you." She appraised him as if he were expensive goods she could well afford. "Don't think you'd be too terribly unwilling." Her husky voice enticed and mocked all at once.

"Really," Jace said with terse regard. "You might be surprised. I don't much fancy a woman with bigger balls than mine."

Garrett gasped.

Heller barked laughter.

Kraft's eyebrow drew up.

"If you're taking notes, sugar-britches, I tend to like my women a touch less deadly as well."

To his astonishment, Kraft uttered a rolling chuckle that enveloped his whole body. "You surprise me more and more, Captain Lawless."

Over the com, a female voice said, "We're locked, Captain Kraft, but his crew can hear us."

"Good," Kraft said. "I hope they're having as much fun as I am. Time?"

"Clear for thirty. Time enough to dance, Captain Kraft."

Jace didn't want to unpack that. What could dancing with Kraft mean?

"Well, isn't this cozy." Jace leaned against the wall, his hands still up. If Kraft literally wanted to dance with him, she'd have to make him do it at blade point.

"Having a good time?" Kraft asked with a bright smile. "I know I am. Too bad I can't offer refreshments and have a proper little sit-down chat, but I'm rather in a hurry."

"Seems to me you're wasting all kinds of time," Danna said from behind her.

Kraft silenced Danna with a glare over her shoulder and turned to Jace.

"How'd you find out about this haul?" Kraft asked. "And before you even think about it, don't lie to me. I'm not in the best mood." Blade tip to his heart, she asked, "Sugar-britches?" She shook her head. "As compelling as you are, Captain Lawless, I'm apt to kill you where you stand."

"Glad you cleared that up," he said, deadpan. "Here I stood thinking you'd come a-courting."

She did it again. She laughed. Not maliciously, but with abandoned delight. Her blade held as steady as her eyes.

"What a package you are. Clever, funny, honorable, and like icing on the cake, you're real pretty too."

Jace thought again of grabbing her blade.

With a raised eyebrow and a light tap that slashed a hole in his shirt without drawing blood, Kraft said, "You're not that pretty." She dropped her smile like a bad habit. "Who sent you here?"

Figuring the truth didn't matter, Jace said, "Feller by the name of Trickster."

Kraft swore in what sounded like German.

"I've got no idea what you're saying, but it sounds awful bad." Jace kept his hands up, wondering what the hell was going on now. This woman changed moods quicker than water went through sand.

She pulled her blade back, and he lowered his hands.

She lifted her blade, and he lifted his hands.

Kraft swore up a streak of German, English, French, Spanish, Japanese and Universal—a cornucopia of international foul words. He understood about half of what she said, but he grasped enough to know how she felt about Trickster. She liked the little weasel about as much as he did. Not much.

"Dammit, Kraft, just do it," Danna said. "We could take the hold, his ship, all of it!"

"I can't." Kraft shook her head.

"Then I'll do it." Danna reached for her dagger.

"No." Kraft lowered her blade and stepped back. "I won't let Trickster set the tune for my dance. Let them go."

"What!" Danna exploded. "We're a heartbeat from scoring—"

"You knew my code when you signed up with me, Danna. I'm not twirling you anywhere you didn't consider going." Kraft kept her voice low and calm, but filled with quiet authority.

"Your stupid code's your own damn problem," Danna argued. "We got nothing. If we don't get this, we're dead in the Void."

"I know," Kraft said. "Likely, so are they."

Behind Kraft's back, a snarl darted across Danna's face, and Jace knew his survival hinged on how well Kraft could control her crew. When Heller opened his mouth to speak, Jace shook his head sharply. Mercifully, Heller closed his mouth.

"Trickster tricked us again," Danna said. "Big surprise! I don't see how it can violate your precious code to take our due."

"If I do this, I lose one of the only two things I have left." Kraft spoke to Danna yet pinned him with hungry eyes.

"Is this about your honor again?" Danna yanked Heller's bonds hard. Heller's face went white with pain, but he didn't utter a peep.

"Stop hurting him, Danna," Kraft said, keeping her gaze pinned to Jace.

"But that's our job!"

"No, it's not. Our job isn't about hurting or killing anyone. Our job is to keep flying. And we can do that. So can they." She nodded to Jace. "There is honor among thieves."

Jace felt a surge of hope that he could get his crew out of this alive.

"Honor, thieves, dancing—half the time I got no idea what you're talking about." Danna loosened her grip on Heller, but Jace could see she had no intention of actually letting him go.

Kraft turned to face Danna head-on. Jace noticed that her linen-bound hair fell to where her fanny met her legs. Clad in faded black dextex, her backside turned out to be just as pleasant to look at as her face.

"Must I dance with *you* again, Danna?" Kraft asked with soft menace.

Even though Danna stood almost as big as Heller, with full body armor and fifty pounds of weapons, she backed off with a snarled, "No."

Danna untied Heller.

Heller immediately attacked Danna.

Kraft sheathed her blade and turned to Jace. "I'll get mine, you get yours."

Jace and Kraft pulled Heller and Danna apart.

"He started it!" Danna kicked at Heller.

"What are you, five? There's no reason for us to fight." Kraft moved Danna back with a glare. "Fair is fair."

"Yeah, and fair is it's ours." Heller lunged at Danna.

"That's enough." Jace placed a hand to Heller's chest. Kraft had him, his back to the proverbial wall, and then let him go. Something about her honor and dancing that he didn't grasp, but thanked his lucky stars for all the same.

After corralling Danna, Kraft turned to him, lifted her hands, palm open and out. "I've got no quarrel with you, Captain Lawless, but Trickster is getting a mite too big for his boots."

In sudden understanding, Jace said, "Trickster sent you along as well." He retrieved his weapons, and Kraft made no move to stop him. The intensity of the moment went from Gunfight at the O.K. Corral to tea with his Aunt Bessie.

"Fetch likes to tweak me. Trickster doesn't take kindly to me being a woman in a man's world." Kraft rolled her eyes. "Boy's got serious issues with his momma, I imagine. He probably figured I'd find the hold empty. Another funny on me. Isn't the first time he's done it. Hell, knowing Trickster? We might *both* find the hold empty."

Before Jace could answer, Danna said, "You let them have this haul, it'll be the last time that fetch tweaks you! You know we don't have the—"

With a glare, Kraft silenced Danna.

Jace wished he had that power over Heller.

Casually, Kraft turned to him. "Way I see it, Captain Lawless, who got here first is up for debate. You want to argue salvage rights until the cold comes?"

"We're all here for the same thing," he diplomatically offered.

"I think so." Kraft nodded. "Me, my crew, we're not looking to kill or rob you and yours. We just want our fair share off this salvage."

"As do we," Jace said.

"Let's take a look-see at what we got then," Kraft said.

"Yeah, and if it's good, you'll be looking—"

"Shut it, Heller." Jace seriously considered getting a muzzle for Heller's big mouth, or a cattle prod. If he couldn't learn

Kraft's stare-down technique, a zap to Heller's crotch might suffice.

Jace followed Kraft to the hole in the floor. Once down the short ladder, she turned on the light, and gasped. So did he.

"I hate to be so bold again, but pinch me." Kraft shook her head. "I think I'm dreaming." She turned and appraised him. "Hell, let me pinch you."

For a moment, he was lost in her eyes. "We hit the mother lode." Cardboard, wooden and metal boxes filled the hold from floor to ceiling and wall to wall.

"Only once—" Kraft grabbed the first cardboard box in front of her then dropped it as if it were full of snakes.

"What's wrong?"

"Nothing." She pulled on a pair of worn black gloves and tossed the box to him.

He chucked the box up, out the hole, to Heller.

"Back on Earth, there was a tale of El Dorado." Kraft tossed him another box. "Man of gold, literally, but too, a mythical city of gold. I don't know about the man, or the city, but I think we found the supply ship."

"Looks like." Jace tossed up another box.

"Trickster had no idea what we would find," Kraft said. "If you got here first, and found nothing, he figured it'd be funny for me to find it empty too."

"Even if I found it intact, Trickster wanted you to find it bare." Jace understood why a misogynistic fetch like Trickster would go out of his way to screw with a powerful woman like Kraft. If not for the problem with *Mutiny's* engine, Jace would have been here three days ago. Kraft would have found an empty hold, and he never would have laid eyes on her.

"That's the general idea." She tossed him another box of freeze-dried food. "If I find a bare hold, too bad. Trickster just covered his deal. If I find the cache, too bad. He knows he can tweak me on the deal." She grimaced. "Either way, the little opportunist likes his advantage."

"Then why do you deal with him?" Jace asked.

Kraft tossed him another box. "Why do you?"

He caught it. "Touché."

To keep flying, a captain of a thief ship *had* to deal with middlemen like Trickster. Jace hated it, but didn't have much of a choice. Captaining a crew of thieves on the Fringe pretty much dictated the bulk of his choices.

Down in the hold, separated from the others, Jace could hear Danna and Heller arguing over how to split the goods.

With an indulgent grin, Kraft asked, "Does it get any better than this?"

Above them, the fighting grew more vocal as Heller and Danna argued over the ammo and weapons.

"Danna is like an unruly child," Kraft said.

"So's he," Jace said of Heller. "An unruly child with a lot of firepower."

After a chuckle, Kraft climbed up the short ladder and popped her head out of the hatch. "Play nice, Danna. Just separate the goods. Portions and merits will be debated later."

When the argument simmered down, she dropped off the ladder and back into the hold. Her thin-soled, worn black boots didn't make a sound. Like a liquid shadow, she turned back to work and tossed him another box.

"Why do you think they amassed all of this?" Jace asked. So far they'd found freeze-dried food, electronics, fabric, guns and ammunition. A major haul easily worth 10K.

Kraft shrugged and kept working.

"Do you think they looked to start a new colony?" he asked.

"No." Kraft removed her gloves. "That first box felt desperate, like they were gearing up for something that wasn't even real." Lifting her hands out to the goods, she made light contact with the tips of her fingers, and then flinched back. "Terror ran this crew."

Jace waited until Heller walked away from the hatch. He touched her bare hand with a cautious finger. "Are you a reader?" Psychic abilities would certainly explain a lot of the questions he had, like how she knew his name, and how she seemed to be able to read his mind.

"After a fashion," she acknowledged, hedging.

"What fashion would that be?" He stroked her hand lightly with his fingertip. Her coffee-cream skin was surprisingly soft and shockingly hot.

She broke the tentative touch by pulling her gloves on and turning back to work. After all her blatant flirting, her retreat from a simple caress surprised him.

"How did you get right behind me without Heller or Garrett seeing you?"

"It's a secret." She winked over her shoulder. "Can't tell you all my super powers, now, can I?"

Without further comment, they stripped the hold and joined the others above. Danna and Heller erupted into a screaming match of epic proportions over the lone Bartlet Blaster.

"Danna, let him have it. You have one," Kraft pointed out.

"This one's better." Danna inspected the weapon critically.

"Fine. Take that one and give Heller your old one," Kraft said.

"I don't wanna," Danna whined.

"The drama of the gifted child," Kraft whispered to Jace.

Raising her voice, Kraft said, "Take the new one, Danna, give Heller your old one, and then we'll split the ammo for it."

"But—"

"Dancing, Danna," Kraft said with a singsong voice. "Don't cut in unless you *really* want to dance."

After darting a glance to Kraft's silver blade, Danna said, "Bavin, go get my Bartlet Blaster."

Bavin trotted off like a faithful puppy. Bavin's clear enchantment with Danna made Jace consider that Kraft, and her whole female crew, might be...lesbians.

Jace cast a speculative gaze to Kraft. She was six-three of dark and deadly Walkyrie with blades and guns strapped to her full, sexy hips. Imposing as hell. Kraft radiated power and authority. Even though he stood a hand taller and outweighed her by fifty pounds, he knew she could take him down without breaking a sweat.

Kraft flashed him that slow, lazy and sexy smile.

Stepping close, she whispered, "Half are, half aren't. I'm in the no pile." As she leaned close, she gave him another taste of her musky perfume and breathed, "I like men."

She ran her gaze over every inch of his body. Jace swore he could damn near feel it, like a good, hard rubdown that touched all his private places with heat. When she finally settled on his eyes, she winked, and he felt certain his decade of celibacy showed in his blushing face.

Lifting her mouth to his ear, she breathed, "I like *you*."

Before Jace could even grasp at a response, Heller screamed.

Chapter Four

"Shit howdy!" Heller yanked open a crate of universal ammo. He fondled the hollow-point bullets with a gleeful, face-splitting leer. He let Danna look, but not touch, and they soon fell to squabbling again.

Kraft wanted to throttle Heller for interrupting her moment with Jace, but realized she didn't have time to linger, not with an IWOG mothership close by.

"I'd still like to know why these folks abandoned ship," Jace said.

When Kraft first touched the ship, the ugly vibrations made her recoil, but her own desire to know overshadowed her reluctant foreboding. Slipping off her gloves, she laid her hands flat against the durosteel hull. She'd read the ship lightly when they docked, just enough to board and secure the vessel. Now she closed her eyes and let her awareness flood deep into the ship.

Emotional residue and disjointed flashes assaulted her in a swarm that threatened to drop her to her knees. A stoic face looming above terrified crew. Bellowed orders and frightened responses. Big eyes and gaped mouths. Hands frantic in work to prepare for destruction. Raw and sharp, the stench of fear and insanity overwhelmed her.

"Captain lost his mind. Apocalypse coming. He ordered all hands to abandon ship, then tossed himself out an airlock." She opened her eyes and looked right at Jace. "Everything hinges on the captain."

Terror crushed her like a vice. The reckoning she'd been running from for eight years felt close. Darkness plunged like sudden blindness. Kraft clasped Jace's hand.

"IWOG mothership approaching," Shar said over the Basic's com. "Please maintain silence on all com channels."

In the dark, she leaned close to Jace. "I hate those bastards."

Almost a decade on the run, and she'd done countless jobs since she'd acquired *Whisper*, but this had to be the most intensely strange of them all. Her terror slipped away when she discovered she liked holding his hand while feeling his body heat in the dark. Too soon, the lights came back on, and she pulled away when she really wanted to press him to the wall and kiss him until neither of them could think straight.

"We're clear, Captain Kraft," Shar said.

"Did they alter course?"

"No, Captain Kraft."

Relief surged. Her time would come, but not today.

"I think there's more than enough for both our crews." Jace nodded to the piles of goods that filled the room.

"Jace! It's ours!" Heller bellowed.

"Technically, the cache is hers," Jace said.

"How do you figure that?" Heller argued.

"Bailey isn't blind. Her ship had to be here all along."

"Intelligent, handsome, honorable and fair?" Kraft poked him with a thrust-out finger, impressed that he figured out she'd docked her ship to the Basic, making her ship look a part of it.

Jace gave her jabbing finger a curious brow.

"Just making sure you're for real," she said, trying to think of other ways to touch him. Any excuse would do.

"That's debatable." Heller kicked a box of ammo and winced.

Jace glared at him, then turned to Kraft. "You've been fair with us. More than. I think we've got a situation with an obvious solution."

"Being honorable thieves." She smiled.

"Such a deal is like to tweak Trickster's nose."

Her smile widened. "It is at that."

"Half?" Jace offered his hand.

Heller and Danna erupted, "It's ours!" then glared at one another.

Kraft clasped Jace's hand and said, "Deal."

As they divvied up the goods, Danna and Heller couldn't stop sneering or lunging at each other.

Jace asked, "How long?"

Kraft tilted her head to the side. "How long is my ship?"

"No." Jace laughed. "How long have you been in the Void?"

Kraft shot him a grin. "Whole of my life." She thought for a moment. "Been flying *Whisper* about five years. You?"

"Never flown your ship." Jace gave her the same cock of the head with a grin. "Been flying *Mutiny* about seven, though."

She laughed. Her gaze drifted to her crew. Her smile faded and her voice dropped. "Gets harder every day, doesn't it?"

His gaze followed hers. He watched their crews move the cache into their respective ships. "I don't know what you mean."

Kraft leaned close, looked right into his eyes, pinned him with both her gaze and rolling whisper voice. "They get like family. More so day by day. More a captain cares, the harder life gets. The Void is a brutal bitch to those who care."

"Makes us special," Jace defended.

"Or crazy." She winked.

Jace blushed. In the whole of his life he'd never met a woman who made him feel like a giddy school boy and a lustful monk all in the same turn. Disconcerting. He managed eye contact, but he couldn't stop blushing as his thoughts turned.

Kraft touched his arm. "I wouldn't live it any other way."

"Me either."

Heller and Danna erupted into another screaming argument they decided to settle by arm wrestling. It degenerated into a mad, grasping tussle on the floor.

"*Mutiny* is an odd name for a ship," Kraft said.

"*Whisper* seems odd to me as well."

"Does it? *Whisper* is descriptive. Is *Mutiny?*"

"You asking me if I stole it?"

"Did you?"

"*Mutiny* is honestly mine. Is yours?"

"Lock, stock and barrel. There's not another ship in the sky like *Whisper*. Best part of my ship is her crew, though."

"Seems like you've got some pretty tough ladies."

"Don't let them hear you say that," Kraft said, leaning close. "Especially Danna. If you want to see her head explode, call her a girl."

"I'll keep it in mind."

"We've defeated Berserkers, more than once," Kraft said, looking at her crew. "My crew knows hell. Does yours?"

"They do." Jace nodded. "We do our best to outrun most."

"As do we." Kraft nodded. "*Whisper* isn't much to look at, but she's fast. She's docked underneath."

"I thought that looked odd." The zeppelin-shaped Basic had a smaller cylinder clinging to its belly, like an overstuffed cigar with a cigarette attached.

"Not odd enough to stay away."

"Script was too good. It's funny how that can sometimes cloud a captain's vision."

"You were willing to give it all up to save your crew."

Incredulous, Jace glared at her. "Enjoy pouring salt into my wound? Would you like a splash of vinegar with that?"

Kraft lifted her hands in surrender. "I didn't mean it like that. You'd give almost any script to keep your crew safe, and you know it."

"You'd do the same for yours," Jace pointed out.

"Touché."

"Ha! Say it, fetch! Give! I *own* your ass!" Danna screamed as she pinned Heller to the floor.

"I ain't giving over to a she-freak!" Heller bellowed.

"Give, or I swear," Danna lifted her hand to draw her blade.

"You'll swear up a whole mess of trouble if you do that," Kraft said. "Leave off your boy-toy, Danna, we gotta go."

"I *so* won," Danna said as she climbed off Heller.

Kraft turned to Jace. "This time? Everybody won. All of us live to dance another day."

Before Jace could answer, Kraft disappeared with a slow, lazy and sexy smile.

Chapter Five

"You've been pissy ever since we salvaged that Basic a month ago," Garrett said after Heller lumbered out of the galley.

Jace let the comment slide as he picked at his plate of nasty glop. "Is the engine fixed yet?"

"Spit and bailing wire, but *Mutiny* will get us to Byzantine." Garrett leaned back in his chair, his own supper mostly untouched.

"When we get there, you get the part to fix the engine, got it?" Jace stabbed his fork around his dinner, searching for something edible amongst the garish goo. Noticing that Garrett had picked out the red bits, Jace rooted around, found one, chewed, then spit it out. "That's the best of it?"

"Want more nasty? Take a bite of the green things." Garrett shivered. "Ewww." His whole face scrunched up. "Red is the best of a bad lot."

Jace tried again. If he didn't think too much, the red bits vaguely tasted of tomatoes. "I can tolerate bad food if the ship is running right."

"Don't get bristled at me, Jace. I told you two months ago to replace—"

"You're right." Jace tossed his fork aside and held up his hand. "You did." It wasn't fair for him to blame Garrett for his lack of script. "I'm going to be plush soon, okay?"

"Okay." Garrett leaned forward with a horse-toothed grin. "You took a shine to that pretty lady thief, didn't you?"

Rather than answer, Jace considered his plate. Dinner smelled better than it tasted, but that wasn't saying much. What looked like wads of vibrant yarn smelled like dirty socks and tasted like something he'd accidentally stepped in.

What I wouldn't give for a decent meal.

"You gonna answer me, Jace, or are you gonna keep making nasty faces at your supper?"

Lifting his gaze to Garrett, Jace said, "Just because you have big eyes for Payton doesn't mean everyone else is looking to hitch up."

"That may be so," Garrett drawled, "my big eyes for Payton, but you didn't answer my question."

"Just make sure we're ready to dock today, okay? Get the part you need to fix the engine when we do."

"Gonna cost at least a grand," Garrett said apologetically.

Jace had at least 5K of goods from the Basic salvage. *Mutiny* needed fuel, water, recyc, parts, food and crew—pretty much in that order. And Jace hadn't paid his current crew in months. How could he take on new crew when he couldn't pay the one he had?

"See if you can find what we need for less." Jace gave the order with a faint hope that Garrett could finagle the part for half. If Garrett could keep *Mutiny* running for just a bit longer with spit and bailing wire, Jace might be able to get them out of the red and into the black.

"I could have taken the part off that Basic," Garrett reminded. "Along with a bunch of other useful electronics."

"You think I'm going to salvage an IWOG credit ship? Are you nuts?" Jace shook his head. "I'm one swift side-step from the edge of the law as it is by salvaging the hold."

"They'd never know," Garrett said.

"The IWOG would slap an Ollie on a part worth a grand." Jace knew the InnerWorld Government routinely slapped trackers all over their credit ships. The only thing the IWOG credit department couldn't track was cargo.

"Ollie-Ollie-Oxen-free." Garrett sighed. "You're right. Not worth the hassle."

"Nothing is worth tangling with those freaks." Because of insatiable IWOG greed, Jace lost his wife, his children, his entire world—and he couldn't do a damn thing about it.

"Never met a woman like Captain Kraft," Garrett said, tipping his battered straw hat off his brow as he lifted his incisive gaze. "Never in the whole of the Void met a woman so much of so many things."

Considering his rejected food, Jace picked up his fork and toyed with the bright strands once again as hunger rumbled his gut. He'd rather think about anything other than Captain Kraft, or hunger. Forcing Senna to his mind's eye, Jace pushed his thoughts down a well-worn, sepia-toned path.

"Beautiful. Powerful. Strong." Garrett kept his voice low and private as he considered aloud, all the while settling his battered hat to his head.

"Senna was such." Jace dropped his gaze back to his plate of garish goo. Senna once stood beautiful, powerful and strong. A tiny sprite with cinnamon hair who loved him through failed crops, three children and a thousand foibles. "And it sounds like *you've* got a crush."

"Not on Kraft," Garrett said. "Payton is all of those things."

Payton. His doctor. "Difference is?"

"Deadly. Kraft is deadly. Payton isn't. Senna wasn't. No matter how finely you slice it." Garrett plunked his hat to the table. "Kraft let us go because she took a shine to you. Here I am thinking you took a shine to her too."

"We're almost a month behind schedule." Resolute, Jace shoved his garish meal away. "I don't have time to consider such nonsense."

"'Specially since you're all crotchety we're late getting to Byzantine, and you're afraid you're gonna miss your opportunity to meet up with Kraft again."

Garrett had been with him way too long. Jace thought he'd been more subtle about why he wanted to hurry to Byzantine.

"That woman would captivate just about anything male." Garrett primped his thinning brown hair. "Thing is, that lady had eyes only for you." Garrett waggled his brows. "Did pretty Captain Jace Lawless take a shine to deadly Captain Kraft?"

"Don't call me pretty." Jace shoved away from the dented metal table, stood and stomped off to the bridge.

Laughing, Garrett shouted after him, "Your pissytude answers my question better than words ever could!"

After docking on planet Byzantine, Jace led Heller and Garrett into the heart of Kali.

Advertisements blared from plasboards. Hucksters hollered

out the wares they had for sale. IWOG consumers, WAG citizens, and Fringe players rushed about in a deafening cacophony. Jace hated being on-world. Sounds and sights and smells made him feel pummeled. Every Fringe planet gave him a headache that didn't go away for days.

Wall-to-wall foot traffic, bodies so dense Jace gagged on the mélange of sweet perfume and fetid unwashed flesh, made the way to Trickster's lair horrific. The stench inside the rubble of his office wasn't much better, just a shade more tolerable than the cluttered streets of Kali.

Trickster welcomed Jace and his crew with an offer of dusty seats and cold IWOG refreshments. Jace declined both with polite suspicion. Trickster repeated his offer with jolly insistence.

"You're all warm and fuzzy today," Jace said. "This puckering because you won the lottery, or I did?" With a subtle flick of his hands, Jace flipped his coat from his guns.

Trickster had never been accommodating before. In fact, he'd been downright belligerent.

Heller snorted and spit on the floor. "If the fetch puckers any harder, his whole head will go right up your ass." Heller settled his gigantic, weapon-riddled frame into a wide fighter stance. At a moment's notice, he could level the building and everyone in it.

"His attitude is unique." Garrett tipped his hat to Trickster and then lowered his hand to his gun. "I'm pondering the weirdness wonder of it myself."

Trickster's private guard, armed with Swain Shredders, tensed.

The whole room of men hit a sphincter factor of seven in less than three seconds.

"Gentleman, please." Trickster lifted one hand to his men, the other to Jace. "There is no call for this. I find I am in a whimsical good mood, that is all. We can conduct our business standing, if you prefer, Captain Lawless."

Bad to worse. Trickster never called him by his rank. Mostly, Trickster hissed Lawless like Jace should live up to the name. While calling him Captain Lawless, the nasty weasel dealt fairly, far too fairly, for the salvaged goods.

Jace chalked Trickster's unnerving attitude up to the fact that Kraft probably made her deal for her part of the cache.

Jace figured Trickster acted strange because he knew he didn't have the advantage this time. Still, Trickster's jolly yet sinister mood kept Jace on guard.

They made arrangements for Trickster's men to unload the goods, at which time Jace would receive his script. Before he and crew could leave, two guards trooped in a bunch of women.

"Stooped to the flesh trade?" Jace knew about the trade in beautiful and skilled women, yet found it personally abhorrent. But most didn't know that. Payton, the doctor on his crew, and her daughter, Charissa were said to be his bought-and-paid for whores. Nothing could be further from the truth, but the tale did lend to his disreputable aura.

"Women are valuable commodities." Trickster ordered them to line the far wall of his ramshackle office. They ranged in height, weight, race and, most notably, awareness.

Captivated, Jace riveted on a beautiful slave dressed in fluffpink. The revealing harem outfit didn't showcase her impossible beauty the way her black clothes and gleaming silver blade had. Tarted up, Captain Kraft looked garish, false, forced to wear a mask that ill-suited her. She stood rigid as a parade-ground soldier, towering over everyone but himself and Heller. Her eyes were so glazed, Jace thought it likely Kraft had no idea where she was.

"Fancy a look at the merchandise?" Trickster sleeked back his greasy hair like a rat grooming his whiskers.

"Already got two whores on my ship. Don't reckon I need another." How had Kraft fallen to this? Jace forced himself to shrug and turn away. He had to grit his teeth not to look back.

"Ah, but these are double-skilled whores you can afford." Trickster lured him back. Jace pretended to consider the offer.

Trickster pointed to each woman as he listed her skills. When he got to Kraft, he said, "This one can cook."

What I wouldn't give for a decent meal.

When Jace hesitated, Trickster licked his thin, chapped lips and trilled, "Let you have her for a fair price."

"A cook for a fair price?" Jace shook his head. "I can't afford a cook. Besides, I'm out two fighters and you know it, since you're the one who stole Moore and Fellows from my employ."

Jace glanced at the two men who now stood as part of Trickster's personal guard. The turncoats met his gaze with cool aplomb. No doubt they told Trickster he'd not made Payton or her daughter his whore, and that he took a strong exception to them trying to do so. Too, they must have told Trickster that he longed to find a good cook.

Coldly, Jace said, "You offer me a boatload of women worth nothing in a fight."

"Men to fight are a dime a dozen. But women, ah, they can warm the bed," Trickster said. "And this one can cook as well."

"Bit tall, don't you think?" Jace looked Kraft over with the discerning eye of a bidder at auction.

"In proportion. Worthy of a man of your stature."

The diminutive scrimshanker buttered him up better than breakfast toast.

"I don't much like the idea of having to subdue my bed warmer every night," Jace said. "Even if she can cook."

"Look. See how docile she is?" Trickster pulled Kraft forward, and she came willingly. She stood straight, towered over Trickster, and tilted her head up slightly toward Jace. He didn't see even a flicker of recognition in her glazed eyes.

"She's docile because she's drugged."

"A bit," Trickster admitted. "And it doesn't take much. You can well afford her."

"Can you cook?" Jace asked Kraft.

She swore up a furious streak in German before Trickster could stifle her with a pinch to her arm.

"Feisty." Jace shook his head and turned away. "Don't need one like that." He stalked off. If he were too eager, Trickster would smell it. Mercifully, Garrett and Heller remained silent.

Jace heard Trickster slap Kraft. Hard. He cocked his head over his shoulder, anticipating the pleasure in watching her rip the weasel apart. But she didn't. Kraft shook her head and stood even more ramrod straight. She must be drugged out of her mind. Barehanded, Kraft could yank Trickster's head right off his scrawny neck and make him do the unspeakable to his own ass.

"She's upset you even ask," Trickster said. "She is the finest cook on the Fringe."

"Really?" Jace didn't believe Kraft could boil water, let alone claim fame as a cook, but he turned back to Trickster with bored indifference.

"You ever heard of Fairing's cook?" Trickster asked.

"Since Fairing is the most epic thief who ever worked the Fringe, I've heard of him," Jace said. "Fairing's cook is almost as epic as Fairing himself."

"This cook-whore is Fairing's cook."

Jace felt his eyebrows rise almost to his hairline. "Not only do you want me to believe she can cook, but you want me to believe she's Fairing's cook?" Trickster wouldn't know the truth if he saw it crap in his hat. "If you're going to lie to me, Trickster, at least make it passable." Turning on his heel, Jace stalked off. "Especially since there's no way to confirm your tale since Fairing died a year ago."

"Fairing speaks from beyond the grave," Trickster said.

"And his ghost speaks only to you?" Jace asked.

"To any who have this."

Trickster waved a paper at him, coyly, like a hanky. He smiled with dark malevolence when Jace reached for it.

Jace read over the holodigitext quickly. The document could be forged, but he didn't think so. Compelling enough as she was, Captain Kraft was more so when he discovered she was, without a doubt, Fairing's cook.

"How do I know she's not riddled with disease?" Jace forced himself to dicker over her finer points as a commodity. He didn't want Trickster, or any other man in the room, to have any notion that he cared about her.

"By this." Trickster handed him a clean bill of health from an IWOG hospital.

"How'd you get this on a cook-whore?" Jace asked.

"There's a doctor at the Kali hospital who has a predilection for the exotic, shall we say." Trickster flashed him an oily grin. "My doctor provides this service for me in exchange for that which satisfies his rather strange appetite."

"Please, don't unpack that." Jace had no interest in some IWOG doctor's perversion. "How much do you want for her?"

"A pittance, really. I have too much stock as it is."

"Fifty." Jace appraised Kraft with a cold eye.

"For a cook?" Trickster asked archly. "Try five thousand."

Jace turned on his heel and strode away. Trickster's smarmy, conciliatory attitude became clear—the fetch wanted as much for Kraft as he'd just paid for the salvaged goods.

Anitra Lynn McLeod

"Three thousand!" Trickster shouted.

Jace stopped but didn't turn around. A two thousand drop in a breath meant Trickster wanted more out of this than money.

"One hundred," Jace countered.

"Two thousand."

"No way." Jace walked to the door of Trickster's lair and turned back like an afterthought. "Two hundred."

"Fifteen hundred."

"Five hundred."

"Fifteen hundred," Trickster said definitively. "I won't go any lower. That's a bargain for a cook. Especially this cook."

Jace looked Kraft over again. Like an oddly dressed tin soldier, Kraft stood boldly proud despite the garish makeup and skimpy clothes. Oblivious because of the drugs, she seemed impossibly vulnerable. He shuddered at the thought of what Trickster would do to her if he didn't buy her. A surge of protectiveness mixed with a feeling of obligation swept him. By her honor, he stood here now. By his honor, he vowed to repay her even if he couldn't afford her outrageous price.

"Deal."

Chapter Six

When Kraft woke up, she saw a gun metal gray ceiling crossed with exposed plumbing, duct work, stabilizer struts. A ship? The air tasted sharp and antiseptic. She touched her body. She didn't have any blades and barely had any clothes. Below her, she found a cold metal table.

Shivering, she took a deep breath and tried to read the table. Confusing images and emotions assaulted her—blood, pain, fear. Overriding them all she felt one word, safety, echo in her mind.

"She's coming around."

Kraft rolled her head toward the lyrical voice. Her blurry vision finally focused on a tiny woman with strawberry blond hair and a sleek, cat-like face.

After speaking into the wall com, the woman gazed back at Kraft with naked curiosity and approached. "How do you feel?"

When the woman leaned over her, Kraft shoved her away and leapt off the table. She grasped frantically for a weapon because she felt too shaky to fight hand-to-hand. Yanking open a drawer, she found a scalpel and brandished it.

"I'm not going to hurt you." The woman held up her hands and backed toward the open infirmary door.

"You got that right." Kraft looked down. "What the hell am I wearing?" She kicked off the ridiculous beaded slippers, flexed her feet and got her bearings for a fight. "Where am I?"

"In the infirmary," the woman, a doctor, said.

"I grasp that part, I mean where in the Void—"

"You're on my ship." Jace entered the room with his gun drawn.

Confused, disoriented, the last month a total blur, Kraft felt the scalpel tremble in her hand as the ravages of powerful drugs coursed through her veins. Her gaze and hand wavered between the targets the doctor and Jace offered.

"I let you go." Kraft tried to comprehend what was going on. "Why are you doing this to me when I let you go?"

"I'm trying to help you," Jace said. "Put down the scalpel."

When she hesitated, he pointed his gun right at her head. The ancient Sod Buster clicked with a resounding boom when he pulled the hammer back.

"Stand down, Captain Kraft. Don't make me kill you to protect my crew, because you know I will."

Kraft struggled to understand the confusing images clouding her mind. She had vague memories of blood and horror. Death like a stench she couldn't ever run from. The scalpel clinked to the floor as she lifted her hands.

"By my honor, I stand down."

"Are you decent?" Jace asked through the closed door.

"Bit of a problem." Kraft tugged at another lacy shirt that barely covered her bellybutton.

"What's that?"

"None of this fits!" Kraft discarded the shirt and realized it was the last one. "Captain Lawless?"

"Yes?"

"I'm asking an awful lot, beggars shouldn't be choosers and all, but, can I have something of yours?" Besides Heller, Jace was the only person on the ship with clothing that would fit.

"So you can read it?"

In her current condition, she didn't think she could read a book, let alone anything else.

His knock against the metal door resounded in the empty storage room. "Are you going to answer me?"

"What if I could read your clothes?"

Without a word, he walked off.

Naked, Kraft waited in a room now strewn with shirts and skirts. She appreciated Payton and Charissa's offer, but most of their clothing flat-out didn't fit her foot-taller frame.

She heard Jace approach. He tapped twice with his

knuckle then opened the door just enough to drop a bundle of clothes.

"Try those." He pulled the door shut.

Kraft picked up a homespun cotton shirt, thick and heavy, dyed in the spring with yarrow root. Youthful hope radiated from soft yellow contours and handcrafted wooden buttons. When she slipped the shirt on, Jace's scent surrounded her. He hadn't worn this in almost a decade. He'd kept it neatly folded in the back of his drawer, like a memory preserved.

She lifted up the brown trousers which were just as faded and worn. She pulled on a dream turned nightmare. Visions of fields filled with rolling grain, and then a woman of home and comfort with three children at her side. Then came a burning sickness. Death. The destruction of all he loved. The resounding echo of her vision in her own heart literally floored her.

Jace must have heard the crash from the other side of the door. He tapped twice. "Kraft, you okay?"

"I'm getting there." She stumbled to her feet and buttoned up the trousers. She wondered how much of what she'd felt was real and how much had been perverted by the drugs. Everything had a surreal chemical edge. Time seemed like salt water taffy in the sun...

"Are you decent?" Jace asked through the closed door.

"Debatable, but I'm dressed."

The storage room door creaked open. Jace wore almost the exact same outfit as she did, but his shirt was battered blue and his trousers were made of denim. He looked at her for the longest time, and she almost lifted her hands to protect herself. How could that man, with his gaze alone, make her feel utterly vulnerable? She chalked the unfamiliar feeling up to the drugs she'd been injected with for the last month.

His clothes fit her well. The shirt strained a bit at her bust and the pants a bit at her hips, but they were about the same size in most places. Kraft took hard-and-fast notice of where they differed.

"I wanted to get into your pants, Captain Lawless, but this isn't quite what I had in mind."

Jace startled back a step. He seemed amazed she hadn't lost her sense of humor. He suppressed a burst of laughter by turning away and coughing hard. Having composed himself, he turned back, but kept his attention on her bare feet. "We'll have to get you some shoes."

"Tell you what, at this point in my life, I'm grateful I still have feet." Her attempt at humor compelled him to meet her gaze. She smiled, but it felt forced, and if his worried brow was any indication, he noticed.

"You're safe."

A thousand questions swirled in her mind, but in the end she shrugged and asked, "Why?"

"You can cook, right?"

Caught off-guard, she laughed. "From captain to cook? I've had quite a tumble from grace."

"But you can cook."

The look on his face brimmed with so much hope, a genuine smile lifted the edges of her lips. "That I can do."

"Then that's why." He leaned casually against the doorframe.

"You needed a cook?" She knew there was far more to his helping her than he would ever admit to.

"Yep. Good cooks are rare. Fairing's cook even more so."

Shock made her drug-ravaged nerves tingle. "Who told you that?"

"Feller by the name of Trickster. He gave me this as proof." Jace pulled a folded paper from his hip pocket.

Pleased to see a well-worn friend, she clutched the paper tightly when he placed it in her hand. "Can I keep this?"

"Then it is yours?"

Caught, she looked up into his exotic-sunset green eyes. "You are so much more than pretty." She dropped her gaze to the paper. "What do you want for it?"

"Cook for me and my crew, and it's yours."

"How long will I be beholden to you?" Despite her best efforts, her husky voice sounded suggestive.

"It's up to you." He shrugged, pulling his soft blue shirt tight across his shoulders. "Whatever you think is fair."

"What latitude." She couldn't help but feel suspicious of his generosity, but trying to read him would probably be a waste of her time at the moment.

"Honor among thieves." His slight smile made her shiver.

"You don't owe me," she defended, dropping any suggestive tone from her voice or posture.

"No, I don't, do I?" He turned and walked away.

She followed behind, mumbling, "Looks like I owe you." She tucked the paper into the pocket of her borrowed shirt.

"He gave me this too." He handed her another paper.

Kraft unfolded a report from an IWOG hospital. Her heart almost exploded. How had they gotten her in there without bells and whistles going off everywhere?

"Trickster said he got that in some kind of hush-hush deal with an IWOG doctor at a hospital in Kali."

"Oh." Kraft thought that explained why she wasn't being tortured at this very moment.

"Next stop, you can get your face cleaned up." Jace pointed to a bathroom.

"What did that weasel do to my face?" She stomped to the mirror, took one look and reeled back. "How the hell did you recognize me under all this crap? I look like a whore!" She turned on a small trickle of water and scrubbed her face clean with the bar of harsh hand soap.

"It's your eyes," he said softly. "Hard to forget."

Looking at his reflection in the mirror, she gave him a speculative once over. Captain Jace Lawless expected her to cook, but what else did he have in mind?

Chapter Seven

Kraft worked behind the stove with skilled and fluid movements, but she shook with fine tremors. As he watched her select tidbits from the meager pickings of freeze-dried food, an explanation for her trembling struck him.

Jace touched her arm. "Are you okay?"

Jerking back, overcorrecting, she stood tall and offered him a wan smile. "Welcome to the wonderful world of withdrawal."

He leaned close. "Payton might have something to help, and we can live one more night without—"

"No more drugs." When she shook her head, her linen-bound hair danced across her back and teased the edge of her fanny. "And I think you're in dire need of a decent meal. You were practically drooling when you asked me if I could cook." Her rolling chuckle enveloped his whole body.

"It has been a long time."

"For a lot of things." She winked and turned her attention back to the stove. "Besides, the only way I'm ever going to get better is if I eat."

He leaned against the counter and wondered how this was ever going to work when Kraft could read him. He feared she found something dark in him, because every time he touched her, she withdrew. As much as he wanted to ask, he didn't want to know.

The delectable aroma of her cooking had been like a siren call through *Mutiny* and everyone gathered in the galley, holding plastiware plates in drooling anticipation. His crew gave Kraft speculative glances, and he knew he'd have to explain, but he hoped to do it after everyone had a full belly.

Kraft served up plates that were fairly snatched from her

hands. When she handed Jace his plate, she said, "You'll know soon enough if you made a good deal for me or not."

He sat at the head of the table on a wobbly wooden bench.

Around a bite of food, Charissa gushed, "This is so yummy!"

"Magnifique!" Payton exclaimed, nodding agreement to her daughter.

"Fabulous," chimed in Bailey, lifting his fork to Kraft like a salute.

Garrett, his mouth too stuffed to comment, rolled back his eyes and moaned.

Jace took one bite and knew fifteen hundred for her was an insult. He hadn't tasted food this wonderful in a decade. How could Kraft make the same freeze-dried dreck they'd been gagging on for months taste like this?

"It's extraordinary." Jace turned from his place at the head of the table to face her.

"Thank you kindly." Kraft bowed from her station behind the stove.

"We can squish over and make room," Charissa offered, more than willing to press against Bailey, the new object of her affection.

"Thank you, but no." Kraft waved off the invitation. "I'm fine right here." She filled her plate and ate standing up.

Jace wondered if she wanted to keep her distance because she was embarrassed about him buying her, or if perhaps the lingering effects of the drugs made her reader ability difficult to control. He turned back to his meal and thought it might be for the best if they kept their distance.

The only sound in the small galley was metal forks against plastiware plates and the occasional sigh of sublime pleasure.

Heller, sitting to Jace's right, glared at Kraft while he shoveled food into his gaping maw. His freshly shaved head gleamed a vulnerable, naked pink under the kitchen lights.

When they'd returned from Trickster's, Heller pitched a fit over how much Jace paid for Kraft despite the fact he'd received full pay. Everyone else took a pay cut so Jace could afford parts and service for *Mutiny*. But it seemed full compensation did not lessen Heller's snarling hate for Kraft.

"You as good a whore as you are a cook?" Heller took

another big bite.

Before Jace could remind Heller to keep his big mouth shut, Kraft softly said, "I might be a cook-whore, but at least none could call me dishonorable."

Everyone stopped eating but for Heller. His grunting chomps echoed in the small galley as everyone exchanged glances and then looked pointedly at Jace for an explanation. This wasn't how he wanted things to play out, but Heller left him no choice.

"What's going on?" Charissa darted her wide green gaze between Jace and Kraft.

"Who is she?" Payton demanded, frowning at Jace with her serious-doctor and protective-mother face.

"I'd like to know too." Bailey primped his pale blond locks with a boyish hand.

Garrett shrugged, leaving the explanation up to Jace.

"She's a whore." Heller leered at Kraft. "A whore that can cook."

"That's enough, Heller." Jace didn't bother to check out how Kraft responded to Heller's comment.

"He's right though, isn't he? That's what you bought me for." Kraft's voice was low and speculative.

Jace turned to her, and she lifted her chin a notch.

"You gonna let all the crew have a go at me, or just you?"

Incredulous that she would even ask him such a thing after what he'd sacrificed to save her, Jace coldly asked, "Is that something you'd enjoy?"

Narrowing her eyes, she asked, "Does it matter? I don't have much of a choice, do I? Your medic could dope me up six ways to Sunday, and I wouldn't—"

"I won't," Payton interjected, looking at Jace with horror that he might even ask such a thing of her.

"I never—" Jace stopped himself from defending something he had no intention of doing. "No one's getting drugged. I want everybody to be quiet."

Silence descended.

"Kraft, please tell them who you are."

"A cook and a whore, apparently." Kraft nodded at his crew.

"Give me strength." Jace rubbed a hand across his weary forehead. After a long, exhausting day, his headache had migrated to every part of his body. He tried to will the tension out of his muscles with little success. "Tell them who you really are."

"Oh, you mean before you bought me as your cook-whore? Well, that's a tall order. What part, exactly, did you want me to tell them? The part where you even the score or the part where I'm humbled?"

She moved to his side and stood at attention with a stony expression on her face. Jace wondered why she felt a need to antagonize him. He'd expected a lot more gratitude and far less attitude.

"Don't worry, I won't make *you* look bad in the telling." Kraft tossed her bound hair over her shoulder and straightened her borrowed clothes. "I look bad enough to blind even the most jaded eye."

Jace crossed his arms and let out a longsuffering sigh. "Would you please just tell them who you are."

"Once upon a time I was captain of a ship called *Whisper.*"

"Captain?" Charissa asked, gazing at Kraft with disbelief.

"Yeah, a bad one." Heller brayed laughter and chunks of food flew from his mouth to the table.

"Really, Heller?" Garrett asked from the other end of the table. "Did you have a lapse of memory about standing down?"

"That bitch—"

"Captain Kraft could have killed all three of us from the hallway," Jace calmly pointed out. "She didn't. Had she been so inclined, Heller, she could have killed us the moment we entered by shutting off the air and locking down the Basic until we suffocated. She didn't. Because of her code, we're alive right now. Captain Kraft treated us honorably, and she will be accorded the same."

Surprise and confusion darted across Kraft's face. Did she honestly think he would treat her in any other way?

"I have to call her Captain Kraft?" Heller squawked.

"You will address her as Kraft. She will address you as Heller, and she will address me as Captain Lawless." He hoped that would define the lines of authority for everyone.

"Call me Garrett." He tipped an imaginary hat Kraft's way.

"I'm Charissa, I saw you when you first got—"

Payton cut her daughter off. "I prefer to be called Payton."

"I'm the pilot, Bailey."

Kraft nodded at each of them, then turned a speculative, stripping gaze on Jace. He couldn't believe how much he wanted to lose himself in the depths of her obsidian eyes.

"Oh, I get it! You're the woman from that derelict Basic ship!" Charissa's youthful face lit up when she figured it out.

"Captain Kraft, at your—ah, right, just call me Kraft." Her stare met his with sudden intensity. "Can't have two captains on the same ship. Causes confusion. I'm just a cook."

"And whore," Heller reminded.

"We'll see," Kraft said, gaze pinned to Jace.

Did she think he intended to make her cook *and* whore for him? If she could read him so well, she should know that he would never... Maybe that's why she pulled away from his touch. Perhaps she read something ugly in him, a bestial animal part of him that wanted her below his sweaty, thrusting body. What man wouldn't? But he would never act on that feeling, and certainly, he would never *force* her.

"What happened after you left the Basic?" Jace asked partly out of curiosity, but more to distract himself from his wayward thoughts.

"How did I fall to the flesh trade?" She laughed. "Well, girls oft go wrong, bad parenting I suppose, and being of wayward youth—"

"Answer. My. Question." Jace spaced the words out with a slow, deliberate tone. He began to suspect the real problem was Kraft didn't know how *not* to be in charge of a situation. If she thought he would give up control to her, she was in for a big surprise. This was his ship and his crew and he was in charge.

Reluctantly, she lowered her face. "It's not a good dinner time tale, Captain Lawless." She flicked her gaze to Charissa, Bailey and Payton. "Not suitable for your crew."

"Report." His imperious captain tone made her stand at attention.

"*Whisper* didn't get far. A Trifecta pinned us. We refused to stand down." She swallowed hard. "I refused to order my crew to stand down. Only Bavin and I survived. Bavin didn't last long with the crew. She killed herself. The Randoms decided I might be worth something on the black market. They were right."

Charissa, Payton and Bailey exchanged horrified glances, and Jace now understood Kraft's reluctance. He knew they were shocked by the tale itself, but also Kraft's emotionless telling. They didn't understand she had to do it this way. By reporting facts, terse and to the point, she blocked the emotional pain.

"Trickster's leer damn near split his head in two when he saw me all trussed up. I figured he'd have a go at me, but, like the Randoms, he only kept me drugged. He saved me. For you."

"Did he." Not surprised, Jace kept his place at the head of the dinner table as he considered her over his shoulder.

"He knew you would buy a cook. Once the drugs wore off—"

"He figured you might kill me to get control of my ship," Jace finished softly.

Kraft gave a terse nod. "I thought the man hated me, but it pales beside how he despises you."

Jace found cold comfort in being right about Trickster's ulterior motives for selling Kraft to him so cheaply. It seemed that Trickster would never forgive Jace for refusing to be one of his minions. Despite the lure of oodles of money, first-rate food and plenty of beautiful and willing women, Jace kept his ship and himself independent. Obviously, Trickster still hadn't gotten over the perceived slight, and probably never would. Likely, Kraft had a similar combative relationship with Trickster.

"Is that something you're likely to do?" Charissa bit her lower lip as she glanced up at Kraft, and then across the table to Jace.

"I don't turn on those who do right by me." Kraft looked long and hard at Jace. "I've got no reason to hurt Captain Lawless."

"Yet," Heller said.

The threat of it hung in the air. Once again Jace considered getting a muzzle for Heller's big mouth. Then again, a cattle prod was looking mighty good too.

"Tell you what, I've got no reason to hurt you either, but that's changing fast." Kraft cut Heller a razor gaze.

Heller threw down his fork. "You wanna go?" He stood, kicked his chair away and puffed out his chest. The fool had a foot in height and a good two hundred pounds of muscle on her. Stupidly, he thought that was enough. If Jace actually let them fight, Heller would be picking his teeth out of the worn neospring floor.

"If you really want to dance with me, Heller, I'd be thrilled to accommodate you." With practiced precision, Kraft dropped into a fighting stance. Bare handed, she could take over the whole ship. All she needed was a reason, and Heller seemed determined to give her one.

Jace stood. "Enough." He wedged himself between them.

"You got used by a whole crew of men," Heller grunted, sidestepping Jace. Lewdly, he yanked the front of his black enotex pants. "What makes you think I won't—"

Jace punched Heller square in the face.

Heller timbered as his nose exploded crimson. The floor reverberated then went still. Blood oozed from between his fingers as he clutched his broken nose.

"I know you won't." Jace leaned close. "Because I'm telling you, you won't."

Heller spewed out swearwords like vomit. "Just because you're a eunuch doesn't mean I am!"

"Are. We. Clear?" Jace punctuated the question with lifted brows. He hadn't mastered Kraft's stare-down technique, and he didn't have a cattle prod, but a classic knock to the nose followed up with clear intent often worked wonders.

"Yeah." Heller cupped his nose as he stumbled to his feet. "Wouldn't want her anyway."

"It's mutual." Kraft relaxed her fighting stance.

Jace shot her a reproving glance, and she clamped her mouth shut even though it took her quite an effort. Clearly, she didn't like the idea of anyone fighting her battles but her.

Holding his nose with one hand, Heller smashed his head into the short kitchen doorway on his way out. He swore up another streak, ducked, then clomped away swearing a profuse and uncreative stream of obscenity. Normally, Jace would remind Heller not to curse, but now wasn't the time.

"Payton, tend to that, if you would." He moved his gaze and chin from Payton to the doorway Heller exited. "Charissa, please find Kraft a place to bunk up on the lower deck. Everyone, let's all try real hard to get along."

Chapter Eight

Arranging things in the sparsely furnished room, humming *Lonesome Road* absently, Charissa showed Kraft around her new bunk on the lower deck. Charissa and her mother had the two rooms across the hall. All the men had bunks on the upper deck, near the bridge.

The room was about twelve by nine, with a small bathroom and an even smaller closet. Not that it mattered. Kraft didn't have anything to put in the closet anyway.

"You wouldn't hurt Captain Jace, right?" Charissa looked almost exactly like her mother Payton, but her hair was more of a brown-blond and her green eyes swam with innocence.

"You don't know me, and I don't know you." Kraft plunked herself down on the narrow bunk—hard as freeze-dried bread. "If I tell you the truth, are you apt to hear it?"

Charissa bit her lower lip. "If it's the truth."

"I've got nothing."

Charissa frowned in a pretty, puzzled way.

"Look at me." Kraft waited until Charissa not only looked at her, but really saw her. "I lost my crew, lost my ship, and I'm wearing borrowed clothes." Kraft looked down at her outfit and then back at Charissa. "No guns, no blades, no weapons but my hands." She lifted them, shrugged. "Hell, I've got no shoes." She shook her head and uttered a harsh laugh. "Whole of my life, I ain't *ever* been this bad off."

Charissa twirled a strand of honey hair around her fingertip as she gazed at Kraft with blinky confusion. Kraft figured at best, Charissa was eighteen. A sweet and sheltered eighteen. Surprising, considering Charissa and Payton had been living on the Fringe for three years, running from an abusive IWOG officer—Charissa's father and Payton's husband. Kraft had read wisps of their struggle from the clothing they'd offered her earlier.

Somehow, Jace protected Charissa from the brutalities of life on the Fringe. Kraft couldn't see how. Jace wasn't ruthless and vicious, but gentle and tenderhearted. She wondered how he survived a day, let alone a decade on the Fringe. But then again, when push came to shove, he'd hauled off and busted Heller in the face.

Kraft fought down a flush of female pride. Even though she could defend her own honor, she had to admit that having a man like Jace step up to do it still felt mighty good.

"Thing is, Charissa, as stripped as I am, I got two things none can take."

"Oh?" Charissa twisted her tiny hands together.

"Honor is one. No power in the Void can rob me of it lest I allow it." Kraft considered Charissa for a long time. "I give you my word, young lady, I'll not betray a soul on this ship." With a sigh, Kraft stood. "Even Heller." Checking the twine of her hair, she flexed her body hard. A good meal helped tremendously with eliminating the lingering effects of the drugs. "Now, I'm going to have to hurt that boy, his fascination for fighting me and all, you understand. But I won't betray him. It's a fine distinction."

"Heller is way bigger than you," Charissa pointed out.

"He's way bigger than Captain Lawless too." Kraft smiled.

"But, well." Charissa screwed up her face as she searched for an answer. "You're a girl."

Kraft chuckled. "You've not ever met a woman who can fight, have you?"

"Well, no. But Heller, he's not a man, he's a beast!" Charissa's eyes went round as her mouth.

"Size matters little against skill." Kraft shrugged. "Sex has nothing to do with it at all."

"Does that mean you're *not* going to hurt Captain Jace?" Pretty and puzzled, Charissa needed a clear answer.

Kraft considered her question for a moment. "Captain Lawless, stripped bare, has his honor."

"I'm not sure I know what you mean." Charissa flushed and turned her attention to straightening the faded silk flowers on the battered table. Kraft could all but taste Charissa's crush. She'd recently abandoned her crush on Jace. Her young heart now fell on Bailey. Not good. Bailey got boy-turning-to-man-gaze and he'd riveted it on Kraft.

"Captain Lawless went out of his way to help me, not hurt me, Charissa. And I'll give him the same measure."

"You won't hurt him?"

"No." Kraft thought about it. "Unless he hurts me first."

Charissa nodded, wary, her delicately arched brows pulling together. "What if he does?"

Kraft gazed right into Charissa's crystal green eyes. Innocence fairly oozed from the girl. Kraft had never looked into the face of a more unspoiled, unsullied young woman.

"Tell you what, I give as good as I get."

"Mind some company?" Garrett asked as he ambled into the galley.

"Not at all." Kraft stowed the last of the now sparkling pots and pans. She set to work on chipping the oven top clean. The Void humbled her back to cook, but she still shined. Fairly amazing, considering what she had to work with in the pantry. *Mutiny* hadn't had a decent cook on it in years, if ever. Hell, if the kitchen were any indication, the ship hadn't had a decent *cleaning* in years, if ever.

Garrett settled himself at the galley table with a worn blue notebook. He flipped through the pages. Ruffles and sighs drifted her way.

After a long while, Garrett asked, "What're you doing?"

Kraft had been banging about in the galley for hours now. She had a feeling Jace, if not all of his crew, had been listening to her via the kitchen wall com.

"I'm attempting to organize this disaster area." She wiped her sweaty brow with the back of her hand. "How could any of you cook in this mess?"

Garrett looked up from his notebook. "I don't think you could call what we did cooking."

"No? What would you call it?"

"Mild poisoning."

Kraft laughed as she continued to chip away at the

congealed glop on the ancient stove top. "What are you doing?"

Garrett shrugged over his notebook. "Nothing much. Fancy myself a bit of a poet. I like to sit in here at night and let my muse have her way with me."

"Feel like sharing?" Kraft chipped a gob off the stove and it landed on the kitchen floor. The patchy mix of neospring and textured durosteel looked almost as bad as the stove top. Once she had the stove clean, she'd sweep the floor, that's if she could find a broom. Cleaning supplies were in short supply around here.

Garrett flipped through his notebook. "How about a limerick?"

"Is it salacious?" She popped another glop of crusty gods-knew-what onto the floor.

"I don't know you well enough for those yet, girl." Garrett flashed her a toothy grin as he tipped back his straw hat.

"Damn shame." She winked and grinned back. "Let's hear a prim and proper limerick, if there is such a thing."

After a few flips, Garrett found the page he wanted. "There was a young girl named Heather, who wanted to be light as a feather. She ate only beans, for she wanted small jeans, but somehow she got into leather."

Kraft applauded. "It's a little risqué."

"Mild. Compared to some I have." Garrett stroked the page fondly. Even from a distance, Kraft felt how important that notebook was to him. All of his hopes, dreams, and fears lay bare within those pages. Garrett presented himself as a jokester, but behind his generous smile was a heart filled with tears and painful longings.

"Ever heard of a place called Nantucket?" Kraft lifted her brow and tilted her head.

Garrett tipped his hat back. "Why, darling, if I didn't know you better, I'd swear you were flirting with me." He flashed her enough teeth to line a keyboard.

As Kraft scoured the kitchen, she exchanged limericks with Garrett. Laughing with him made her feel more comfortable on *Mutiny*, and the exercise from cleaning the kitchen helped to dispel the last of the drugs from her system.

In the back of her mind she knew that if Jace thought for half a second she posed a danger to his ship or his crew, he'd chuck her out the nearest airlock. And her honor would compel her to let him.

But apparently all Jace expected her to do was to cook for him and his crew. She felt a twinge of disappointment that she wouldn't be sharing his bed, but she liked his crew. Well, his crew minus Heller.

Chapter Nine

Jace found Kraft sitting in the kitchen, looking out the window in the ceiling, a dented metal cup in her large, calloused hands. Without her black clothes, wearing his castoffs, she didn't seem smaller or less deadly. She seemed a tiger, slowly twitching her tail, poised. She sat with one bare foot up on the counter, her knee cradled by her arms. The length of her hair, bound in black linen, draped her back, then snaked around her hip to her thigh.

"You all right?" Jace asked.

"Most of me." She didn't even turn when he spoke. Kraft continued to consider the Void out the tiny and oddly misplaced window in the kitchen ceiling. "How's Heller's face?"

"Ugly."

Kraft laughed, low and deep. She crossed her legs then spun on her behind to face him. "Before or after you smacked his snout?"

"That's a hard call." Jace chuckled. "But he'll live."

"Aye, there's the rub." She sighed. "I don't relish starting over."

Jace leaned against the opposite counter. "You could give up, I suppose."

"Nope. That'd be easy." She sipped from her cup. "I don't seem to take to things simple or easy." She shook her head, causing the tail of her hair to brush her thigh. "Tell you what, I have a knack for finding the most onerous road and then running down it headlong. Usually blindfolded to boot."

"Makes you special." He nodded.

"Or crazy." She winked.

Jace looked at the cup in her hand.

Kraft tipped her head. "On the stove."

As he plucked his cup from his locker in the galley, he swore he felt her gaze running up and down his backside. When he turned, she held out the soup pan and carefully filled his cup.

"I'm a lucky lady."

Her comment jolted him. He sloshed his drink, recovered, then leaned against the far counter.

"I'm still alive." She set the soup pan aside and grinned. "I've gone from captain to cook—such a tumble from grace—but I can start over. I've done it before."

"After everything—"

"How can I still be standing?" Kraft said it very slowly, enunciating each word. Her huge, extraordinary eyes focused on the small swath of Void out the window. "If I let it break my spirit, it wins. But more than that, I lose."

Kraft turned her pinning gaze on him. "Tell you what, I don't like to lose." She thought for a moment. "The Void can kick me, beat me, and spit in my face, but I'm not dead yet."

Flashing her teeth, not in a smile, but in a baring of them, as if for a fight, she looked out the window again. "I think that's what irks the Void so. I just flat-out refuse to die."

"Because death is too easy," he said softly.

"Sure enough. Death makes everything real simple. Life is what gums up the works." Kraft took a deep breath. "Captain Lawless, there's something I need to say to you."

"You don't—"

"Yes. I do." After looking at the now-clean floor so hard she might have been trying to burn a hole in it, she turned her razor attention to him. "I flew with my crew for five years, and I don't recollect ever saying thank-you to a one of them, because I was too busy being strong. I thought gratitude would make me look weak." She shook her head. "I have nothing to give you but my gratitude. Thank you."

"You're welcome." It tumbled from his mouth prompt and automatic. His upbringing demanded his response. Thinking of what she had done for him, he softened his voice. "You're welcome."

Kraft nodded, cupping her drink. "I'll pull my weight on

your ship and follow your orders. It's how I got my start—Fairing's cook. I guess it's not the worst thing I start over as a cook." She paused. "On a ship called *Mutiny.*" She paused again. "For a man called Captain Lawless." She chuckled, shaking her head. "Does the Void get any more perverse than this?" Kraft looked at him as if they shared a private joke.

Jace had to admit, in all respects, it was nothing short of strange. But when he pondered what Garrett called the weirdness wonder of it all, Jace thought more about its wonderful weirdness. Huge, so vast, each person a grain of sand in the desert of the Void, he'd found Kraft. Twice.

"Explain to me how a cook becomes more renowned than the captain." Jace took a deep swig of his drink. Swassing. He hadn't had swassing since he'd been on Tyaa. Swassing that Senna had forever simmering on the back of the stove. Never had the tart and tangy drink tasted this good. Maybe he held the explanation for Kraft's notoriety in his hand.

"Fairing, Fairing." Kraft lifted her cup to the Void. "A fearsome captain." She took a sip to his memory then eagerly launched herself into the tale. "Smart, deadly, and even though he was a thief, he was an honest one. If Fairing gave you his word, you could count it script. He took me on, raw, didn't believe I could cook, but he gave me a shot in the kitchen. Turned out I wasn't lying. I could take the nastiest crap in the Void and make it ambrosia." Pride made her smile wider as she kept her gaze on the window.

"I'm mighty impressed with your ability to make swassing out of my own pantry." Jace saluted her with his cup.

She laughed, low and deep. "You're easy to impress, Captain Lawless. Swassing isn't much. You ought to try the other delights I can craft with my hands."

Her hands were big, strong, well-calloused, but also had a slender, dexterous grace. His thoughts turned and he yanked his gaze to the floor. He gave her his back to hide his blush by taking a strong and sudden interest in making sure the galley lockers were firmly closed.

After a chuckle, Kraft said, "Fairing had a rule on his ship—every man by his own worth. The more one made toward the common good, the more one would be paid. As you know, good cooks are rare unless you pay them high. Fairing paid high because the man did so love to eat."

Once the heat drained from his face, he turned. "It's not surprising, considering the man weighed three hundred pounds."

Kraft nodded. "Fairing had vast appetites, food being only one, but he also had a knack for culling the best from his crew. He played no favorites when promoting. If you were the best, you took the front, no matter how long you'd been aboard. In three weeks, I became his head cook."

"I'll bet that got some folks a bit upset." Jace noticed the kitchen was spotless. The room probably hadn't been this clean since the ship was new a hundred and thirty years ago.

"It did, it did." Kraft sipped her drink. "Ansley, who'd been Fairing's head cook for years, didn't take kindly to my usurping his role. He decided to take me down a peg by bashing in my face."

She spoke so matter-of-factly that for a moment Jace thought he hadn't heard her right. "Ansley beat you up?"

With an are-you-kidding-me snort and a mischievous lift of her brow, Kraft said, "Ansley never got close." She refilled her cup. "The coward couldn't even face me. He swung a pan at the back of my head. I ducked, grabbed his arm, and pinned his face to the floor in front of the whole kitchen staff. Poor bastard, he was so..." Kraft searched for the word.

"Embarrassed?" Jace supplied.

"Close." She nodded. "Anyway, Ansley outweighed me by a hundred pounds, stood a hand taller and was twice my age."

"Moreover, a man defeated by a woman." Jace knew that alone would chafe a male ego. He'd been none too pleased when Kraft got the drop on him. Things would have been bad enough if a man bested him, but that a woman did just seemed to pack his wounds with salt.

Kraft nodded. "Emasculated. That's the word. Anyway, I told Ansley things were the way they were, and he'd do best to accept them. I made it clear that if Ansley cut in on my dance with Fairing again, I would cut off his legs."

"Fairing found out," Jace guessed.

Kraft nodded. "Ansley demanded an audience with Fairing then insisted I be cast to the Void for attacking him unwarranted. Ansley made two fatal mistakes. He demanded of Fairing." Kraft shook her head slowly back and forth with her brows lowered. "One could request, not demand. Fairing stood by no man's laws but his own. But Ansley didn't stop there. He lied." Kraft shook her head, side to side, more vigorously. "No matter how ugly or painful the truth, one did not lie to Fairing, because Fairing never acted rashly. He always found out the truth."

"What happened?" Jace asked, riveted by both her sharp beauty and her compelling tale.

"Fairing cast me and Ansley in the brig, questioned the kitchen staff, then tossed Ansley out an airlock while I watched. Fairing turned to me, and said, 'Liars bore me. Don't bore me.'"

Kraft took a sip of her drink. "I faced him, nothing more than a scullery maid in his employ for three weeks who overnight became his head cook. I told him precisely what I had done and why. My honesty impressed him. Fairing asked me to demonstrate my skill on his guards. I took down twenty men before he called them off. Fairing laughed as I stood trying to catch my breath. Fairing had never heard of a cook who could also fight, especially a woman. The idea of it intrigued him. I offered him a deal. I would cook and fight for more script. I became a warrior-cook, very rare, and worked my way up from there."

With her tale fully spent, Kraft lifted her drink to the Void once again, as if saluting Fairing.

"But why are you known only as Fairing's cook?" The cramped galley suddenly felt large and Jace wanted to compress the space to echo the intimacy he felt with Kraft.

"Ah, well, that was Fairing's ego, another vast appetite. Part of our deal included I would only be known as Fairing's cook."

"You know everyone assumes his warrior-cook to be a man?"

"Yes." Kraft smiled as if she'd gotten a joke over on the whole Void.

"And you had no problem with that?" Jace didn't understand her. Most men would be scrambling all over themselves to get recognition in their own name to build a reputation.

"I did my job." Kraft shrugged. "I cooked, I fought, and I built Fairing's legend. Tell you what, I've got no desire for notoriety in my own name."

It struck him suddenly that he knew very little about her, and he asked, "Is Kraft your first or last name?"

"Kraft is my name," she said shortly. She looked out the window again. "Fairing's reputation grew along with my script."

"To buy your own ship."

"*Whisper.*" She closed her eyes and swayed slightly on the countertop.

Jace wanted to pull her into his arms and comfort her, but she clenched her jaw and shook off her obvious pain.

"Fairing knew I wanted to captain my own ship, and that I'd do anything to get her. That letter Trickster gave you is the only proof I have that I am Fairing's cook. After losing my crew and my ship, it means the world to me to have that one remnant back." She covered the breaking of her voice by sipping her drink.

Her vulnerability startled him, because Kraft seemed so strong, almost indestructible. But she was human after all.

"I'm glad I returned it to you."

She took a deep breath and a sip of her swassing as she kept her gaze on the window in the ceiling.

He let her take all the time she needed to collect herself.

After several minutes of companionable silence where the only sound in the darkened galley was the ticking of the stove-top clock, Kraft lowered her chin, then turned her gaze to him.

Softly, she said, "You'll find I'm as good in your kitchen as I am by your side during a fight, and I'll pay you back what you paid to Trickster."

"It's not necessary."

"Yes, it is. I pay my debts, Captain Lawless. But I don't know if I can ever really repay you for what you've done."

Jace pushed away from the counter. "Just keep cooking meals like that, and I'll be happy."

After a long pause, Kraft asked, "You really have no intention of making me your whore?"

With his back to her, he said, "I won't make you do anything you don't want to."

When she remained silent, he turned.

Kraft gave him a really hard, tilted head look. "Are you, like Heller said, a—eunuch?" Up her eyebrow went as she cast a dubious gaze to his trousers.

Jace laughed. "Life would be simpler if I was, but, no, I'm not a eunuch." He looked out the window to the fathomless

Void. "It's funny, in a way."

"What?"

Jace looked her dead-on. "If I hold you to whore, I'm suspect. If I don't, I'm even more so. Even by *your* standards."

Kraft opened her mouth to speak, then clamped her jaw with an audible click. She leaned back and considered him for a long, quiet time. Her gaze held the same intensity she'd had when she held him at the tip of her blade. "You're right. I guess I've come to expect the worst. I've forgotten."

"Forgotten what?"

"That you are so much more than pretty."

"Don't know about that." Jace rolled his eyes. Why did she keep calling him pretty? Didn't sound like an insult the way she said it, but it didn't sound quite wholesome either.

Kraft unfurled herself from the counter like a deadly cat and looked down at herself. "My back is to the proverbial wall, Captain Lawless. I got no ship, shirt, or even pants but at your discretion."

Looking up at him from a lowered face, she said, "Were you in mind, you could strip me bare and toss me out an airlock, and that's either before or after you make my last hours hell. Lord on high, I'm at your mercy. You and I both know it."

Jace nodded. "I once fell to your mercy."

"And you were willing to give up everything just to save your crew." Kraft frowned. "I don't have *anything* to bargain with."

"Is that why you spared me?" He'd long and deep into the night pondered why Kraft had let him go. In her hand, at the tip of her blade, she could have taken everything—his ship, his crew, his life. But she didn't. She left him with everything intact and 5K in script goods. Kraft split the haul so even-steven he still couldn't grasp why.

"Spared you?" Kraft shook her head and chuckled. "Heller could have killed us all in an instant with his Gatewin Gusher. If anybody did any sparing that day, it would be him." She tilted her face to the window in the kitchen ceiling. "I danced. And while I danced with you, I found out you are smart, honorable and fair."

"Don't know about honorable. I am a thief after all." Jace turned his attention to the swath of Void out the window.

"Being honorable in a dishonorable Void is a mite difficult, isn't it, Captain Lawless?" Her voice rolled out to embrace him.

He looked at her, compellingly dressed in his own clothes, and felt his desire for her rise such that the heat would make him blush if he didn't turn away. Suddenly, Senna filled his mind. He felt an almost crushing guilt and turned his back on Kraft.

"It is at that, Kraft. Being honorable in a dishonorable Void is mighty difficult."

Chapter Ten

Within three days, Kraft's life aboard *Mutiny* settled into a pattern. She cooked while Heller needled her every chance he got, Garrett took great pleasure in tossing limericks back and forth, Bailey developed a crush on her, and Payton and her daughter, Charissa, seemed endlessly fascinated by heavily censored tales of her derring-do.

Jace made himself scarce.

Kraft saw him, or at least his backside, only at meal times. She found her gaze drawn to his slightly too long black hair that curled against his shirt collar and brushed the expanse of his shoulders. His utensils looked small in his broad hands and drew her attention up his sinewy forearms, dusted with black hair, to his biceps below the folded sleeves of his homespun shirts.

Kraft found herself inordinately pleased when Jace maintained a reverent silence during meals. Talking took time away from enjoying his food. The others talked and joked, but the only time Jace responded was when one of the others complimented her on the meal; he would nod vigorously, but keep eating.

Bailey constantly groomed his blond locks and riveted his pale blue eyes to her. Ripe with his boyish crush, he determinedly made room for her at the table, but she refused.

"The cook does not eat at the table."

Crestfallen, Bailey sat beside Charissa with a pout on his rounded young face.

"I'm not shunning your hospitality or your kindness, Bailey. I'm simply following a tradition long in standing. The cook serves herself last and eats in the kitchen. But if all are so inclined, I can converse from here."

"The cook speaks when spoken to." Heller, sitting to the right of Jace, rammed a fork-full of food into his mouth as he glared at her over the swollen purple of his broken nose.

"No, that's children," Garrett said from the long end of the table, directly across from Jace. "That would be you, Heller, not her."

"Huh?" Heller turned his attention to Garrett.

"You're acting like a child with a diaper full of piss and vinegar." Garrett took another bite of his supper.

Heller glared, flexed his hands into fists and plunked them on the table, rattling the plates against the metal surface.

For all Kraft could see, Jace sat at the head of the table and continued to eat. What kind of a captain was he? She would have put a stop to this squabble as soon as she got wind of it.

"Don't get bristled with me, polecat." Garrett set aside his fork and looked at Heller like a father disciplining his son. "Since you can't seem to grasp, let me lay it out." Garrett took the napkin from his lap, tossed it on the table then stood. "Kraft has gone above the bend to get along with you, but you just keep sticking burrs in her boots. Get over it."

"Got nothing to get over." Heller settled in his chair, crossing his massive arms over his bulky chest.

"Kraft bested us," Garrett said. "Not just you or me or Jace. All of us. Get over it."

"Yeah, well, look who got bested now." Heller shot her a malicious snarl.

Not wishing to change the beat, Kraft continued to watch Garrett dance with Heller. Jace had to step in, not her. She couldn't believe Jace sat at the table calmly eating his supper while two of his crew members geared up for a show down.

"Bested? You think *her* bested?" Garrett laughed. "Who the hell do you think made the food you're shoveling into your greedy, gaping maw?"

"Jace's cook-whore." Heller tossed off the insult like a gauntlet, then stood. At seven feet and a good three-fifty, he almost filled the galley with his mass. Heller's eyes, rimmed black like a raccoon from Jace's punch, challenged her.

Garrett tapped the table with one gnarled finger. "You stop glaring at her and look at me, Heller, since I'm the one talking to you."

Heller's head swiveled like a haunch of pork on a meat-hook. He sized up Garrett with the cunning eye of a beta dog probing for weakness in an upper pack member.

Even though Garrett was a tall, thin drink of water who was half Heller's size and twice Heller's age, Garrett stood and faced Heller unafraid. Garrett's stance spoke volumes. Kraft knew without a doubt that if Heller physically challenged Garrett, Heller would get beat down. Not by force, but by skill. Garrett might come off as simple and ambling, but the man had dexterous speed where Heller had only bulk. Experience counted on the Fringe, and Garrett had a lot more than Heller.

Jace barely looked up from his dinner at the drama unfolding before him. As pleased as Kraft was that Jace found her cooking so distracting, she wondered if Captain Lawless really was the alpha dog on the ship. Garrett certainly seemed to be taking that position at the moment.

Payton waved her hand in front of her face. "Could we tone down the billowing clouds of testosterone? You two are spoiling an exceptional meal."

Kraft wanted to applaud Payton for bringing the moment from a swift tango to a waltz.

"I agree." Garrett plunked himself down and tossed his napkin in his lap. "You've done a fine job, Kraft."

Kraft nodded. "Thank you kindly."

Heller stood nonplused for a moment, looking around like a little kid trying to find his toys so he could take them and stomp home. No one challenged him, and he didn't know what to do. In the end, he focused his burning eyes on her and mouthed the words, "Cook-whore".

Kraft held his gaze and took a bite of her dinner. She refused to take his bait, but she didn't back down from his challenge either.

"She bested us, Heller," Jace said matter-of-factly. "She isn't grinding it in your face. Sit down and let it go."

Heller sat, but he shot Kraft a foreboding glare.

Kraft thought that Heller was like Smug, a terrible mean dog she knew once upon a time. Vicious and deadly, Smug had to be shown, clearly and sharply, who not to tangle with. Heller was by far stupider than Smug. Since Jace's sharp rap across Heller's snout hadn't brought him into line, she would have to find another way. And she didn't have to wait long for the training to begin.

At lunch the next day, Bailey stood first in line, but Heller shoved him aside and thrust out his plate.

Kraft waited for Bailey to recover, took his plate and said, "Fair is fair, Heller. Bailey was first." She fixed Bailey's plate and he sat at the table.

She took Heller's plate and heaped it high. She held it out to him. He took it, looked around and snarled, "How do I know you ain't poisoned it?"

"Cheery thought, but don't you think—oh, wait." Kraft deliberately turned her back on him. "You don't."

"What?" Heller asked.

"Think," Bailey said, taking a bite. He grinned at Kraft like a well-trained puppy.

"That's it!" Heller slammed his plate down on the counter, splattering food everywhere. "We're going."

Kraft sighed and rolled her eyes. "Fine. Mano-a-mano?"

"What?" Heller's face wadded up like a piece of paper trash.

"Hand-to-hand, no weapons," Bailey translated, gripping his plate of food protectively.

Heller tossed aside his blade. "That's all I got on me."

Kraft shrugged. "I can't toss aside my weapon so easily."

"Cheater."

"No." She shook her head. "But I'll tell you my weapon first."

"Go ahead." Heller drew up until he loomed almost a foot over her.

"I have two fingers. Well, one finger, one thumb."

"That all?"

"All I need."

Heller spat, then motioned her forward with two flicking fingers. "Come at me, freak-show, and I'll ram your two fingers up your fucking nose."

Kraft smiled. For the most part, Heller only swore when Jace wasn't around. "You'll be on your knees before you can even process my threat."

"Didn't Captain Lawless tell everyone to—" Before Bailey

could finish, Kraft grabbed Heller's right hand with her thumb and forefinger, flipped his hand up and back, then forced him to his knees with steady pressure.

Bailey dropped his fork in open-mouth shock.

Heller's eyes went wide. He twisted his hand this way and that, but only managed to make matters worse by giving her a better hold. He flailed his left arm, but his thick muscles prevented him from lifting his arm high enough to disengage her.

"Let go, bitch!"

She leaned close and whispered, "Stop challenging me, Heller. You stop right now, or I promise, I'll wrench your hand so hard I'll break it along with your arm, your shoulder, your back, and then I'll get to work on your legs."

His face went white, except for the still purple mask across his eyes and nose. If she were inclined to fight dirty, all she had to do was poke his schnozz and he'd scream uncle.

Jace entered the kitchen, considered their tableau for a moment, and calmly asked, "What's going on?"

"An understanding." Kraft spared Jace half a glance.

"You freak-show bitch!" Heller gurgled in pain as he knelt in front of her.

"Not the understanding I'm looking for." Kraft tweaked the pressure point harder.

Heller yelped.

Looking down at him, using the rolling power of her whispered voice, Kraft said, "You got no reason but hurt ego to be fighting with me. I got no compelling reason at all to fight with you."

"I'll kill you when you sleep!"

Jace only watched with a curious indifference, and she began to appreciate his quiet authority. He didn't have to constantly step in and take charge. He let his crew work things out amongst themselves, stepping in only when he had to. Jace didn't step between Garrett and Heller because Jace knew Garrett could hold his own against Heller. Apparently, he felt the same about her.

"Heller." Kraft tweaked his hand hard, causing him to almost go fetal on the floor. "Stop cutting in."

"You crazy bitch!" Heller tried again to worm his way out of her hold.

Kraft could keep him pinned for the rest of her life. "Do we have an understanding?"

"Jace is the captain, not you!"

Kraft lifted her gaze to Jace. "I know. He's my captain too. I'm dancing with him and you keep cutting in." She turned her attention back to Heller. "Now, I'm all for a bit of healthy competition, but you got the wrong idea of it. I'm not your enemy. I've got no mind to hurt anyone, even you. Give over that we won't fight each other anymore."

Releasing the pressure, she gave Heller a reprieve from pain but made it clear she could reimpose it with a pinch.

"I think you better do what she says." Jace squatted down to Heller's level. "Seems to me my cook can more than handle herself."

My cook? Kraft couldn't decide if the possessive nature of that comment pleased or enraged her, but she kept her focus on the matter at hand.

It seemed to take forever, but eventually, Heller gave in with a snarled, "Okay!"

Kraft released him and went back to the stove as if nothing had happened.

"I just thought she might be trying to poison us, is all." Heller grabbed his plate and moved to the table. He shook his hand and cupped it to his chest, rubbing his palm carefully.

"I wouldn't kill anyone with food." The very idea went against everything she held to as a cook. "If I wanted to kill you, Heller, I'd want to get up close and personal. Poison is a coward's way." Kraft looked right at Jace. "I only kill when I have to and only with regret."

A small frown wrinkled the edges of his mouth, and she wondered what caused his displeasure. Was he angry at her for the way she'd chosen to deal with Heller? Surely, Jace understood that Heller wouldn't respond to anything but a clear and decisive physical besting. Jace himself resorted to physical violence when he'd punched Heller in the face. Perhaps Jace worried that she might turn her trick on him at some point.

Charissa sat at the table. "Did you cook on your ship?"

"I did, I did." Kraft served up plates to the rest of the crew as Heller mumbled to himself. "Everybody took a turn, even me. There was a lot of gluttony on the nights the duty fell to me, and a lot of fasting on the nights it fell to Danna. That woman could fight an army, but couldn't serve fresh fruit without disaster."

Kraft shook her head and laughed as she handed a plate to Jace. For a brief moment, they both touched the plate, and she tried to read him through it, but found conflicting thoughts and feelings. Some of her own emotions charged back at her with a curious feedback she'd never encountered. Her inability to read him startled her, and she let go of the plate so abruptly it almost dropped.

His lightning-fast reflexes saved his plate from crashing to the floor. After settling it within his grasp, he narrowed his eyes and his frown deepened.

He didn't go to sit at the table, but stood with her in the kitchen as she fixed her own plate. Jace seemed in no hurry to move away. She enjoyed looking at his front-side for a change, but felt confused by the look on his face—concerned, compassionate, yet oddly carnal and compelling. Unable to read him, Kraft turned away.

"I remember this one time when we pilfered a ship full of apples that rapidly went bad. Within a week, we had to unload them, eat the damn things, or eject them into the Void."

Horror filled her when tears welled up in her eyes. Frozen with shock, she locked her gaze on Jace, and felt desperate to find a way to leave without drawing attention to herself.

Jace seemed to understand that she was suddenly overwhelmed with memories of her dead crew. "Kraft, before you eat, I want you to check that freeze-dried food in the lower storage area." He took the serving spoon from her, blocked her from the view of his crew at the table, leaned close and whispered, "Go."

After giving him a grateful nod, she left the kitchen and strode swiftly down the main hallway then the catwalks aft. She refused to let gathering tears blind her. She'd rather die than let anyone see her cry. Somehow, that Jace understood and spared her made her tears more thick and shameful when they erupted.

She crossed the floor of the hold and ran into her room. She slapped at the wall com, shut the door and tumbled to her bed. Hard and racking, her body shook as Danna, Jinj, Shar, Tan, Bavin, Path and Road all ran through her mind.

Danna, so fierce, a fighter through and through, yet so tender to Jinj, their doctor. Shar, able to fly *Whisper* like gossamer thread through a theoretical needle. Tan, small but deadly, able to make *Whisper's* engine do the impossible. Path, a computer whiz, Road, her sister, just as brilliant. And Bavin, young and fiercely enamored of Danna. Bavin had been too new to learn much before her life ended. From all the women of *Whisper* could have taught her, Bavin showed the most promise as a cook.

"I refused to stand down."

Burying her face in the pillow, Kraft tried to quell her hot tears of regret and shame. She blamed herself for all of their deaths, because she was the captain. If she'd been a better captain, all of them might still be alive.

Kraft and her crew danced their way through the Void for five years. There had been times of men—crew members, companions, lovers—but they never lasted long. Very few men could handle the women of *Whisper*. In the end, what drove them away was Captain Kraft. A woman in charge chafed.

Through it all, Kraft kept *Whisper* flying. She lived for her ship. The crew might flux, but the crew always held to the ship. *Whisper* defied the Void, over and over, until the odds got too long and the Void took a terrible vengeance.

Out of eight women, only Kraft survived.

She'd been drugged, bound, bought and sold, but still she drew breath, and she found herself beggar for that—Jace could toss her out an airlock at any moment if he were so inclined.

And they both knew it.

Even though she could best him in a fight, she wouldn't, because she owed him her life.

Her gaze riveted on her bare feet. Through the prism of her tears, her feet seemed terribly far away and far too small to hold the weight of her body, let alone her conscience. She wiggled her toes and, like a fun-house mirror, her tears made them look huge then small.

"At least I've still got feet."

If she had feet, she could stand, and if she could stand, she could fight. Even though, sometimes, she didn't really know what she was fighting for.

Kraft shook her head and looked around the bedroom Jace allowed her to use. There were little Charissa touches everywhere—a fancy stitched pillow in a rainbow of colors, a vase of faded silk flowers on the battered table, a crazy quilt formed out of everything from supple leather to cotton grain sacks. All in all, a warm and inviting room.

Mutiny rocketed her through the Void as Captain Lawless held her life in his hands. In the blink of an eye, she tumbled from captain to cook-whore. She found herself compelled to cook but rejected as whore by a man with as much honor as she.

Kraft made her way up the catwalk then down the main hall to the kitchen to begin dinner. With the limited supply in the pantry, she would have to exercise the very depth of her cooking skills. Flexing her mental fingers, she relished the challenge. Good food made life bearable. Good food on *Mutiny* was akin to making it rain in the desert.

Jace strode down the hall from the bridge.

She found herself at the opposite end of the long hall that ran from the bridge in the fore of *Mutiny*, to the catwalk around the cargo bay aft.

When she looked up, she found her gaze riveted with his.

Lord on high, that man had beautiful eyes.

The moment spun out, and Kraft felt a giddy thrill run through her. Part sheer desire, part outright fear. She felt vulnerable around him. He held her life in his hands, and he had seen her cry. Not a soul in the Void had ever seen her cry.

Tension filled her as she walked toward him.

Jace went past her.

He didn't stop her and demand an explanation for what had happened at lunch. He didn't give her so much as a curious look, or even one brimming with pity. He simply nodded and walked on down the hall, intent on his business.

At the doorway to the kitchen, she turned and watched him walk away. For such a tall and heavy man, Jace walked with an unusual rolling grace. Her gaze dropped to his fanny, which was nicely outlined by his trousers and the low slung double-holster around his hips.

Damn it all, but that man had a nice backside.

Damn it all, but that man, coming or going, would make

anything female sit up and take notice.

Damn it all, but Jace Lawless was so much more than pretty.

Getting emotionally entangled with him would be the stupidest thing she could do. Kraft vowed again to hold to her honor. By honor she would cook for him as a member of his crew, and if he demanded it, she would be his whore, but she would keep her heart to herself.

"We should arrive at Dahank in a few hours, Captain Lawless." Bailey sat at the table for breakfast. He smoothed his wayward blond locks as he looked at her.

"What city?" Kraft asked from her usual place in the kitchen. She studiously ignored Bailey. His crush grew like a weed. Maybe it would be better if Jace made her his whore. At least Bailey would get the hint and stop looking at her with winsome-puppy eyes.

"Jade." Jace kept his back to her as he sat at the head of the table.

"Ever been?" Garrett asked from the other end of the table, flashing her a horse-toothed grin.

"I have, I have." In between bites of breakfast, Kraft washed up the dishes. "How long will we be docked?"

"A few hours," Jace said, over his shoulder. "Why? You need something?"

"Well, I'm running out of options in this pantry of yours."

Day by day, the food Kraft served grew less spectacular, but only because the pantry pickings became sparse.

"I got no problem kicking in for more grub," Garrett said, "provided you'll be around to cook it."

Bailey, Payton and Charissa agreed by nodding vigorously since all their mouths were stuffed with food.

"Who's gonna pay her share?" Heller squawked. Food flew from his mouth to the table. He pointed a meaty hand at her. "Ain't fair I gotta pay for freak-show."

"I'll—" Garrett offered.

"No, I'll pay," Jace cut Garrett off.

Garrett grinned. "That's right, she's *your* cook, isn't she?"

Before Garrett could goad Jace further, Kraft said,

"Actually, Captain Lawless, give me a thousand—"

"A thousand!" Heller shot from the table. "That makes my share..." His brows lowered when he tried to divide a thousand by seven.

"That seems a bit much," Jace said.

Heller's face cleared and he grinned at her like he'd won.

"You didn't let me finish, Captain Lawless. Give me a thousand. I'll get what we need and bring you back the thousand. I'm not asking to keep it, just to borrow it for a while."

"I'm afraid you're going to have to unpack that." Jace left off his meal and turned on the little bench to face her. "Seems to me it's not a good idea for you to be stealing."

Jace might be a thief, but he was an honorable thief. He didn't condone stealing just because it was the easiest way to make a living on the Fringe. Kraft saw a lot of Fairing in Jace.

"I'm not aiming to steal anything, but if you have a problem with gambling..."

"Shit howdy!" Heller snarfed. "This gets better and better—your cook-whore has a gambling problem."

Jace caught her gaze. "Does she."

Giving him a slow smile, she shrugged and said, "Isn't much of a problem if I win."

"A thousand is an awful lot to risk," Garrett said, darting a suspicious glance between her and Jace.

"Unless there is no risk." Jace flashed her a knowing grin.

She could see it in his eyes. Jace grasped instantly what she planned to do. "Only other thing I need is a pair of shoes." Her gaze bounced to her bare feet then up. "Some of Jade's gambling hells are pretty ratty, but shoes would be a real plus for getting in the door."

Jace nodded. He pulled a blackened leather wallet from his hip pocket and counted out battered script. When he came up short, Garrett, Payton, Bailey and Charissa helped him out.

Heller kept his arms crossed and refused to pitch in so much as a five-flat note. "What's to stop freak-show from taking your script and running?"

"Her honor, Heller, and I'd appreciate it if you'd shut your big mouth."

Tsking and rolling his eyes, Heller made it clear he thought they were suckers for trusting her with any money, let alone a bundle like that.

Jace stood and handed her the stack of multi-hued script. When the worn notes hit her hand, she felt fleeting emotions of what money meant to them—security, freedom, a future. They had so little, but had no problem sharing what they did have, and they trusted her because Jace did. She'd never touched such emotionally pure script in her life.

"I have an old pair of boots that might fit you." Bailey leapt up from the table and ran from the room.

Charissa watched him with a sullen frown.

In Jade, Heller followed Kraft into a hell called the Double Whammy. It didn't take long for her to walk away with over two thousand in script. When she left, Heller had to run to keep up with her. She ducked around the corner of a shabby two-bit hotel and restaurant.

Heller clomped his way round the corner to find her standing there with her hands on her hips.

"Instead of following me, Heller, why don't you walk with me? You're acting awful suspicious, and we don't want the IWOG to start sniffing around."

Kraft darted a gaze to the crowded streets of Jade. IWOG officers, with their swath of maroon-red against their royal-blue uniforms, stood out amongst the teeming masses.

Turning on her heel, her feet tight in Bailey's boots, she walked away, crunching down the side street.

Heller fell into step beside her. "How'd you do that?"

"Know you were following me?" Kraft pointed at his thick-soled black boots. "You got some mighty big feet, and you don't walk so much as you stomp from place to place."

Heller took the subtle reprimand under consideration, then blurted, "No, how'd you win like that at the Double Whammy?"

"Just got a knack, that's all." She shrugged. If Heller didn't know about her reader ability, she wasn't about to enlighten him. "Do you gamble?"

"Not no more." Heller spat on the ground.

Not since Jace took you from the grunt and groan of street

fighting in Kali, Kraft thought. Curious as to why Jace kept Heller around, she'd found the answers when she read the crazy quilt in her room.

After the IWOG killed Heller's parents, he joined one of the street gangs in Kali. He was ten. At nineteen, he started fighting in caged death matches. Jace took him away from all that, and Heller looked upon Jace as a combination of father, brother and captain.

Softly, Kraft said, "You sure know how to make a mighty fine crazy quilt."

Heller stopped dead in the street. "Don't know—"

"Keep walking."

He kept pace with her only by sheer determination and outright indignant curiosity.

"None of them know, do they?" Kraft asked.

"If you tell—"

"I'm not going to tell anyone." If she were so inclined, she could probably blackmail Heller with the information he enjoyed quilting. "I won't blow your manly cover."

"How'd *you* know?" Over the fading purple bruises on his face, Heller gazed at her with eyes that vacillated between fury and fear.

Kraft shrugged and sighed. "Just got a knack, that's all. But thank you for letting me use the crazy quilt. It's a true masterpiece."

"Wasn't my idea." He snorted deeply and hawked a loogie to the street. "Charissa took it out of the rec room."

"Do you want it back?" Kraft turned down another street.

"Didja mess it up?"

"No." Kraft walked with great strides. Even with his long legs, Heller had to shove hard-forward to keep up. Under the weight of his weapon-riddled body, he gasped at her pace.

"Slow down," Heller snarled. "It's like you've got a Preston Protofuse drive strapped to your ass."

She laughed and eased her pace. "You are so determined to hate me, aren't you?"

"Something about you ain't right."

A shifty-eyed huckster clad in a mishmash of old and new clothing from all ends of the Fringe turned his assessing gaze on them. He recognized Heller and dismissed him, turning his intent gaze on her.

The huckster took one step toward her then stopped when she peered deep into his eyes. His dirty face filled with confusion as he backed away. It didn't take long for him to find another target. The other street hustlers met similar fates. Heller didn't notice and they continued to walk together without being bothered.

"Is there anything I could do to build even the smallest bit of truce between us?" Kraft asked, eyeing the clothing stores with a wistful sigh.

"No truce without trust." He spat on the street. "Don't trust you. Never will."

"I appreciate your honesty." Kraft turned onto the chaotic market street. Scoots, small electric carts, darted around the stalls, shops and street carts as IWOG consumers, WAG citizens and Fringe players tended to their singularly important business.

On a deep breath, Kraft tasted a slew of foods, spices, colognes—the wonderful depth and breadth of humanity. As a Fringe planet, Dahank, city of Jade, was a crossroads to all the human animal could aspire to. As much as she enjoyed being on-world, she still preferred being on-ship.

Pulling herself from her thoughts, Kraft turned to Heller, and said, "Trust me or not, at the moment, you can help me shop."

"I ain't here to help you," Heller said, his gaze darting to the many offerings of female pulchritude. Market street offered the basics; food, clothing, and sex. Heller seemed well acquainted with the various whorehouses, and cat-calls from the ladies residing there made it clear Heller was not only known, but welcome.

"You might want to rethink that. He who helps the cook oft finds his plate filled with that he likes best."

"What?" Heller's face twisted up with confusion.

Just like Danna, Kraft thought. Most of the time, Heller had no idea what she was talking about. She stopped to examine a pen of bright white chickens. "Best way to man's heart is through his stomach."

"Only if you jam your hand in and make a sharp left." Heller mouthed the quip sideways, out the corner of his lips, and then focused his leering gaze on the woman who tended the penned up chickens.

Kraft laughed. "I think it best if I go through your mouth, don't you?"

Chapter Eleven

"What's that?" Garrett peered at the thick brown soup Kraft boiled on the stove as Jace watched from the kitchen doorway.

"Nectar of the gods." Kraft stirred the pot and turned back to chopping large white onions. "Or it will be in a week."

Garrett sniffed the pot dubiously. "It smells like candy."

Kraft uttered her enveloping chuckle. "There's a saying from Earth—candy is dandy, but liquor is quicker." With a deft swipe of the broad knife down the cutting board, she dumped the chopped onions into a sizzling cast-iron pan.

"Guess that depends on what you're looking to get," Garrett said, tipping his hat to Kraft. "Right pretty as you are, I don't much fancy having Jace punch my ticket." He flashed her a huge, buck-toothed grin.

Kraft darted her gaze sideways to Jace and laughed. He thought no one had noticed him watching from the doorway, but she noticed, and perhaps even suspected why. Spying on his crew was not the norm for him, but having Kraft aboard wasn't normal either.

"It's wort." Kraft nodded to the pot of thick brown soup.

"That helps me exactly—none." Garrett lifted his hands palm open and up. "Can you frame that such an engineer like me can grasp?"

After grooming his pale blond locks, Bailey came forward and sniffed the pot.

"Wort is the precursor to beer." Kraft gave the pot another stir.

Garrett looked happy enough to hug her.

"Hey!" Bailey almost sang. "I can't think of the last time we had decent beer on board."

"You ain't old enough to drink, pup." Garrett wrapped an arm around Bailey and ruffled his hair with his free hand. "You best leave the beer to old timers like me who can show it the proper respect."

Bailey wriggled out of his grasp. "I'm old enough!" He put his hair in order as his gaze darted to Kraft. "I am."

"Barely." Garrett tried to grab him again, but Bailey ducked.

"Well, give me a week, and fine beer will be a staple around here." She checked the stove-top timer, stirred the pot of wort, flipped the onions, then sprinkled a handful of green herbs into the pan. A pungently sweet scent of something like mint mixed with the strong odor of onions. Jace's mouth watered when he took a deep breath. He had no idea what she was making for dinner, but he couldn't wait to find out.

He'd almost laughed when Kraft apologized to him for the weight the fresh food would put on his ship, but he'd dismissed her concern. Freeze-dried food took up far less room and weight, but it couldn't compare to fresh food. Just the smell of raw vegetables took him back to his life on Tyaa.

"And if you want to thank someone for the beer," Kraft said, "thank Heller, it was his idea."

A bell pinged.

"That'd be my bread. Excuse me."

After Bailey and Garrett stepped back, Kraft pulled four gleaming brown loaves from the oven. Jace found his gaze drawn to his old homespun pants drawn tight across the full of her hips as she bent over.

Kraft popped the loaves from the pans onto a wire rack then stroked butter over the crust. If heaven had a smell, her cooking was it. He dropped his gaze and blushed when he found himself aroused by the sight of her bare feet against the decimated floor of his galley.

He kept thinking of that Earth phrase about keeping a woman barefoot and pregnant. Sexist in the extreme, it also clashed horribly with Kraft's true nature. Kraft was a warrior-cook. Taming a woman so elemental went far beyond his grasp, and how could he dare do so? Besides, even if he did somehow win the lottery and make his way to her bed, he'd just bet a sophisticated woman like Kraft had the latest and greatest B-chip. No way would Kraft allow herself to get pregnant.

"I could so get used to this," Garrett said.

"Couldn't we all," Bailey agreed. His gaze fell on Kraft, and it didn't take a reader to see the poor boy was almost sick with infatuation. Jace hoped his own lust wasn't quite so apparent to everyone.

"You seem very happy puttering about the kitchen," Jace said from the doorway. He'd been covertly watching them, a bit envious of how easily Kraft managed to insinuate herself into life aboard *Mutiny*. In some ways, she made him sharply aware of how much he missed Senna. In other ways, Jace felt guilty because he was glad Senna was not here.

He'd been diligent in his efforts to make sure he was never alone with Kraft. Not that he didn't trust her. He didn't trust himself. Avoiding her allure seemed to be the most prudent course of action.

Kraft did exactly what she said she would. She'd taken the thousand script, outfitted the pantry and returned the script to him, plus two hundred extra.

When their hands touched, she jerked back, and again he wondered what darkness in him pushed her away. Jace became even more determined to make sure they never spent time alone and that he never touched her.

Jace knew every moment of her leave from *Mutiny* because Heller fairly documented it. He seemed furious that she'd done exactly what she said she would. Heller found conspiracy in that Kraft returned the script plus without buying anything for herself. Jace knew she'd used her psychic ability at the gambling hell, and he wondered why she worked as a thief when she could obviously make a living as a gambler, or a cook. He had a strong notion he would never understand her.

"I am happy." When Kraft flashed him that slow, lazy and sexy smile, he frowned. He'd thought that smile was just for him, but he'd watched her turn the power of it on both Garrett and Bailey.

All at once, the smile fell from her face, and she turned back to the stove. She stirred the pot, flipped the onions and herbs and said, "I haven't run a kitchen in a long time. I forgot how much I enjoyed it. It's like rediscovering an old friend."

As Jace watched her from the doorway, he wondered how long her joy in being a cook would last. She shone as a cook and she took tremendous pride in it, but in her heart of hearts, she'd always be Captain Kraft. There may be honor among thieves, but there could never be two captains on the same ship.

Jace watched his crew fall inevitably into her dance as he held himself back like a wallflower. Kraft, a dust devil, twirled ever faster on her way right out of their lives. He couldn't bear to feel her wind in his hair only to watch her move inexorably on. Touching Kraft would be like touching a fine glass figurine and dropping it with a clumsy hand.

Late that night, finished cleaning the kitchen, Kraft made her way to the bridge. Silently, Jace followed behind her.

Bailey fiddled with a guitar, obsessively tuning strings that sounded in perfect order to Jace's untrained ear.

"I didn't know you played," Kraft said, entering the bridge.

Bailey fumbled the battered instrument. He looked up with big blue eyes. "I'm watching the Void too. I'm not slacking."

Kraft stepped back, lifting her hands palm up. "I didn't say you were." She plunked herself down, cross-legged, on the ratty neospring floor. "You got an ear and eye to the Void, but you got another for what's in your hands. And I'd like to hear you play. Hell, you've been tuning her endlessly. Let me hear you wrest a song from her before you tune her to death."

Kraft relaxed against the lockers that lined the port side of the bridge. She closed her eyes. She looked exhausted but content.

Bailey grinned impishly as he caressed the neck of the guitar then strummed softly. An impossibly sweet chord filled the bridge.

"Do you play anything?" Bailey asked.

Kraft popped open one eye. From the doorway, Jace watched her suppress a burst of laughter, then say, "I play no instruments, but I do dance."

Bailey fumbled his guitar again as he flushed bright red.

Jace wondered if he looked that stupidly boyish when Kraft made him blush.

"I do not dance in a literal sense, Bailey." Kraft shook her head. "But play me a lively tune, and I will dance in my mind with it."

Eyes closed, Bailey played a mix of sweet and sour, fast and slow notes that told a story.

In the hallway, spying, Jace allowed the music to embrace him. He tapped his toes as his body swayed, but he held his cover in the shadow of the doorway. He felt like a dirty thief for stealing a moment that didn't belong to him.

Bailey finished his musical tale.

Kraft opened her eyes and applauded.

Bailey looked to the console. "Could you fly her?" Bailey took obvious pride in the fact that he was, for the moment, in full command of *Mutiny*.

"In a hard pinch I could manage." Kraft stood, brushed her fanny off and looked down at the array of components. "Frankly, I know just enough to be dangerous."

Bailey uttered a giddy, high-pitched schoolboy laugh that made Jace cringe. After dealing with Charissa's crush, he wondered how Kraft would deal with Bailey's.

"I don't have the knack Shar did or you have," Kraft said. "I hear tell you once outfoxed Berserkers."

Jace doubted she'd heard that information. More likely, she'd read it off the ship. He wondered what else she'd read just from touching things on his ship.

"You heard that?" Bailey flushed with pride. "Yeah," he said, trying to downplay it and be cool, "I made *Mutiny* fly."

Kraft and Bailey looked out the window, and Jace followed.

Berserkers, Randoms, IWOG officers—any number of vicious brutes could descend at any moment. There was such a dangerous freedom on the Fringe.

"What brought you out into the Void?" Bailey asked.

Kraft looked out to the black. "Freedom. And I love the feel of a ship, the rumbling low bass of the engine. When I'm on-world, I feel constricted and claustrophobic. Out here I feel free."

Bailey nodded. "Me too."

Kraft looked down at Bailey's young head with a fondness only a mother could bestow. She lifted her hand as if to smooth his hair, but thought better of it and lowered her hand to the back of the pilot chair.

"My space is limited by my ship, but I still feel like a bird in the sky. Like I can go anywhere the wind takes me." Kraft shook her head, her twined hair dancing down her back. "Well, listen to me wax poetical. Give me a moment and I'm liable to burst into song."

"Here," Bailey said, ready to flip a switch, "we could pipe it over the com."

"That'd be fun. Wake up *Mutiny* to a voice that's a cross between a pernickety engine and a burning cat." Kraft covered his hand on the com. "You got some beef with the crew I'm unaware of?"

Bailey flushed when she touched his hand then burst forth a nervous, delighted giggle. Kraft patted his hand the way one would pet a puppy then pulled her hand back.

Jace felt a surge of dismay that she didn't flinch from Bailey's touch the way she did from his. Apparently, Bailey wasn't filled with a repulsing darkness. Again, Jace wanted to know as much as he didn't.

"Your voice can't be worse than mine," Bailey said.

"Yes it can." Kraft laughed. "Unless yours is more annoying than two alley cats going at it in the dark."

Jace wondered if the cats were fighting or—his mouth dropped open at the very idea, but Bailey didn't even blink.

"I've heard alley cats fight," Bailey said, lifting his chin. "I've been around."

Kraft barely suppressed a smile. "Tell you what, you still can't sing worse than me."

"Do you know *Running the Line*?" Bailey asked.

"I do, I do. You willing to sing it over the com?"

"No!" Bailey shook his head.

"Then why are you asking?"

"We could just sing it, you and me, for fun." Bailey flashed her an engaging, child-like grin. He strummed out the simple beat for "Running the Line".

Kraft sang in low alto, "Ain't gonna fly with you today, ain't gonna fly at all that way, I don't care what they say, I be running the line."

While playing the beat on his guitar, Bailey, in a clear high alto, sang the second verse, "Got my ship in the sky, love the view up so high, got no time to wonder why, I be running the line."

Together, Kraft and Bailey sang the chorus as Jace mouthed the words. "Tales they tell don't matter much, I know right from wrong and such, and when they tell their tales of me, everyone will finally see, I've been holding the line."

They finished, high-fived each other and laughed. More than ever, Jace felt like a dirty thief for obsessively observing a moment that didn't belong to him, but he needed to know more about Kraft. He thought watching her interact with his crew would reveal her true self. All he'd discovered so far was that he was powerfully attracted to her. Not only for her exceeding beauty, but her generous nature and infectious laughter. She was so open and honest that he worried she was *too* open and honest.

"I don't think they'll be booking our act anywhere soon," Kraft said. "On that note, I'm going to get some shut-eye." She turned to leave, and added, "There's swassing in the kitchen."

"Oh, hey, thanks." Bailey settled into the pilot's chair and began obsessively tuning his guitar.

Jace made a beeline down the hall.

Kraft walked away from the bridge.

"Hey," Bailey said.

Kraft stopped and looked back.

Fumbling, shy, Bailey caught her gaze. "I don't know what else you are, but you're a really good cook."

"Thank you kindly." Kraft bowed her head. "You play one hell of a tale. And my understanding is you're one hell of a pilot too."

Bailey blushed. He seemed impossibly young yet tested beyond his years.

With a shy smile, he said, "You can't sing worth a damn."

"You either." She offered him a gentle grin filled with sisterly camaraderie.

"So we're even?"

"We're even. Got no reason to be at odds."

Turning away, she left the bridge. Poor Bailey, he was so enamored. Kraft shook her head. In many ways, the sweet and impressionable Bailey reminded her of Bavin, with her big brown eyes to Danna, who scarce took notice. Kraft noticed Bailey's infatuation, but ignored it studiously. The best way to cure a crush was to refuse to feed it.

Bailey's song echoed in her mind as she walked through the velvet dark of the main hallway. Rounding the corner, heading down the catwalk to her bunk aft, Kraft plowed right into Jace.

She hit him so hard and fast she knocked him right off the steps to the metal floor above the hold. The crash of their two bodies hitting the membrane of metal to a now empty hold shook the entire ship like a strike against a drum.

Mutiny reverberated then went still.

Gasping on the floor with the wind knocked clean out of her, Kraft lay panting in the dark. Two feet to her right, Jace lay just as beached fish as she.

Within seconds, lights flooded the bay.

Garrett and Heller leaned over the railing and pointed Sharp Shooter rifles at her.

Chapter Twelve

Jace shot to his feet with a mortified glance up to Garrett and Heller. "It was an accident." Jace felt stripped-naked exposed when he hadn't done anything wrong.

Payton and Charissa peered down, then Bailey joined them.

"You accidentally floored Kraft?" Garrett winked and pulled his gun up. When Heller didn't, Garrett pushed Heller's barrel to the sky. "What a happy accident."

Jace felt a flush rush up his face and he gritted his teeth to force it down. "Go back to bed." He ran an impatient hand through his hair. "Bailey? Get back on the bridge and do anything but sleep."

Kraft dusted herself off. "I apologize, Captain Lawless. I didn't see you." She started to walk away.

Jace waited until his crew left. He grabbed her arm and spun her around.

"Hey! What are you—"

"So now you've taken up flirting with Bailey?" Fury filled him when he thought of her casually touching his pilot when she couldn't bear to touch him.

"What?" Her eyes went wide.

"I heard you on the bridge, singing and laughing with him." Jace knew he turned his embarrassment into anger then dumped it on Kraft, but he couldn't seem to stop himself.

"Oh, the horror!" She lifted her hands to the sky. "Would you rather I make the poor boy burst into tears?"

"Leave him alone," Jace said with soft menace. "Isn't it enough you've got Garrett wrapped around your little finger?"

Her jaw damn near hit the floor.

"Bailey's young, and he's got a crush on you something fierce. Don't be jerking his heart around. Throw your favors at Heller. He's the one you gotta warm up." Jace couldn't believe how cold his voice sounded. He had no idea where all his anger sprang from, or why he inflicted it on Kraft, but he also couldn't seem to silence himself.

Kraft went from stunned silence to a furious whisper so fast it made his head spin.

"What kind of a person do you think—wait, don't bother to answer, because it's *obvious* what kind of a person you think I am. An any-way-the-wind-blows harlot with an itch so deep that apparently *anything* male can scratch it."

"I never—"

"Said it?" Kraft cut him off. "No. But you don't have to. You think it, and act accordingly. Is that why you were lurking around in the dark? So you could spy on me?"

Before he could respond, Kraft leaned close. "I've been doing so much cooking in your kitchen, I don't have the energy to get cooking in the sack—with anybody—not even myself."

Jace knew what she meant, and it took all his willpower not to blush. He'd done *that* more than once since she'd come aboard. At first, out of loyalty, he'd thought of Senna, but Kraft danced into his mind until—

"If you're so worried about who's diddling who, I'll show you how to tap the com in everyone's bedroom from the bridge. And if I scrounge up the energy to diddle anybody, even myself, you have my permission to stand right in the room and watch."

A muscle twitched in his jaw. "As captain of *Mutiny* I have the right to be anywhere I want on my own ship. At anytime. Day or night. Your permission or not."

Emotion drained from her face as she came to attention. "I apologize, Captain Lawless."

"You've had military training." Nothing else could account for the sudden shift from angry woman to subordinate crew member.

"Yes, Captain Lawless, five years." Kraft stood with her shoulders back, head held high and her arms at her sides. Barefoot, still clad in his castoff clothes, she had a bearing nothing short of fiercely proud.

"You may call me Captain."

Kraft nodded. "Thank you, Captain."

"At ease."

Kraft clasped her hands behind her back then took a half step to the left.

Jace felt instantly more comfortable in the role of captain to crew member, but being alone with her played havoc with his nerves. He found his gaze drawn to her wide, sensuous mouth. Repeatedly, he had to remind himself to look at her eyes. The fathomless depths were distracting, but less so than her lips.

"Is there a problem with me observing your behavior on my ship?"

"No, Captain."

"As I understand it, our agreement is you cook and I keep you safe."

Kraft frowned, but didn't say a word.

"You may speak freely."

She took a deep breath. "I cook and you don't toss me out an airlock. I'll tend to my own safety." From her lowered face, she caught his gaze. "Allow me to venture forth on jobs. I seek not a wage, but a percentage."

"I'm no Fairing," Jace said with naked honesty. "A wage might well be higher than a percentage. That derelict Basic was a fluke for us. We're fairly low budget."

"I'm willing to accept that risk."

"I'm not so sure I am." Jace shook his head.

"Because I'm a woman?" Kraft kept her gaze on the floor.

He thought that was part of his reluctance, but not the whole. Kraft was not a fragile sprite like Senna. Kraft was six-three of dark and deadly Walkyrie. With two fingers, she'd dropped his most powerful fighter to his knees, but right after, she'd fled in tears when thoughts of her lost crew overwhelmed her. Kraft was strong yet vulnerable. The combination damn near devastated him. Ten years of resigning himself to lost dreams of what was seemed swept away by new dreams of what could be, with a woman who wasn't anything like anyone he'd ever known. A woman all at once everything yet nothing like his dead wife.

Captain of a thief ship wasn't the life Jace planned for himself, not even remotely the life he wanted, but Kraft seemed to suddenly make all of the scrambling, the fear, and the ever-present threat of the Void worthwhile.

"Captain?" Kraft asked expectantly. Her eyes, huge and dark, filled with unplumbed depths, peered up from her lowered face. A bare hand shorter than him, she managed to make him feel a foot taller by tilting her face like that.

"I think it best for now if you remain only a cook."

Kraft scowled at the floor. "I've clearly shown proficiency in battle."

Jace considered. In his heart, he knew Kraft could take him down, but she belonged to him in a way. Her safety was his utmost concern.

"You will cook and nothing more." To his own ears, his voice sounded imperious. He couldn't believe she hadn't challenged him physically for control of the ship. Did her honor hold her back, or had she taken a shine to him as Garrett had suggested?

"Permission to speak freely?" Kraft almost burst at the seams like a child in dire need of the restroom.

He nodded.

"I'm a better fighter than a cook. If you use only one of my skills, let me fight."

"I hired you to cook."

"You *bought* me to cook."

"I bought a cook-whore. Do you think I should hold you to the full of that?" His voice came out brutal and dark, surprising him but not her.

"Frankly, Captain, if you demanded it of me, I would honor that contract between us."

Jace didn't know what to say. By her honor she would submit herself to him? He didn't blush at the thought of commanding her to his bunk. Instead, even worse, he got hard. Just the fleeting thought of her lovely body in his lonely bed...

"Now that you've got me, shouldn't you actually use me for what I'm good at?" Kraft peered up at him from a lowered face. Again, she managed to make him feel a foot taller.

Did she mean fighting, cooking, or whoring? Deciding to play it safe, Jace put on his best captain voice. "You're more than a good cook. You're an excellent cook. And I think that's where your true talent lies."

"Can't I have more than one true talent?"

Warrior, cook, whore. Jace wanted her so profoundly he

shook. "I'm finished arguing this."

Kraft nodded, resolute. "Fine. I'm *your* cook. Please inform *your* crew not to talk to me."

"That isn't—"

"Yes, it is."

Finished being a submissive crew member, Kraft became an angry woman and lifted her face. All at once he lost a foot in height.

"I won't be able to talk to your crew because I might *laugh* with them, which, for some insane reason, has a ring of sleaze in your pretty head." She turned on her bare heel. "When I'm not cooking, I'll stay in my quarters. If you want me to be your whore, let me know."

Her dismissive attitude grated his nerves. "I think you're forgetting who's captain on this ship." Jace couldn't refrain from digging a bit further, just to see if he could goad a physical attack. He had a perverse need to see just how far he could push his authority over her.

"How could I forget you're the captain?" Kraft spun and faced him. "You remind me every time I turn around. Lord on high! What do you want me to do? Genuflect every time I see you? Bow and mumble, 'I'm not worthy'? Salute you? What?" Up her hands went. "You've made me your cook, rejected me as whore, yet seem furious at the very idea I might sleep with another man on your ship."

Jace met her blazing gaze. "Bailey's hardly a man."

Kraft rolled her eyes and said something low and guttural in German. Before he could ask for a translation, she said, "I would no more go to his bed than Heller's. Or Garrett's. I've got even less interest in Payton or Charissa. Guess that leaves you, Captain." She lifted her brows and put her hands on her hips. "Until I'm released from my contract with you, I won't take any man into my bed *but* you. Satisfied?"

Stunned by her forthright declaration, Jace said, "I want you to cook and keep your hands off my crew."

"But I didn't—"

"You touched Bailey's hand."

She took a deep breath to retort, but changed her mind. Instead, she saluted him. "You got it, Captain. I'm your cook and nothing more." She tossed a smoldering look over her shoulder as she stalked off. "Tell you what, you'll regret that a hell of a lot more than I will."

Kraft created incredible meals, and Jace found himself looking more and more forward to mealtime. Before Kraft, the galley had been a place to avoid, but not any longer.

After she served everyone, Jace would step forward and she would have a plate waiting. Once she served him, she fixed up a plate for herself and went to her room. When everyone left the kitchen area, she returned, cleaned up and went right back to her room.

Phantom cook.

His crew assumed he punished her for the fiasco in the cargo bay, but they were too intimidated by his sullen mood to ask.

After three days, nine incredible meals, terse orders and tense silence, Garrett set aside his fork and boldly asked, "I'm apt to regret this, but what's going on, Jace?"

"Nothing." Jace glared at Garrett down the length of the kitchen table. "Just eat your lunch and get back to work."

"You all bent at her because we caught you on the floor with her?" Garrett grinned. "Hell, Jace, not a one of us is teasing you about it. If you've got something with Kraft—"

"There's nothing going on." Jace turned his attention back to his meal.

"Your pissytude indicates *something* done crawled up your butt and died." Garrett tossed his napkin aside. "Hell, we'd all like to know what it is before we hold you down and have Payton forcibly remove it."

Payton gasped at the vulgarity.

Charissa and Bailey giggled.

"Did that bitch do something to the ship?" Heller asked.

"Stop calling her a bitch." Bailey spoke to Heller, but kept his eyes on his plate.

"Shut up, boy, or I'll rip out your tongue." Heller lunged at Bailey from across the table. Bailey flinched, splattering half his food to his lap. "I owe you two for flinching."

"If Jace refuses to let anyone speak, could we also refrain from bickering during meals?" Payton asked.

"I'm all for not fighting, but we got us some serious jawing to do," Garrett said. "Kraft is a bought woman, Jace. *Your* bought woman." He passed his napkin along to Bailey, who cleaned up while Heller grinned at him. "She's cooking up a storm, yet she's being shunned. If you're going the way of the WAG Amish, that's fine, but at least give a heads up on *why* we're gobbling up her victuals, but eschewing her company."

"It does seem unfair," Payton said.

Charissa nodded.

Bailey nodded and took a wary bite while he kept his gaze on his plate.

"Did Kraft do something wrong, Captain Jace?" Charissa asked. "If she did, shouldn't you—"

Payton shook her head at her daughter, forbidding her from interfering.

"I'm just asking, Mom!"

Bailey looked at Jace. "You said to treat her honorably, but you—"

"Shut up, boy." Heller lunged at Bailey.

Bailey didn't flinch this time, but he did drop his gaze.

"Heller," Garrett said, "you lunge at him one more time, and I promise you, I'll—"

"Everyone, stop." Jace slapped his hand to the table, rattling the plates. "Kraft didn't do a damn thing wrong. Neither did anyone else. I did."

Resolved, he left the galley and walked directly to Kraft's room. Using his knuckle, he tapped softly against the wall com on the outside of her door.

"What?" Her voice sounded tinny over the speaker, but bellowed through the metal door.

"We need to talk." Jace pressed the com and her bedroom door pocketed to the side with a dull thud.

"Are you sure you're willing to risk it? I might make you laugh." Kraft ate while sitting cross-legged on her bed, reading the paperback Garrett had taken from the derelict Basic.

Jace wondered if the western was any good. "I don't feel much like laughing." He closed the door by slapping the wall com inside her bunk door.

"Really? I'm stunned." Kraft glanced at him, and then turned her attention back to the book. "You're usually such a bundle of giggles."

"Could we *not* fight, please?"

"Of course." She set the book aside, crossed her arms and glared at him. "I can't flirt, can't fight, you don't want me to do the other big F, fornicate, so, forgive my confusion, but what *do* you want me to do, Captain Lawless? I mean, besides be *your* cook. I got that part of my indentured servitude down."

Her tone and the look in her eyes could freeze the fires of hell. Jace turned to go. He thought he might try again later when she was less angry, but he realized she had a right to be upset, and walking away now would only make matters worse.

He faced her and softly said, "I want things to go back to the way they were."

She smiled sickly sweet and snidely asked, "You mean when I was throwing myself at everyone on your crew?"

Jace took a deep breath and sat on her bunk. "Kraft, I'm really trying here."

"Aw, hell. I know." She sighed and pushed her plate aside. "I'm just bitchy from looking at four walls for three days. I'm willing to give right in." She leaned forward. "Look, Captain, I like your crew, and I think they like me, well, except for Heller. Singing and talking and laughing is not flirting. Most people call it fun."

"I know." Jace looked at the cover of the paperback western and wished himself that man with his gleaming white hat tipped back off his brow, riding a midnight-black horse through an untouched prairie of pale grasses. That painted-picture man stood forever in a position where he could still triumph. Jace envied him that, since he had already lost his battle to protect all he loved.

"Then why did you think I was flirting with Bailey? Because I sang a song with him? Because I laughed with him?"

Jace shrugged. How could he explain his actions to her when he didn't understand them himself? Looking up, he caught her gaze.

Sudden understanding flashed across her face. "You were jealous."

When he tried to stand, she touched his arm, and he stopped. He sat down but wouldn't look at her. After a long stretch of silence, he asked, "Are you reading me?"

"Like a fifty foot plasboard." Kraft pulled her hand back to her lap. "If you mean do I have my psychic hat on, then no, but right now, I don't need it. You were jealous, weren't you?"

Reluctantly, he nodded. He saw no point in lying to her when she could read the truth anyway. "I don't even understand why. I know you're not interested in Bailey, you were just being nice to him." He kept his gaze on that captivating painting of a man with so much to fight for. "I guess, what made me jealous, was how fast you became a part of the crew. How quickly everyone accepted you, like you've always been here."

He finally braved a look at her. Sadness cast hunger deep in her fathomless eyes.

"And you're afraid I'm going to break their hearts when I go," Kraft said softly.

Jace nodded.

She looked at the paperback book. "I'd like to be that man too."

"Dammit, you are reading me." Jace stood from her tightly made bunk, turning his back on her.

She laughed gently. "You think because I told you I can read objects, I fudged a bit and can really read people."

He nodded without looking at her.

"Well, in a way, you're right. Sometimes, when I look at someone, I just know what they're thinking."

"I knew it." He felt so utterly exposed he wanted to double-check that his pants were still buttoned.

"It's nothing magical, Captain. I can read you just by watching what you do and listening to what you say. You broadcast your feelings more clearly than anyone I've ever met."

Her comment didn't surprise him. He'd never been very good at hiding his emotions, and it caused him more trouble than not. But he also felt Kraft wasn't being completely honest with him.

"I know you can read people better than that." He glanced at her closed door and thought he should have left it open. Just being alone with her made him feel jittery. "That's what you did at the gambling hell, isn't it?"

"No. Contrary to what you're thinking, I can't read people the way I can read objects. At the hell, I read the table and the cards, not the people." She sighed. "Look, it's complicated, and I really don't feel like telling you the details about my super powers."

He turned to face her. She looked suddenly small and vulnerable while sitting on the narrow bunk. When she lifted her gaze to him, he saw a deep pain, almost shame, on her face, but it vanished when she shook her head.

"Captain, the thing is, you have a tendency to make your feelings perfectly clear, then totally obscure." She shrugged. "It's like you're dancing a very tight one step forward, one step back with me."

"Why do you call it that? Dancing, I mean." That she chose that particular metaphor spoke volumes to him. Night after night, he locked himself to his room to dance in his mind with his wife. He'd stopped of late, because he no longer imagined Senna in his arms, but Kraft.

"Because life is like a dance with daggers drawn. You can make it stylized or you can make it deadly. Just depends who you're dancing with and why." Kraft stroked her hand over the paperback. "I don't want our dance to be deadly."

Jace considered her for a very long time. "Neither do I."

She looked up and offered a tentative smile. "I think, if we both try a little harder, we can make this work. But you have to stop thinking that I'm some kind of walking freak-show."

"I don't think that," he blurted, surprised that she would accuse him of agreeing with Heller's assessment of her.

With a grim frown, she said, "Yes, you do. You think I know everything about everyone all the time, but I don't. I'm a reader, Captain, but my skill is not remotely on the level you think it is. I'm not omniscient."

"If I said something that offended you, then I apologize."

"Okay." She smiled up at him. "Permission to leave my quarters, sir?"

"Permission granted." He nodded. "Grab your plate and come back to the kitchen."

"Yes sir!" She stood, saluted him sharply, and picked up her plate.

He slapped the wall com and opened the door.

"So, can I grab your butt on the way too?"

He spun around.

"You said you wanted things back the way they were." Kraft winked at him. "I assumed that meant I could flirt with *you* again."

"Beware what you ask for." He turned away before she could see his smile.

"Captain?" Her low voice held no trace of joking.

He turned and looked her right in the eye.

"If you really hate my flirting with you, I'll stop."

"I don't hate it, *annyae*."

The endearment surprised her. In Universal, an *annyae* was a tiny gold trinket worth not for its weight in gold, but its fierce sentimental value.

When Kraft blushed, he was more than a little pleased with himself for turning the tables on her.

She glanced away, then back. "That's good, because I don't think I could. Stop flirting with you, that is. You're just way too pretty."

He grinned and she echoed with that slow, lazy, sexy smile that touched him to his toes. It didn't bother him so much anymore that she kept calling him pretty, because he understood she meant it as a compliment. He felt an overwhelming urge to reach out and stroke her flushed cheek, but held himself back. He didn't want to watch her flinch away from the darkness of his touch.

After a decade in the Void, he'd never met a woman who attracted him like Kraft. To splash vinegar to the salt-filled wound, the object of his desire was now a part of his crew, which made her totally off limits to him. No matter how enticing, it would be inappropriate to make her his lover. No matter how badly he wanted to.

Chapter Thirteen

When they returned to the kitchen, Jace took his place at the head of the table. Kraft stood by the stove, looking at his broad back and thinking of how much she wanted to embrace him—the hell with all these stupid rules of honor.

His gentle honesty touched her deeply, and his clear love for his crew, that he worried about her breaking their hearts when she left, almost brought tears to her eyes. Behind that simple truth lurked the fact that his heart would be broken too.

She wanted to allay his fears about her psychic abilities by disclosing the full of her powers, but she couldn't. They were both safer with him not knowing.

Very soon, they would have to talk about the length of her contract. She couldn't be his cook forever, yet she couldn't leave until he released her.

She should have confronted him long before now and set limits to the fuzzy contract, but she honestly didn't want to. For the moment, she wanted to stay. She felt safe and had no responsibility other than to cook. Once they agreed to a definitive time limit, they would both have to stick to it. With everything unspoken, they could take advantage of the wiggle room and keep dancing.

"Were there any romances on your ship?" Charissa cast a wistful look at Bailey.

When Bailey cast a wistful glance at Kraft, she realized she might be better off staying in her room.

"I thought your crew was all female," Payton said with an odd hesitancy. Just the thought of same-sex love made Payton distinctly uncomfortable, and it showed on her pinched face.

Payton's attitude didn't surprise Kraft in the least. Payton lived most of her life on the IWOG worlds where homosexuality was forbidden by law and punishable by death. As a doctor, Payton had been forced to report any questionable relationship to the IWOG officers stationed within her hospital.

"Yeah," Heller grunted. "Tell us all about it."

Dismissing Heller with a roll of her eyes, Kraft looked to Charissa. "There was romance on my ship." She thought of Danna and Jinj, and how they'd snuck around for months even though everyone knew what was going on.

"Did anyone fall in love?" Charissa lifted her innocent green eyes to Bailey, but he didn't notice because he was too busy taming his wayward locks as he looked at Kraft.

After a brief hesitation, Kraft reluctantly said, "Yes."

"You make love sound like it's not a good thing." Charissa frowned in her pretty, puzzled way.

"Well, love isn't bad, such as it is." Kraft really didn't want to have this conversation now, but after what she and Jace had discussed, now might be the time to remind him not to fall in love with her. "But love can sometimes make folks do all kinds of strange things."

Charissa looked confused and everyone else got a lot more interested about eavesdropping. Even Jace perked up his ears.

"Surely, love is better than hate on a ship?" Payton cast a fond gaze to her daughter and then a quick sidelong glance to Garrett.

Payton just proved her point. In a desperate situation, Payton would choose her daughter over anyone else on the ship, no matter what orders Jace gave. That's what made love so dangerous. It muddied the waters and made the chain of authority fuzzy.

"Love can cause more problems on a ship than hate ever could." Kraft scrubbed the dishes clean and stacked them on the sideboard.

"But if two people love each other..." Charissa trailed off with a wistful voice as she looked at Bailey. Everyone noticed *but* Bailey, who kept his pale blue eyes riveted on every move Kraft made.

"Love can far outweigh a captain's orders and make life more—fudgy. Not bad, just more complicated around the edges."

Heller snarfed. "Who gives a rat's about love. Just tell us

the juicy parts." He laughed like a grunting pig. Heller, like most Fringe men, embraced female homosexuality with a leering salaciousness. If Kraft attempted to tell him about the men she'd known who were in love, he'd snarl and curse his way out of the room.

Charissa frowned at Heller then turned her big green eyes to Kraft. "You forbid it?"

Appalled at the very idea, Kraft shook her head. "No. A captain can't dictate matters of the heart." Finished with the dishes, she methodically wiped down the stove and countertops. "I just made it clear that their allegiance to the crew always came first. Not to me, mind you, but to the whole of our ship."

"Yeah, bet you had all kinds of fun with your allegiant crew." Heller flashed her a nasty smirk.

It took all her willpower not to force Heller down on his knees and make him apologize for being such an ignoramus. Lord on high, Heller had all the appeal of a festering anal fissure.

"You never fell in love?" Charissa asked.

"I fell in love with each and every member of my crew."

"Yeah, I'll bet you 'loved' them." Heller slashed quote marks in the air and his implication was unmistakable.

"There is love without sex, Heller, just as there is sex without love. I'm not surprised you don't understand the difference."

Her gaze settled on Charissa. "I loved my crew. Much like your mother loves you." Kraft nodded to Payton, and understanding filled Payton's eyes.

Kraft dried and stowed the dishes. "It's funny that our Universal language knows only one word for love when there are many kinds of love, and all are special. But all can cross a captain. Love is a dangerous thing on a ship."

Kraft knew Jace listened intently, but he never turned around. In a way, she felt she spoke directly to him, warning him not to fall in love with her. And perhaps reminding herself that such an emotional entanglement between them could only end badly. More than anything, she didn't want to repay his kindness by hurting him.

"Bet that didn't stop you from getting a little thrust and wiggle." Heller made a rude hand gesture as he flashed her a perverted grin.

Coldly, Kraft said, "I never touched a member of my crew in such a manner." But she thought of the times she'd held them as they cried over a real or imagined loss. She'd been like a protective mother. Her embrace had been the only place Bavin could find peace within her last hours on the Random Trifecta. Kraft had not been able to soothe Bavin's shock and pain, and a feeling of failure crept over her again.

"They ain't around to deny it, are they?" Heller's eyes glittered.

Wanting to bash him in the nose like Jace had done, Kraft instead looked Heller in the eye. "Ugly fits you like a tailored suit."

Heller sat stock still as he digested her comment.

When she turned around, she found Jace watching her speculatively.

"Tell you what, I like men in my bed, notably pretty ones." She winked at Jace, who blushed just a bit. She found his blushing sexy. Maybe because it made her feel like she seduced a man about three steps from the priesthood, especially since he had a decade of celibacy under his belt. She still couldn't believe he was thirty-five and knew only his wife. She hoped her open and blatant flirting made it clear she didn't take anything too seriously, and that he shouldn't either.

"What man would want a ball-buster like you?" Heller asked.

"A man with a hefty set?" Kraft dipped her gaze to Heller's crotch. "Guess that leaves you out."

Heller puffed himself up, but backed off when she pressed her index finger to her thumb.

"As charming as this conversation is," Jace said, "we've got a job to do."

After washing their dishes and stowing them, Payton and Charissa left the kitchen.

Garrett, Heller, Bailey and Jace sat around the table while Kraft dawdled near the stove.

Jace cleared his throat. "You're excused, Kraft."

She left before she gave in to her desire to argue but it damn near killed her. She wouldn't have a notion of what they were planning to do. Even as a raw recruit on Fairing's ship, she'd always heard enough scuttlebutt to grasp the plan. Not so on *Mutiny*.

"Unless I tap the kitchen com from my bedroom."

Kraft considered the idea. *Mutiny* was a 2xBasic with limited upgrades. Mucking about with the electronics would be child's play. Open any com panel, twist three wires, and she'd be privy to everything on the ship.

"I'd also kiss my honor goodbye."

Jace had every right to spy on her but she had no right to spy on him. He was the captain and she had to follow his orders.

Kraft waited until she heard the port shuttle disengage from *Mutiny*, then she made her way to the bridge. She looked out the main window. "Is that the ship they're salvaging?"

Bailey nodded, obsessively tuning his guitar.

"Lord on high, do any of you know what that is?"

"Sure," Bailey said, "it's just an old IWOG scout."

"No, it's not." Kraft yanked the guitar right out of his hands. "That's a Runner ship." She set the instrument aside. "That ship is loaded with deadly hardware."

"How can you tell it's a bounty hunter's—"

"Do you have a com link to them?"

"Sure." Bailey nodded to the console.

She activated the com. "Captain Lawless?"

"Kraft? Get off the com," Jace ordered.

"You are in danger, Captain Lawless." She kept her voice calm even though her heart tried to pound its way out of her chest. "Stop where you are, turn back, and get off that ship right now."

"Everything looks—"

Rapid gun fire crackled over the com, causing both her and Bailey to wince.

"Activate the other shuttle," Kraft said.

Terror-filled, Bailey froze.

"Now, Bailey. I don't have time to explain."

Bailey just gave the com a wide-eyed look of fear.

Kraft grabbed him by the shoulders and gripped him hard enough to hurt him, but the pain made him focus on her.

Calmly, she said, "If you don't activate the second shuttle, they are going to die over there." Kraft let the truth sink in. "Trust me. I can save them."

Bailey slapped at the console.

She ran to the second shuttle, fired it up, disengaged from *Mutiny* and made her way to the IWOG scout. To her relief, the shuttle had a small cache of guns. She picked the best of a bad lot.

It took forever to double-dock her shuttle piggyback to Jace's on the cargo bay of the Runner ship. When she did, she touched the airlock. The entire ship was filled with autofire weapons. Jace and his crew were pinned down, unable to retreat.

She walked along the central hall. Thanks to Bailey's boots, she had two thin surprises in conjunction with her crummy gun. She touched the walls, read where each autofire weapon was located and blasted it to smithereens with a shot. Or two. Her gun had a sight off by about five degrees. Annoying, but she had the ammo to take at least three shots for every solid hit.

Kraft yanked out the spent clip, slammed up another and continued down the hall, hoping like hell she wasn't too late.

Finally, she found Jace and his crew bunkered down behind a pile of wooden crates, hiding from the infrared sensors of the autofire modules. Dodging, using the crates to shield her body heat, she made her way toward them.

To her horror, Jace stood when he saw her.

She jumped in front of him and took a shot in her left arm as she tackled him to the floor. Before she could enjoy the feeling of his rugged body below hers, she scrambled up, spun around and shot the autofire weapon apart.

"What are you doing here?" Jace put his hands around her waist and pulled her behind a crate. He pushed up her sleeve to check her arm.

The bullet grazed a three inch long and inch wide gash across her upper left arm. The wound looked a lot worse than it felt. She rolled the fabric down and a crimson blossom seeped ever larger against her yellow sleeve.

"I'm okay."

"Shit howdy! What's freak-show doing here?" Heller had to lie flat to hide his bulk.

"I'm selling cookies." Kraft rolled her eyes. "What do you

think I'm doing here?"

"You made this ship do this!" Heller's eyes were wide and he looked on the verge of a full blown attack of hysteria.

"No, but I could have told you to expect this if you would have let me be a part of your little planning session." Kraft touched the floor, rose over the crates, took out two more autofires with three shots and dropped back behind the crates.

Jace looked at her with an expression she couldn't figure out, and after their chat earlier, she didn't want to violate his privacy by trying to read him through the floor, which they both touched. She also didn't want to feel that odd feedback that blasted her when she'd tried to read him through his plate.

"Yeah, I forgot you know everything," Heller snarled.

"I think the gun in my hand is more capable of coherent thought than you are. Lord on high, we're not done yet."

Touching the floor, she waited. A roving autofire rolled down the hall. Popping up, she blew it away with three shots. It slumped down to a quivering mass of snapping electronics.

"Now we're done." She yanked out the spent clip, flipped it over her shoulder, then slammed up another. All of the sudden she realized the crummy gun she held was far superior to the ancient Sod Busters Jace chose to arm himself with. She wondered why he didn't upgrade his guns, and then decided he had a fondness for them or felt more comfortable with them, just as she did with a modified Katana. And such a random thought didn't really matter at the moment.

"Well, that went simple." Garrett blew across the barrel of his gun and holstered it.

Heller grunted and slapped his back.

"I vote she goes with us next time, Captain," Garrett said.

Heller shoved Garrett hard for betraying him.

"If you folks keep pulling boners like this, there isn't gonna *be* many more next times." She winced as she pressed her sleeve against her wound. Focusing her mind, she made the injury stop hurting, but let it bleed. She wanted the wound clean before she shut it down.

"How did you get over here?" Jace demanded.

"My fairy godmother flew me over." She shook her head. "No, she was gonna, but I thought it would be faster if I just took the other shuttle."

"You shouldn't be here," Jace said, his voice rising.

"Tell you what," she said, raising her voice, "neither should you."

"Everything was just fine—"

"Until you almost got shot!"

His gaze fell on her bloody arm. Lowering his voice to an intimate whisper, Jace said, "I wouldn't have stood up if you wouldn't have come in the room."

Glaring at him, Kraft whispered, "Oh, goody, let's play blame the victim."

His voice rising again, Jace said, "You are so far from a victim, lady, it makes my head spin."

Climbing to her knees, Kraft said, "That bullet would have literally made your pretty head spin. Lord on high, Captain Lawless, you're just embarrassed because your cook-whore saved your ass, or rather, your head. Oh, and by the way, you're welcome!"

Kraft found herself practically nose-to-nose with Jace. She wanted to shake him for almost getting himself killed. She realized he wanted to do the same thing to her. Fury erupted because they were both safe. Getting pissed off was a hell of a lot more comfortable for both of them to deal with rather than the underlying emotion of affection.

Looking up, locking her gaze to his, Kraft knew down to her bones Jace had the same insight. They were furious at each other because they cared about each other. Simple and complicated all in the same breath.

"Would you two stop squalling?" Garrett shook his head at them as if reprimanding children. "Ponder the weirdness wonder of it all, but we're safe, and we still have to salvage this ship of horrors. That is, if it's safe to do so."

"We're clear." She shook from the surge of adrenaline and the sudden connection to Jace. Gathering her wits, pulling herself from the knowledge in his eyes, she touched the floor, read lightly, confirming, and said, "We're clear."

Garrett stood, stretched, and settled his hat. "Let's get moving on this then."

Jace also stood.

"You're taking the word of freak-show?" Heller's hands shook as he clutched his Sharp Shooter rifle. His breath, short and gasping, burst from him like ten lions in a crowded cage.

"Why would I lie?" Kraft looked at her wound and then at Heller. "Did I come over here to make sure you all got shot or just me? How stupid are you?" She deliberately goaded Heller. As soon as she did, his fear turned from free-floating rage to self-preservation. Heller got a very hard and fast grip on himself.

"Stop calling me stupid, she-bitch." His hands steadied on his gun.

"If the boot fits," she drawled, "you best take it from your mouth."

Heller took a deep breath and stood, looming over her. He touched the butt of his gun to his crotch then flicked it toward her face. "I've got something nasty to shove in your mouth, and it ain't no boot."

Before Jace could punch Heller again, she smiled up at Jace then turned her gaze to Heller. She gave a calm, cool assessment up his massive frame from her submissive position and pressed her right index finger to her thumb, over and over.

Heller backed off so fast he almost tripped himself with his own big feet. Embarrassed by his fear, he recovered, lowered his gun, flicked off the safety and pointed the barrel at her head.

Kraft laughed. "You think?"

Doubt flickered across Heller's face.

Kraft smoothed her hand down from her waist, along her thigh, to the top of her borrowed boot. Her fingertips stroked the handle of the thin blade tucked between the seams.

Heller's gaze followed her stroke.

"I got fast hands, Heller. How fast are yours?"

Meeting her gaze, Heller clutched his gun and swallowed.

"Do you think I can knock that gun from your hand before you can shoot me?"

Heller's brows lowered as he considered.

"Enough." Jace wedged himself between them.

Heller yanked his gun up and flipped on the safety.

Jace wouldn't let her do it because he knew she could. One flick of her hidden blade and she could take off Heller's hand long before he could pull the trigger.

"Garrett, Heller, start stripping the ship."

They set to work. Kraft found herself alone with Jace.

"What of me?" She peered up at him. When he noticed her mouth was level with the worn edge of his button fly, his gaze jumped to hers. She smiled and winked, but he didn't blush. He got hard. She could see his reaction and sure as hell he could feel it.

Jace stepped back and turned away. "Get back to *Mutiny*."

She stood. "Captain, if I could suggest—"

"I think you've done enough for today. You best be on your way and have Payton look at your arm. If you're able, then rustle up some dinner." He couldn't even look at her when he spoke with his imperious captain voice.

"Oooo, nice way to put me in my place, Captain." When he turned, she snapped him a sharp salute. "But before you leave this ship, you might want to strip it of the electronics. Runners typically have some of the best tricks."

"This is an IWOG scout, not a Runner ship."

"Some Runner bought this IWOG scout and upgraded the hell out of it so he could use it for bounty hunting. Had you paid more attention to details, you would have known that."

"How was I to know autofire weapons would be around every corner?"

Kraft gave a short, exasperated sigh. "Because it's a Runner ship."

"It looks like an IWOG scout."

"It is. One that a Runner upgraded."

"But it looks like an IWOG scout."

"It only looks like that if you don't look hard enough!" She lowered her voice. "Didn't you notice the larger port aft?"

"So?"

Resisting the urge to shake him, she calmly said, "This ship is a flying blow torch. It's faster than almost anything in the Void."

Jace pondered for a moment. "You knew by looking?"

"Just at the back end." Kraft nodded. "It's an IWOG scout, just as you were told, but they hoped you wouldn't notice the wider exhaust port, and you didn't. Do you realize you could have come into this ship and found a prisoner on the loose? Who knows who this Runner transported?"

"Kobra never mentioned—"

"And you didn't know enough to ask."

Jace gritted his teeth.

"I'm not trying to grind it in your face. I'm just suggesting, in the future, for the time I'm on your ship, it would behoove you to accept my input." She grinned. "Yes, I'm a girl, a lady, a chick, a she-bitch, and Heller's personal favorite, a freak-show, but I also know a thing or two about the Void that maybe you all don't. I won't expect you to do what I say, but at least *give* me a say." She shrugged and winced. She held pressure to her arm and mentally forced the wound to stop bleeding. "Even if you all point and laugh at me right after I open my mouth, at least give me the chance to speak before you relegate me to the kitchen."

Jace cast a curious gaze around the storage room. "You knew this was a Runner ship?"

"As soon as I saw it from the bridge of *Mutiny*."

Jace leaned close. "How do you know so much about ships just by looking?"

"I told you that I had five years of military training. I know ships and I know upgrades, or the signs of them, anyway."

"Which military branch?"

She'd rather do anything other than answer that question.

"Captain!" Heller yelled, puffing into the room. "Garrett says you gotta see this bridge!"

Jace watched Heller lumber away. "Why is he so excited?"

"It's loaded with tricks." She silently thanked Heller for her reprieve.

"What tricks?"

"You want my help or not?"

"Fine. Take whatever you want. Just don't bleed to death."

"Yeah, wouldn't want to deprive you of your captive cook." Kraft turned on her heel and stalked off to the shuttle bay.

"The next time I get an itch to do a good deed," Jace said, "I think I'll shoot myself in the head."

Kraft turned. She looked at him for a long time. "I didn't ask for your help."

"I didn't ask for yours either."

"Touché."

Kraft's injury hampered her movements in the kitchen. She

made a simple dinner and ate standing, but she couldn't manage to clean up one-handed afterwards.

Against her best efforts, she managed to maneuver the large pots and pans right to the floor. Her shoulder just wouldn't grasp more than ten puny pounds no matter how angry she got.

She fumbled a pot. Before it could hit the floor, Jace caught it.

"Here, I got it."

When he bent over to put the pot away, she admired his backside. Jace Lawless had a fanny that any woman would want to squeeze, or wrap her legs around.

"Feel like explaining why you're doing this now?" Jace closed the cabinet and faced her.

"Just wanted to see you bend over before I went to bed."

She hoped for a smile, but instead, he only looked at her with concern in the depth of his eyes.

"I seem to have a real fascination for your backside." She smiled at him, but he wouldn't echo it.

"How's your arm?" He lifted his hand as if to touch her, but seemed reluctant to actually make contact. His hand fell back to his side.

"It's fine." She shrugged. "It's one of the lesser wounds I've had."

"You took it for me," Jace whispered, his gaze riveted to the bloody mess on her left sleeve.

She hadn't had time to ask him for a new shirt or clean up this one. After what happened on the Runner ship, she didn't think asking him for any more favors would be a wise idea.

"You're my captain," she said simply.

"So you'd give up your life for me?"

The dance felt way too intense, and she pulled back. "All I did was give up a chunk of my arm for you. It's not that big of a deal."

"It is to me." He stepped close enough for her to smell the subtle musk of his body. It wasn't fair that he smelled even better than he looked.

She hadn't thought before she'd leaped out in front of him. She'd automatically reacted. The more she thought about her reasons for doing so, the more she wanted to pull away from

Jace. His scent and the plaintive look in his eyes made her feel uncomfortable in her own skin.

"If I hadn't leapt forward that bullet would have hit your neck. Didn't I once confess I'd hate to muss your hair let alone your pretty neck?" She desperately tried to keep the conversation light with her joking question and her jaunty attitude.

"You don't owe me your life, Kraft." He frowned with his face and his entire body. Jace slumped, looking dejected, embarrassed and apologetic.

"You think that's why I protected you? Because I feel guilty about owing you?" She turned away. "Well, I must say, you've got me all sussed out, Captain Lawless." She dodged past him, thankful that he'd given her the opening she needed to exit.

"Wait."

"What? You wanna toss it in my face some more?" Hands on her hips, she continued, "Haven't you ground my nose in it enough that I owe you? You keep ascribing it to me, but you're the one who keeps bringing it up." She lifted her arms and winced when doing so reopened her wound. She swore up a German streak.

"Here, let me—" He reached for her.

"Don't you dare." She pulled back. She was unbalanced enough without adding the confusion of his touch to the mix. "I swear, if I had a purse of script I'd hurl it right at your pretty face. Since I don't, you can just keep my share of the job, okay? Consider it a downpayment on my contract."

Turning away with a dismissive toss of her head, she took two long strides to the door.

"Stop."

"Is that an order, Captain?" she asked mockingly.

"Turn around."

His tone brooked no argument. With a deep breath, she faced him, her chin high.

"Go to my bunk and wait for me there."

Startled by his command and the smoldering heat in his eyes, Kraft had to clench her jaw tight before shock allowed it to fall off her face. Would he make her his whore just to assert his authority over her?

Cautious and respectful, she asked, "Are you ordering me

to your bunk to..." She let her voice trail off because she didn't know how to finish.

Stepping close, he lowered his voice. "You said you would honor the full of the contract between us."

Chapter Fourteen

Jace strode down the hall and found Kraft standing by the door to his bunk. Seeing her dressed in his old flax trousers straining against her hips attracted him on a deep physical level, but his too-small yellow shirt now ripped and stained from a gunshot to her upper left arm repulsed him with a hefty dose of guilt. Kraft had damn near killed herself to protect him.

She'd been forced to put herself in jeopardy to save him from his own bumbling. He should have known the information Kobra gave him on the salvage job was flawed, but he needed the money and the job looked okay. Once again, even though he'd gone by the book, everything went wrong. He felt inept, ashamed, emasculated, and he'd taken his frustration out on Kraft because she saved him without a single thought to her own safety.

His decade of surviving the Fringe was a drop in the bucket to her shark-infested depths. Just by being a woman, Kraft opened herself up to a seamy-underbelly of the Fringe that he never had to deal with. Most established worlds, be they IWOG, WAG, or Fringe, still considered women chattel. Men could be bought and sold as labor slaves, but few were bought or sold as sexual slaves. Women were far more valuable commodities. Women could be sold as cheap labor, breeders, or thralls. A thrall, a sexual slave, especially an attractive woman with cooking skills, was the most valuable of all women on the Fringe.

Cook-whore.

Freeze-dried dreck in knowing hands could be most pleasurable. And if the cook-whore couldn't cook all that well, then at least she could still whore. Even if the woman put up a fight, a strong man could force her to provide the basics of pleasure. Or drug her so she might not care so much. Or restrain her until she had no choice.

Kraft willingly cooked, willingly fought, and claimed she would willingly whore. By her own honor, she offered the full of herself up to him, but Jace sensed that she expected him to restrain himself by his own dictates of honor. Asking her to cook and fight was one thing, but asking her to whore? Well, that was an entirely different matter.

When she saw him approach, Kraft stood at full attention with her face demurely lowered. All at once he felt a foot taller than her when he wasn't.

He'd ordered her to his bunk as a spur-of-the-moment way to get her to stop defying his authority. He never thought Kraft would actually obey. Now that she had, he wasn't sure what to do with her. Feeling awkward and shy, he thought the first thing he should do was explain and apologize.

Embarrassment at her having saved him and his crew fueled his need to remind her and himself that he was in charge. As he drew close to her, he longed to reach out and touch her face. On a rush of emotion, he wanted to confess that he didn't always know what to do, or how to proceed, and sometimes acted rashly, fueled more by his heart than his head.

As a captain, Jace wanted to ask for her help and make her his partner in crime. Perversely, he felt he shouldn't need her help and should make her his partner in bed. As a man, Jace wanted to possess the full of Kraft. He wanted to protect her even though he knew he couldn't. Worse, he knew he didn't have to coddle Kraft, which only increased his longing to claim her as his bedwarmer. Beyond that corral of confusion, Jace knew Kraft shouldn't have to protect him.

Instead of saying anything, he unlocked his bunk with a slap of his hand to the wall com. The metal catch released with a soft snick that vibrated the floor below their feet.

Her braless breasts jiggled against the worn yellow fabric of his secondhand shirt. The enticing movement caught his attention, and he forgot what he intended to say. Instead, he found himself imagining what she would look like topless.

"If you'd like, I could put the harem outfit on."

His gaze went from her chest to her mouth.

Lifting her lowered face a fraction, Kraft met his gaze, and whispered, "Someone placed the costume in my closet." She flashed him that slow, lazy and sexy smile.

Jace had no idea who put the outfit in her closet, but he wouldn't mind seeing her in that getup again. Fluffpink clinging and exposing the full promise of her undeniably strong and sexy body was certainly worth a second look. After seeing her in the revealing outfit, he knew her nipples were large and toffee-dark against her skin. He remembered the snug slit of her innie bellybutton drawing his gaze down to the wide pleasure of her hips. Between her lush thighs, he would find another snug—

"Should I fetch that costume, Captain?"

Her seductive, superior attitude dispelled all his thoughts of apologizing. Kraft didn't worry one bit about him taking charge, because she assumed she had the upper hand. His blushing and backing off made her think she could say or do anything, and he'd just turn away. Normally he would have, but not this time.

Slipping a finger under her chin, he lifted her face until she met his gaze. Fathomless black eyes held a smirk that he wanted to quash in a sudden rush. For the first time, she didn't flinch away from his touch. She melted to him as he stroked his finger across her full, sensuous lips. More than anything in the Void, he wanted to kiss her. He wanted to taste every bit of her luscious mouth. Kraft had a body built for sin, but she had a mouth destined for seduction.

Jace lowered his voice as his mouth descended on hers. "Seems like a waste of time for you to put on all those complicated clothes when I'm just going to make you take them off."

Her eyes widened.

Placing his mouth to her ear, he whispered, "Or did you want to dress up and then strip for me?"

She tensed and swallowed with an audible click.

He pressed closer. "I've never had a whore in my bed. If you're familiar with the concept, maybe you could walk me through it."

Kraft pulled back and narrowed her gaze. "After ten years of celibacy, I think a walk is all it would take."

"Is that so?" Refusing to back down, Jace traced his finger along her ear to her neck. "Since it's been a decade for me, I'm thinking you won't be able to walk by the time I'm satisfied."

Her jaw damn near hit the floor.

Jace took a perverse delight in shocking her, and her dismay made him even more determined to make her back down this time. Even if he had to say the most vulgar things in the Void, he would force her retreat.

"I can't believe you're surprised." He stroked her lips with a forceful fingertip. "You can read me so well, right?"

She darted her gaze to the floor. "I told you, I can't read you like that. I can read—"

Plush lips gave way below the thrust of his silencing finger. When her hungry eyes met his, he said, "Don't try to distract me. I don't care what you can read. You don't have to read me. I'll tell you what I want."

Lowering his mouth to her neck, he nipped lightly. "I want you." After pulling her mocha skin, marking her, he lifted his mouth to her ear. "I want you writhing and panting and sweating below my thrusting body."

She placed her large hands on his chest, pushed him back and looked him right in the eye. The depths of her black gaze swarmed with heat, smoky and slightly unfocused. "You want me by force?"

He heard the catch in her voice and sensed her desperation. He smiled at her as he answered her question with one of his own. "How can I force you when sex is part of your contract, my lovely cook-whore?"

Kraft withdrew with a startled step back. She pressed against the metal door of his bunk and flattened her palms against the smooth durosteel to steady herself.

Closing in on her, he took a half-step forward and placed his palms on the door, encasing her with his arms. In a tingling rush, a fleeting ripple washed over his body, and he wondered if he could actually feel Kraft trying to read him through the door. He forced himself to contain the rush by focusing his mind and constricting his body to a tense stance.

Kraft stood taller. Confusion and fear darted across her expressive face. He wondered if the darkness in him caused her reaction, or if he'd succeeded in preventing her from reading him. Either way, he sensed his advantage.

Pressing his mouth to her ear, he whispered, "What's wrong, sugar-britches? I thought you were all for this kind of dance between us, especially after what you said in the cargo bay."

With her back to his bunk door, she lifted her face and the whole of her body until she met his gaze with level intensity. Since she couldn't force him to retreat verbally, she now tried to force his retreat with the fierceness of her gaze, and it almost worked.

He fought down the urge to step back by moving closer. She radiated the scents of cooking, but below, he found that enticing hint of her musky perfume. Her scent was rich, intoxicating and alluring. He wanted to find the source of her fragrance and lose himself in it.

"Just give me the order, Captain Lawless, and I'll ride you until we both collapse."

One fleeting vision of her proudly riding astride him caused him to blush and turn away. The triumphant look on her face clarified she thought such a command a distinct impossibility.

She seemed pleased that she'd finally forced him to back down. He watched Kraft's pulse jump below the smooth skin of her neck when he closed in on her and said, "That's an order I'm not likely to give."

Her lips parted in surprise. She lowered her face but not her gaze.

"I wouldn't order you to ride me because I like to be on top."

He forced her chin up so their lips came close without touching. "Stop giving me that submissive face when you've got nothing behind it but arrogance."

Kraft stood tall. "I thought you preferred submissive women?"

"As a matter of fact I do." Tracing his finger along the open V of her shirt, he smoothed the fabric against the curve of her breasts and popped open one of the small wooden buttons. "Do you like submissive men?"

She closed her eyes, took a deep breath, but it caught in her throat. When he looked down, he discovered her nipples were pressed tight against the soft yellow fabric of his old shirt.

He chuckled and stroked the barest brush of his fingertip over the swell of her nipple. "Obviously not."

Pulling back, Kraft lifted hungry eyes. "Are you taking me to your bed, or are you planning to fuck me in the hallway?"

The vulgarity hit him like a cold water slap, but he would not retreat. "Don't swear at me. I don't like it." For a brief moment, he almost told her to go. This had gone far enough, and no matter what darkness filled him, he could not command her to his bunk. Once behind that closed door, all his self-control would vanish in a consuming fire of need, but he had yet to taste her mouth. More than anything, he did not want this moment with her to end until he'd kissed her.

Coldly, he said, "I prefer a wife in my bed. Seems to me I should take my whore in the kitchen." He inclined his head toward the galley doorway.

With a dismissive lift of her chin, Kraft strode into the darkened galley. He followed, his gaze riveted on the sway of her fanny below the soft homespun of his secondhand trousers.

The luscious scent of dinner still wafted through the silent galley. Jace turned the lights low. With his hands to her hips, he lifted her to the counter, placing her below that oddly misplaced window in the ceiling.

"Rather dangerous place for a tryst." She pressed her legs together. "Anyone could walk in."

"It's late, and everyone is in bed." Running his hands up her thighs, he gently forced them apart. "If anyone interrupts, I'll just order them to leave. That's one of the benefits of being the captain—I get to order everyone around." He stepped between her parted legs and settled his hands on her hips.

Kraft sat very still, as if waiting for him to pull her forward, so he didn't. The anticipation of feeling her fully pressed to him was intoxicating enough. Just the thought of possessing her made him strain against the front of his trousers.

Along with swirling desire, a fear trickled down his spine like rainwater. He'd already gone too far to back down without losing face, and a deep masculine pleasure filled him when he thought about commanding a woman far stronger than himself. He wanted to know if Kraft would let him or fight him. Adrenaline surged with the thought he might very well die for his perverse curiosity.

"There's a dark streak in you, Captain Lawless. You want your crew to see us like this." Kraft placed her hand to his chest and toyed with the black hairs that peeked from below his shirt. "You want them to know that you took me down a peg by making me submit to you."

"Perhaps." He tightened his grip on her hips. "But then again, I don't really care what they think."

"Yes, you do." She lifted one brow as she popped open the top button of his shirt. "I usurped your authority today. You're doing this to reclaim your power."

Her insight into his motivations clarified that she could still read him on some level, but he refused to back down until he had tasted her. Once he knew the full of her mouth, he would never touch her again.

"Maybe this is the only way to make you understand that I'm in charge of this ship, and everyone on it, including you." He leaned close to kiss her, but she turned her head away before he could. Confusion washed over him. She seemed willing to let him touch her, but she would not kiss him, and he wondered why. Was all her pointed flirting just an act?

"I'm not disputing your authority, Captain. You don't have to do this in order to discipline me."

"You make it sound like I'm going to turn you over my knee and paddle your butt." He paused. "Not that it isn't an intriguing idea."

Fury drew her brows low. "You wouldn't dare."

"Keep defying me, and I might." With an insistent stroke of his fingertip, he pushed the V of her shirt apart until he exposed the inner curves of her breasts. Her soft skin melted under his touch. She arched back with a sigh of encouragement.

"Captain—"

"Silence."

Harsh and impatient, the command rushed from his mouth. Using the length of her bound hair, he pulled gently until he exposed her neck, making her vulnerable to him. He nipped her flesh as his voice shook a tremble in her body.

"If I want you to speak, I'll tell you what to say."

She tensed, and he thought he'd finally pushed her too far, but then she gripped his shoulders, encouraging him.

He kissed the space between her breasts as he worked the small wooden buttons of her shirt apart. Pounding blood coursed through him and echoed her pulse. Lips pressed to her flesh felt each push of her heart mimic his. He cupped her breasts through the worn yellow shirt, and her nipples tightened below his fingers.

She leaned back, balancing herself on one hand against the counter. With a soft moan, she cupped his head, trying to draw his mouth to her breast, but he refused and continued to tease the inner curves with his lips and tongue. She uttered a groan of frustration that became a gasp of surprise when he gripped her hips and pulled her tight against him.

Her heat burned through his trousers, arousing him beyond rational thought. Jace felt drugged yet alert. Digging his fingers into the flesh of her bottom, he held her still as he stroked slowly against the center of her spread legs.

Ten years of painful, lonely celibacy turned his gentle thrusts to gripping intensity. Losing control, Jace uttered her name with a breathless plea. He wanted her, all of her, here and now. He didn't care if a member of the crew entered the galley. In his current condition, he didn't think he would notice. Nothing existed for him but Kraft. The intoxicating pleasure of riding his swelling need against the slick moist heat of her trapped behind his castoff trousers rendered him an animal. He damned himself to the hot place for what he was doing, then damn himself even more for not insisting she wear a skirt.

Blind with passion, Jace pushed aside Kraft's shirt, lowered his head to her breast and took her swollen toffee peak into his mouth. He rasped his tongue and the sharp hairs of his new beard against the sensitive bud of her swelling breast.

Yanking her shirt from her pants, Kraft pulled it off and flung it away. She angled him to her other breast with a guttural command in a language he didn't understand, but he didn't need to.

Lifting and pressing her breasts together, he used his rough beard, his lips, his teeth, his tongue and his softly twisting fingers to provide the pleasure she sought. He pulled away and discovered her eyes closed, her head moving side to side, and her breath catching and releasing with delirious need. He cupped her beautiful bare breasts with his hands and firmly twisted her nipples between his fingers and thumbs.

With a startled gasp, she drew close and wrapped her legs around his hips. She lowered her hands to grip the tense muscles of his buttocks. Arms and legs working in tandem, Kraft crushed him against her so tightly he could barely move.

The power of her body, the painful press of his need, the passion of her embrace, compelled Jace to lift her from the countertop and plaster her against the thrust of his body.

Kraft curled around him, embracing him with strong arms and solid thighs. Only layers of clothes separated them. Even though she was heavy, adrenaline and lust filled him with power. Kraft felt feather-light in his arms.

He lifted his mouth to her ear, and she lowered her mouth to his. Panting, gasping, he was inflamed by the feel of her moist breath against his neck and ear. The moist heat below, rocking, twisting, crushing against him, almost brought him to climax.

When she lifted her hands and entwined them in his hair, he wrapped his arms around her, clutched her bottom and buried his face against her neck. At first, he nibbled and chewed the tender skin of her throat, but her groaning compelled him to bite harder. He knew he marked her, but he didn't care. Jace wanted to mark Kraft as his own. He wanted to claim her. He wanted to kill any man who even thought of touching her. She belonged to him and he would never let her go.

Lowering her to the countertop, he leaned back enough to let the buttons on his fly ride against her. Kraft uttered gasps of increasing pleasure. With a few more strokes, he feared they both would climax.

"Kraft, tell me to stop."

"No."

She wrapped her legs even tighter around him and encouraged him to continue rocking against her.

More than anything, he wanted to taste her mouth. He would not let her deny him this time. He angled away and grasped her shoulders to pull her close and force her to accept his lips against hers. He would penetrate her mouth then rip off her pants and know the full of her body right here in the kitchen.

When his hands gripped her, Kraft uttered a fractured gasp of pain and reeled back. Shoving his right hand away, she clutched her upper left arm.

"What—" He stepped back and looked down at his hand. With a wince, all his desire abruptly left him. "I'm sorry, I—"

Eyes wide with shock and pain, she looked slapped awake from a beautiful dream. She shook her head. Her baffled gaze darted away from him as she climbed off the counter. Her legs trembled as she retrieved her shirt, clutched it to her chest and then stumbled to the short kitchen doorway.

One shaking hand clutched the doorframe for support. Her other hand, her left, clenched to a fist. Blood oozed in sluggish drops to the floor. After a deep, gasping breath, she recovered and exited the kitchen without turning back.

Jace watched her go and now understood the darkness in him that pushed her away. His aggressive, possessive passion was his darkness. In that moment, he hadn't cared if he hurt her, or if she wanted to kiss him. He intended to force her by grasping her shoulders hard enough to reopen the gunshot wound.

He washed her blood from his palm and knew he could never face her again.

Chapter Fifteen

Kraft wasn't surprised when Jace didn't come to the galley for breakfast. She was even less surprised when Jace ordered Bailey to bring his meal to the bridge.

"Why does Captain Lawless want to land on Dahank?" Bailey frowned at the plate she handed to him. "I've done it a million times."

Kraft knew why Jace wanted to stay on the bridge, but she kept her voice casual. "Practice, maybe?" She shrugged. The movement caused Jace's secondhand shirt to smooth over her shoulders and stroke her breasts and belly. The shirt smelled of harsh hand soap, but it was clean and stitched. Only a fading maroon swath marked the bullet wound below.

"Practice?" Bailey asked.

"Perhaps Captain Lawless wants to make sure that he can still fly the ship in case of an emergency." She had done the same on her ship and it seemed a likely excuse that Bailey would accept.

"Captain Lawless isn't getting rid of me, is he?" A frown creased the smooth plump of Bailey's face.

Since they both still touched the plastiware plate, she read Bailey through it. She discovered Bailey feared that Jace knew and resented his interest in her enough to kick him off the ship.

"Of course not." She handed Bailey a cup of swassing. "I'll bet Captain Lawless would appreciate your help, though."

Reassured, Bailey trotted off to the bridge with Jace's breakfast.

Kraft turned her attention to her own meal. She'd eaten two bites and could feel them sitting in her belly like lumps. She wasn't hungry and pushed her plate aside. After a sleepless night pacing the floor of her bunk, she couldn't decide what she wanted more, sleep, sex, or salvation.

With methodical precision, she washed the breakfast dishes. Lemon-scented suds popped along the top of the wash water and puffed up along her forearms. She enjoyed the sensual feel of the warm water with a greedy pleasure. The other crew members thought doing the dishes a nasty chore, but not her. Warm water and fluffy bubbles soothed as her mind drifted in thought.

In a way, she was relieved she didn't have to face Jace this morning, because she had no idea what happened last night. She remembered feeling almost desperate to get him to back down. By the most remote fringes of honor, Jace should have folded faster than a market street huckster. Manipulating him should have been child's play. His blushing and turning away from her slightest provocative overtures filled her with confidence that she could force him away with her pointed flirting and, if that failed, she had the power of her gaze.

But then the so-much-more-than-pretty Captain Jace Lawless touched her and a surging resonance multiplied her passion until desire filled every cell in her body. The power of his touch had been strong enough to wipe away her genetically ingrained self-preservation. She could not have fought him even if she wanted to. Honor did not hold her back nor compel her. Something far more dangerous made her his virtual slave, and it wasn't lust.

Jace evoked desires in her that went far beyond carnal needs. He compelled emotions so intense she couldn't defend herself from the onslaught. He enthralled her with his strong hands, direct words and erotic need to possess her fully. His control excited her to a degree she didn't think possible. She never let a man take charge the way she let him.

Well versed in bedroom power plays, Kraft always found herself still able to ultimately take command and walk away. No man was *that* good. But for Jace.

The only thing she refused him was a kiss. The sweet intimacy of locking lips with him would have sealed her fate.

Submissive did not come to her by nature or design. She could *play* a submissive woman, but she could never actually *be* one. Assertive and aggressive in both body and word came automatically to her. Never had she felt so consumed. Never had she allowed a man to so fully command her. But for Jace. The things he'd said. Those wicked words and harsh commands...

If Jace hadn't accidentally grabbed her injured shoulder, she would have let him take her right there, on that kitchen counter where she now stacked the dishes to dry. Just looking at that innocuous piece of countertop made her nipples and passage tighten.

She danced such a tight two-step with Jace that one wrong move would send her spiraling out into the Void. She lifted her gaze to the window in the ceiling and saw strands of brightening sunlight fill the mocking darkness of the Void.

The kitchen wall com squelched, and Jace said, "Everyone, we're about twenty minutes off Dahank. Prepare for landing."

Kraft stowed the dishes and battened down the hatches. Just the sound of his husky voice issuing curt commands made her physical condition almost unbearable, and she knew, in that instant, she had to prepare not for landing, but for leaving.

After Kobra's men carted away the goods from the Runner salvage, Jace divvied up the script from the job. Since she'd convinced him to strip the ship of both equipment and electronics, the job netted a solid 10K. If Jace considered the Basic 5K a fluke, the Runner salvage coming in at that price must have made his head spin.

Despite Heller's bitching and moaning, she received a fair percentage. Not that she got a chance to defend her rightly deserved portion. Not that she'd needed to. She'd been trapped in her room while Jace, Garrett and Heller loudly argued in the cargo bay. She could have left her room, but her only escape was to cross the hold where the three men argued. Just about the last thing she wanted to do was run into Jace when he had a full head of steam. She paced her room and listened to his imperious captain voice via the air vent.

It seemed that once Heller clapped an eye to 10K he got mighty greedy mighty fast. He made no bones about wanting his fair share, and he thought he deserved more because he'd carried all the heavy equipment.

Jace allowed that Heller had earned a fair ten percent by doing the bulk of the grunt work.

Heller thought he'd earned at least double what Kraft did.

Jace calmly reminded Heller that if not for Kraft, they'd probably still be bunkered down, hiding from the autofires.

Heller insisted she hadn't helped enough to deserve ten percent. He thought two percent was more than fair. For a man who couldn't count, Heller quickly calculated out her take at a paltry two percent.

Garrett thought ten seemed low after what Kraft contributed to the job itself and her work running the kitchen.

Jace agreed.

Heller resisted, citing the fact Jace took fifty percent for the ship.

Kraft thought fifty low. She took sixty for *Whisper* and that didn't include her wage.

Heller made the colossal mistake of reminding Jace he'd spent fifteen hundred on a freak-show cook-whore who didn't belong on the ship in the first place.

There was a long stretch of dead silence, and she wondered if Jace would end up punching Heller again.

"I'm splitting the job the way I think is fair. If you don't like it, you can leave," Jace said with his imperious captain voice.

The argument simmered down after that, and she could only hear snatches through the duct work. She didn't mean to eavesdrop, but she really couldn't help it, trapped as she was in her room. She felt inordinately pleased when Jace stood up for her in his straight-shooting, no-nonsense way. But then she wondered if he wanted to give her a solid ten percent to assuage his guilt over last night.

Looking at her reflection in the small bathroom mirror, she touched the marks Jace had made on her neck. Her now clean and stitched shirt kept them well hidden, but she shivered every time she thought of when he'd put them there; how she allowed him to put them there; encouraged him to mark her as a way to claim her as his own. She felt a surge of fear when she'd felt his determination to never let her go. By honor, if he refused to release her from the contract, she would have to stay. She found the thought both profoundly erotic and deeply terrifying.

While she waited, she prepared herself to face Jace. She decided the best way to handle the situation was to act like it wasn't any big deal. What happened last night was just a pissing match that got out of control and turned sexual.

She jumped when she heard a rhythmic tap from the wall com speaker and then ran to open the door. It took mounds of effort to hide her disappointment when Garrett stood on the threshold.

Garrett handed her a bundle of battered and smelly script. Everything that Kobra touched ended up reeking of sweat from Push addicts. Before she could read further into the money, Garrett flicked the brim of his hat and drawled, "Far as I'm concerned, you done earned more'n that." Garrett nodded and ambled off.

Kraft closed the door and thought it might be for the best if she avoided Jace for a while. Through the script, she felt Jace's shame for hurting her, and his determination to keep their relationship honorable. Mixed up with his erotic need and lust, lingered his emotional fear and confusion. She understood, for she felt the exact same way.

Once Jace and crew departed the cargo bay, she left the ship and made her way into the cluttered streets of Jade.

She quadrupled her script at the Double Whammy, bought herself some blades, a gun, some clothes, a decent pair of boots, and a clutch of personal items. She also restocked the kitchen. She hired a jobber to take the goods to the ship so she could continue to shop.

"Heller, are you trying to follow me around again?"

Heller stepped out of the alley, glared at her, then spat a wad of brown-green rubtab that exploded, splashing the street and building. A combo of rubber and tobacco, rubtab continued to be one of the most despicable, disgusting and destructive habits.

"Since you're so eager to spend time with me—"

"Just keeping an eye on you."

"Any particular reason why?" Kraft stopped at a window display of chic dresses. She'd love to wear something so dramatically beautiful, but such a getup wasn't practical, and she moved on. With a flush of female pleasure, she wondered what Jace would think of the lacy black bra and panties she now wore below her crisp new dextex shirt and pants. She had a feeling he would find them nothing but in the way. And he would probably like her to wear a skirt, so he could just yank it up when—

"Maybe you're a spy or something."

Heller's comment jolted her from her flight of fancy.

She kept walking but turned to him. "A spy for who?"

"Maybe Trickster."

She laughed at the absurdity of his accusation. After what Trickster had done to her, she wouldn't help him on pain of death. "What could I possibly tell him?"

"Don't know." Heller was distracted by a scantily clad huckster at the doorway to a touchy-feely show. "But you should be off our ship by now."

"How do you figure that?" Kraft glanced at the exhausted woman below the bright makeup and garish clothing. The woman's voice rang shrill and desperate. When Kraft slipped a ten-flat to her small hand, she felt the pressure behind the woman's struggle to support her three children after the IWOG killed their father, her husband, over a drunken exchange outside this very establishment.

"You could wager your script up and buy your own damn ship and get the hell off ours." Heller's words rushed out in an annoyed tumble.

Turning away from the woman after the brief exchange, Kraft thought that was a grand idea, but it simply wasn't practical.

"There's a limit to how much I can win at one time, Heller. If I took a thousand and tried to run it up to 500K, I'd get myself banned from every hell on every planet in a matter of hours. I need to start with big money and go up from there."

"You ain't ever leaving *Mutiny* are you?" Heller turned his gaze to a small boy herding goats through the street with a sapling stick.

"Believe me, Heller, as badly as you want me off the ship, I want it a thousand times more." *For reasons you couldn't comprehend.*

Day by day, she felt more comfortable on Jace's ship and enjoyed her respite from the pressures of being in charge. And Jace, well, he became ever more interesting when he decided to take charge. She didn't think she could handle another encounter like last night without taking it to a soul-shattering climax.

Her determination not to kiss him wouldn't last long under the wicked seduction of his touch. She didn't have to read him to know how badly he wanted to kiss her. Jace lost his focus when he gazed at her mouth. His striking green eyes went all soft and dreamy, and he damn near licked his lips with anticipation, just like he had when she confirmed she could cook. Hell, he wanted to kiss her so badly he almost forced her. If not for a shock of pain, she would have let him. And then she would have been lost forever.

She had to get off his ship, and fast. It'd be too easy to fall into a life where all the burdens rested on a captain who wasn't her. Falling in love with that same captain would be disastrous. To her *and* him. Eventually, she'd want to be in charge and run the ship. No matter what power games they played in the bedroom, when it came down the sticking place of who gave the orders, she would take control.

Ingrained reactions, inculcated in her from the day of her birth and in her genes, Kraft had to take control or die. Self-preservation ran so strong she would kill anyone and everyone to protect herself. But for Jace.

For the first time, she found herself in the impossible position of putting another human being before herself. It ran counter to her rational mind, her training, her genetic code— the very foundation of her being.

Putting another before herself was suicide.

Only her heart understood.

Submitting to Jace in the galley, willing her body to him by clinging to her honor, she almost allowed the Void to take the last thing she had left.

As if a talisman, she held back her kiss. If only she didn't lock lips, she would not fully lose her heart to him. Determined to give up any part of herself to his pleasure, she would hold that one compelling intimacy back, almost like an ace up her sleeve.

Her refusal to kiss confused Jace to an alarming degree. Kissing loomed primary to him. He couldn't envision penetrating her body in any way until he took possession of her mouth. By her refusing him that, he refused her everything else.

Stalemate.

Her little chat with Heller made her realize she needed a big haul to start over and get her own ship. As they walked the market street, she set her mind to scheming and came up with the perfect plan.

"You want to knock off an IWOG transport station? Did you get brain-bashed on Dahank?" Clean-shaven and smelling of spicy aftershave, Garrett tipped his new straw hat off his brow as he propped his feet, clad in shiny-new snakeskin boots, on the kitchen table. "Lady, I got all kinds of faith in your ability to kick some serious behind, but this is just plain crazy."

"Could be." Kraft darted a quick glance to Jace at the other end of the table. He kept his gaze riveted to his cup of swassing. He'd been avoiding her all day. This was the first time they'd faced each other since last night. Jace refused to meet her gaze, but he listened to her plan.

Unlike Garrett, Jace hadn't spent his script on new clothes. Jace wore a decimated homespun shirt and faded dungarees. He hadn't even bothered to shave. He looked scruffy and harsh. She stopped looking at him when she found herself wondering what his beard-shadow would feel like against her skin, especially the exquisitely sensitive skin along her inner thighs.

"Those fetches play rough, darling, and there's got to be at least a hundred of them on that station." Garrett looked around. "We got you, me, Jace and Heller. Four fighters against a hundred?" He looked down at her new boots. "Are your toes starting to stress that leather?"

It took her a moment to grasp what he meant. "You think I'm getting too big for my boots?" She laughed. "Maybe I am, because if you think four fighters against a hundred is crazy, how does one grab you?"

"One? You mean one person?" Garrett leaned back in his chair and tilted his hat further back. "Let me guess, you?"

"Just little old me." Kraft smiled, leaned forward and gripped the table. "Why send an army, or even four, when you've got me?"

Garrett whistled. "Jace had it right, lady, you've got bigger balls than any man I ever met. Hell, you got more in your sack than the three of us combined."

"Garrett!" Bailey, sitting to the left, slapped his arm, clearly horrified he would say such a thing about the all consuming object of his puppy-love. "And there's four men here, not three." Bailey sat a bit straighter and tried to broaden his chest by extending his slender arms.

"We already know her balls are bigger than yours." Heller slapped Bailey on the back so hard the poor boy struggled to keep his seat.

"It's not that, Bailey." Garrett glared at Heller. "You'd be flying, not fighting. We got four fighters, one pilot, and two docs." Garrett considered. "No, wait." He lifted a gnarled finger. "What we *really* got is one bonafide crazy lady, three fighters, one pilot and two docs." He winked at Kraft. "You crazy, girl, but you got a mind for mischief on you, and I'm willing to listen."

Kraft followed Garrett's gaze down the table to Jace. Captain Lawless sat at the other end with his attention on his cup of swassing. He just listened while his crew discussed the possibilities of the job.

"It's impossible," Heller said. "We can't even get close to the damn thing without them seeing us coming."

Bailey looked up at her. "It's true," he said apologetically. "*Mutiny* doesn't have any way to jam their sensors. They'll see us coming from at least ten minutes off."

"Ye of little faith." Kraft sighed. "They won't see us at all. And there won't be any record of our visit. What we need is exactly what we got."

"A crazy lady?" Garrett looked at her black boots again.

"A shadow," she said. A quick glance to Jace revealed he still paid full attention to his cup.

"A what?" Heller asked.

"Someone quiet, invisible. That'd be me."

"I ain't letting my hide hinge on you, freak-show." Heller shoved his chair back from the table and crossed his bulky arms over his chest.

Kraft rolled her eyes. "Could we lay off the nasty names for awhile? And how about, just for fun, I present the whole plan before you rip it apart?" She laid out a detailed schematic of an IWOG transport station. "Before anyone asks, I acquired these blueprints on Dahank."

"Finagling black market goods. Another interesting skill you have." Garrett grinned. "I'm starting to think you got full right to some mighty big boots."

"Thanks for the lone vote of confidence," she said, hoping

Jace would finally look at her, but he continued to stare into his cup. Disappointed but not surprised, she turned her attention to the blueprints. "Now, let's go over the plan."

Chapter Sixteen

Relieved that he had something to focus on besides his now empty cup, Jace studied the diagram Kraft laid out on the kitchen table. IWOG transport stations were 10xBasic. The zeppelin shape became a cigar with a bite off the front end. The bite opened into a huge cargo bay with the bridge riding up and behind the mouth, like a leviathan from the bottom of the Void. The hatch of the transport cargo bay would fit to the docking bay of *Mutiny* perfectly, like a lip-locked, T-shaped kiss.

Before his weary mind could start wandering down the trail of kissing, Jace asked, "Could you get in?"

So far, he'd just sat back and listened. Right from the start, he didn't like the job, but Kraft's voice compelled him to consider the particulars. And it gave him an opportunity to face her and hopefully put behind them what happened last night. But he still couldn't bring himself to look directly into her eyes. He couldn't even face himself in the mirror long enough to shave.

He was ashamed for losing control and hurting Kraft by grasping the raw wound on her arm. A wound caused by his own bumbling. Her blood on his hands was a reminder of all he feared. Claiming her as his own, possessing her, trying to protect her, then failing her so miserably. Just as he'd failed Senna.

When Kraft paused in answering, he finally looked up and caught her gaze. He felt the space between them compress. His heartbeat shot up to a painful twirling-dervish pace, but he didn't see what he expected in her fathomless eyes. Rather than fear or regret, he found that smirky flirtatious arrogance.

Kraft cocked her hip, lowered her eyelids and her voice, and said, "With the right gear, I could get in, lock it down, and we could grab whatever we take a fancy to." She arched one brow and gave him a saucy wink.

Confused by her casual attitude, and the potential double entendre of her statement, he dropped his gaze from her face and noticed she wore a new black dextex shirt, dangerously unbuttoned and tucked into tight black dextex pants.

The fabric clung to every curve she possessed and caused interesting things to happen in his own clothing. When she leaned forward over the blueprints, she gave him an enticing hint of a lacy black bra. He wanted to rocket to his feet and yank the rest of the buttons apart, but then he noticed a bite mark on her neck, and he dropped his guilty gaze back to his empty cup.

"How?" As soon as he asked, he knew he'd just swallowed her lure like a greedy fish. Garrett may think her crazy, Heller might hate her guts, Bailey might lust her every step, but Jace seemed to believe her every word. As much as she tried to act flippant about last night, she seemed to be doing so for his benefit. As if she were saying their encounter didn't mean anything to her so why should it mean anything to him?

"Okay, what we got is a supply station with a skeleton crew. We hit them at the right moment and half the crew will be on down time. I enter here." Kraft pointed to the diagram.

Jace forced himself to keep his gaze on her finger and not look at her cleavage.

"That's the sewage line." Bailey's whole face pinched up in squeamish distaste.

"That's where they're weak," Kraft said. "And don't worry, I'll be in a suit. Since the IWOG runs everything like clockwork, they're gonna clean the line in two days."

"Don't they have recyc?" Heller asked.

"They do, they do. Lucky for us it's old and inefficient. Couple of times a year they clean it out. It's cheaper for the IWOG to pump and dump than to upgrade the technology. You know how they are about the bottom line." She looked right at him and Jace saw a curious sad hunger in her eyes, something almost like an apology.

More than anyone at the table, Jace knew too much about IWOG greed. When the vast agricultural WAG world of Tyaa had become profitable, the IWOG unleashed a virus that killed almost everyone on the planet while leaving the plants and animals intact. Jace survived and he'd been almost mad with grief when the IWOG showed up in biosuits and mobile body disposal units to clean up the dead. As they dug up the four bodies he'd carefully buried, Jace snuck aboard the IWOG scout and eventually ended up on planet Byzantine.

"How do you know they're gonna clean it out in two days?" Garrett asked, pulling Jace from the past to the present.

"I bought the information with the blueprints." Kraft shrugged and Jace noticed she winced slightly as her shirt pulled on her upper left arm. "Anyway, the Dungslurper—"

"The what?" Heller asked.

"The pump and dump ship. Let's just call it the IWOG Dungslurper." Kraft smiled brightly. "Now, the Dungslurper has limited instruments and no sensors aft."

"Right! Who'd want to rob a ship full of shit?" Heller was clearly delighted he'd figured something out on his own for a change.

"Exactly." Kraft nodded. "Anyway, using a shuttle, approaching the Dungslurper aft, where it has no sensors, you drop me on it."

"I'm all for that," Heller said. "But only if you ain't wearing a suit."

Kraft straightened and put one hand on her hip. "When this job is over and you've got 100K script in your pocket, I'll let you decide whether or not you want to toss me to the Void without a suit."

There was a long run of hushed silence. Jace let the number roll over his brain as his gaze traveled the enticing thrust of her hip.

"No way can *you* run a job that will bring that kind of script," Heller said.

Despite his biting comment, Jace saw respect in Heller's eyes. Since they'd met Kraft, their score on jobs had climbed exponentially.

"Finish running it, Kraft." Jace met her gaze and held it only by the sheer force of his will.

She stepped forward and pointed to the diagram. "The Dungslurper will dock here, to the sewage hatch. Once it starts to pump and dump, nobody is going to notice me getting onto the transport station. I wait until they're done then use a flashpop to open the airlock, but I probably won't need it."

"Yeah, why lock a door that holds back megatons of shit?" Heller laughed and, for the first time since Kraft had come aboard, Heller seemed to be enjoying himself in her company. And Jace let the swearing slide since now wasn't the time.

"Absolutely." Kraft nodded. "I get in through the recently cleaned lines. Then, look." Using her index finger, she traced her way through the schematic. Jace noticed her nails were short and buffed, newly manicured and feminine despite the strength evident by the rough calluses that no amount of moisturizer would ever soften. "From the sewer to the hall to another and—"

Dropping his feet to the floor with a solid *thwump*, Garrett whistled out a long sharp tone. "Well, glory be, girl. You went from shit to shinola!"

Jace retraced her path. "You're in the control room." He triple checked the schematic. No way could it be that easy.

"Yep. And all it's gonna cost is one suit. After trudging through there, I don't think you'd want it back."

"No." Jace shook his head, still considering the schematic with a worried frown. "I think we can spare a suit."

"Anyway, I leave the suit in the line and make my way down this hall. At best, two men will be on duty in the main control room. Most like, one of them will be sleeping while the other ponders IWOG sanctioned porn on the Tasher."

"Cameras." Garrett pointed. "Trained on the hall."

"The IWOG guards won't be looking at them," she said. "Even if one of them is, he won't see anything."

"So you'll just sneak up and kill 'em?" Heller was enthused about the idea of killing as many IWOG officers as they could during this job.

"No, I'll sneak up and make sure both of them sleep."

"How?" Jace asked.

"Want me to demonstrate on Heller?" When she moved behind him, Heller shot to his feet so fast he knocked his chair clean across the room.

Jace knew Heller had a healthy respect for Kraft's physical prowess. Once again, he wondered why she hadn't fought him last night. With two fingers, she could have dropped him to his knees in begging agony. Instead, she'd allowed him to grasp and fondle her body like a greedy kid in a candy store. Was it because of their contract or did she actually welcome his embrace? In a million years, he felt he'd never understand her.

"I won't hurt you." Kraft smiled at Heller as she rapidly touched her forefinger to her thumb. "Much."

Heller pulled his hand to his chest. "Stay away from me, freak-show."

"Why don't you demonstrate on me." Jace challenged her with his gaze. She seemed so casual, cocky even, like last night hadn't even happened. He wanted to find out just how disinterested she was.

"Ain't the best idea you've ever had," Heller said. "She-bitch could kill you."

"Hell, lovely lady has already saved him twice, why would she kill him now?" Garrett dropped his hat to the table and primped his freshly cut hair.

Jace thought Garrett looked like a proud peacock with his new duds. It worried Jace at first that Garrett had turned an eye to Kraft, but over dinner it was clear Garrett still wore his heart on his sleeve for Payton. And he'd seemed a mite more than pleased when Payton had taken pleasurable note of all his efforts. Compared to Garrett, Jace looked like a market street bum. With his scruffy face and slept-in clothing, all he needed was a paper-wrapped bottle to complete his dreadful appearance.

Kraft obviously spent a large portion of her share of the job on clothing. He'd seen her enter the cargo bay wearing a new belt with blades and guns. She'd strode in like she owned the place and never looked up at him. But he'd had a feeling she knew he was there and watching her.

"Go ahead, Kraft," Jace said. He felt a perverse thrill in ordering her to embrace him while his crew looked on.

"Oh, goody goody fun fun. I always did wanna hold you in my arms." Kraft smiled, slow and lazy and sexy. She got behind him. "Now, just relax." She cupped his face with her left hand and pressed her body to his back as she slid her hand to cup his neck. He caught a whiff of her perfume and his whole body felt electrified.

In a flash, she lowered her right arm and crooked her elbow against her hand. She squeezed.

Jace couldn't move, couldn't scream. His vision went grey

around the edges.

Kraft released the pressure, but kept her body pressed against his as he sat on the little bench at the head of the kitchen table. If she hadn't held him gently, he would have tumbled to the floor.

"Wasn't that fun?" she whispered to his ear with a moist wind that made it impossible for him to stand up anytime soon.

"Only if you're a masochist." Jace shook his head. "Where in the Void did you learn that?"

"Charm school." She dropped him a curtsy with an imaginary skirt.

"I couldn't even breathe." Jace shook his head. If she'd been so inclined, she could have killed him right then and there. Why in the Void had she allowed him such liberties last night when she could have killed him with a flick of her damn fingers?

"I know, too much pressure in the right places. It's a quiet way to get folks out of the way without killing them or raising a fuss." She pointed back to the diagram. "So, now, the two guards are out. I gag them, bind their hands with their own hardware, lock the door, and I've got the main control room all to myself."

"And you can run it?" Garrett asked.

"IWOG controls are so simple even Heller could likely fall on the right ones." Kraft winked and Garrett laughed.

"Freak-show," Heller snarled.

"Village idiot," Kraft returned.

"Unruly children." Garrett tsked and sighed.

"Get on with it!" Jace bellowed, poised on the edge of his seat.

"From that room, I lock everything down but for the hatch where you'll dock." Kraft pointed. "We can strip them bare and be gone before the guards ever wake up."

"Sounds too easy," Garrett said.

"Too good to be true," Jace agreed. Every single time he found a job that looked easy, it turned out to be anything but.

"Lord on high. Look. The only place they can override my lock down is from here." Kraft pointed to the only other security cell. "And we're gonna let them think they have."

"Feel like a repeater, but how?" Garrett asked.

"Bailey will help me build a False."

"A what?" Bailey asked.

"A False. A wireless contraption that I'll put on this wall, here." She pointed to the diagram. "Don't worry, it's on my way up the hall to the main control room."

It was the back wall of what should have been a sealed-off security cell, but it wasn't separated from the main by more than a wall. The IWOG went cheap on routing expensive wires and com boosters to the Tasher drive. They thought that separating the cells with a wall would be good enough.

"And what's this False gonna do? Pipe in the latest IWOG commercials?" Garrett asked.

"That's an interesting idea for a torture device, but, no. It's gonna look to those IWOG officers like they've sounded the alarm and all hands are responding." Kraft grinned, her wide and luscious mouth bracketing her perfect teeth. "Don't you get it?" She leaned forward as if she expected them to get the obvious joke. "It's gonna be a False—a computer loop that will keep them occupied for the time it takes us to strip them bare."

"And you really think this will work?" Jace asked.

Kraft lowered her head and winked. "I know it will."

A sudden surge of lust made Jace want to order the others out of the room so he could take Kraft hard and fast right on the kitchen table. Even if it killed him, he wanted to find out if she'd obey or object.

Before he could issue the order, Garrett asked, "You've done this before?"

As if she read his mind, Kraft smiled at Jace. "Oh, yeah, I've done this before." She turned her gaze to Garrett. "Once. The station we hit had 100K in script goods *after* being stocked for a month. This station just got restocked two days ago." Kraft paused and let that information sink in.

"It's got to have at least..." Heller trailed off, and Jace could practically see smoke coming out of Heller's ears as he tried to calculate.

"Almost a Mil, maybe more." Garrett shrewdly assessed the schematic again.

Kraft nodded. "And that ripe chunk of change is just sitting there in that cargo bay, waiting for us."

"But the hallway, here," Garrett said, pointing. "There's

bound to be guards stationed. How are you gonna get past them?"

"I'm a shadow," Kraft said.

"Unpack that," Jace said.

"Well," Kraft hesitated. "Guess I gotta show you one of my super powers."

Kraft disappeared.

"What the hell?" Jace looked around.

"Looking for me?" She appeared on the other side of the table and touched Jace's shoulder. He almost shot from the bench in shock.

"How'd you do that?" Garrett asked.

"It's a trick of the mind. I make you forget to see me."

"There's a thought," Heller said.

Jace now understood how she snuck up on him in the derelict Basic. "You walked right past Garrett and Heller. They didn't see you because you didn't want them to."

Kraft smiled and nodded with abashed assurance.

"I pondered that for days!" Garrett leaned back. "I thought you were some kind of magician."

"See, she's a freak-show!" Heller glared.

"That may be true, Heller, but my talents could make us all the richer." Kraft moved back to the other side of the table. "Isn't it best to have the freak-show on your side?"

"But they'll alert the whole quadrant about the stolen goods. We won't be able to unload them." Jace looked desperately for holes.

"Nope." Kraft shook her head and grinned. "They won't say a word."

"*Mutiny* strips an IWOG transport and they don't put out a lure on the Tasher? Are we blessed, or did they get real stupid real fast?" Garrett asked.

"To add insult to injury, a splash of vinegar to their salt filled wounds, they're gonna think it was an inside job," Kraft said. "They're gonna be real quiet about it."

"Beginning to feel like an IWOG ditto-head, but how?" Garrett asked.

"When we're done with the False, it melts down and starts a fire. They'll be dealing with that while we make a fast get away. And, since they had no indication of a ship approaching, they'll think it was an inside job by the two guards who'll swear up and down they ordered the crew to respond."

"That's fairly evil," Heller said with admiration, and a low, deep chuckle. "I'm beginning to like this job more and more."

Jace realized even Heller had been swayed. Script and revenge at the expense of the IWOG was a combination all of them could appreciate.

"I've got no problem making them chase their own tail," Kraft said.

"We'll have to maintain com silence. How will I know when to approach and dock?" Bailey asked.

"I'm going to invite you to dock," Kraft said.

"You're mad!" Garrett exclaimed.

"No one but *Mutiny* will hear it, and I'm going to erase even the tiniest smudge of it from the IWOG computers."

"They won't have a record?" Garrett asked.

"Not after I get done with the computers." Kraft gave Garrett a saucy wink.

Later that night, Jace found Kraft sitting at the kitchen table, fiddling with circuit boards and wires. She bit her bottom lip, one corner tucked below her perfect gleaming teeth as she concentrated. A soldering iron smoldered next to her, and she picked it up, dabbed it to the works, then considered the wires again.

Even though she seemed oblivious to him, Jace felt her awareness that he entered, yet her gaze never left her task.

"You'd be taking all the risk." He poured himself a cup of the ever-present swassing that simmered on the back of the stove.

"Risk is minimal, but I would be taking it all." Kraft focused her attention on building the False. "Call me greedy." She smiled then frowned. "If something goes wrong, you hightail it out of there."

"Fancy yourself captain?" Jace plunked himself down in the chair opposite hers.

Kraft stopped what she was doing and caught his gaze. "I didn't mean it like that."

"Yes, you did." He sipped his drink. "Right under my nose

you're running the show."

"It's a good plan."

He nodded. "But you're still taking all the risk. And I'm beginning to feel like window dressing, being so pretty and all."

"Is that what this is about?" She pushed the gizmo aside. "When I call you pretty that's just my way—you're like a fancy package—hell, you're making this job so much harder than it has to be."

"My ship. I'm captain. We run a job only if I say." To his own ears, he sounded like a tyrant, one desperate to assert his authority. He'd never felt a need to declare himself the alpha dog with any of his crew in such a surly manner, until Kraft came along, all powerful and enticing.

"I'm not disputing that."

"Not overtly."

"I'm taking the risk, sure, but we'd all make out like Berserkers." She slapped her palms to the table. "What is this really about, Captain?"

"If they catch you, they'll kill you. I won't be able to save you." He took a casual sip of his swassing.

"I'm not asking you to." Kraft gave him a sharp one-eyebrow-up look. "You can't honestly think I don't know how to take care of myself."

He didn't dispute that for a heartbeat. Kraft could take care of herself and just about anyone else. Dropping his imperious captain tone, he quietly asked, "Is it so bad here that you're willing to take this risk just to get away from me?" He looked deep into her fathomless eyes. "What happened last night won't happen again."

"That's too bad." She winked. "I'd like to finish what we started."

Anger surged at her smirky tone. "It's not funny. I hurt you, and I didn't mean to. Why are you acting like it wasn't any big deal?"

"Because it's not." Kraft shrugged. "Look, I know you've only been with your wife, but if you're thinking you're the second or third in my line, you're sadly mistaken."

So now she was trying to push him away with her experience or his lack thereof. "You make it sound like you've done half the Void."

"Well, probably less than half, but I'm working on it." She winked and flashed him that slow, lazy and sexy smile.

His answering frown dropped the grin right off her face.

"Anyway, last night has nothing to do with this. If you don't want to do this job, then pull rank and put the synch on it. I've got no desire to step on your captain toes. And if that's what you think this is about, some kind of pissing match, then say."

"Fine. I'm saying no." He leaned back and took a swig of his drink. Her excellent swassing rolled over his tongue.

"Fine." She pushed away from the table and tucked her chair neatly beneath it. She unplugged the soldering iron with a yank. "Night, Captain."

"Night, Kraft."

She made it all the way to the door before she turned back.

"You know—"

"I know there's no way you're giving up without an argument." He kicked her chair out from under the table. "Plunk yourself right back down and let's have it out."

Kraft smiled and poured herself a cup of swassing. "And you think only I can read you." She sat down and leaned back in her chair. "Are you saying no just to keep me on your ship?"

"Do you want to do this job just to get off my ship?"

"We could play dueling questions all night." Kraft leaned across the table, her palms flat to the battered surface. "Or we could just cut the crap."

"Ladies first." Jace didn't touch the table, because he didn't want her to read him through it. Drawing his body and mind tight, he forced a mental shield around himself.

Kraft uttered an annoyed sigh. "If I sit at the table and touch it when you do I can read you." She stood. "Just so we're real clear on the concept, I'm going to stand over here." She leaned against the wall that separated the kitchen from the main hall. "I want to do this job so I can get back to where I belong—on my own ship."

"You expect me to put you in a terrible position."

"That's what a captain does."

"Did you?"

"All the time." Kraft nodded earnestly. "I put Danna and Tan into the mouth of hell, over and over, because that's what our life demanded. It was my call not to stand down, and my call cost seven women their lives. Don't look at me like I don't know what it's like to be captain."

In her eyes he saw the pain that made her flee the kitchen in tears. She would have sacrificed her ship and all her cargo if only she could save her crew. Kraft had never been given the option and only a flimsy piece of paper had kept her alive.

Jace knew what crushed her was not the loss of her ship or her cargo, but the loss of her crew. Kraft failed to protect them. As she said long ago, everything hinges on the captain.

"And now you're punishing yourself for surviving."

"I'm not." Kraft looked offended at the very idea. "I'm not going to get a ship of my own again with piecemeal jobs. I need something big. I could take my share from this job and wager it ten times over."

Jace saw her frustration building.

"Look, you gotta use your people for the skills they have. You wouldn't take Bailey off being pilot because it was risky, right? No one but me has the skill to pull off a shadow. Not even you. Let me do what I'm good at."

"Use you." Suddenly, the thought of her in his bed, captive to the needs of his body, made him look away.

"If that's the way you want to look at it, fine. Use me. You've had no problem making me cook."

"You're not likely to die from it."

"Is that the rub?" Kraft frowned. "You're all for letting me use my skills as long as I'm safe? You hold Garrett and Heller to that too?"

"We're not talking about them."

"No, but maybe we should be. You're holding *me* back. And for the life of me I don't know why. If *you* were taking all the risk, you'd be all for it, and you know it."

"I guess that's the problem," he said. "I'm sitting back, safe, while you risk your neck."

"I've got no problem with you sitting back and being captain, while I, your intrepid cook, bring down an IWOG transport. Sure, I risk my neck, one person, one you know you can spare, to bring a bonus—what you paid Trickster for me would be returned to you a thousand times over. Or more."

"I should gamble you to that?" Jace was sickened that she wanted him to approach this with such a casual attitude. Like he shouldn't care if she got hurt or died for she only cost fifteen hundred.

"Look at the odds on this job. You'd have to be blind or daft not to take them. It's a good plan."

"I still don't like it."

"Well, you don't have to like it, but do you see any holes in it?"

"No, but—"

"Just leave it at no. Don't give me any buts. This will work. When we pull this off, you could get real picky about taking jobs. You could even go legitimate if you wanted to."

"That's if your plan succeeds."

"True enough." Kraft nodded. "But if it doesn't, you're out a cook and one suit."

He was appalled that she expected him to consider her no more valuable than that. "You're not just a cook."

Kraft groaned. "I'm a woman you paid a fifteen hundred for." She looked like she wanted to shake some sense into him.

"That's not what this is about. It's not that you're a cook I bought from Trickster, nor is it about how much I paid for you. It's about you."

"Fine. Let me be who and what I am. Let me fight, let me cook good food, and if you want, let me fuck."

The vulgarity made him shoot to his feet. "Don't swear at me. I don't like it." If he wouldn't tolerate cursing from Heller, he certainly wouldn't let Kraft get away with it. He slammed his cup to the table and strode over to where she leaned against the wall.

"I apologize, Captain Lawless." She stood at attention and kept her gaze on the floor.

He had an overwhelming urge to pick her up and place her back on the kitchen counter. Her attitude about last night filled him with confusion and anger. If it didn't mean anything, then why hadn't she kissed him?

Sudden understanding filled him and he leaned close. "You know, I think now is the time to discuss the payout on your contract."

"After this job, I'll be able to pay you in full."

"I never agreed to that." And he knew she already had that amount from wagering up her take from the Runner salvage job.

Kraft looked up and frowned. "You want more than the fifteen hundred?"

"I don't want money at all, because money doesn't mean anything to you."

"Then what do you want?"

"One night."

Her breath quickened and her breasts rose and fell against the plunging V of her shirt as she looked up at him. "If all you want is one night of wild sex then I'll happily pay you tonight."

Stroking his finger over her lips, he said, "I didn't say anything about sex."

She swallowed hard and narrowed her gaze. "I don't understand."

"One night, you in my bunk, and all I want to do is kiss you."

Turning her head, she closed her eyes. "I don't like kissing."

He believed that was the first lie she'd ever told him. He cupped her chin and turned her face back to his. "I guess that's what makes kissing me a payment." No matter what she said, he knew why she hadn't kissed him and why she feared doing so. Kissing would make their liaison mean something. She could keep him at arm's length and keep it casual as long as she didn't share that sweet intimacy with him. Now that he understood, kissing was all he wanted from her.

"One night of nothing but kissing?" she asked, keeping her gaze demurely lowered.

"Are you afraid you won't be able to handle it or I won't?" He leaned closer. "After a decade of celibacy it might be a little difficult for me, but we can keep all of our clothes on, maybe even wrap ourselves up in separate blankets."

"One night?"

"Eight hours. We can set a timer." He couldn't believe he was actually suggesting this, moreover, defining the particulars when he had no intention of ever forcing her. In the back of his mind he thought she might not ever leave if he made the payout difficult. But he knew she would leave. Eventually. And he would do everything he could to delay that day.

"Fine. I'll settle my contract after the job is over."

Pulling away from her, he returned to the table and

wondered if she hoped she'd never have to pay because the job might go south. But he couldn't believe she'd put herself in danger just to avoid kissing him. She had a solid plan with minimal risk to everyone but herself. Like a burr in his boot, the fact that Kraft could be hurt dug at him. He couldn't stand the thought of never seeing her again. But whether he held her back or not, he couldn't hold her forever. Eventually, she would have the script to start over and she would leave *Mutiny*.

The question was how long did he want to delay the inevitable? Would it hurt worse to let her go now or a year from now?

"You're sweet on me." Kraft frowned. "And I'm real sweet on you too. But that can't enter into this. This is about captain and crew. You're a good captain and you take good care of your people. Right now, I'm one of your people, and you don't want to see me hurt, and I appreciate that." Her hungry eyes pinned him. "This job is solid and will satisfy my needs, yours, and will also toss a snag into the IWOG machinery. It's bonus all around."

"You don't just think this will work, you know it will." She couldn't be more convincing if she had proof in her hand.

"Again, I don't have a psychic hat, but I've run this job once before. The damage to the bottom line of the IWOG was so minimal they didn't bother to upgrade anything, especially since they thought it was an inside job."

Jace considered. Kraft laid it out, step by blessed step, and for the life of him, he couldn't find a single hole. Every job he'd ever run looked just as solid until real life showed up, and he knew if it looked too good to be true...

"You wanted the derelict Basic to be a cakewalk, right?" Kraft asked.

"You heard me say that?"

"We tapped the Basic a full hour before you showed up. We heard everything. Hell, we tapped your ship thirty minutes before you docked your shuttle. How did you think I knew all your names?"

He'd thought she'd read them by touching the ship. "With that kind of power, how—"

"My crew was skilled, and we had our tricks, but we weren't perfect." Kraft shook her head. "My point is, this job is a total cakewalk. It's practically a skip to the bank. Another bonus is we don't have to deal with Trickster or any of his ilk. I know someone who will take it all. Not full price, mind you, but we won't have to worry about any deadly dancing with middlemen like Trickster or Kobra."

Kraft could sell a glass of water to a drowning man.

"We'll run it," Jace said. For the life of him he swore he heard a tsunami approaching.

She grinned. "You won't be sorry."

As the tsunami crashed over his head, Kraft refilled his cup with swassing.

"That remains to be seen." Jace plucked it off the table and hustled out of the room.

Whether the job went south or not, he would be sorry to see Kraft go, but he couldn't hold her. He wondered how Fairing had coped with it. Surely, Fairing had not been in love with Kraft—the realization in his own head made Jace stop dead in his tracks. Swassing rolled from his cup to splash on the worn neospring of the main hall.

He heard Kraft returning to her work at the kitchen table as Bailey obsessively tuned his guitar on the bridge.

Jace stood in the dark hallway and listened. Bailey had been tuning his guitar the whole time he'd been in the kitchen with Kraft. He hadn't paid attention to it until now.

Bailey tuned and tuned.

Kraft sighed, sharp. Once, twice. He could hear her stand and slap the galley com. With a rolling whisper, Kraft said, "Bailey? Play her or I swear, I'll march in there and play her myself."

The hall went silent.

"You don't know how," Bailey said. A honey-sweet chord made a trip down the hall.

"I know," Kraft returned, her voice clear in the dark hallway. "I'll march up to the bridge, open the ship-wide com, play her and sing. Now that would be just be ugly all the way around. If you're going to help me build this False, you best play her and not tune her to death."

Jace heard Bailey laugh as he plucked against the strings, making the battered guitar play like gold struck with a careless god's hand. In the year Bailey had been pilot, Jace had no idea that he could make music better than he flew *Mutiny*.

Kraft knew.

Jace wanted to walk right back into the kitchen and demand to know what else she knew of his crew. What stopped him was the truth in his own heart. If she knew all the secrets of his crew, what must she know of him?

Waiting had been the hardest part. Kraft had almost two hours of air in the suit and it took almost an hour for the Dungslurper to finish and pull away.

Jace practically felt his black hair turning grey.

The twenty minutes it took Kraft to make her way from the sewage line to the control center seemed more like twenty years.

"She's fine, Captain," Garrett said as they all clustered on the blacked-out bridge of *Mutiny*. "Lady knows her stuff."

"She's a freak-show, but she's our freak-show," Heller said. It was as close to an endorsement of Kraft that Heller had ever gotten near.

"See? Even Heller gives her the nod." Garrett slapped Heller's wide back. "As a betting man, I'm all for this being the first time it's gonna run easy."

Kraft had been inside for ten minutes, halfway through the sewage recyc line. She had a com unit in the suit but she'd disabled it. They couldn't utter a peep or they'd alert the IWOG crew.

Mutiny hung just out of range, ten minutes off, hiding in the disturbance caused by the wake of the Dungslurper.

Jace waited for her screams. He shook his head. He wouldn't even get that. Kraft was incommunicado for at least five more minutes. His breath came in pained gasps as he waited. He wished he'd had the guts to kiss her before she left. He'd thought about it, come close, but pulled back at the last second because of that deal he'd made with her. One night of kissing that might never be.

"She placed the False," Bailey said.

On a com pan, Jace read what the two IWOG guards in the secondary security cell thought they were doing. They banged out commands that the False answered in perfect IWOG code. The guards locked down their room. The False kept them occupied as Kraft made her way up the main hall.

Bailey turned his attention to the console. "Everything looks good."

"Too good to be true." Jace shook his head. He couldn't help but expect this job to go horribly wrong. He gripped the back of the pilot chair so hard he left permanent dents in the worn pleather.

"Relax." Garrett pulled Jace's hand off the back of the chair. "Everything's fine."

"It's been too long—"

"This is IWOG transport station Delta Alpha Two Three Fifty-nine," Kraft said, in a clear, delighted voice over the main com. "*Mutiny* may dock at the cargo bay." She uttered that rolling chuckle of hers and his whole body sagged with relief. "The crew may sing, dance, or howl like banshees if they are so inclined."

As *Mutiny* came to life and surged forward, Jace could well imagine her dancing around the main security cell of the IWOG transport. He wished himself beside her so he could sweep her into his arms and dance with her.

Bailey docked and locked the ships together. When the airlocks opened, Kraft stood in the jam-packed cargo bay. She stepped to a forklift filled with goods and drove it forward.

"Cakewalk," she said, as she went past him and deposited a load of goods into *Mutiny's* cargo bay. "We have about twenty minutes to do our damage. We can do it best with all hands."

Jace's crew didn't need his command. They all came forward and tossed boxes into the mouth of *Mutiny*. Jace looked around the cargo bay of the IWOG transport. If the Basic was a treasure drove, this was ten times more. He tossed boxes and tried to clear his head.

"Just once, you wanted it easy." Kraft smiled. "Pinch me or let me pinch you, neither one of us is dreaming."

He nodded but thought back to the comment she'd made that nothing worth having comes easy.

In less than twenty minutes, his 2xBasic sucked down almost the whole total of a fully stocked 10xBasic.

With a grin, Kraft slapped the com of the IWOG transport then scampered aboard *Mutiny*. "They'll never even know we were here."

Garrett lifted his hand and Kraft high-fived it.

As soon as the airlock closed, Bailey piloted *Mutiny* off the transport. Gravity shifted and Kraft fell against him, giving him an enticing hint of her strong body and wicked scent.

Righting herself, she said, "Sorry, Captain. It's a bit crowded in here at the moment."

"We're clear, Captain Lawless," Bailey said over the com.

"I don't care how big your boots get, girl," Garrett said. "Let your toes stress that leather all they want, and I'll give you my own hard-won leather to patch them!" Garrett swept Kraft up into his arms and twirled her in a dance around the crowded cargo bay.

She flung her head back and laughed like a delighted child. Her hair, forever bound in the twine of black linen, whipped out and almost hit Heller. He flipped it away with a grin.

Garrett saw the frown creeping down Jace's face and carefully set Kraft away.

With shining eyes, Kraft turned to him. She went from happy to confused in the blink of an eye.

Jace left the cargo bay without a word, and made his way up the catwalk.

As he entered the hallway, he heard Heller ask, "Why is Jace   pissed?"

Chapter Seventeen

Kraft didn't say much about the world they traveled to, but she didn't need to. All of them had heard of Windmere and Michael "Overlord" Parker. After insisting he was real and would pay a fair price for the goods, she refused to confirm or deny any of the gossip with a pointed, "He's just a man, not a myth."

Kraft knew Michael would be inordinately pleased by the rumors surrounding him. Beyond a doubt, Michael "Overlord" Parker could give the mythical Narcissus—he who fell in love with his own reflection—a run for his money.

Since Michael had bought the goods from the first transport job she'd run, she assumed he wouldn't mind buying the goods from the second job. Unfortunately, the limited range of the com on *Mutiny* meant she had to wait until they were closer to contact him. If Jace had a Tasher on the ship, Kraft could have contacted Michael in real time, but the low-budget ship didn't and she'd have to wait. Had she realized *Mutiny* didn't have a Tasher drive, Kraft would have kept the one they'd salvaged from the Runner ship.

Jace had been avoiding her like a sink-full of dirty dishes since the transport job. She thought he'd be insistent about that night of kissing, but he hadn't mentioned it. Boldly, she'd gone to his bunk door and offered herself up for payment, only to be told to go away. Perhaps he thought that if he delayed the payout, she wouldn't leave. And on that score he was correct. Or maybe he changed his mind and wanted something else from her to pay off her contract to him. She didn't know and couldn't try to get a handle on it if he refused to come near her.

Perhaps *that* was why Jace was avoiding her. He didn't want her to know what was going on in his head. Jace didn't know that she found reading him increasingly impossible. As her inner turmoil rose, so did his. Frankly, her ability to flat-out read a book became debatable.

As she pondered all of this, Jace entered the kitchen.

"Can't sleep?" he asked, probably drawn from the bridge to the kitchen by the enticing smell of the midnight snack she concocted for herself. She'd heard Bailey begging Jace to go check it out and bring back a bite or two of whatever it was.

"No, I can't sleep." Kraft nodded to the stove. "You want one?"

"One what?" Jace cast a dubious glance to the pans on the stove.

She considered. "A moment?"

"Of what?"

"Time." She flicked off the stove. Taking a deep breath, she straightened her shoulders and met his gaze. "Throughout that job I could practically feel you worrying about me."

As Jace looked down into her eyes, she felt the heat of his body against hers. But he backed away.

"Captain, I'll give you every bit of my share of the job if you'll just tell me why you've been avoiding me." The cache from the job filled the cargo bay and at even one-fourth its value it would fill all their pockets to overflowing.

"You honestly think you have to pay me to tell you the truth?"

"Do I?"

"It's complicated," Jace said.

"The good things always are." Kraft nodded. "Truth even more so."

"You want the truth?"

She nodded. "Even if you think it might hurt my feelings."

"I felt...emasculated."

Her jaw almost fell off her face. "Why?"

"You're better than I am." Jace held her gaze with a deep shame in the depths of his eyes.

"I am not!" It popped out of her mouth automatically.

"You're a better thief. With one job you've made more for my crew than I have in a decade." He hung his head and turned slightly away.

"Whether that's true or not, I didn't do it to show you up."

"I know. Somehow that only makes it worse."

His broad shoulders slumped a bit more, making her want to embrace him from behind. But she didn't, because her coddling him in anyway would only increase his feelings that he'd failed as a man. Kraft felled many a man for his misogynistic arrogance, but Jace's turmoil was borne of a more basic male pride: he wanted to be her protector and defender—it shamed him utterly that she had become his.

"I'm not better than you," Kraft said softly. "I have different skills than you do. There's plenty of things you can do that I can't."

"Name one." Jace kept his back to her.

"You can pee standing up."

The comment caught him so completely off guard he laughed and faced her. It pleased her to no end to see him smile.

"Anything else?" he asked, chuckling. "I'd hate to think that was my big claim to fame."

"You're better at keeping your crew safe," she pointed out.

He frowned. "That wasn't your fault. I don't think I could have fought down a Trifecta either."

"If I could have one wish granted, it would be that you never have to find out." Again, she felt an overwhelming urge to touch him and refrained only by fiddling with the pots and pans on the stove.

"You honestly don't think you're better than me, do you?"

"I don't think I'm better than anybody. I think I have my tricks, but that doesn't make me any more worthy to draw breath than anybody else." She shrugged. "And frankly, Captain, you did something I couldn't."

"What's that?"

"You saved my life."

"No, I—"

"If you hadn't bought me from Trickster..." Her voice trailed off because she really didn't want to think about what could have happened. "Because of you, my dance didn't end. And something else—you let me lead. I've never allowed what you did. I never let a member of my crew lead a job. I'm a bit too much of a control freak. You don't seem to have that problem."

"You pull no punches, do you? Even on yourself." Jace

straightened up a bit, losing that dejected edge.

Kraft smiled, then frowned. "I learned long ago to accept myself for all I am, be it good, bad, or ugly. I'm far from perfect, and I make terrible mistakes, but I strive to learn from them." Lord on high, she sounded like a woman with a lot of therapy under her belt.

Jace looked at her for a long time. "Would you consider this a mistake?" He stepped close and lowered his head.

By a breath, his lips brushed hers. Her resolve not to let him kiss her wavered as her hunger to taste him became uncontrollable. Throwing caution to the wind, she lifted her face.

"What the hell is that smell?" Heller asked from the kitchen doorway.

Jace stepped back from Kraft, cursing Heller with every swear word Heller had ever spoken. He'd been so close to kissing her that his whole body surged with thwarted desire.

Kraft relit the burners of the stove.

Jace touched her hand, softly, as if to convey they would take this up at another time, then turned to Heller. "A victory surprise."

"A celebration party," Kraft agreed, nodding to his brief touch.

It pleased him to no end that she didn't flinch away. Whatever darkness she'd once felt had apparently been altered. He wondered if things had changed because he understood that darkness better and had even come to accept it as a part of himself.

Capping his anger over being denied kissing Kraft again, Jace walked over and slapped the kitchen wall com. "This is the Captain, I need all hands in the galley."

Bailey wandered in and took a seat at the table across from Heller.

Garrett ran into the room with big eyes as he strapped his holster to his hips. "We under attack?" His brown hair practically stood on end.

"Well, the sandwiches I'm making are likely to give you a heart attack, but that's probably a few years down the road," Kraft said.

Payton and Charissa laughed from the doorway.

"Come on in and join the party," Jace said. Getting everyone in the room forced him to put a damper on his raging hormones. But still, he wanted to kiss Kraft so badly he could barely keep his gaze off her mouth. By a damn breath he'd missed his opportunity.

Everyone gathered around the table while he stood watching Kraft in the kitchen.

"What are you making?" Bailey asked. "It smells incredible."

Kraft said something in German.

"One more time, in Universal, please," Payton said.

"Hamburgers with fried eggs."

Kraft worked the stove like a virtuoso. She slung spatulas and pans and in all her fury she created a stack of sandwiches.

"Now these have no redeeming nutritional value whatsoever, which is what makes them so irresistible. And, you can't eat these without some of this." Kraft slapped her hand to a squat metal tank.

"I know what that is," Garrett said, rising from the table.

"Use those," Kraft said, nodding to a box.

"Real glass!" Garrett exclaimed, lifting out thick mugs.

"Can't have decent beer in anything less."

Garrett dispensed tall steins of beer to everyone.

"Beer's not ice-cold." Heller grunted.

"It shouldn't be," Kraft said. "If it's too cold, you lose all the subtle flavor of the hops."

"After eating these gut bombs, I'm not so sure we'll be able to taste anything subtle," Garrett said.

The stack of greasy sandwiches didn't last long. His crew polished them off with much licking of fingers and long sips of beer. Jace hadn't had a beer in so long the alcohol went right to his head, then migrated to a few other places when he glanced at Kraft. He decided one would be his limit and nursed his mug like a miser.

"You're gonna make us all fat!" Charissa giggled.

Payton moved Charissa's glass away.

"Hell, we could all use a little more meat on us." Garrett polished off his third beer. His face had a soft red sheen. "And what you doing way over there, Kraft? Come join the party."

"Here," Jace said, scooting over on the little bench at the head of the table. "There's room."

Everyone's head swiveled toward Kraft. Jace could tell she felt pinned by the scrutiny.

"Really, Kraft." Heller grunted. "Damn rude of you to stand way over there." He lifted his arm and sniffed. "I done took a shower."

"Hell, darling," Garrett drawled. "You best get over here after an invite like that. I do believe that's the first time Heller's ever called you by your name."

"It is, it is." Kraft sat on the little bench to the right of Jace and near Heller's left.

Jace almost groaned at how good it felt to have the side of her body pressed fully against his. She gave off an incredible heat and she smelled like the food she'd made, but below lingered the scent uniquely hers. Like a mélange of food and sex. Jace thought of how close he'd come to tasting her wide and luscious mouth. He would have to be the last one to leave the table because if he stood up now, everyone would see how much he enjoyed sitting next to Kraft.

"A toast." Kraft lifted her glass. "To good food!"

"To good beer!" Garrett lifted his glass.

"To good times!" Charissa giggled, plucking her stein back from her mother.

"To good money!" Heller growled.

"To good company!" Bailey said.

"To good health!" Payton chimed in.

"To the best crew in the whole of the Void!" Jace said.

Everyone clinked their glasses together and drank.

"You know what this party really needs? Music." Jace nodded at Bailey. "Go get your girl, Bailey."

"Oh, I don't know." Bailey blushed, but Jace could see he just needed a little coaxing.

"I could always sing," Kraft threatened.

"Come on, Bailey, play for us," Jace encouraged, eyeing Kraft warily. "You really don't want her to sing, do you?"

"Okay." Bailey went to the bridge and returned with his guitar. "What should I play?"

"Play *Lonesome Road*. I believe Charissa here knows the words." Kraft nodded to Charissa.

Charissa blushed then smiled at Bailey. "I'll sing if you play."

They made a lovely combo. A sweet tune brought to life by Bailey's skilled fingers and Charissa's wonderful soprano voice.

As everyone applauded, Jace suddenly felt that they made a family together. It pleased and dismayed him, but he focused on the good emotions inside. He wanted only happiness in his heart right now, and for once, the past didn't haunt him. For a decade, Senna and their children darkened every pleasurable moment when Senna would have been appalled at such an attitude in him. For the first time, he felt that Senna wanted him to move on and open himself to love again.

"Play something we can all sing to," Heller demanded.

Bailey played *Life in the Void* and everyone sang with far more enthusiasm than skill. Heller whapped his hand against the table, beating it like a drum, and Garrett slapped his hands double time.

Jace tapped his toes to the tune and he sharply wanted to stand up, pull Kraft into his arms and dance the night away with her...

They sang, they drank, they laughed.

Jace didn't want the evening to end. Kraft sat snugly to his side, swaying into him as they sang, and when she laughed, he felt his body shake with it. And she laughed a lot. The moment in time was so sweet he longed to bottle it up, like a fine wine, so that he could sip from it whenever he felt the need. But time moved on and the evening ended.

Payton took the slightly tipsy Charissa out, Heller lumbered away, Bailey staggered to his bunk and Garrett offered to stand watch on the bridge.

"I don't think so," Jace said, grinning. "You can't even stand, let alone see straight!"

Garrett laughed and stumbled happily to his bunk.

Kraft washed the dirty dishes. "I could stand watch, Captain." She didn't look up. "I've had one beer."

"No. I'm fine." He cast his gaze to the door that would take him to the empty bridge.

"Yes, you are. Very fine." Kraft said it with her rolling whisper voice.

"What?"

"It's fine. Go watch the Void. I'll put the galley to right again." Kraft waved him away with soapy fingers.

"Seems unfair that the conductor of the evening is stuck mucking it up."

Kraft looked up from the sink. "You could rinse, if you're so inclined."

Jace stood beside her at the sink. Into his hand, Kraft slipped soapy steins. Then heavy pans. When she finished, she pulled a dishtowel to her hands and twisted them dry.

"Thank you." She nodded to the stacked-to-dry-dishes on the counter beside the sink.

Jace remembered her on that counter with her legs twined around his hips. "You're welcome." He took the towel from her hands, dried his own and tossed it aside. He stepped close, and her heat, her scent, her presence, engulfed him.

"You should get to the bridge," Kraft blurted. She danced back a step then turned away. She grasped the discarded towel and swabbed it liberally over every inch of countertop.

"Come with me," Jace said.

Kraft kept her attention on the counter. "To the bridge?"

"For starters." Jace deliberately pitched his voice low.

"A start to what?" She stopped swabbing the decks but didn't turn around.

"I don't know. I'm offering you a dance, Kraft."

She tossed her head back and laughed. Her bound hair swept along the edge of her fanny. "I honestly don't know if I can do this, Captain Lawless."

"Then we're even."

"You—you are so much more than pretty." Kraft turned. "What makes you think I can dance like this with you?"

Jace stepped forward, tossed the rag in her hands aside, cupped her hand and then coaxed her to the bridge. He didn't stop tugging until Kraft stood in the center of the small room. He shut the door and turned down the lights. The only illumination came from the green indicators on the main console.

"At this moment, at this time, it's you and me against it all." Jace squeezed her hand. "Feel *Mutiny* below your feet, over your head. Look out to that fathomless black. It's nothing but us in here against everything out there."

"Berserkers and Randoms and all things dark and dangerous," Kraft said. "IWOG worst of all."

"Yes. All that out there and my tiny ship. Since you came aboard, Kraft, I'm a lot more confident when I face that blackness." He squeezed her hand. She squeezed back. "You could kill me, my crew, and take this ship in under sixty seconds."

She gripped his hand a bit tighter as she laughed. "I'm unarmed, Captain."

Jace twined his fingers tighter to hers. "You have your hands. You dropped Heller with two fingers. Since you dropped him, you know you can drop me."

"I wouldn't."

"Why?" He had to know.

"Because you're my captain." She clasped his hand tighter and tingling rushed through his body. "You give me greatly yet hold back from your own crew."

Jace let go of her hand. "I didn't ask you here for a reading, Kraft."

"They know me better than they do you. I know you better than they do, and I've been here only a few weeks."

"There's nothing wrong with me being a private person."

"Private or paranoid? What is it about yourself that you are so afraid for everyone to know? You go off by yourself, lock yourself down for hours in your bunk, and you won't tell anyone why. Your crew gossips endlessly about it."

"Why is it you throw yourself at me every chance you get, but when I take you up on your offer, you run away?" Jace was so frustrated he wanted to bellow.

"Back to playing dueling questions, are we?"

"I think you're deliberately trying to start a fight." He pulled her into his embrace. "The last thing I want to do right now is fight with you."

Peering up at him with her extraordinary eyes, Kraft said, "You could compel me to your bunk."

"What?"

"You bought me as a cook-whore."

"You'll come to my bunk if I demand it?"

"Yes."

"But you won't come of your own free will?"

"This isn't about my will."

"Do you want to come to my bunk or not?" He was sick to death of playing games with words.

"It's not a matter of what I want. By honor, by the unwritten contract between us, I have to if you demand it."

"But you don't want to."

"Captain—"

"Don't you dare start flinging platitudes at me again." He pulled her tighter. "Do you want to dance with me or not?"

"If you want me to be your whore, I will."

"My whore?" Jace pushed her away. "You think that's what I want from you?"

"That's what you bought me for. I'm your cook-whore. If that's what you want—"

"I want you in my bunk because I thought the attraction between us was mutual."

"Are you demanding this of me?" She kept her gaze out at the blackness of the Void.

For a moment he almost reminded her of the agreement to pay off her contract with a night of kissing, but he didn't want her to come to him because she felt she *had* to. "No."

"Then I'm your cook and nothing more." Kraft left the bridge without another word.

Jace plopped down in the pilot chair. He cast his gaze out to the fathomless Void. All he could think of was Kraft's hungry eyes, and how he'd been bitten by his own words.

Kraft slapped the com and closed her bedroom door. After chucking her boots off, she curled up on top of her bunk, but couldn't sleep. Why was doing the right thing so damn hard all the time? Honor compelled her to be his whore should he demand it, and a part of her wanted him to demand it. She wanted Jace to haul her to his bunk with no questions asked. She'd like him to enforce that kissing contract to pay him off, but he wouldn't. She knew that. Jace wouldn't force any woman to his bed, not by contract or strong-arm tactics.

Kraft wanted to go to his bunk. "Tell you what, I'm amazed I haven't hauled that man to the floor and had my wicked, wicked way with him." She'd wanted to undress him like a fancy-wrapped gift since the moment she laid eyes on him, but she would only go to his bunk if he demanded it.

"Doing the smart thing is hell." Kraft knew if she went once, she'd never leave. Counting on the fact of Jace's honorable heart, she challenged him, knowing he would take the high road. He wouldn't force her. A part of her longed to submit to every naughty whim he could concoct, but the smart part feared the emotional enslavement that would ensue.

She held to only two things. Honor dictated her actions, her code. The other didn't dictate as much as it compelled sacrifices.

"No power in the Void can rob me of love lest I allow it."

Only by her own heart could she grant it. Kraft granted it to her crew. She loved them dearly, deeply. She would have died for them. She lived because of them.

And now a man who accepted that she could best him but wouldn't, a man who wanted her more because of it, a man who wouldn't force her but could compel her—Jace didn't know it, but so far, he was the most dangerous man she'd ever met. He could best her. He just didn't know how.

Kraft wasn't about to tell him. It wouldn't take much to enslave her heart and soul to him. One kiss would seal the deal. She knew it as sure as Jace knew she could break every limb in his body if he tried to force her to kiss him.

"I've got to get off this ship."

She slept fitfully.

In the morning, she entered the galley to find Garrett walking wounded from the party the night before. She couldn't resist teasing him.

"Got a hangover?"

He grumbled something unintelligible.

"Want another beer?"

Garrett looked up with a face tinged green.

"Would some lukewarm pork help?"

He covered his mouth like he was on the verge of blowing chunks.

"Don't pick on him." Heller slapped Garrett's back. "I think he's learned his lesson."

"I'll never, as long as I live, ever do that again." Garrett cupped his head in his hands and curled to the table.

"Have you done it before?" Kraft readied the kitchen

equipment and food.

"Yes."

"Then you're apt to do it again."

Kraft created a huge breakfast, but made a special drink for Garrett. "Here, try this."

Garrett looked at it warily. "What is it?"

"Trust me, it'll help."

Garrett took a dubious sip. "It tastes awful!"

"I know, but in half an hour you'll feel a lot better."

"I better." Garrett drank it down. "If I don't, and I feel the urge to hurl, I'm gonna do it on you."

"Fair enough."

Jace strode in from the bridge and made a point of not looking at her. He heaped his plate high and took his place at the head of the table. "Looks like everyone survived."

"Barely," Garrett said.

"Well, you're lucky because we have a two day cruise to Windmere. You should have ample time to recover."

"How come you look all frisky this morning?" Garrett took a sip of his hangover drink, tweaked his face, then glared at Jace.

"I was smart enough to stop at one. How many did you have? Six? Seven?"

"I don't want to talk about it." Garrett polished off his drink and curled his head to the table.

"What kind of beer was that, Kraft?" Jace asked without turning around.

"A variation on the classic German Pilsner."

"And the alcohol content?"

"Seven percent. Give or take a percent."

The kitchen table stifled Garrett's groan. "Next time I vote you make something a bit lighter."

Kraft knew there wouldn't be a next time. When they finished their business on Windmere, she would disappear.

Jace turned around and gazed at her speculatively.

She read in his face that he knew it too. Within a week, she'd be off *Mutiny* and appointing a crew to her newly bought second ship.

"I thought next time you were gonna let me make it?" Heller dropped her an I-knew-you-were-lying look.

"That's right. I'll walk you through it today if you want."

Kraft shot back an I-meant-what-I-said nod to Heller then glanced at Jace. Every line of his expressive face and body drew into a tight, knowing posture, as if he'd accepted the inevitable. Like a clock loudly ticking, their time together drew to an end.

"That won't be an improvement," Garrett slurred against the table. "Heller turns everything into a weapon. He'll make beer more deadly than yours."

"What makes you think I'm gonna share it with you?" Heller settled at the table with a heap of food on his plate.

"What makes you think I want you to?" Garrett asked.

"Next time you shouldn't be such a guzzler." Heller shoveled food to his face.

"Like you didn't—"

"Enough." Jace held up his hand. "We have some decisions to make."

Kraft cast her gaze to him with a wary quiver in her gut. He could refuse to let her buy her way out of the contract, or demand a payment she didn't want to make. And they both knew it.

"After Windmere, we'll have some serious script in our pockets. We need to decide what to upgrade on *Mutiny*. Any suggestions?"

Chapter Eighteen

"Tell your crew to stand down." Kraft lifted her hands to her shoulders.

"I thought you said you knew this guy." Jace lifted his hands into the crisp, dry air of planet Windmere. It would have been a beautiful autumn day if not for the thirty men with Slim Shot rifles surrounding them. "You said we could sell the IWOG transport goods here without the hassle of Trickster or his ilk."

Their reception on Windmere went splendidly until they'd opened the hold of *Mutiny* and displayed their ill-gotten goods. Now they stood on the cargo bay ramp with their hands up.

"That's what I thought." Kraft flashed him a wan smile.

"We've got enough firepower pointed at us to chew away the side of the ship in two seconds." Jace had never seen so many bright barrels all pointed his direction.

"I can see that, Captain."

"Michael 'Overlord' Parker, a mythical figure who just happens to be your friend." Jace shook his head but stopped when the guard below tensed. "I'm an idiot for believing you. I'm thinking the IWOG owns this planet."

"Look at them, they're not IWOG." Kraft rolled her eyes and flicked her chin to the men below. "Michael told his henchmen to greet us like this. As to why..." Her voice trailed off and she shrugged.

Jace noticed the men below didn't dress in uniforms, and certainly not in IWOG uniforms, but most of them wore light-colored fabrics and sturdy boots that matched the high-desert colors of the land surrounding them. The only thing they had in common was their rifles and the intensity in their eyes.

"I honestly don't know what in the Void is going on, but

we're dead if you don't order the whole crew to stand down."

Jace considered. He'd surrendered once to Kraft and it'd turned out okay. If he didn't surrender to her supposed friend, he would be responsible for killing everyone.

With a longsuffering sigh, he said, "This is Captain Jace Lawless ordering the crew of *Mutiny* to stand down."

"I'm sorry, Captain," Kraft whispered.

Out the side of his mouth, he whispered back, "Since I say that so much, I'm going to have that phrase tattooed on my chest. That way, I can just rip open my shirt and make this faster for everyone."

To his amazement, Kraft laughed, really loud. She actually doubled over and dropped her hands on her knees to steady herself. When the men below tensed, she again stood straight and lifted her hands, but she kept on chuckling.

"You surprise me more and more, Captain Lawless."

A man with dusty blond hair approached Kraft. "Remove your weapons."

Kraft dropped her hands to her hips. "Only if you say please."

The man lifted his rifle to her face.

"Golly-gee, Duster, with your gun up my nose, I guess I'd better obey." She unbuckled her belt and tossed it aside. A guard grabbed the belt of weapons from the ramp and backed away. Jace noticed he never took his eyes off her.

"Remove your boots," Duster said.

Kraft complied, but chucked her boots at him. He sidestepped and kicked them to another guard.

"Socks too."

Kraft pulled her socks off, wadded them up and tossed them into the circle of men below. They rippled away like water in a pond. "No bombs, boys, and they're clean."

"Remove your pants."

Jace startled at the command, but Kraft laughed.

"How about some bump-and-grind music?" As she peeled off her black dextex pants, she uttered notes to enhance her show. She did it in jest, mocking, but Jace found her display provocative nonetheless. He couldn't believe he was getting turned-on watching her in the midst of such a dangerous situation.

Kraft twirled her pants above her head and tossed them into the crowd of men. They backed away then cautiously approached her discarded clothing.

Jace was horrified that she was being ordered to strip in the company of nothing but men, yet Kraft laughed as she did it, making a crude joke of everything when he didn't find the situation at all amusing. He wanted to protect her, but had no idea how.

"Now your shirt." Duster gave the order without a bit of leering in his gaze. In fact, he seemed afraid, not titillated.

Jace assessed the guard and realized they were afraid of not only her, but her clothes. Did they think she had weapons hidden in them? They must, by the way they were behaving.

Button by button, she undid her shirt then slipped it off her shoulders. She spun it over her head then tossed it into the crowd below. They all backed away and the black dextex landed on the tarmac with a *fwump*. Standing in nothing but a pair of lacy black panties and bra, her creamed-coffee skin glistening in the sunlight, she didn't seem to be embarrassed, intimidated, or even slightly perturbed, not with that bright smile on her face.

"If you don't stop this, Duster, I'm going to die of amusement." Hands on hips, absolutely unfazed by her undressed state, she further offered, "You'd have to cut off my arms, legs and hair to render me weaponless."

Duster's right eye twitched to a narrow slit. "You talk like her."

"What do you mean I talk like her?" Confusion replaced the amusement on her face.

"Kraft's dead. We have her ship."

"*Whisper*? My ship is here?" Kraft cast her intense gaze around the tarmac.

Jace heard the longing in her voice.

Duster checked her forward momentum by lifting his rifle.

Kraft held her place. "So that's what this is all about. Michael thinks I'm an imposter?"

"That's about the speed of it."

"You really think I'm not me?" Kraft advanced again.

Jace wanted to yank her back, but didn't dare.

"You know I'm me, Duster." She winked. "You know I'm not

into faking it."

Jace lifted a brow at her comment. Just what kind of relationship did she have with Duster, not to mention the mythical Michael?

"We'll see." Duster snapped his fingers.

Kraft dropped to her knees.

Jace knelt beside her and she slumped into him. She yanked a dart from her neck and tossed it aside. Her eyelids fluttered. "I'm so sorry, Captain. This is all my fault."

Before he could respond, Duster jabbed his rifle into his chest and bellowed, "Back off."

Jace didn't have much of a choice but to comply. He stood and backed away from Kraft. Clad in racy undergarments, profoundly beautiful in her vulnerable state, she lay panting slowly on the cargo bay ramp.

Duster snapped his fingers. A guard bigger than Heller stepped forward and flipped Kraft over his shoulder.

Jace was ordered to remove his weapons and his boots. He was relieved that he didn't have to strip down to his skivvies like Kraft, but he panicked when they bound his hands and ankles, then blindfolded and gagged him. He didn't know what to expect, but so far, things weren't going well.

Shackled hand and foot, Kraft stumbled her way to Michael's office. The cool, moist air inside his base command caused goose bumps to rise on her mostly naked body. She couldn't believe Michael had her strip practically naked to ensure she had no weapons. Or maybe Michael thought a semi-dressed state would unbalance her. She'd face him or anyone else buck naked without a bit of modesty. In fact, her nudity would give her a distinctly distracting advantage over a male opponent.

Behind her, she heard a troop, but Duster refused to let her look back. "Captain Lawless?"

She heard him gurgle behind a gag.

"Shut up." Duster yanked Kraft to a standstill, waiting for the other group to catch up.

"Tell you what, Captain Lawless, Michael has a gigantic ego, bigger than this whole planet. Duster here? Well, he's got abandonment issues."

"Kraft, you best shut it." Duster nodded to the tranquilizer rifle in another guard's hands.

"So you admit I'm Kraft." Pleased as punch with herself for trapping him so easily, she smiled at Duster and winked.

Duster frowned. "You work it out with him." Using his shoulder, he pushed open a set of gigantic swinging doors.

Michael "Overlord" Parker stood in the center of the room. Red Dardinian silk shimmered down his muscled chest to his black leather clad hips. Michael was gorgeous and he knew it. At seven feet tall, he towered over everyone in the room.

"Kraft?" Michael's voice rumbled like gravel in a swiftly running creek.

"Expecting the CEO of the IWOG?" Kraft noticed how the lights hit Michael just so. "Very theatrical, Michael. You haven't lost your flair for the dramatic, have you?"

He tossed back his head and laughed, exposing his perfect white teeth. The strategically placed lights highlighted his golden-brown hair and eyes. Causally, he plunked himself down on the edge of his desk and drew up his leg. Big, bold and blasé, Michael Parker moved like he owned everything in the Void, but found it all exceedingly boring.

"You look like her, you talk like her, but I have no proof you actually are the elusive Captain Kraft."

"Why would I lie?" She shrugged and noticed his gaze lingered on her chest. Michael always did have a fascination for her breasts. She used his interest to her advantage by lifting them a bit higher. The delicate scrap of black lace barely covered her nipples, which were hard from the cold and not Michael's lustful gaze. At one time, that smoldering look of his could have melted her into a mass of gooey lust, but not anymore. Her infatuation for him and been fully spent a long time ago.

"Just a hologram of me is worth a fortune. My hide alive considerably more." While he spoke, Michael ran his gaze all over her. He did it as if hoping the pointed look would intimidate her. When he realized she moved and preened under his inspection, a tiny frown darted across his lips and he stopped.

"Lord on high, Michael." She chuckled. "You really think I'm going to crash your planet by pretending to be nothing but a cook-whore on a ship called *Mutiny*?"

"Under the command of a Captain Lawless." Michael tucked his chin to the fully bound aforementioned man. "Sounds like nothing short of total crap."

"I'm thinking you're the one full of it." Kraft refused to let her gaze linger on Jace. The last thing she needed to do was pique Michael's ire.

"Indeed?"

"You haven't changed." Sadly, time had not blessed Michael with a sense of humor. He never did like the idea of anyone laughing at him.

"You have." Michael looked her up and down. "A long time ago we once saw eye to eye."

"And what changed it?" she asked archly, knowing he would never admit to his dark and dirty past. Of course, she wouldn't want to fess-up to hers, either.

"You tell me," Michael returned easily.

Kraft lowered her voice. "You stopped seeing faces and saw only script."

Michael walked forward, cupped her face and placed his lips a breath from hers. "I took you against an alley wall like a cat in heat."

Kraft yanked her head back. "I kicked you from my ship three months later." She tried to keep her attention on the situation at hand, but a fleeting thought of what Jace might think made its way into her mind. Would Jace think her some kind of slut who bed-hopped her way around the Void? Probably. But she couldn't do anything about his opinion at the moment.

Michael flashed her his trademark half grin. "Why?"

"You know why." She held his gaze.

"If you are Kraft, you can offer—"

"Don't get into a posturing contest with me, Michael. If it's a pissing match you're looking for, you might want to think twice about taking me on. If you want me to tell everyone in this room what an unbelievable bastard you were, I'd be thrilled."

She surged against her restraints. Five gigantic guards grasped her arms at the wrist, her legs at the ankle, and the odd man out lifted his fist to the start of her ponytail at her scalp. His guards held her in check so soundly she couldn't move an inch. Obviously, Michael wasn't taking any chances with his personal safety.

Kraft lifted her head despite the fierce hold on her hair. "I'm Kraft and you know it. Hell, Michael, you just got up in my face so you could sniff me and confirm my identity."

That comment caused him to narrow his gaze. Michael's ability to read scents wasn't common knowledge. He called himself an emotichemical perceptionist, and his reader ability allowed him to smell subtle changes in humans, chemical changes in their pheromones.

"You let Captain Lawless and his crew go. You do it now."

Michael's eyes and nose flared with anger at her demanding tone. "You're not in charge this time. You're not even a captain this time." Michael settled back to his desk. "He's captain." Michael nodded to Jace. "You're nothing but his cook-whore."

Jace struggled against his gag to say something. She wanted to beg him not to, but ordering him around wouldn't look good right now. Michael flicked his chin and a guard removed Jace's gag. A small relief filled her when they didn't remove his blindfold.

"She may be my cook, but I wouldn't make any woman my whore."

Pleased as she was that Jace would defend her against such impossible odds, she knew Michael could destroy him with a flick of his fingers.

"A man of honor." Michael ordered his men to fully unbind Jace. "I will offer you a deal."

"Don't you dare." Kraft tried to lunged forward, but restraints and five guards held her in check. Michael would offer Jace a terrible choice with no right answer. And now that Captain Lawless had seen Michael's face, he would never let him go. Very few people in the Void actually knew what Michael "Overlord" Parker looked like.

"Put her in lockdown." With a snap of his fingers, Michael had Kraft escorted, struggling and screaming, from his office.

Jace moved to defend Kraft, but a guard shoved a gun into his chest. Up his hands went. He wanted to be heroic, not foolish. After they hauled her away, Jace got his first good look at the mythical Michael "Overlord" Parker.

Michael stood seven feet tall and a good three and a half

feet wide. He probably tipped the scales at a solid three hundred pounds. Dressed in red and black with military short hair, he was also a man who took great pride in his appearance. No wonder Kraft had slept with him, Jace thought. What woman wouldn't be attracted to a man who looked like that? But then again, Michael was a total bully. How could an honorable man have a woman strip down in front of all those male guards?

"Here's the deal, Captain Lawless." Michael nodded. "You take your ship, your crew, yourself and a Mil in script for whatever goods you have."

"In exchange for what?" Jace didn't think he would like the answer.

"Kraft."

"You expect me to sell her to you?" Disgust twisted Jace's face.

"If that's the way you want to look at it, yes." Michael crossed his arms over his chest. "You will sell her to me for your ship, your crew and a Mil in script."

"We've come here to sell you IWOG goods. You buy them or not. If you want to deal, that's the only thing I'm putting on the table. Kraft isn't for sale." Jace stood his ground.

A slight smile twisted Michael's lips. "By her own admission she's your cook-whore."

"Not anymore." Jace didn't like the emphasis Michael kept putting on the word whore.

"You've promoted her?" Michael smirked and straightened the papers on his desk. "To what? Full-time whore?"

Jace gritted his teeth. "Stop calling her that. Kraft is a warrior-cook, Fairing's cook."

"Kraft is a beautiful woman," Michael pointed out.

"She is." Jace shot a quick glance to the door she'd been dragged out of.

"You haven't taken her to your bed?" Michael relaxed to his desk.

"That's none of your business."

Michael snapped his fingers and a guard pressed his gun to Jace's temple. "I'm making it my business."

Gritting his teeth hard, Jace managed to say, "No. I haven't taken her to my bed."

"Is she unwilling?"

"Ask her." Jace wouldn't mind finding out the answer to that question himself.

"You could force her."

Jace laughed even as the gun pressed to his head. "No, I couldn't, and neither could you."

"I didn't have to force her." Michael smirked. "She came very willingly."

"Once upon a time, perhaps." Jace shrugged. "She doesn't seem all that willing now." He nodded to the doorway where Michael's guard had taken Kraft. "In fact, she seems downright repulsed by the very idea."

Michael frowned. "What did you pay for her?"

"None of your—" The gun pressed a warning to his head and he reluctantly answered, "Fifteen hundred in script."

"That's all?" Michael was appalled at the low figure. "I will give you ten thousand times what you paid for her."

"No."

Michael frowned when Jace didn't hesitate. "That's 15Mil, Captain Lawless, in script. How can you refuse?"

"I can count, and I just did. The answer is no. Kraft isn't for sale."

Michael catapulted off his desk. "I could kill you right now with a snap of my fingers. I could torture and then kill your crew. I'm offering you an honorable escape." Michael was bigger and clearly in charge, yet Jace heard a desperate edge to his voice. "Take my deal."

"Me and my crew for a woman. A woman who obviously doesn't want you. You offer not a deal but a despicable choice." Jace stood his ground. Perhaps all his dealings with Trickster paid off in some strange way.

"Kraft would sell you in a heartbeat."

"Bring her back in here and ask her." Jace knew Kraft would take the same stand as he.

"Take the money and run or I'll kill you."

"Kraft will rip off your head for your trouble."

"You think she holds to you?" Michael asked.

Jace nodded. "Her honor compels her to."

"Your owner is an interesting man." Michael's voice sounded amazingly crisp over the prison com.

His guards had left her bound and tossed her into lockdown. "Jealous much, Michael? Still haven't gotten over our breakup? Tell you what, five years is a long time to hang on to a three-month fling."

"We had more than a fling." Michael leaned against the plexiglass of her prison cell.

"Hardly. Why don't you tell me what this is really about? I saw you a year ago and you weren't remotely interested in me. Why the sudden change?" Kraft couldn't read him very well, not from inside the glass walls, but she could sense his agitation and frustration.

"I thought you were dead." His gaze bored right into hers, and that's when she saw his pain.

"Punishing me for being alive?" She kept her tone flippant.

"I want you to stay with me." For all his posturing, Michael was vulnerable, and what he said shocked her. They were over a long time ago.

"Is that why you bought my ship? You figured I'd eventually come looking for it and we could have some kind of magical happy ever after?" Kraft settled herself, chains and all, on the narrow prison bunk. Comfy. Far softer than her bed on *Mutiny.*

"I can offer you a lot more than he can." Michael's sleek eyebrows snapped together.

"You mean all this could be mine?" She lifted her bound hands to the prison room.

Michael actually looked chagrined. "Pot to piss in. Ever heard of it? He's captain of a rust bucket."

"It isn't about money, Michael, it's about honor and respect and—" Kraft shook her head, frustrated she could not describe what bound her to Jace Lawless. "It's everything I stand for."

"You don't love him." Michael lowered his gaze to the textured durosteel floor.

Kraft lifted a brow. "All I know is I owe him. I don't know how to convey to you—"

"That I can't compete."

She wouldn't have believed it if she hadn't seen it with her own eyes: Michael Parker, one of the most respected and feared men in the Void, was sulking like a child.

"This isn't a competition. You think if not for Jace I would rush into your arms, but I wouldn't. We burned up all the white fire-bright passion between us. Jace or no, I wouldn't jump into your bed again." She took a long breath. "I'm also starting to suspect you only want me because you think he does."

Michael straightened, regaining his air of authority. "And what of Jace Lawless, Captain of *Mutiny*, the rust bucket you're calling home now? As, of all things, a cook-whore?" Michael seemed to be furious that she'd allowed herself to be put in such a position.

"I don't owe you an explanation for anything." Despite her scantily-clad state, Kraft lifted her head with the dignity of a queen.

"He claims you cook yet refuses you whore."

"Your point is what, Michael?"

Michael lifted his gaze to the guard station. "What do you think your honorable captain would do if I offered him 15Mil for a cook-whore he paid fifteen hundred for?"

Kraft wondered how Michael knew how much Jace paid for her. "You already tried it, didn't you?" A dull fury burned in Michael's eyes, confirming what she already knew. "He turned you down, didn't he?" A warm shiver ran through her. "I know it's difficult for you to swallow, Michael, but not everyone in the Void is as hung up on money as you are."

Michael strapped plastimetal bracelets to Kraft and Jace then set them loose in his techno-house. Combination locator, locker and luller, the bracelets tracked their movements, denied access to most of the rooms, and also would inject them with powerful drugs if they tried to fight their way out.

Even so, six fully armed guards, changed every hour, stood vigilant by every door. Male, female, tall or squat, every guard had the same focus. If Kraft came near the door, they tensed. The closer she got, the more they gripped up on their weapons. If Jace came near, they tracked him with gleaming eyes as if they were begging him to try something so they could blow him away.

Jace wisely didn't try anything. At the moment, he sat in a dining room that was bigger than his ship, but only three people sat at the lavishly appointed table.

Kraft picked at her dinner like a finicky child. Michael had given her back her clothes, but he kept looking at her like he wanted to order her to take them right back off. Behind her, ever vigilant, stood five men as big as Heller. One false move and the guards would grab her arm, her leg, or her twined hair.

Michael wasn't at all concerned with keeping such tabs on him. As Jace sat at the table, picking at his dinner, the only person who stood behind him was a painfully young serving girl named Clara. Michael's dismissal of Jace as any kind of threat made him feel far more emasculated than Kraft's big score on the transport job.

"You planning on keeping us here forever?" Kraft asked.

"I haven't decided yet." Michael sipped from his crystal wine glass. He sat at the head of the enormous table with Kraft to his right and Jace to his left.

All through the painfully awkward dinner, they made wary eyes at each other. Jace wanted to pull her close and reassure her, and he discovered a similar desire in her gaze.

"What exactly do you want, Mr. Parker?" Jace didn't have any appetite at all. His stomach rolled and clenched so tightly he didn't dare eat.

"You will address me as Commander Parker, Captain Lawless." Michael nodded to Jace. "What I want is very clear. I want Kraft."

"It's not mutual." Kraft pushed back from the table and all five men behind her tensed.

"It isn't your decision, is it?" Michael turned the full intensity of his gaze on Jace. "Captain Lawless owns you."

Jace crossed his arms. "I already told you she's not for sale."

"Indeed. You won't sell her because you are a man of honor. I find honorable men most interesting." Michael took another sip from his wine. "What about you, Kraft?"

"What about me?" She leaned back in her chair.

"What's your price for Captain Lawless?" Michael twirled his wine glass. "What will you sacrifice to save him?"

Kraft caught Jace's gaze. "Let him and his crew go, and I'll—"

"No!" Jace shot to his feet. "No way am I letting you sacrifice yourself to save me and my crew!" As if she hadn't done enough for him already. He wouldn't allow her to sell herself to protect him, especially not to a man with about as much honor as Trickster.

Michael considered them both with a satisfied smile. "It seems you two have something to discuss." He dabbed his napkin to his lips. "You can either sell Kraft to me, or she can stay here to save you and your crew. That's the deal. I'll give you twenty-four hours to decide."

Chapter Nineteen

"Why is he doing this?" Jace threw a pillow and blanket on the floor.

"I don't know." Kraft sat on the edge of a massive green silk-clad bed. Her head felt heavy with all the questions in her mind. "I told you I would sleep on the floor, Captain."

Jace shook his head. "No. You sleep up there."

"You could sleep up here with me. It's a huge bed." The beautiful bed was big enough for six people to sleep comfortably, or eight people to sleep sensuously.

"Everything in this mausoleum is huge." Jace rubbed his hand over his exhausted face. His stubble rasped against his palm.

"Including Michael's ego."

Jace laughed and punched the pillow. "I think that's what he wants." He glared at the bed. "Michael wants to see if I'll try to claim you like some kind of macho Neanderthal. He wants to see if you'll let me, or kill me." Jace shook his head, threw himself down on the floor, then glared at the ceiling. He lowered his voice. "I'm curious about it myself."

Kraft sat very still. Too afraid to meet his eyes, she cast her gaze around the bedroom. Silk, velvet, rich wool, luxurious flowering plants hanging from the ceiling and growing up from large pots on the floor—everything earthy and sensual. Michael, that prick, knew just what buttons to push. If he tested Jace, he just as surely tested her. She didn't think it was any accident that all the shades of green complemented Jace's eyes.

"I know he has cameras in here." Not that she cared in the least. This might be her last night with Jace, and if it was, she wanted him in the lush bed with her. She wanted to touch and taste every last bit of him. She wanted to straddle his hips around every corner of the bed before she had to say goodbye.

"I'm sure he does." Jace cupped his hands behind his head as his gaze wandered speculatively around the walls and ceiling of the room. "Cameras and coms."

But, if somehow they got out of here *after* she indulged the last bit of her erotic mind on the so-much-more-than-pretty Captain Jace Lawless, Kraft knew she'd never be able to *tell* him goodbye. One kiss and she'd be hooked for the rest of her life. She knew that down to her toes. Honor bound her to Jace, but love would enslave her to him.

"Coms and cameras and security right beyond the door." Kraft nodded to the gigantic door about fifty feet away.

"At least he didn't send those five guys in here to guard you all night." Jace considered. "Let me guess? I make a move on you and the testosterone freaks rush in here and do the unspeakable to a delightful combination of my own face and my own ass?"

She bit back a laugh. "Not on my watch, Captain."

"There's no way in or out of this room but for that door?" He nodded to the gigantic door.

"Only that door."

"Those five guys are just waiting for you beyond that door, right?"

"Most likely."

"We can't get out of here any other way?" Jace perused the ceiling.

"No."

"If you were alone, could you get out of here?"

"No." Kraft considered as she looked around the decadently lewd room. Michael had the tightest security in the whole of the Void and he'd more than trebled security to contain her. She had a few tricks up her sleeve, but she was reluctant to share them with Jace when there might be an open com.

"I'm not holding you back, am I?"

The way he asked it, barely a whisper, stunned her for a moment. "Holding me back how?"

"You tell me." Jace kept his attention on the ceiling.

"You think this would be easy for me if only you weren't here?"

"Would it be if not for me?" Jace sat up. He drew close, trying to whisper to her without a com picking up their conversation. "Michael is terrified of you. Even with the security bracelet on your wrist, he has five hulking guards follow your every step. Every single person in this house is tense, waiting for you to do something, Michael most of all."

Kraft nodded. "I know."

"Michael doesn't stand a chance against you, and he knows it. Care to explain that to me?"

Kraft shook her head. She didn't want to discuss her past history with Michael.

"You could kill him, couldn't you? You know it, he knows it, his guard knows it, and now I do too."

Kraft looked away. "Are you demanding that I fight him?"

"What?"

"I could take him down, given half a chance. Is that what you want me to do?"

"You'd have to seduce him to get half a chance, wouldn't you?"

Kraft swallowed hard. "Yes."

"Could you?"

"I don't know. Do you want me to try?"

"You'd really do it if I told you to, wouldn't you?"

"You're my captain."

"No, I don't want you to—I'm not going to use you—he really is Overlord, isn't he?"

"Yes."

"He's the only man to defeat an IWOG civilization attempt."

"Yes."

Jace clearly admired Michael for not only standing up to the IWOG, but defeating them. Given Jace's past with the IWOG, his attitude didn't surprise her in the least.

"Do you love him?"

"No." Straight from her heart, she told Jace the truth. She'd never loved Michael. She'd been soundly in lust with him once, but that was very different from love. Only two things did she cling to—her honor and her love. Not a force in the Void could wrest them from her without her permission. She gave honor to Jace in full and equal measure as she received it, but she had never given her heart to any man.

"If he were in here with you, would you want him sharing that big bed with you?"

"No."

"But you want me there."

"Yes." Kraft finally met his eyes. Now wasn't the best time to get into this, but now might be the only time they had left. "Tell you what, Captain Lawless, if I had my pick of any man in the whole of the Void to spend my last night with, I'd pick you."

Reclining on the floor with his hands behind his head, he pinned her with his exotic-sunset green eyes. "I'd pick you. But not when I feel like I have to. I don't want you to feel like you have to." He let out a longsuffering sigh. "I don't like feeling I have to claim you in some twisted way to prove I'm a man because of some pissing contest with Michael." Jace tore his gaze away to focus on the ceiling of the plush bedroom they shared. "I don't want it to be like that with you."

The longing in his voice touched her deeply. "I'll stay. You take the money and go. Trust me, Captain, I'll escape."

"You want me to sell you for 15Mil." Jace said it dispassionately, looking at the shadow thick ceiling. "What a tidy profit on fifteen hundred."

"I'll stay here just so you can get away. Take the damn money. It's bonus all around."

"No."

She was simultaneously pleased and angered when he didn't hesitate. "Captain—"

"What was the deal with you and Michael?"

Reluctant to answer, she stalled for time by slipping her boots off. "We were lovers for three months, but that was five years ago."

"It ended badly?"

Very badly, she thought. "Michael went his own way." A way she refused to tolerate.

"Why does he have your ship?"

"Randoms must have sold it." No matter how much she loved her ship, after what happened on it, she didn't want to ever set foot on it again. The emotional residue would drive her crazy.

"He's behaving either like a man in love, or a man hellbent for revenge, or both. Explain that to me."

"I can't." She removed her socks. "I've been racking my brain ever since we got here. When I pulled the IWOG transport job the first time, I sold the goods to Michael—about a year ago. It seemed to me we were friends." Michael's sudden shift in attitude baffled her, and her attempts to read him and the objects in his base hadn't clarified why.

"Did you sleep with him then?"

"Talk about not pulling any punches."

"Report." Jace used his imperious captain voice. "Did you or did you not sleep with him the last time you were here?"

"No."

"Did he want you to?"

"If he did, he didn't mention it. I flew in, made the deal, had dinner with Michael, and I left." Kraft shrugged. "That's why I thought we would be fine coming here. I really don't know what's going on." She tried to rub the exhaustion out of her eyes with her fingertips. "Whatever the reason, it's clear he wants me to stay, so maybe it's best—"

"For the last time—no." Jace climbed off the floor and sat on the bed beside her. "I'm not selling you to him."

"Don't think of it that way. Think of it as saving your ship and your crew."

He frowned. "*You* are part of my crew."

His intensity caused her to glance away. "If I had any idea, I never would have brought you here."

"I know." Tentatively, he took her hand. "We'll work it out, *annyae*." His beautiful green eyes searched her face. "I won't leave you here."

Kraft knew, at that moment, simply holding his hand while they sat on the plush bed, she fell hopelessly in love with Jace Lawless.

Deep in the night, shrouded in the darkness of their shared bedroom, Jace awoke on the floor to find Kraft kneeling above him.

She pressed a finger to his mouth before he could speak, lowered her head to his and whispered, "I have a plan." With that, she crawled on top of him, pulled the cover over her and pressed her body against his.

After a deep groan of pleasure, he managed to whisper back, "And your plan involves straddling my hips?" Not that he minded in the least. So far, it seemed like a grand plan.

"No." She smiled against his neck. "That's just a bonus."

He chuckled softly. "I'm not sure I have enough blood left in my brain to actually think at the moment." All the blood in his body migrated to his hips.

Snuggling a bit firmer, she sighed. "Actually, Captain, I forgot what I was going to say."

"Something about a plan?" he prompted, calling on every shred of self-control not to rock his hips.

"Right."

With her lips invitingly close to his ear, she told him her plan. He argued against it. She insisted the scheme would work. He found new ways to nix the idea. She found a way to allay his concerns. After a long debate, he admitted to himself he was arguing with her only to prolong having her draped over him.

Kraft felt nothing short of wonderful. Her husky voice filling his ear compelled his whole being with a deep longing he hadn't known in a decade. He didn't want her to move away. For a few brief moments, he could pretend that she was his.

After he'd dragged out the debate for as long as he could, he said, "Okay, we'll run with it."

Kraft lifted her head and smiled down at him. "I know you're going to have to put a lot of trust in me, but I hope I've proved to you that you can." She moved to go.

"Don't go yet." With his hands to her wide and sexy hips, he pulled her right back down.

She whispered something guttural in German then tried to kiss him, but he moved his head to the side.

Kraft tensed and whispered, "What's wrong?" She lifted her head. "I thought you wanted to kiss me?"

He cupped her lovely face in his hands. "Believe me, I want to kiss you so badly I'm literally shaking not to." His hands trembled against her face. "But not here, not now, not like this." He traced his finger across her sensuously full lips. "When you come to me, I don't want there to be anything between us but..." He didn't know how to finish because he wanted only love between them but couldn't bring himself to say those telling words. "I just want to hold you. Please."

Reluctantly, she settled against him. "I'm not crushing you, am I?"

"No. You feel wonderful." Lifting his hands, he stroked her back, marveling in how sexy her muscles felt below his hands. He never would have imagined himself so attracted to a woman so much stronger than himself, but that was one of the things that made her so compelling, her physical strength. "Kraft, there is so much I want to say to you, but again, not here, not now, not with so much hanging over us."

"You are so much more than pretty, my captain." Lifting up, she touched his mouth. "I'm afraid if I don't kiss you now, I never will."

Tears fell down her cheeks and he brushed them away.

"Then maybe that's as it should be." He pulled her tight and nestled her face against his shoulder.

"What have you decided?"

Michael once again sat at the head of his massive table as she and Jace picked at their dinners. Michael was the only one who had an appetite. He also had an annoyingly smug smile on his arrogant face that she wanted to slap off. But she remained seated and nodded to Jace.

Jace placed his napkin on the table and stood. "We've decided you can keep us both."

Michael lifted one brow and leaned back. "That's not a part of the deal I offered."

"It's our counteroffer." Jace shrugged, pulling his battered blue shirt tight across his shoulders. Despite the shadow of his beard and the darkened circles under his eyes, he looked wonderful. "If you want Kraft to stay here, I'm staying here with her."

"I'm not interested in you, Lawless." Michael stood, looming his superior height over Jace.

"I'm not interested in you either, Parker." Jace didn't back down. "I'm also not selling Kraft to you, or trading her to you, or leaving her with you—deal with it."

"You think you can protect her from me?" Lifting a brow, dropping his bottom lip to a crooked half grin, Michael smirked as he took a step closer to Jace. "You can't protect yourself,

Lawless, let alone her."

Jace straightened. "I'll die trying."

Michael laughed. "I could take you down without breaking a sweat."

"I know." Jace lifted his hands to his shoulders, the universal sign for surrender, then lowered them to his sides. "Give me guns at thirty paces and I might have a chance."

Jace was playing the situation exactly how they'd discussed last night; be calm, be clear, but above all, offer no challenge.

Michael took a breath and resettled himself, clearly perturbed by Jace's attitude. Michael wanted to fight. The fact that Jace didn't unbalanced him. Kraft knew the time was right.

She stood, ignoring the guards behind her. "Think you could take me down without breaking a sweat, Michael?"

"I'm not offering to fight you." Michael spoke to her but kept his gaze on Jace.

"You were right," Jace said to her with a shake of his head and a bemused smile. He turned his attention to Michael. "She told me you wouldn't fight her because you know you'd lose."

Michael went rigid at the insult and quickly offered one of his own. "Enjoy hiding behind a woman?"

"I'm not hiding behind her." Jace chuckled and pointed. "She's way over there with five heavily armed guards." Jace shifted his gaze to Michael. "I know you're not afraid of me, but you're afraid of her, and I don't blame you. I'm afraid of her too." Jace winked at her. "Thing is, she's on my side. She could best every man in this room without breaking a sweat."

"Not with that bracelet on her wrist."

Kraft glanced at the bracelet. It would inject her with powerful drugs if she raised so much as a finger against Michael. This was the one problem they could not overcome, but she and Jace had come up with an alternate plan. She'd worried that the very idea would anger Jace, and it had, but he'd finally agreed.

She approached Jace. "I offer a challenge to you, Jace Lawless of the ship *Mutiny*. Will you fight me?"

Jace didn't hesitate. "Nope. You can have my ship, my cargo—the whole shebang. Knock yourself out." He bowed formally and took a step back.

Baffled, Michael cast a curious gaze to Jace.

"Thank you, Captain Lawless. That means the challenge Michael offers to you now falls to me." Kraft peered up at Michael.

"I offered to him, not you."

"I just commandeered his ship."

Michael snapped his fingers and pointed at Jace. "Put him in lock down."

Jace didn't fight as he was taken away, but he looked back over his shoulder at her, and she nodded—she'd told him to expect this. Her heart swelled with pride that he trusted her enough to let her take the lead, but her heart broke that she'd lied to him. As she watched the guards drag him away, she wished she'd kissed him goodbye last night.

Michael ordered the rest of the guard to leave. Once they were alone, he eyed her shrewdly. "Your plan won't succeed. I will not fight you, and I will not let you go. If you refuse me, I will torture him to death while I make you watch."

Kraft didn't flinch. She'd known this was coming too. "If you harm him in any way, I'll kill you."

Michael flared at the threat.

"If you let him leave, I'll stay."

Surprise widened Michael's golden-brown eyes. "You were playing him." He stepped close.

She nodded reluctantly. "I had to. He refuses to leave without me. Now that I have command of his ship, he'll have no choice."

"You know I can't let him go. He knows what I look like."

"No matter how much money was involved, Jace wouldn't turn a sketch of you over to the IWOG. He hates them more than he could ever hate you."

Michael flashed her a dubious frown.

"Jace is from Tyaa." She knew that explained everything. Rather than declaring war on the agricultural world, the IWOG unleashed a devastating virus. "The IWOG killed his wife and his three children. Do you really think he'd do anything to help them?"

With a grimace, Michael shook his head. "I'll let him go if you stay."

"I'll stay." She would stay until she knew Jace was safely away and then she would escape.

Michael smiled with triumph, grasped her shoulders and pulled her close. After a deep breath he stepped back as if burned. Shock then fury twisted his face.

"You love him. I can smell it."

Her heart lurched. Now that Michael understood the depth of her feelings for Jace, she had no idea what he would do.

"I still can't believe he just let us go." Jace sat at the galley table. "Especially after buying all the goods at a fair price."

Kraft nodded as she cleaned up the dinner dishes. She didn't feel like talking, especially not about what had happened on Windmere.

"What did he say to you before we left?" Jace asked.

"It's really not important." She secured the pans behind the locking galley doors.

"I still want to know."

Kraft paraphrased it. "Michael said it wouldn't be long before I figured out how weak you are. That once I did, I would return to him." Michael had been more explicit than that, more brutal than that, but that was the gist of what he said. Michael also realized that since she was in love with Jace, there was no hope of rekindling a romance between them. Defeated, he couldn't get them off his planet fast enough. Michael never had been one to linger when he clearly couldn't have his way.

"How weak I am?" Jace asked curiously.

"Michael apparently still operates under the delusion that might makes right." She wiped the stove top and counters.

"Doesn't it?"

"No."

"You really could have taken him down, couldn't you?"

Kraft nodded. "Good night, Captain." She left the galley before he could ask her anything else.

Hours passed. She was settled into her bunk with a paperback when she heard Jace tap twice with his knuckle against her bedroom com.

"May I come in?"

Say no, say no, her mind begged, but her mouth said, "Yes."

He wore that battered green shirt, the one that matched his

eyes, and simple cut flax trousers. He looked scrumptious.

"What do you want, Captain?" She set the book aside.

"You."

It took all her will not to react on the outside, but her heart pounded triple time in her chest. He had no idea how her feelings for him had changed, and she was determined that he would never find out. As she'd said in the galley, love was a dangerous thing on a ship. Loving Jace made her far too vulnerable. Walking away would be difficult enough with her heart broken. She didn't need to break his too.

Jace leaned casually against the wall. "You could have taken Michael down. You could level me. Yet you said I could compel you to my bunk by your own honor."

Swallowing down every carnal need in her body, Kraft boldly returned, "Is that what you want, Captain? Me in your bunk by my honor?"

He considered her question for a long time. His quiet speculation caused her nipples to tighten below her lacy bra and clinging shirt. That he noticed her reaction but didn't blush or turn away made her flush ever so slightly. After the longest time, he said, "I want you there because I think you want to be there."

"Just because I want something doesn't mean it's a good idea."

Jace considered again then nodded. "I didn't say it was a good idea. Just—an idea. You come to me if you want to. I won't make you, I won't compel you, I'm offering. You accept or decline on your own."

Kraft watched the rolling grace of his big body as he strolled away after telling her in no uncertain terms that all she had to do was just show up at his bedroom door.

"Lord on high, he won't even make me ask."

Chapter Twenty

Two days later, Kraft waited by the door of Jace's bunk. She wore all of her gear but her boots. She'd spilled water on them and they were drying out in her room. So, her feet were bare. She'd also left her bra off, but didn't want to think about why, so she didn't.

When he came down the hall she quietly said, "I guess you know what I want to talk to you about."

Jace tapped the com and opened his bedroom door. "You want to flirt with me some more?" He stepped inside and nodded to her.

She followed him in as if they'd done this a thousand times. His room was sparsely furnished. No pictures or knickknacks detracted her attention from the tidy bunk against the port wall.

"Flirting is fun, isn't it? But I'm a lady with a plan." She deliberately kept her tone bright. "I have enough script to start working toward getting another ship. I think it's best if I do it somewhere else."

"You know, you're welcome to stay." Jace closed the door without looking at her. He perused a clipboard of reports.

"I know." Kraft hesitated. "That makes it real hard to leave."

"Is it Heller?"

"No." She laughed. "He's like Smug—a mean dog I knew back when—just gotta show him who's boss. Heller's not the reason." She dropped her flippant tone. "Your ship feels more and more like home every day. That's the reason I—you're the reason I have to go."

"Me? What have I done?" He cast aside the clipboard of reports he wasn't really looking at anyway.

"Nothing. Everything." She met his gaze. "Staying here is like watching my dream die. Honor among thieves is one thing, but a ship can't have two captains, and I can't be just a cook."

"You've held on this long."

"Because I owed you." She held up her hands to stop him from denying the truth. "I think I've more than paid my debt to you. I have to get back to my own life."

"Maybe this is your life."

She shook her head. "This is your dance, and I've cut in far too much already."

"Leading or following, you make a mighty fine dance partner." He smiled grimly once he realized he could not sway her off her chosen path.

"You once said you wouldn't make me do anything I didn't want to." As soon as she said the words, she wanted to take them back. She'd known why she'd come to his room at night, after everyone else was in bed, without her boots or her bra. "But there's something I've been wanting to do ever since I saw your pretty face at the end of my blade." She walked forward and mussed his hair. "I'll bet you thought I was going to kiss you."

"Wishful thinking on my part, apparently." He straightened his hair absently.

"Do you want me to?" She knew what she was doing was downright crazy, but she couldn't stop herself.

He kept his gaze on the floor for the longest time then met her eyes with a guarded expression. "I don't want you to go."

"I know. And there's a part of me that longs to stay. But it'd never work. We'd be fighting all the time. Every time I got put in danger, you'd tussle with it. You'd have a hard time splitting your loyalty between me and the rest of the crew. I'd have a hard time not being in charge. It's a road you know we can't go down."

He nodded with bleak resolution. "I thought you expected your life to be difficult?"

"I've got no problem making my life difficult, but I have a big problem making yours so."

He touched her face. "You are so impossible."

"Am I?"

"Impossibly strong. Impossibly beautiful. Put your lips on mine, Kraft."

Never had a man so sweetly inclined her to kiss him. She tilted her head and brushed her lips to his. A chorus of warning bells went off like a klaxon in her brain and she tried to pull back.

Jace danced her into his embrace with firm insistence.

Keeping his lips pressed to hers, he lifted his hand and gently fingered her lips until she opened to his tongue.

Sweeping slow, tender and deliciously erotic, Jace nudged her lips until she gave herself up fully. She kissed him more intimately than any man she'd ever known. Losing herself, feeling the fall in slow motion, she shook herself awake then danced back with a gasp. One kiss. One sweetly seductive kiss and she'd do anything for that way too pretty man.

"Now that was worth waiting for." She took a deep breath. "And all the more reason I have to go." She turned to the closed door of his bunk.

"Stay here, tonight, with me." His voice was soft and plaintive. Gently, he turned her around.

She hesitated even though this was what she'd been after all along. "It'll only make it harder to walk away."

"I know." He reached for her belt of blades. "But didn't you tell me you have a knack for running down the most onerous road headlong?" He lowered his lips to her ear and breathed, "Blindfolded to boot."

Fascinated and frightened, she watched him cast her belt of blades aside. Normally, when she desired a man, she just strode right up and asked for what she wanted, but with Jace she felt unsure and awkward.

"I would like it very much, Kraft, if you ran down this road with me headstrong and eyes wide."

Jace blushed so many times at her ribald comments that she found it entirely fitting it was she who blushed now. Not at what he said, but at the way he looked at her. He gazed at her with such intensity she felt utterly desirable yet vulnerable.

Behind her, less than a quick turn and one step away, was the door to safety. In front of her, looking at her so openly and intently, stood Jace. She knew her life would be much simpler if she ran out his door right now.

Jace hit the com panel to his bunk. The heavy door locked

with a *thunk.*

"You locked the door." She gulped.

Jace nodded. "If you honestly want me to, I'll unlock it."

If she asked him to unlock his bedroom door, this strangely compelling dance would end. If she didn't, she was about to dance her way down a road that might be fatally disastrous. Or at least extremely painful. Ever practical, she said, "Bailey could tap the com."

"Not to my room when it's locked." Jace shook his head and gave her a slight smile, as if he applauded her effort. "Bailey can talk to me, but he can't hear me." Jace leaned close, put his hand to the top button of her shirt. "If you're in here with me, that means he can't hear *you* either."

"Oh." For a moment, she didn't understand why she was so flustered. It wasn't like she'd never been with a man before, but this was the first time she'd been with a man she loved. Everything was different, more intense, because with Jace, sex actually meant something.

"So, tell me, Kraft, should I touch that button?" He nodded to the com. "Or this?" He nodded to her shirt where his hand hovered.

"Captain, this—"

"Was inevitable." He unbuttoned her shirt with a slow, deliberate hand as his gaze held hers. A slight smile lifted the corner of his mouth when he discovered she wasn't wearing a bra.

"I'm your cook." She offered it up as a last ditch effort to stop what happened between them.

"I thought you were only a passenger now?" He hesitated at the top button of her dextex pants.

"It'll look bad."

"Yes, it will look like I'm diddling my cook." With a twist of his fingers and thumb, he popped the button and grasped the zipper tab.

"Captain, your crew will think—"

"A bunch of things I can't control."

He lifted his hand to her chin and slid his fingertips down her neck and between her breasts. His slow, languorous stroke thrummed her body and tightened her nipples.

"You once said you wouldn't mind a quick dance in my

trousers. How would you feel about a long and slow waltz?" He held his hand to her zipper.

"You have no idea what kind of trouble this would cause."

"I really don't think we're going to have a bit of trouble if we do what I have in mind." He let go of her zipper and unbuttoned his own shirt with that slow, deliberate hand. He shrugged his shoulders and the faded blue homespun fell to the floor behind him.

Black hair that she'd only seen peeking out of his shirt collars now compelled her gaze down. He held his hand to the top of his button-fly trousers.

"Tell me, Kraft. Do we dance this dance or not?"

She stood still, her chest tight with a mixture of desire and confusion. A thousand dreams and fears rushed through her. Eight years of calling her life a dance when it was so frenetic it could be only be called running.

"I'll follow your lead." She had much to lose, but more to gain.

"No matter where I twirl you?" He offered a welcoming smile.

"No matter." She grasped the edge of his fly and popped the top two buttons with one hard yank. Her boldness surprised him, and she offered an apologetic grin. "I'll try real hard not to step on your toes too much."

"You lead this dance any time you have the notion to." Jace slid down the zipper of her pants. He slipped his hand lower, between her legs, pressing his palm against the moist fabric.

Overwhelmed by the rush of pleasure, she rolled into the arc of his arm and squirmed wantonly against his powerful hand. She wanted her pants gone and his strong, thick fingers thrusting deep inside her.

"This dance would be better without all these clothes." He slipped her unbuttoned shirt off. He brushed his fingertips gently over the swell of her breasts then tugged a turgid peak with forefinger and thumb. As his mouth replaced his hand, he reached for the waistband of her pants.

She felt again at crossroads. If she kept her pants on, nothing more would happen than just a taste of pleasure. He sensed her hesitation and moved back slightly.

"Tell me to stop if that's what you want." His eyes were heavy-lidded with longing, but also filled with concern. Even if thwarted lust killed him, Jace would stop if she asked.

His compassion, his genuine desire to please her, stripped away the last of her reluctance. Whatever may come from one night with him, she would gladly pay the consequences.

Unable to find her voice, she pressed her face to his neck and bit him softly.

Groaning low and deep from his chest, he slipped off her pants and toyed with the top edge of her panties.

"Black lace against your exquisite mocha skin—and what's this?" Before she could respond, he kissed his way down her belly and knelt on the floor. "A little red bow on a fancy wrapped gift."

Her smile became an O of surprise when he pressed his mouth against her sex and exhaled a hot, moist breath. Ribbons of need encircled her nerves and she parted her legs to allow him greater access. Through the lace, he nibbled her clit to throbbing intensity. Her eyelids drifted closed and her head went back.

He continued his wicked ministrations until her groans turned to gasps. Lightheaded and close to climax, she trailed her fingers through his silky black hair and cupped the back of his head. With a final teasing bite, he slid his fingers under the elastic and pulled her panties down and off.

Breathless, she waited for what felt like a lifetime, but when he didn't continue, she forced her eyes open and looked down. He met her gaze, parted her inner thighs, and slipped his tongue between her secret folds. Pleasure consumed her with such intensity her eyes snapped shut and she jerked back. He grasped her hips, steadied her, and twirled his tongue ever faster and bolder.

Burning for release, she tilted her hips and parted her knees. His long, thick fingers swirled against her core, but he made no effort to fill that ever tightening passage. A scream of frustration built in her chest, but before she could bellow out a command, he stood, pressed her against the wall, and thrust his fingers inside her.

Her held-back bellow became a gasp that he swallowed by capturing her mouth with his. He kissed her like the thirstiest man in the Void. Tasting her passion on his lips compelled her to rock against his thrusting hand. She clutched his shoulders, clinging to him, afraid that if she let go she would explode into a million shards.

"Come for me."

The command in his husky voice pushed her over the edge. Her climax was a rainstorm that swept the desert of her body with a sudden and frightening intensity. Trembling legs couldn't hold her against the onslaught, but when she faltered, Jace steadied her by holding her and pressing her to the wall.

His lips found hers again. He kissed and stroked her gently as the waves of pleasure subsided. For the first time in her life, she felt vulnerable without feeling afraid. She'd surrendered to him and discovered, much to her surprise, that capitulation empowered her.

"Captain, I—" She stopped speaking when he withdrew.

"Is that why you..." Confusion deepened the lines around his eyes as his gaze searched her face. Relief melted the lines away when he smiled. "Call me Jace."

"Jace." She called him by his first name for the first time. On the derelict Basic, she addressed him as Captain Lawless to show respect. Held captive on his ship, she called him Captain Lawless again, only calling him Captain when he gave her permission. She hadn't even been aware she'd been waiting for his permission to call him by his first name. "Jace."

Here and now, in this moment, he was only a man who wanted to be with her as a woman. He didn't want her as his captive cook, as a proud warrior beaten, or the humbled female captain—Jace wanted her, the woman, the soul behind all the masks.

"Jace." She cupped his face and kissed him.

A surge of need possessed him as her tongue danced wantonly with his. Jace wanted to possess her, to fill her. He didn't need to be a reader to know Kraft felt exactly the same way, but he didn't want to rush this wonderful fulfillment of all his longings.

Murmuring words of how beautiful and special she was, he drew her to his bunk. Kraft reclined and pulled him with her, but he shook his head. He lifted her hand and placed a gentle kiss in the center of her palm.

The liquid heat in her eyes deepened as he kissed his way to her wrist where her flesh pulsed with her heartbeat. Ever so slowly, he worked his way up her arm to the sensitive skin of her neck. She arched her head back, encouraging him with low rumbles of pleasure. Teasing her with teeth and tongue, he explored her upper body until she grew restless and tugged at the fly of his pants.

"Not yet." He captured her hands. He feared one touch of her naked body against his would compel a climax he wouldn't be able to stop. Slipping on top of her, he straddled her hips, pressed her hands above her head, and lowered his face to hers.

Jace explored her beautiful high cheekbones and the angles of her jaw. He pulled her full bottom lip between his and sucked lightly.

Sliding his hands down her arms, he kissed the tops of her breasts and the full inner curves. Her toffee dark nipples strained as he nipped close without touching. Kraft writhed below him, groaning out guttural commands and straining to angle her breasts toward his mouth. He waited until her frustration became fever-pitched then he took one toffee peak between his lips.

Breathing heavily, she cupped the back of his head, trailing her hand through his hair as he continued to torment her exquisitely sensitive breasts. His name escaped her lips in a begging chant.

When he angled up, he discovered her eyes were heavy-lidded and sweat beaded on her forehead. Her strong hands gripped his shoulders as if she would flip him over at any moment.

"You find it very difficult to be passive, don't you?" He sat up astride her hips and unbuttoned his trousers.

"Almost impossible." She flashed him that slow, lazy and unbearably sexy smile as she pushed his pants and boxers aside, exposing his now painfully hard penis.

Before he realized her intent, she lifted from the bed, grasped his hips, and took the tip of him into the warm hollow of her mouth. Shock and pleasure surged, tightening every muscle in his body. Slowly, she eased her lips over his shaft. She encouraged him to rock his hips by gripping his buttocks and easing him back and forth.

Close to climax, he retreated. The sensation of cold air on his wet erection cooled his ardor. He climbed off the bed and quickly shucked his clothing.

She watched him with hungry eyes.

For a moment, he simply stood by his bunk, amazed to find such a lovely woman waiting for him. Trepidation filled him as he sat down beside her.

"Jace, what's wrong?" With a hand to his cheek, she turned his face to hers. "I have a B-chip."

He wasn't worried about birth control, but he didn't know how to express his concern that he could never measure up to the men of her past.

"Is it your wife?" Pain filled her eyes.

"No, no." He embraced her, kissing her cheek and nuzzling her neck. It never occurred to him that she would have her own apprehensions about measuring up to *his* past. The realization melted away his worry. "I'm afraid I won't last."

A relieved chuckle escaped her and puffed along his shoulder in a moist wind. "We can go as fast or as slow as you want. And then we can do this again. And again."

"Slowly," he managed to say, lowering her to the bunk and slipping between her legs. After waiting a decade, he was determined to make this last longer than ten minutes, but her lovely scent and passionate embrace made ten seconds seem out of his reach.

When he touched the tip of his penis to her slick core, she tried to wrap her legs around him and pull him deeper.

"Don't move." Gritting his teeth, he eased into her as he kept her gaze.

Her eyes remained open and widened as he entered.

The intensity almost hurt.

Ten years of celibacy, ten years of clinging to the past, ten years of denying himself fell away as Jace claimed Kraft.

Ever so slowly, she rolled her hips, encouraging his thrusts, until they worked frantically against each other.

He slid his hand between their sweat-slicked bodies. Kraft jolted when he flicked a fingertip across her clit. Rocking ever faster, Jace said, "Stay with me, stay with me."

As her climax rose, Kraft answered, "I'm here, I'm here."

Her body clamped down around him, tight and full, as the most intense orgasm ripped through him.

Fusing flesh.

For a brief moment they were one. Jace buried himself within her as if that could bind her to him. Where everything would be simple as one. Drawing her willing body to his, Jace knew they could not be.

Chapter Twenty-one

"We'll be docked for a few days," Jace said idly, after *Mutiny* touched down on Byzantine.

Kraft nodded, feeling a strange tug between freedom and Jace as she made a list of what the kitchen needed. Over the last few days, when she hadn't been sharing Jace's bed, she'd been composing a book of recipes. Doing so reminded her she would be leaving, and that day had finally arrived.

"I know you have work to do, but you have to sleep somewhere." He looked right into her eyes. "I suppose here is as good as any digs you'd find in Kali."

The longer she lingered the harder it would be to ultimately leave. "I think I could stay one more night."

"One last night." His voice sounded wistful.

"Jace, if it's going to make matters worse—"

"No." He cut her off. "One last night. We'll make it one to remember."

She forced herself to smile and lightly say, "I'd like that."

Kraft left *Mutiny* with almost 150K tucked to a money belt wrapped around her belly. At the ready to her right was a modified Katana. To her left were a dagger and a revolver. Her black shirt, tucked into her black pants, tucked into calf-high black leather boots, were topped with a black duster. Her black hair was pulled back, folded in half, twined with black linen like a rope down her back.

She swept through the darkening Kali streets like a liquid shadow. Children scrambled from her path. Men and women, rich or poor, all instinctively moved aside. Kraft didn't smile or frown as she strode past them.

Scores of IWOG officers on leave in the seamier part of Kali could have stopped her and demanded to see her bonafides, but they didn't dare. Not a soul willingly intersected his path with hers as Kraft sought a hideously garish hell called the Den of Ishtar.

In the midst of the most atrocious poverty, the IWOG ran a decadent hell decked in red velvet with obscenely huge gilded doorways and mirrors. A shot of whiskey would run you ten—if you didn't bat an eye at that, you would be allowed to enter and then encouraged to see how much you'd sell your soul for. There wasn't a damn thing you couldn't wager yourself into at the Den of Ishtar.

A quick flash of her script got her in the door with no questions asked. The IWOG didn't scan high-roller gambling dens; it wouldn't do to have valid proof of their own corruption.

Kraft picked her marks, settled at the table and got the usual little lady crap until she won the first hand. The joking ceased entirely when she took the next three.

Carefully, losing a bit, winning more, she worked her way up to 500K. To these high-ranking IWOG officers, what she took really wasn't much. They resented her as a woman, but in the end, they enjoyed the experience so much they were smugly condescending. To her, 500K would buy her a ship and outfit a crew. To them, they probably pissed away that much in a month on their mistresses.

Kraft tucked her winnings to her money belt and thanked the men for a lovely evening.

They let her go with a cheery wave and a lifting up of their three hundred script drinks.

In the heart of Kali, dickering over some upgrades for his ship, Jace found himself surrounded by Trickster's men.

"Trickster wants a chat."

"I got nothing to say to that scrimshanker." Jace turned his back on them as he considered again the electronics huckster.

A gun clicked and Jace felt a barrel pressed into his spine.

"He didn't say it was optional."

Jace went with the men to Trickster's lair. It was as filthy as ever. "Some things never change."

"Actually, change is the only constant in the Void." Trickster leered from behind his cluttered desk.

"What do you want? I've got people to see, places to go."

"I imagine you do. What with all that script burning a hole in your pocket." Trickster's upper lip curled.

"Is there a point to this?"

"Cut the crap, Lawless." Trickster leaned back in his chair. "I know you knocked off that IWOG Transport station. I know Kraft ran the show."

"So?"

"Maybe I'm hurt you didn't think of trading with me."

"Too bad. You're not the only show in town."

"I know a lot more about the show than you do." His smarmy smile exposed a row of crooked yellow teeth.

"What is this? Extortion? You expect me to pay you to keep your big mouth shut?" Suspicion twisted his gut with foreboding.

"Not at all. I'm wise to the ways of the underworld."

"That's only because you've got your dirty fingers in practically everybody's pie. You're just upset that you didn't get a piece of this one."

Trickster nodded. "I think you're going to give me a piece of it, a token piece."

"Out of the goodness of my heart?" Jace wished the little rat would get to the point. He wanted to finish his business in Kali and then prepare for his last night with Kraft. Already he'd bought new sheets for his bunk, a pricy bottle of wine, and a tin of powdered honey—the bright-eyed clerk assured him brushing the substance on wasn't nearly as fun as licking it off.

Trickster picked up an envelope and tapped it on his desk. "I think you'll be happy to pay me for this." Dust poofed up and danced in the fading sunlight that managed to slip through the grungy windows.

"If you're waiting for me to ask you to unpack this, you're gonna be waiting a long time. I've got no interest in playing any of your games, and there's no way I'm going to pay you for the privilege of jerking me around."

"I know you'd be interested in this." Trickster tapped the envelope to his greasy head. "More a man knows about his crew, the better off he is."

"I know my crew, Trickster. Seems to me you're the one who didn't realize how valuable Kraft was. You're just looking to get a bit more script for her, that's all. That's also too bad because that deal is long past being done."

Trickster nodded. "But new information has come into my possession. Information I think you'd pay handsomely for."

Jace laughed. "About Kraft? All I have to do is ask her. She'll tell me anything I want to know."

"Will she?" Trickster considered for a moment. "I believe she would. Provided you asked the right questions."

"Are we done?" Jace sighed. "Because I've got no intention of buying what you're selling."

"You have no desire to know who she really is? No curiosity about how she knew so much about an IWOG Transport station?" Trickster pushed the envelope toward him with skeletal fingers. "What's in this envelope will explain everything, and I'll sell it to you for a paltry 3K."

"That's twice what you sold Kraft for."

"Information is far more valuable than any woman."

Jace looked long and hard at the envelope. He knew if he bought it, it would be a betrayal of Kraft. If he didn't, it would be a betrayal of himself. Either way, he wouldn't be able to stop thinking about what was inside.

"I'm so certain you'll want this information that I'm willing to make you a deal. You give me half, then open it up. If you agree with me that it's worth knowing, you give me the other half."

Jace counted out fifteen hundred to Trickster's desk and tore open the envelope. He found a single piece of paper. He read the information again and again. He counted out the rest of the money with trembling hands.

On the way back to *Mutiny*, Jace made several purchases then waited in the kitchen for Kraft to return.

Chapter Twenty-two

Plush with money, flush with the thought of spending a last night in Jace's arms, Kraft practically ran back to *Mutiny*. The ship was unnaturally quiet, but she didn't give it much thought as she made her way to the galley.

"Did you have a good time?" Jace sat at the kitchen table clutching a piece of paper in his fist.

Disconcerted by his mood, she evenly offered, "I got what I wanted."

"How much did you take them for?" His voice was flat and emotionless.

"Five."

"That's more than enough for a new ship, a new crew, a new life. Maybe even a new name."

Foreboding raced her heart and her mouth went dry. "Jace, what's going on?"

"I think it best if you call me Captain Lawless."

She stiffened at his demanding tone. "I'm not your cook anymore."

He didn't speak and didn't look at her, but his anger came across crystal clear by the tension in his neck and face. A vein throbbed from his shirt collar to his jaw.

"If you want to make our last night something to remember by fighting, then tell me what we're going to be fighting about, because I haven't got a clue."

Jace stood and hit the wall com. "It's time to go."

Below her feet, *Mutiny* powered up. "What are you doing?"

"We're leaving."

"Fine." She turned away from him. "I'll be on my way." She

didn't know what was going on, but her instincts told her not to hang around and ask.

"You're not going anywhere."

In a flash, he handcuffed her hands behind her back.

"What are you doing?" She was so shocked she didn't struggle.

Holding her wrists, Jace leaned intimately close, and whispered, "I'm taking care of some unfinished business."

Garrett entered the kitchen and stopped dead. "You two playing some kinky game?" He lifted a brow at the cuffs. "I could come back later if you all want to be alone."

"The games are definitely over." Jace practically spit the words into her ear. "Tell Heller to get up here."

With a concerned and confused frown, Garrett called Heller to the galley as *Mutiny* lifted off.

Her heart pounded all the way up to her throat, making it impossible for her to breathe. A huge fear welled up and she tried desperately to quell it. Even cuffed, she could use her abilities to escape, but quickly realized she had nowhere to go. And she couldn't bear the thought of hurting Jace or his crew.

Heller entered, examined their tableau for a moment, and asked, "What's up?"

"Kraft's number." Jace ordered Heller behind her and he held onto the chain between the cuffs.

Jace faced her and glared at her with full-blown hatred.

"Why?" Her voice quavered when she asked.

"I paid good money for you."

"This is about money?" A faint hope glimmered. "I have over 500K, Captain Lawless, and every last bit of it is yours."

"Where the hell did she get—"

"Shut up, Heller." Jace met her gaze with narrow slits that completely obscured any kindness. "It's not enough. Where else could I find a cook, a warrior and a willing whore all wrapped up in one woman?"

Her mouth and eyes went wide at the word whore. "You bastard."

"I'm no bastard, you bitch." Jace slapped her.

Garrett grabbed Jace's arm. "I don't know what's going on, but I'm not about to stand aside while you strike a bound woman."

Jace strode to the table. "Before you leap to her defense, you might want to read this." He retrieved the paper he'd been clutching and shoved it into Garrett's hand.

When he finished reading, Garrett glared at her like he itched to slap her himself.

"What the hell is on that stupid piece of paper?" Her face throbbed from Jace's slap, but it didn't hurt nearly as much as her heart—it was bad enough she fell in love with him, and had to leave him, but to have him despise her as well?

Jace flashed her a very nasty smile.

"This isn't funny." Being called a whore and then struck like a wayward child stung her deeply.

"No, it's not, is it." Jace literally shook with rage. "To have everything change in the blink of an eye. Difficult to get your bearings, isn't it, Julie?"

Realization hit and almost knocked her off her feet. "Oh, God." She closed her eyes against the tremble that raced through her body. The paper was a warrant.

"I don't think God would lift a finger to help an IWOG assassin." Jace was shaking with fury.

"She's IWOG?" Heller yanked her cuffs.

"I can explain." She searched Jace's face, looking for one scrap of understanding, but found only disgust.

"I'm certain you can. Lying seems to be your best skill."

"I never lied to you." She may have danced around the edges of the truth, like she'd done at Michael's, but she'd never once outright lied to him about who she was. When he'd asked, she'd told him she'd been in the military for five years. She just never specified which military.

Jace dismissed her claim with a roll of his eyes. "I guess it's my fault for not asking the right questions."

"What did you expect me to do? Blurt it out the first time I laid eyes on you? I was afraid to tell you. Afraid of what you'd think of me." She struggled in her handcuffs. "Afraid of what you'd do to me."

Heller yanked up, but she refused to even wince.

"You should be afraid. If you feel anything right now, which is probably a real reach for an IWOG fetch, you best feel stark terror. Because I got a world of possibilities at my fingertips, Julie. I could do anything I want to you. Maybe I'll turn you in for the reward."

"I've already given you ten times that. I'm willing to give you fifty times it or more."

"I've been harboring an IWOG fetch." Jace leaned close to her face. "One I actually paid good money to save. You think any amount of script is going to pay me back for that?"

A tremble raced through her.

"I'll bet there's a boatload of folks who'd pay handsomely for you, given the sum total of your skills: Fairing's cook, an object reader and a fully trained IWOG assassin. You're worth a fortune."

He touched her face possessively and she flinched.

"Perhaps my little investment with Trickster wasn't such a bad one after all. I could parlay you into a hefty retirement fund. Go legitimate, like you suggested."

"Do you have any idea what will happen to me?" Her belly clutched at just the fleeting thought.

"What do I care?" He shrugged and winked. "I got my use out of you."

She closed her eyes, wishing that when she opened them, she'd be almost anywhere but here.

"And I've got no problem selling a heartless killer back to her own kind."

"You don't understand."

"You're right, I don't. I don't understand how anyone could willingly work for those bastards. Frankly? I don't want to wrap my head around such a conundrum because I really don't care. You're lucky I didn't just blow your worthless head off when you walked in here."

Kraft nodded, amazed she was still alive. Apparently, the Void wanted her last hours to be filled with nothing short of pure misery. "What are you going to do with me?"

"I have to collect some bids. And thanks to you, I got plenty of money, therefore, plenty of time to decide who I'm going to sell you to."

Jace ordered Heller to escort her to her room. Jace had prepared it by stripping the room of everything but the bed, the table and a chair. Jace took her inside while Heller stood guard at the doorway.

"Okay, Julie, this is the drill—I'm going to un-cuff you then re-cuff you with the longer pair. If you so much as wink, Heller here is going to blow your head off. We clear?"

Kraft looked into Jace's deadly-serious eyes, then down the barrel of Heller's gun. Heller would gladly blow her away at the slightest provocation. "Crystal clear, Captain Lawless."

Jace slipped off the cuffs then slipped on a pair with a long chain that looped to one of the huge, exposed pipes. "Hands up, Julie."

Kraft lifted her hands and Jace removed her belt of blades. He tossed them on the bed then opened her shirt to get at her money belt. He slipped that off and tossed it to the bed. He didn't bother to button up her shirt.

"Enjoying the view?" She nodded to the bed. "You leave that in here for me, or you?"

Jace's eyes narrowed at her suggestive tone. "Heller, take her stuff and stow it in my bunk. I think little Julie and I need some alone time."

Heller leered at her, scooped up her gear and left.

Jace slapped the com and locked the door. "You think I'd toss it all aside for another tumble with you?"

"No, I'm just wondering how much you're going to wring from me before you toss me to the wolves. You seem to be a man who's mighty concerned about getting his money's worth. So, tell me, are you going to make me cook and fight while you hold me captive for sale, or just whore?"

"Perhaps." Jace stepped forward and unbuttoned another of the small black buttons on her shirt.

"You've got a dark streak in you, Captain Lawless. Just the thought of having me at your tender mercies is making you harder than that gun at your hip."

"Maybe it's the thought of killing an IWOG bitch that's got me all hot and bothered." He grabbed her wrists. "And I ain't letting you get your hands on my hardware."

"Can't blame a girl for trying."

"I thought being called a girl would make your head explode."

"That was Danna, not me. The only thing I don't like being called is Julie, which will ensure that's all you'll call me."

He yanked her against his body. He looked down into her face. "You really want to explore my dark side? You might want to think carefully about that. I've got a powerful hate for anything IWOG."

"So do I."

"Maybe you're as hot as a firecracker because you think once you get me between your legs you can kill me."

"Why would I do that?" She undulated against him. "I want all that anger and fury pounding into my body. So do you."

Jace kissed her hard and merciless. Even knowing what she was, he still wanted her. With a gasping groan, he pushed her away and wiped his mouth with the back of his hand.

"Deny it to yourself, but you still want me, Captain Lawless."

"You're my big payday, nothing more. Maybe I'll sell you to Michael for 15Mil. I wonder what he'd do to you if he knew you were IWOG scum. Because, surely, he doesn't know."

"No, he doesn't, but I thought you were too honorable to sell me to a man who—"

"I no longer care." He slapped the com and the door opened. "And apparently there really isn't any honor among thieves."

Jace kept her chained up in her room. She searched it from top to bottom, but didn't find anything she could use to escape.

Her chain allowed her the run of the room and the bathroom, but not a one of her considerable skills would get her out of this fix. Even with the right tools it would take hours to pick the lock on the cuffs. A week with a very sharp file would hardly make a dent in the thick chain. She'd have better luck trying to teleport herself off the ship than she would bringing down the pipe her chain was affixed to. The pipe was made of durosteel and was as thick as her thigh.

Jace had put some serious thought into keeping her captive.

"That man is so much more than pretty." She shook her head and looked around the room for the umpteenth time, hoping against hope she had failed to see something she could use to get out. "Even if I do get out of here, where the hell am I going to go?"

"That's why you're not getting out of here." Jace entered the room with a plate of food. "If you did, you'd kill me and my crew and steal *Mutiny.*" He set the food down on the table.

"Lord on high! If I wanted to steal your ship don't you think I would have done it when I had the run of it? Don't you think I would have done it then when it was a mite simpler? Or hell, maybe you think I'm insane and really like to challenge myself." She flung her arms up and the chain clinked merrily.

"Or maybe I just think you didn't have a compelling enough reason until now."

"Ah, yes, trust issues. I've treated you so horribly since the moment I met you. I only saved your life—how many times?"

"How do you justify being an IWOG assassin?"

"I don't."

"You mean you can't." Jace crossed his arms.

"That too."

"What did you think I was going to do when I found out?"

"I didn't give it much thought."

"You didn't think I'd ever find out."

"I'd hoped."

He grabbed her shoulders and shook her. She refused to fight back. She went limp and closed her eyes in resignation.

Jace let her go. "You don't even care, do you?" His breath came in short, painful gasps.

"No." She shook her head. "I don't see why I should. I don't have any control over what you do, knowing my truth or not."

"It changes everything."

"Does it." She spoke without asking a question.

"Stop doing that." He clenched his hands to fists to keep from shaking her again.

"Just tell me what you want and I'll do it."

"How dare you turn this back on me!"

"That's exactly what this is about."

"It's about me? You unbelievable—"

"Bitch? Fetch? IWOG ditto-head?"

"Stop it!"

"Got ya. It's okay for you to call me all those names, but I can't do it." She took a deep breath. "How does this grab you? I'm nothing but a worthless IWOG fetching ditto-headed bitch."

Jace recoiled.

"Too much or not enough?"

"This isn't going to work."

She laughed. "You seem staggered that I agree with you. Oh, I get it. You thought I was going to stand here and *defend* myself. Well, you know I'm not an idiot. Why the hell would I waste my time? You don't want to hear an explanation. Even if you did, you wouldn't believe it. There's nothing I could say that would justify my life to you. And frankly? I thought you'd seen enough of my present that my past wouldn't color me that darkly."

"I never could manage to look through black."

Kraft tilted her head curiously. "The black of my past invalidates everything I've done since I left the IWOG eight years ago." She nodded. "Hell, I guess I should have just stayed with them. According to your philosophy, what's the point of correcting a mistake?"

"A mistake? That's what you call it?"

Kraft shrugged. "Okay, a big mistake."

"You killed innocent people!"

"Did I."

Jace shook his head as if one of them was completely insane and he was utterly baffled as to which one.

"You seem to be of the mind you know my whole life story so why don't you just tell it to me."

"Stop turning this back on me."

"Again, Captain Lawless, this is more about you than me. I've dealt with what I did, you haven't. All you hear is IWOG assassin and that sets you to hating me."

"Did you think it was likely to do any else?"

"No, I didn't. But I thought you knew *me*. I thought you knew enough about me that maybe you'd ask first before you condemned me. But, hell, I guess it doesn't matter who I am to you. Seems to matter a hell of a lot more who I *was*."

Jace considered the floor for a moment, glanced up at her face, then to her restraints. With a wince, he turned on his heel and left the room.

Kraft felt sorry for them both. It seemed inevitable that they would dance this terribly awkward painful dance and she wondered how deeply their daggers were going to cut.

Chapter Twenty-three

Jace brought in a plate of food. The last plate sat congealed and untouched.

"Hunger strike?"

"Yeah." Kraft nodded from her cross-legged position on the narrow bed. "I've opted for slow death rather than an instant death by eating that garbage."

"You think it's poisoned?"

She snorted laughter. "I wouldn't feed that dreck to my worst enemy." She waved her hand in front of her face. "If it smells that bad, how good could it possibly taste?"

"It'll keep you alive."

"Well there's a selling point." She rolled her eyes. "I should eat that garbage because I've got so much to live for." She made a face at the food then laughed. "Do me a favor, Captain Lawless, if you're not going to kill me outright, at least don't try to kill me with a sorry excuse for a meal. Let me cook." Kraft flung up her arms and the thick chain danced and clanged against the metal frame of the bed. "Hell, *make* me cook. I'd rather do that than just sit here contemplating my navel."

Heller leaned into the room. "Chaining her to the stove ain't a bad idea. I wouldn't be against putting her through her paces in here either." Heller cupped his crotch and leered at her.

"Come near me with that in mind, and I'll kill you." Kraft said it utterly deadpan. "I won't even think twice."

Heller flinched then pointed his gun at her head. He cocked it and the click resounded in the mostly bare room.

"Pull the trigger." She lifted her hands, palm open, to her shoulders. "If I'm dead you can do whatever you want to me, because at that point I will cease to care. But you damn well better make sure I'm dead first."

"Maybe I'll get a little something from the doctor," Heller threatened.

"Payton better be awful quick. Anyone comes at me with a loaded syringe and I'm apt jam it in their eye."

"Really?" Jace asked. When she turned her razor gaze on him, he almost flinched. Bound, Kraft seemed far more dangerous than when she'd been free. Confinement did not sit well with her, and captivity not at all. But in her eyes he saw her weakness. When she'd glared at Heller, she'd meant every word she said. But now, when she looked into his eyes, Jace saw the smallest flicker of doubt. "If I came at you with a loaded syringe, would you jam it in my eye?"

When she hesitated, he smiled. "Heller? Go get Payton. Tell her to bring her bag."

Heller's leer about split his face. Thundering footsteps pounded down the hall to the infirmary.

"You wouldn't." Her face went pale.

"Give me one good reason why I shouldn't."

"I'll give you the only thing I have left."

"I'm not much interested in your honor at this point."

"What about my love?"

Jace didn't move a muscle as he contemplated Kraft, sitting motionless on her bare prison mattress. A part of him wanted to believe that she loved him, but he feared it was only a trick to get him to relax his guard.

Heller almost shoved Payton into the room. Her hair was in wild disarray, a cloud of strawberry blond around her startled green eyes.

Casually, Jace turned to Payton and said, "She's got scratches on her wrists that need tending to." He turned and walked away.

"Aw, Jace!" Heller whined, following him.

Kraft let out a wavering sigh of relief.

Payton found herself alone with Kraft. "This would work better without the cuffs..."

"I have a feeling they're not ever coming off."

Payton examined her wrists. They were badly scraped from three days and nights in the cuffs. Payton's questioning gaze kept darting to her face. "There's not much I can do. I can wrap them in gauze. That should help."

"I'd be grateful."

"Just doing my job." Her tone was colder than the Void.

"One you'd rather not."

"The IWOG has never granted me any favors." Payton worked meticulously.

"I'm not IWOG, Payton."

"Jace said you were. I saw the warrant." Payton wrapped her battered wrists and left.

Kraft sank to the bed. Jace, the man she loved, hated her. His crew, those she had grown to care for, hated her. Her own parents would gleefully turn her into the IWOG regardless of the bounty. Fairing was long in his grave. So too were the seven women of her crew. There wasn't a soul in the Void who could or would help her. Not even Michael would if he knew.

She covered her face with her hands.

"Aw, is the big tough lady gonna cry?" Heller leaned against her doorway jeering at her.

"I will if I have to eat any more of the slop coming out of the kitchen. Did you make that abomination?" She nodded toward the strange, gaily colored mixture on the table.

Obviously disappointed when she didn't burst into tears, Heller snarled, "You're lucky we're feeding you at all."

"Well, lucky's not what I'd call it. Torture's what I'd call it."

"There's an idea." Heller pulled a wicked dagger out of his hip holster, but he frowned when she laughed.

"Could you be any more pathetic? I'll bet you'd take real pleasure in slapping babies and kicking puppies."

"Nothing's more pathetic than an IWOG fetch."

"That's true enough." She sighed. "Are we done yet?"

"Done what?"

"Dancing."

"You know," Heller said, looking up and down the hallway. "Jace isn't around."

"Let me point out the obvious to you, Heller. Even if Captain Lawless was around? I don't think he'd stop you."

Heller took a step toward her and she stood, her body poised for defense. "Of course, I don't need him to, chained up or not. If you'd pull your head out of your butt for half a second you'd remember a little interlude involving me, your hand and a lot of tears. Notably *not* mine."

Heller yanked his hand to his chest as if to protect it. She could practically hear the rusty wheels grinding in his head. In the end, Heller decided to play it safe.

"I don't know why, but Jace wants you alive."

"I imagine cashing me in for 15Mil gives him quite an incentive."

"Maybe he won't sell you. As soon as he gives the word— *eerk!*" Heller swiped his blade in pantomime across his neck.

"Then I guess we're all waiting on Captain Lawless to set the tune."

Heller didn't understand what she meant. He shook his head. "Maybe he'll want to kill you himself."

"Maybe."

"You don't seem to care."

"About dancing with you? You're right, I don't. You're an annoyance, Heller. Captain Jace Lawless is the man I have to worry about dancing with."

Kraft sat on her bed in the dark, repeating every recipe her grandfather and Parkhill taught her. As she thought of the recipes, she went through the motions in her mind, visualized herself preparing each dish just so. She became so focused she could almost smell the creations.

An impossibly sweet chord filled her room.

A green light glowed steady on the com next to the door— the only thing she couldn't reach in the room.

From the tinny com speaker came a melancholy tune. Slow and sad, filled with a curious longing.

Bailey. Sitting watch on the bridge. He'd tapped her com so he could play for her. Bailey played stories without words long into the night. She didn't know if he could hear her or not but she finally curled for sleep on the bare mattress and whispered, "Thank you."

The whole crew, minus Jace, sat around the kitchen table, picking and poking at the oddly festive glop on their plates.

Whatever Charissa made for dinner terrified everyone. Not just for its garish color, but its lively stench.

Everyone took a bite, to be kind, then pushed the food around their plates.

"Remember that Rinderbraten Kraft made?" Bailey asked. "You could cut it with a breath it was so tender and juicy."

"Kung Pao chicken." Charissa nodded. She too pushed around the gaily colored goo. "I've never had anything so—"

"Sublime," Payton said. She caught herself and nodded to Charissa. "But this is, well—" Payton looked down at her plate. "This is—"

"Horrible," Garrett said. "I'm sorry, Charissa. I appreciate your effort and all, but I'm tired of beating around the bush. Three days of nothing to eat has made me more than a mite crotchety."

Jace rolled his eyes. "This can't be that bad." He sat down, ate one bite, gagged it down and then shoved his plate away.

"Look everyone, I know it's terrible," Charissa said, "but you guys don't know how to cook with Kraft's stuff either."

"And since we have Kraft on board, it seems logical to ask her to cook," Garrett said.

"That whore is chained to a bed—just where she belongs," Heller said.

"Kraft is a prisoner," Jace said. "And she stays right where she is."

"Indefinitely?" Bailey asked.

"That's up to me." Jace stood.

"Eventually we're gonna have to do something," Garrett said. "Rather, you have to do something, Jace. You gotta decide. Push comes to shove. You can't leave everybody hanging by a thread. It's cruel to leave Kraft twisting in the wind."

"Julie, not Kraft," Jace corrected. "You still have a notion she needs your protection?"

Garrett stood. "I saw the warrant, Jace. Clear as day her pretty face, but that was eight years ago. Kraft's not once given us a wrong turn. That lady could have killed us all from the moment we stepped into that derelict Basic. Whatever Julie was, Kraft became. Despite her past, or maybe because of it, Kraft wouldn't hurt a one of us."

"Unless we hurt her first," Bailey said.

Charissa and Payton nodded.

"Are you?" Bailey asked.

"What?" Jace asked, glaring down at his dinner.

"Going to hurt Kraft?"

"It's on a need-to-know basis." Jace picked up his fork and toyed with the glop on his plate.

"Let me guess, I don't need to know?" Bailey asked.

Jace refused to answer and kept his attention on his plate.

"Hate to say it, Jace, but I'm getting the feeling even you don't know what's really going on," Garrett said.

"I know enough."

"Maybe we should interrogate her," Heller said with obvious relish. "We could get all kinds of information with the right tools."

Jace looked at Heller for a long time then marched away. Heller tried to follow him. "You stay here."

Grumbling with disappointment, Heller threw himself back into his kitchen chair.

Chapter Twenty-four

As Jace approached her door, he could hear the chains rattling. He slapped the com and the door jerked open.

Kraft had slung the chain over her shoulder and was practicing some kind of martial art.

"Did you think I was trying to escape?" She wiped the sweat from her brow with the back of her hand.

He closed the door behind him.

The look on his face made the hairs on the back of her neck stand up and goose flesh break out over her body. In the whole of her life, she had never been so afraid. She could take him by physical force, but her honor and love held her back. Hurting Jace would be worse than hurting herself.

"We need to chat. Sit down."

She sat gingerly on the bare mattress.

Jace stood right in front of her, forcing her to crane her neck to look into his eyes.

"I don't even know where to start."

"I never lied—"

"We've had that conversation. Why did you join the IWOG?" He leaned over and practically screamed in her face. "You explain to me how someone like you could align herself with butchers."

When she flinched back, Jace grabbed her shirt collar.

"Tell me how you could condone killing innocent people."

"I didn't—"

His fists tightened. "You were an IWOG assassin!" He realized she made no effort to fight back and let go.

"I didn't know any better," she offered softly.

"You didn't know it was wrong to kill innocent people?"

"They recruited me when I was barely sixteen." She drew a deep breath. "All I'd ever known was life on IWOG planet Banna. To me, it was normal to live in a rigidly controlled society where everyone spent at least four years in the military." After a very long pause, she said, "I thought I was doing the right thing."

Jace snorted with derision. "You helped them bring fear and chaos."

"I know that now. I didn't know it then. Has no one ever tricked you? Taken advantage of your naiveté?"

"Besides you?"

She winced.

"Why? How? Tell me your life story, Julie, and don't lie to me or I swear, I'll kill you."

"I'll tell you. And you can kill me if you want, but when you do, I'd appreciate it if you called me Kraft."

Jace refused to look at her.

"I grew up on Banna. My parents were high-ranking officers, so it seemed natural that I would follow in their footsteps. I thought our way was the only way. And I trained so well. There wasn't anything I couldn't learn. Flying, computers, martial arts. In five years they crafted me into an incredible weapon. Contrary to your opinion, I never went after an OuterWorlder."

"Then who did you go after?" His face was drawn and haggard.

"My targets were high-ranking officers from the very organization that created me. I was a tool they used to keep their own people in line."

"Assassins go after OuterWorld targets."

"Some do. I didn't. There's a lot about the inner workings of the IWOG that even most IWOG officers don't know."

"Why would they kill their own people?"

"As Garrett would say, some of them just stressed their toe leather too much. They didn't follow the code. That's a very big no-no to the IWOG. The code is almost as sacred as the bottom line."

"They would tell you who to kill and you would just go do

it?" Jace asked.

Kraft nodded. "They'd brief me on the target and I'd shadow them until I found the perfect opportunity. My superiors liked that I could make it look like an accident or natural causes. I hate to say it, but I was very, very good at what I did."

"Why did you run?" Some of his fury had lessened but he still couldn't seem to look her in the face.

"Parkhill."

"Is that a person or a place?"

"A person. A retired officer. When they briefed me, they said that Parkhill had outlived his usefulness, that he practiced a way of life that ran counter to the ideology of the IWOG. They didn't give me specifics. I shadowed the man for three days. And what I saw...I couldn't kill him."

"Why?"

"Parkhill reminded me of my grandfather. He eschewed the Tasher and all forms of media, preferring instead to read banned books. But most of all, he cooked. My grandfather taught me how to cook. It was a dangerous game we played because my parents would have turned him in for teaching me."

"You mean he cooked with raw ingredients, not the IWOG packaged food."

Kraft nodded. "I was shadowed in Parkhill's kitchen, watching him. When he finished making dinner, he set two plates at the table and asked me to join him. I don't know how he knew I was there, but he didn't seem concerned. It's funny, in a way, but it's a lot harder to kill someone after you've supped with them."

She gave Jace a meaningful look. "Well, perhaps that only applies to cooks. Anyway, Parkhill was a wonderful cook. Far better than me or my grandfather. And while we ate he taught me his recipes and I taught him mine. When dinner was over, he wiped his hands, stood and said he was ready."

"For what?"

"For me to kill him." She paused, remembering exactly how small and harmless Parkhill had looked. "I couldn't do it. It would have been like killing my grandfather. Killing myself." She took a deep breath. "You see, I never got so close to a target before. I watched where they went and at what time. I didn't really think about who they were or why the IWOG wanted them dead. Believe me, Captain Lawless, with most of them it wouldn't have mattered. They were terrible people doing horrible things. But when I think back, I think in my zeal, my misguided youth, I may have killed men like Parkhill without even knowing it."

"What did you do?"

"Put Parkhill in my IWOG fighter ship and flew him to Kali. There I sold the ship and went to the Den of Ishtar and wagered up the script. I gave most of it to Parkhill so he could live a good life while in hiding. While I was in the Den of Ishtar, I heard of Fairing, that the man was always looking for a good cook." Kraft sighed. "You know the rest of the tale from there."

Jace sat down heavily on the bed. He rubbed a hand against his exhausted face. "What happened to Parkhill?"

"I don't know. When I gave him the money I told him to go into hiding. If the IWOG caught me, I didn't want them to be able to extract the information, so it was best I didn't know. Sometimes I think of him, hope he's still alive, but I honestly don't know."

"And your parents?"

"Again I don't know. I could find out, but honestly, I don't really care. I know that sounds horrible, but you have to understand how they are. They'd turn me in without a second thought."

"Your own parents?" His eyes went wide.

"They'd turn on me in a flash. Not for the money, but for the glory of doing the right thing. Turning in your own flesh and blood is considered one of the highest marks of honor to the IWOG. There's even a medal for it."

"So you went at life utterly alone."

"For the last eight years I've lived by my own code. I've tried so hard to atone for what I did. Because if you think you hate me for it, you ought to try it from my shoes. Repeatedly, I put myself in danger hoping to die. I hated myself that much. But death would have been easy, a blessing, so I just wouldn't die. It was more of a punishment to live. If there's anything I could do to make up for what the IWOG did to you, I swear, I'd do it."

"How could you make up for me losing everything?" Jace shook his head. "Everything I believed in. Everything I fought to protect they destroyed. They killed my wife, my kids. Every person I ever knew. And not even in war."

"Tyaa Plague."

They sat together in profound silence for a moment.

"I never even got sick. Out of all the surrounding farms, I was the only person left standing. For the life of me I don't know why I was spared. I would have rather died with them, because being the sole survivor damn near drove me mad. A month later the IWOG showed up in bio-suits and cleaned up. Know how I survived? Stowed away on one of their ships until I got to Byzantine. Worked as a mercenary for brutal thieves. Killed men I had nothing against. Stole what wasn't mine. I went from being an honorable man to man who would kill anyone who stood in his way. I named my ship *Mutiny* to remind me how I got her. I committed mutiny against my own honor. How could you make up for that?"

Kraft shook her head. "I can't. I simply can't change the past. If I could, I would. Yours and mine. If you think selling me will give you the life you want then—"

Jace shot to his feet and turned on her. "You're giving me permission? How dare you? You got a real knack for cutting deep wounds, packing them with salt and then splashing vinegar all over them! You're unbelievable."

"Impossible." Her throat constricted, making her voice almost harsh when she asked, "What are you going to do with me?"

"Why don't you tell me?"

She was stunned. What did she really want? Did she want her freedom or did she want to stay? Where her choice had seemed clear, now that she realized she loved him and admitted it...

"You think on it and let me know."

"Jace, wait."

He turned.

"Do you believe in me?"

He closed his eyes. The simple question seemed to cause him tremendous pain. He left without answering.

She buried her face into the mattress of her bed. She dug her fingernails into her thigh and gritted her teeth, but her tears came anyway. She couldn't stop them and wiped at them furiously, her chains clinking loudly in the stripped-bare room. The hate for herself that had filled her for so long grew again with a vengeance. She hated her past. Hated her weakness. Hated that Jace could see them both.

Her room was dark and she blinked, bleary with sleep, when the door came open. Jace stood, backlit, with something in his hand.

She didn't move. Maybe this was it, the end. Since she hadn't been able to decide, maybe he had decided for her. She took a deep breath, tossed up a cross between a prayer and a desperate plea to the Void, then waited.

Jace stepped forward and unfurled a blanket. He didn't say a word as he tucked the edges around her.

In the morning, Jace came into her room. "I'll make you a deal."

Kraft sat on her bed, wrapped up in the blanket. "This deal, it have something to do with your crew being hungry?"

Jace smiled, albeit reluctantly. It was the first time she'd seen him smile in days. It amazed her how much that simple act lifted her spirits.

"It does. If you agree to cook, I'll agree to stop calling you Julie."

He was utterly deadpan and Kraft laughed. "Well, that is quite a deal." She wanted to ask if he was going to kill her or sell her, but she didn't. One step at a time. "Do I actually get to eat what I cook?"

"Of course."

"Do I have to do it chained up?"

Jace frowned and toed the floor.

"It's okay, Captain Lawless. I understand. You have to protect your crew. I could swear up and down that I'd never hurt a one of you, but you'd be wise to make sure of it. If I were in your boots, I'd do exactly the same thing."

"No offense taken?"

"No."

Jace un-cuffed one of the cuffs from her wrist, un-looped it from the pipe, and placed it on his own wrist.

She giggled.

"What?"

"There's a song from Earth about a bicycle built for two.

This is kinda the same idea."

"Actually, it made me think of men who call their wives the old ball and chain."

"Lucky for you I'm only your prisoner."

Jace frowned. "If you'd rather not do this—"

She lifted her hands, palm open. "I didn't mean it like that. I'm so hungry you could strap Heller to my back and I'd still want to cook."

"Heller hates you so much he most like won't eat anything you've touched."

"Yes, he will." She smiled. "He may hate my guts, but he's never had a problem eating my cooking. As soon as I get in there and start up, everyone on this ship is going to come running to the galley. You and I both know it."

"Actually, they're already there. I called a meeting this morning and we kicked the idea around. Heller cast the only vote against you."

"Let me guess—Heller voted to toss me out the nearest airlock?"

Jace nodded.

"Would say I'm surprised, but it'd be a lie. He's got all kinds of justification for hating me now."

"Can you blame him? The IWOG killed his whole family, right before his eyes. He lived out of the garbage cans of Kali until I took him on when he was nineteen."

"Seems everyone on this ship has a good reason to hate the IWOG. I'm not surprised at them hating me. And I don't expect any favors. Just let me cook and what you finally do with me is still entirely up to you."

"Even if I choose to sell you?"

"Even if you do." Kraft shrugged. "If nothing else, I'd like to meet my maker with a full belly. It'd be cruel for a cook to go to the fiery pits of hell without a last meal."

The whole crew sat around the table with hungry and somewhat guilty eyes as Kraft worked silently in the kitchen. Jace watched everything she did, but Kraft didn't mind. If she were so inclined, it wouldn't be that hard to make something right under his nose that would make everyone sick. It wouldn't kill them, but they would wish it had. But she wouldn't. She could never deliberately ruin a meal.

"It's ready."

"We're going to run this a bit different. You're going to eat first," Jace said.

"Of course." Kraft served herself a plate and almost passed out when she took a bite. Real food after days of nothing almost brought tears to her eyes. When she looked up she almost laughed at the hopeful yet fearful looks.

She knew she'd probably regret it, but she couldn't help picking on them a bit. She clutched her throat with both her hands and uttered a strangled gasp.

Everyone shot to their feet with eyes that damn near swallowed their faces.

"I told you she'd poison it!" Heller yelled.

Kraft laughed. "I'm kidding!" She straightened up. "Sheesh, you guys, it was just a joke." She ate another bite. "It was a little too intense in here."

"That really didn't help the tension level," Jace said.

"Well, it's up to you if you want to eat what I made or not, but I'd appreciate you not looking at me as if I'm some freak in a side show while I eat."

"Hell," Garrett said, stepping forward and filling his plate. "I don't care if it does kill me, I'm not real keen on starving to death." He sat down and took a bite. His eyes rolled back in his head with ecstasy. "At least this will be a quick death, right?"

"No. Slow and painful," Kraft said. "Not only am I a sadist, but I'm a masochist too." She said it utterly deadpan and everyone stopped. Heller stood there about to scratch his head trying to figure out what she meant.

Kraft raised her hands. "Kidding. Did everyone's sense of humor starve to death already?" Everyone glared at her. "I'm sorry. No more jokes. It's fine, it won't kill you." She ate a few more bites. "Well, at least not right away."

"That's enough." Jace filled a plate and stood up in the kitchen and ate. "Go ahead and eat. I watched her and she didn't put anything deadly into it."

Everyone filled their plates and began eating. Even Heller.

"Besides, why would she kill herself?" Charissa asked.

"Good point," Bailey said.

"Right, why would I kill myself when I've got so much to live for?"

Everyone dropped their forks.

"One more word—"

"I know, I know, I'll have to go back to my room without dessert." She ate without further comment.

Everyone ate slowly but she noticed it was more from savoring the meal rather than fear of it. She waited patently until Jace finished. He took her right back to her room.

"You really didn't gain yourself any points with that little show," Jace said as he chained her back up.

"Probably not. But I thought it was funny. And at the moment that's really all that counts."

"You're not going to make this easy, are you?"

"No. If I made it easy, the Void would have done me in by now, don't you think? Besides, who wants to go out crying when they can go out laughing?"

"Captain, I need you on the bridge." Bailey piped his distress call over every com of the ship but Kraft's prison. He didn't like that she was being treated like a slave, but Jace wasn't making her do anything she didn't want to. Still, piping in music to her was one thing; piping in anything else would be nothing short of mutiny.

Jace sat just down the hall in the galley. He damn near broke his own neck rocketing from the little bench at the head of the kitchen table. He ran to the bridge and scanned the console.

Everything glowed ruby red.

"Report."

In a quavering voice Bailey said, "There is an IWOG attack ship twenty minutes aft. They've scanned us and know we're here."

"Have they hailed us?"

"No."

"If we run they'll wonder why."

"Yes."

"Does their path look to intersect ours?"

"No. From aft, they will pass us on our port side." Bailey

automatically pointed left.

"Stay on our original heading. If we don't bother them, they probably won't bother us." Jace took a deep breath and crossed his fingers.

"Sounds good to me." Garrett joined Jace and Bailey on the bridge. "Low profile is always best."

All three men looked at the glowing red console.

"We really ought to put a more soothing color on that thing for times of crisis." Garrett nodded to the red console. "I think a cheery lemon yellow—"

The com pan went from steady to flashing.

"They sent up a flare." Bailey's hand hovered over the com.

"Shit," Jace muttered. If he didn't open up his com it would look mighty suspicious.

Both Bailey and Garrett gulped. Jace did not swear. That he chose to do it now with a soft voice and a visible cringe shocked them both.

"Someone wants to say howdy." Garrett fought down his fear by cracking wise.

"I think they want to do a lot more than that." Jace nodded to Bailey. "Open the com."

"This is I.W.G. Majestic hailing Basic2X to our fore. Identify your ship by captain, class and commission."

Jace leaned over the console and touched the send button of the com. "This is Captain Jace Lawless of the modified Basic2X commissioned as *Mutiny*."

"Thank you, Captain Lawless."

A long pause spun out.

"They're looking it up," Garrett said.

"We're clean," Jace said.

"Not with that IWOG bitch aboard," Heller snarled, joining them on the bridge. "She makes all of us dirty."

Jace turned. "You didn't."

Heller flinched back. "Didn't what?"

Jace grabbed Heller by the collar of his shirt and almost shook him out of his boots as he pounded him against the wall. "Did you call those bastards down on us?"

Grasping instantly, Heller's eyes went wide. "No! No! I'd never call those shanks!"

Jace let him go. He turned back to the com and waited.

"They seem to be spending an awful lot of time looking at our dance card," Garrett said.

Jace had a sudden image of dancing in his sheets with Kraft.

Another light on the console went from steady to flashing.

"The IWOG ship has altered course. In twenty minutes they will intersect ours." Bailey looked to the console again. "Correction. Fifteen. They've also increased their speed."

"Why don't we just ask them what they want?" Heller asked.

"It doesn't matter," Garrett said. "Like a boy with his prom date, they'll say anything to get us to lay still for them."

"Crude but accurate," Jace said. "Bailey, squelch the com."

Bailey did. No response.

"They've increased their speed," Bailey said. "We've got ten minutes at best." Another light flashed. Bailey typed rapidly into the Tasher that Kraft had recently installed. "They have a warrant."

"For who?" Garrett asked even though everyone knew the answer.

Bailey gulped and turned to Jace. "Kraft."

"Who told them—"

"Trickster." Jace cut Heller off.

"That would explain why they didn't just blast us to smithereens. They want to make sure she's on board," Garrett said.

"What can we do?" Heller asked.

"Fight," Jace said. "We can't run, we can't hide, we've got no choice but to fight."

"An IWOG attack ship of that size has at least fifty fully trained and heavily armed fighters." Heller checked his body for weapons and found himself woefully lacking.

"I know. Garrett, Heller, load up. Strap everything we've got to yourselves and make a pile of everything else in the cargo bay."

Garrett and Heller left to follow his orders and Jace wondered if they would be the last he would ever issue.

"Cut the com, Bailey."

Bailey slapped it off. "I could try a hard burn."

"Would it buy us at least five minutes?"

"Yes."

"Do it. But save us enough to limp away if by some miracle we survive."

Chapter Twenty-five

A deep throbbing in the ship woke Kraft. Just by the sound and feel she knew *Mutiny* went for hard burn. Her heart kicked up into high gear and she leapt to her feet. Chained, she had at least the nasty weight of it for a weapon. And her tightly bound hair. She flicked her head twice, testing the limits, then tested the chain as a weapon.

Jace entered her room and tossed her boots and her belt of blades to the bed.

"We're being chased by an IWOG attack ship." He unlocked her cuffs.

She yanked on her boots and strapped on her gear. Her stomach rumbled loudly. Startled, they looked at one another. She looked to her belly then Jace. "I guess it's just thanking me for a great last meal."

Jace tossed her another gun. "If you're as good in a fight as you are in the kitchen, it won't be your last meal." He tossed her three clips.

"I take it you're not turning me in." Kraft checked the sight of the gun. Off by less than two degrees. She nodded as she holstered it on her back butt-cheek. She liked her blade to her left so she could draw it with her right hand as primary weapon, but the gun drew second. She could yank it off her fanny faster than most men could blink.

"Not after Trickster turned us all in."

"He what?"

"The details are sketchy, but most like that scrimshanker told them my name, my ship, that you were on board, and that we were responsible for the IWOG transport job."

"If we survive this, Captain Lawless, Trickster is going to have to pay. That fetch cuts in way too much on my dancing and the only way to stop him is to cut off his damn legs."

"On that, we agree. But we got bigger and better at our back door at the moment."

"How long do we have?"

"Not long at all."

She followed Jace from her room to the cargo deck. Garrett, Heller and Payton waited.

As soon as Kraft set foot in the room, Heller lifted the gun strapped to his chest. He flicked off the safety and pointed it right at her head.

"What's she doing here?" Heller snarled. It was the first time he'd seen her unchained in days.

She lifted her hands, palm open, to her shoulders.

Jace stepped directly in the line of fire.

Heller yanked his gun to the sky. "Shit howdy, Jace! Don't step in front of my gun like that!"

"Then stop pointing it at my crew." Jace's hands hovered over the pistols in his double holster.

Heller flipped the safety on and let his gun fall back to his chest. "She's part of the crew again?" Heller looked baffled then betrayed.

"Ten minutes, Captain Lawless." Bailey did his best to calmly report the moment of doom, but everyone heard naked fear in his voice. Bailey didn't have to say what all of them were thinking.

They were going to die.

No two ways about it.

Mutiny would vanish and none of them would be so much as the tiniest fleck of rain in the most vast desert of the Void.

The IWOG attack ship had fifty fighters. *Mutiny* had, as Garrett once said, one crazy lady, three fighters, one pilot and two docs. It was so hopeless Jace almost burst into hysterical laughter. Nothing had ever come easy. Anything that looked easy turned out to be anything but. This situation was so hopeless from the get-go he almost wanted to toss himself out an airlock. He couldn't run. He could fight but he'd never win.

They were going to die.

"Look, I don't want to step on your captain toes, but I know about that ship," Kraft said. "I know how they're going to attack. And even though they have three times the crew we do, we can win."

"They have ten times the crew we do," Garrett pointed out. "Stress that toe leather all you want, girl, but we're screwed."

"No, we're not." Kraft shook her head. "*Mutiny* is small, so we can't outrun them, but we can fight. Being small in a fight isn't always a bad thing."

"You couldn't fight off a Trifecta," Heller snarled.

"Because Randoms don't run the same plan every time they attack." Kraft flipped her hair over her shoulder. "The IWOG does."

"By the book," Jace said.

Kraft nodded. "The IWOG runs seek and destroy by the book. And I know the book. They need to confirm the kill. That's why they haven't just blown us apart. They need to board the ship which means they are going to take certain steps." Kraft looked to them all. "The IWOG is nothing if not consistent. They have their code of conduct. That's why they're gonna make this a lot easier than it should be."

"She's got a point, Captain," Garrett said. "If she knows them, what they'll do—"

"She's just laying a trap for us!" Heller was a twitch away from pulling his gun on Kraft and shooting her without further ado.

"Where my own neck is like to get yanked?" Kraft glared at Heller then looked at Jace. She dropped her hands to her hips. "I don't know about you, but I've got no strong desire to die today. If they board *Mutiny*, you know for a fact there won't be a one of us who'll live to tell about it."

"Maybe they're only here to arrest you," Heller said.

"That's about as likely as them being here to exchange recipes. They aren't here to arrest anyone. They're here to kill everyone." Kraft looked him full on. "Call me IWOG scum or not, Heller, they'll kill me too. I've been gone too long to be an effective weapon for them anymore. They aren't gonna waste their time brainwashing me when they got legions of folks who are more advanced than me."

"Captain? Five minutes." Bailey's voice crackled with tension.

Everyone revved up a notch.

"The wolves are baying at the door, Captain Lawless. You're gonna have to decide if you trust me or not. If it helps, I swear to you, I don't want to die today."

Jace looked at her for a long moment. Hatred for her past battled with a longing to trust her. In the end, his own desire to live won out. "Run it, Kraft."

Nodding, she pointed to the main hatch. "They're gonna latch to that airlock, so we narrow it down."

Under her direction, the crew pushed everything in the hold against the airlock.

"Don't block it all the way yet. Okay. Who are your two best sharp shooters?"

"Heller and Garrett," Jace said.

"Garrett, you stand up there on that catwalk. Find a rope so that if we need you, you can slide down. Heller, you do the same from that catwalk. Both of you pick them off as they come in. Take those flood lights and train them on the hatch. Jace, you and Payton are down here. If Garrett or Heller misses one of them, you pick them off from here."

"Where are you going to be?" Jace asked.

"I'm going to be in the airlock."

Everyone looked at her as if she was completely mad.

Kraft shook her head. "They won't see me. I'm a shadow, remember? I'll kill as many as I can as I shadow my way onto their ship. Once in their ship, I'm going to muck it up and lock it down then blow it up—take care of our mutual problem."

"I'm not even going to ask if you know how. I got a feeling you do."

"I told you once I don't care much for killing, but we've got no choice this time. We can't leave a single one of them alive. If we fail, even if we limp away, our lives are gonna get a hell of a lot more dangerous. So we have to kill them all. Since they're IWOG scum, I don't imagine this is much of a problem for anyone."

Nobody said anything.

"Glad we're all in agreement."

"How are you gonna get back onto *Mutiny*?" Jace asked.

A part of Kraft wanted to be nastier than hell at that moment. She wanted to turn to him and jeer, *Don't you want me to die with my IWOG brethren? Isn't that what you're all hoping for?* But she didn't. Because she really didn't want to die.

"If I make it back, I do. If I don't, as soon as the airlock closes, you run. And don't look back. You ever been to Corona?"

"No."

"Perfect. You go there, to Borealis. After this you won't ever be able to go anyplace where anybody knows you. You understand?"

"What are you going to do?"

"I'm going to blow that ship apart and you don't want to be anywhere near when I do."

"How do we know she ain't setting us up?" Heller asked.

"You don't," Kraft said. "I hate to say it, but you're gonna have to trust me."

"There's an idea. A very bad one!" Heller yelled.

"Do you not grasp this, Heller?" Kraft shook her head. "Everyone's butt is in a sling, including mine. We either stick together and fight, or we're all going down. I've never crossed you or a soul on this ship, and you know it. You've got about sixty seconds to decide if you want to die today or not."

Heller clambered up onto the catwalk. "I swear, if you're lying—"

"If I am, you have my permission to kill me. But let's survive this first."

Everyone got into place as Bailey allowed *Mutiny* be locked to the IWOG ship.

Before she slipped into the airlock, she looked at Jace. "Once it starts, you run your crew without a thought to me. When that lock closes, you go. Go to Corona. Take that money in my money belt, change your names and go legitimate. Okay?"

"I'm not ever going to see you again, am I."

Kraft laughed, then winked as she grinned. "The Void has a powerful hate for me, but it hasn't killed me yet. And I really don't feel like dying today."

Kraft slipped into the airlock and Jace crouched behind the mound of goods that cluttered the passageway to the airlock. He could hear the IWOG ship dock, just as Kraft said they would.

"Let her be right about everything else." Jace heard his

crew cock their guns in the darkness, waiting for the airlock to open. When it did, huge lights blared into the mouth and blinded the men who tried to breach it. They staggered forward, blinded by night vision goggles.

What men Garrett and Heller didn't pick off from above, Jace and Payton got from below. They didn't have a chance. It was like shooting fish in a barrel.

As his crew picked them off, they sent in more and more, eventually, by sheer luck, they hit one of the flood lights and Jace's crew lost a bit of advantage. But not for long. The opening was still too narrow and made the IWOG soldiers easy targets. All he could think of was Kraft.

Kraft shadowed her way through the IWOG attack ship. Blade hacking, she cut down IWOG soldiers. The hallway became slick with blood. Following their code to the letter, they didn't stop coming even though they could see something killed the men in front of them. Even the strangest phenomena couldn't break their code.

She locked down rooms and outright killed anyone who got in her way as she ran to the bridge. It didn't take more than twenty seconds to break the code and enter.

The IWOG officers turned to the open door. Careful of the computers, she shot them all and then locked the door behind her.

She shoved the dead body away from the main console, ignored the blood and flung herself into the chair. She let her fingers fly like a furious virtuoso on keyboards. If anyone were to look over her shoulder, the commands would be flying so fast they wouldn't understand a tenth of what she did. At her feet, the body leaked crimson from a perfect hole centered in his bald head.

Time pressed on her like the pull of thirty Gs and she worked as fast as she could. Entering the last of her commands, Kraft stood, looked around and said, "This is the last time I let you cut in on my dance."

She left the control room, fused the door closed and headed back to *Mutiny*. She killed more fighters on the way back. Her blade, her arm, all the way to her shoulder, became saturated with blood and gore, yet she refused to think of it. Her mind focused solely on completing her mission. She became a machine, mindless in pursuit of her goal.

"Get home. Get home."

When she got to the corridor formed by the airlocks, the sheer volume of IWOG soldiers had breached *Mutiny*. Jace, Payton, Heller and Garrett were all on the main floor.

An alarm went off and the yellow light above the airlock flashed. The huge doors started to close.

Kraft leapt into *Mutiny*'s airlock as the IWOG soldiers retreated. Jace took a shot right to his chest. He glanced down as if shocked. Staggering backwards, he slipped and fell onto his side.

"No!" She rushed forward, forgetting to shadow.

She took a blast squarely in her belly. Now she understood his stunned surprise. The impact was so painful she fell on her back. Using her elbows, she crawled backwards to the huge doors where Jace lay. She tried to drag him onto *Mutiny*, but she could barely drag herself.

The airlocks were going to separate at any moment. If they didn't get inside, they were going to be sucked out into the Void. Since she had to choose, Kraft gave up trying to drag them both and tried to shove Jace home.

Heller grabbed Jace by the arm and yanked him away from the closing doors.

Garrett struggled to drag Kraft in.

"Leave her!" Heller bellowed.

"No!"

If Garrett didn't hurry, she was going to be cut in two when the huge doors closed.

Payton rushed forward, grabbed Kraft's other arm and they barely managed to yank her onto *Mutiny* before the airlocks closed. She left a long streak of bloody gore.

"Go, Bailey!" Garrett screamed into the com.

Mutiny darted away. Heller dragged Jace into the infirmary as Garrett and Payton struggled to drag Kraft.

"You heavy, girl," Garrett said, grinning down at her.

"All bone and muscle, darling." Blood trickled out the corner of her mouth. It tickled and she wiped her face with her shoulder. "Do we all live to dance another day?"

Garrett and Heller lifted Jace up to an infirmary table. Payton and Charissa set to work on him.

"Help me get Kraft up," Garrett said.

"No." Heller leaned over Jace. "You should have just let that bitch die in the airlock."

"Dammit, Heller, she saved our lives!"

When Charissa and Payton came around the table to help, Heller pulled his gun and flicked off the safety. "You stay right where you're at and fix Jace."

Payton flinched. "How dare you?" She shook with rage.

"I ain't letting him die and neither are you. Get back to work."

Garrett came around and Heller swung the gun at him. Garrett lifted his hands. "This is mutiny, Heller. I'm second in command, not you."

"You think I give a rat's? I ain't letting Jace die, not to save that worthless IWOG bitch."

"We can save everyone if you'd just let me—"

"I ain't fooling here!" Heller swung the gun back to Payton. "You work on Jace and only Jace!"

"Then let me work on her," Charissa offered. Tears of anger and fear ran down her cheeks.

"She's IWOG scum."

"Kraft damn near died fighting to protect us," Garrett said. "And since Jace is down, I'm in command, not you. I'm giving you a direct order to stand down. Payton will work on Jace. Charissa and I will tend to Kraft. We can save them both."

"That bitch," Heller said, glaring down at Kraft, "covered her own ass and you know it. She's IWOG scum. The only reason we're all still alive is 'cause it suited her. I'll bet the only reason she did anything is she wants our ship."

"This isn't about you, Heller." Bailey pointed a gun at Heller's head.

Looking over his shoulder, Heller sneered. "You don't have the balls to shoot me, little boy."

"Do you really want to find out?"

From her position on the floor, Kraft could see the gun trembling in Bailey's hand.

"Get back on the bridge, Bailey," Heller snarled.

"I will just as soon as you drop that gun."

"I do believe he's serious," Garrett said. "Drop your gun, Heller."

Heller did. He turned and faced Bailey with his hands up. "You're making a big mistake, little boy."

"I don't think so." Bailey tossed a pair of handcuffs to Garrett, who clicked them down hard on Heller's wrists.

"She's IWOG—"

"I heard you the first time!" Bailey yelled. "And the second, and the third, and I heard Captain Lawless say it too. And everyone else. That may be so, I don't know because I wasn't in the need-to-know loop. But I do know whatever Kraft was before, she certainly isn't that now. I like her. She's a hell of a fighter and one hell of a cook."

Heller glared. "You just got itchy pants for her, boy."

"So? Gives me all the more reason to want to save her life, doesn't it?" Bailey cocked the gun and Heller flinched. "I owe you two for flinching."

"I'll take that." Garrett took the gun from Bailey. "You best get back to the bridge."

"Let me help you get her on a table first."

It took Garrett, Bailey, Payton and Charissa to lift her up to the table.

"Damn, she's one heavy lady." Garrett pulled the shredded fabric of her shirt and pants aside then examined her injury. "Oh, mother of mercy. I've never seen a wound this bad."

Bailey took one look at the bloody mess, fought back rising gorge, then fled back to the bridge.

Charissa leaned over and winced. "Mom? This is really bad."

Payton examined Kraft carefully. She shook her head and looked again. "I don't believe it."

"What?" Bailey asked over the com.

"It's not bleeding. It's like it's been cauterized. Most of this blood isn't hers."

Payton checked her heartbeat. "Slow, steady, but only about ten beats a minute." She shook her head. "Pack the wound, set up an IV." Payton turned back to Jace.

"How's his?" Garrett asked, nodding to Jace as he packed Kraft's wound.

"Clean through and through."

"He better live, Payton or I'll—"

"You threaten me one more time, Heller, and I will march over there and sedate you." She set up an IV on Jace. "My operating room is tense enough at the moment, thank you very much, and I won't stand here and let you exacerbate matters because your ridiculous ego feels slighted by Kraft yet again." Payton sighed hard. "You either control your testosterone or I will."

"Chemically or surgically?" Garrett asked, as he ran an IV to Kraft while Charissa packed her wound.

"Clip him or slip him," Payton said.

"What?" Heller snarled.

"I could castrate you or inject you with estrogen." Payton looked up at Heller. "It's how the IWOG handles violent male prisoners. If you promise to sit quietly, I'll do neither."

Heller leaned back against the wall with a face so suffused with fury it turned crimson.

"Jace will recover, Heller." Payton kept her voice calm and soothing. "Relax. In two days he'll be on his feet."

"And most like punching you in the face for what you did today," Garrett added.

"What about Kraft?" Bailey asked over the com.

Finished stabilizing Jace, Payton moved to Kraft's table. She peeled back the bandage and sighed. "She needs hours of surgery, Bailey. And even then..." Bailey couldn't hear Payton shake her head but her trailing voice made the outcome clear enough.

Voices swirled around Kraft's ears and she felt weightless as she listened. Her hands gripped the cool metal of a table. She'd been on this table before. She'd been in far less dire straits then as compared to now.

The scatter blast to her belly caused devastating damage. Automatically, her body shut down, conserving blood, energy, resources, but Kraft knew it was the worst wound she'd ever had. There wasn't a knowing in her body that it could recover, and it frightened her.

As the voices rose and fell like crashing waves, she took stock of her body. Too much damage. Way too much. Kraft shut everything down. As the voices became a rising drone, she forced her body lower, even though she knew without surgery she would die. She'd led a good dance through the Void and realized she'd have to take her last dance with fate.

Chapter Twenty-six

After dumping Heller in Kraft's bedroom-turned-prison-cell, Garrett returned to help Charissa assist Payton.

"You sure she's not dead? She's hardly breathing."

"Kraft is in a self-induced state of suspended animation," Payton said, using delicate stitches in the open wound. "Don't ask me how, but she is. Right now, it's the only thing keeping her alive."

Hours later, Payton stood away from Kraft and stretched. "Dressing, please, Charissa."

"Will she live?" Garrett asked.

"I've done everything I can. All we can do now is wait." She snapped off her latex gloves and threw them away. "Charissa? Will you take the first watch, please?"

Charissa collapsed gratefully into a chair as her mother and Garrett left. She watched Jace's chest rise and fall.

When she had first come to *Mutiny*, she developed a terrible crush on Captain Jace. Awkward and painfully shy, she mistook his kindness for interest. Her grand seduction scheme had been a crushingly painful defeat when Jace gently but firmly explained she was far too young for him. He called her a daughter and it had been months before she'd been able to look him in the face again.

But now, years later, she did see him as a father. Her young heart had fallen instead on Bailey. When he'd come aboard a year ago, it was as if Jace had never taken place in her heart at all. But Bailey was just as shy as she. And as soon as his eye had started to fall her way, Kraft had shown up.

All tall and dark and scary and sexy—Kraft made Charissa feel more boring than oatmeal. But Kraft treated Bailey the same way Jace had treated her. She'd watched, jealous at first, as Bailey followed Kraft around like a puppy. To her horror, she realized she once followed Jace around the exact same way. Her jealousy gave way to empathy. Eventually, Bailey would realize the futility of chasing after Kraft.

Even though he'd stood up to Heller in Kraft's defense, Charissa sensed it was more from caring than infatuation. It seemed Bailey had already made peace with it. For surely he knew like everyone else that Jace and Kraft had been sleeping together. The two had been almost inseparable the three days before the dung hit the duster in Kali.

Jace moaned and Charissa leaned over him.

"Don't worry, Captain Jace, everyone is fine."

Jace blinked, nodded and fell asleep.

With a sudden inspiration, Charissa pushed the two tables close together and put Kraft's hand into Jace's. They both gave a curious little squeeze then held on to each other. Charissa burst into tears.

When Payton came back two hours later, Charissa flung herself into her mother's arms. "Oh, Mom, I don't want them to die!"

Payton wrapped her in a fierce hug. "Honey, we've done everything we can." She pulled back and looked into Charissa's face. "Remember, we're doctors, not magicians. We can only do so much."

"But they have to live because they love each other so much."

"Sweetheart, we're just going to have to wait and see." She noticed Charissa had linked their hands. Her eyes watered at the picture Jace and Kraft made, bloodied and bandaged, tubes and wires dangling from their damaged bodies as they held hands, like lovers ready for an evening stroll.

Payton knew Jace would be able to get up and stroll away. Kraft might never even wake up again. If she managed that, she might not be able to walk again. Some of the blaster shot could have nicked her spinal cord. Payton didn't have the equipment to find out. Only time would tell.

"Nice to see you back on your feet, Captain," Garrett said, two days later.

"I won't be entering any dance contests anytime soon," Jace returned, sitting down with an old man's grace at the kitchen table.

"Least you still can dance, albeit slowly," Garrett tossed the comment off, then thought about it, thought about Kraft still laying motionless in the infirmary. "Aw, hell! I didn't—I hope—I'm going to shut up while I only have one boot in my big, fat mouth."

"Don't worry about it, Garrett. I know what you meant, and we're all worried about Kraft."

"Except for Heller."

"I still can't believe he tried to take over the ship." Jace scratched at his bandage.

"If Bailey hadn't stopped him, Kraft would have died on the floor. But, to be fair, he wasn't out to kill her so much as he was out to save your hide."

"I've taken that into consideration."

"You gonna leave him locked up?" Garrett asked.

"For now. Kraft is utterly helpless and I can't risk him going in there and—" Jace shook his head. "He's safe where he is and so is Kraft. It's the best I can do at the moment."

"Hey, I'm not faulting you. I'm the one who threw him in there in the first place."

"You did the right thing. So did Bailey."

"Not to mention Charissa and Payton."

"I was getting to that." Jace touched his bandaged chest. "Cut me some slack for being a bit slow on the draw for a while. I know everyone tried to do the right thing."

"Funny kind of irony about it, though, Heller locked into the prison he took such delight in keeping Kraft in."

"Poetic justice." Bailey entered the kitchen and plunked down at the table.

"Don't you go and get a big head about it, Bailey," Jace said. "You did right to protect a member of the crew without bloodshed but don't you be lording it over Heller."

Bailey flushed. "I won't. But he needs to stop picking on me. I'm tired of his, 'I owe you two for flinching'. If he smacks a noogie onto my arm again—"

"Down, boy!" Garrett slapped his back. "One taste of power and the boy's like to run mad with it."

"And that's another thing!" Bailey yelled, standing up. "Stop calling me a boy and stop hitting me!" Bailey shook with indignation. "I'm fed up with being treated like the ship's stupid but lovable mascot. You all make jokes about me right to my face, slap me, punch me, ruffle my hair whenever the whim strikes like I'm your little brother! Well, I'm not! I'm a damn good pilot who deserves your respect. If you can't give me that then you best leave me at the next port!"

Bailey's outburst rendered Garrett speechless.

"Bailey?" Jace asked quietly. "Have I ever done any of those things to you?"

"No, Captain, not you, but they—"

"Are going to stop. Right here and right now. They are going to treat you the way I do. Is that agreeable to you?"

"Yes, Captain." Bailey turned to go.

"Bailey?"

He turned back.

"You were right to stand up for yourself. I'm proud of you."

"Thank you, Captain."

"You were right to stand up for Garrett."

Confusion washed down Bailey's face.

"Heller disobeyed his direct order and you were right to treat it as a mutiny."

Bailey nodded. "Thank you, Captain."

"You can call me Jace."

"Really?" Bailey's voice broke with excitement. He swallowed hard and strove for a casual face.

"Really. You've earned it."

Bailey stood a bit straighter. "Thank you, Jace."

"One more thing before you go." Jace looked at him long and hard. "We're all worried about her."

Bailey nodded and went back to the bridge.

"Will wonders never cease." Garrett shook his head. "I didn't think he had it in him."

"He's right, you know." Jace was exhausted after the brief exchange. His energy level was low to start with and even minor movement drained away what little he had.

"Hell, I know it. I just didn't think he did."

"First time a boy knows he's a man is when he starts looking at women." Jace toyed with his cup of water, wishing it was swassing.

"That's a fact," Garrett said. "Kraft's one hell of a woman to set his cap for, though. He ought to do himself a favor and aim elsewhere."

"If I told you that about Payton would you?" Jace asked.

"Hell, no!" Garrett slapped the table. "Even if you were chasing after her, it wouldn't change my mind."

"Payton is a wonderful woman."

"So's Kraft."

Jace nodded.

"You think Bailey grasps your cap is set for her too?"

Jace laughed, but winced when it rattled his chest. "You think it matters much? Every man in the Void could flash an eye her way, but she's the one who decides. What makes you think she'll want anything to do with any of us when she wakes up?"

"If she wakes up." Garrett groaned and covered his face. "Aw, just shoot me now, I did it again!" Realizing Jace had been shot he slapped his own face. "I just did it again! Stuff your boots in my mouth before I do it again, Jace!"

"Captain?" Payton called over the kitchen com.

"Yes?"

"Kraft is waking up."

Kraft blinked. The first thing she saw was the grey ceiling of exposed pipes and stabilizer struts.

"Don't try to move," Payton said. "Just relax."

"Wasn't gonna go for a jog." Kraft wondered what that burbling was, then realized it was her voice. What she tried to say came out as a bunch of gurgling whistles.

Payton helped her sit up. "Try to clear your throat."

Kraft did. It hurt. Payton lowered her back to the table.

"Can you understand me now?"

"Yes, I can." Payton smiled.

Jace leaned into her field of vision. "As impossible as you are, you're apparently impossible to kill too."

Kraft smiled. "I told you, I just refuse to die."

"Makes you special."

"Or crazy." She winked very slowly, almost a blink. "Are you okay?"

"I'm fine." If that didn't beat all. Her first concern wasn't for herself, but him. If he didn't grasp it before, he certainly did now. He loved her. "Everybody, including you, lives to fight another day."

Kraft blinked slowly. "That's good. Told you I didn't want to die. But, Captain, and I'm only saying this as your cook, but if we could lay off fighting for a while, I'd really appreciate it." She touched her bandaged belly. "I wouldn't want to pull out all the fancy stitching."

"Your wound was so bad it was more like knitting," Payton said, leaning over and cupping Kraft's face as she shined a light into her eyes.

Kraft laughed and winced. "It hurts when I laugh. I hope that's not a permanent condition, because I do so love to laugh." She looked up into Jace's eyes. "I do so love to dance. Dancing with you was such fun I didn't want anyone to cut in." Kraft touched Jace's face. "Because you are so very pretty and I do so love...you." She fell asleep.

Jace looked down at her for a long moment. He turned to Payton. "How much of that was the drugs you got pumped into her?"

"Don't try to foist that off on me." Payton fiddled with the tubes and wires hooked up to Kraft. "I haven't given her anything but antibiotics."

"Come on, she's barely lucid. You must have given her something for the pain."

"She's not in pain. I don't know how or why, but her brain is doctoring her better than I ever could. I'm just a cheerleader on the side, lending support."

"I don't understand."

"I didn't save her, Jace, not really. Her body is healing so fast I feel like I'm watching a time-lapse."

"What are you saying, Payton? She's human, right?"

"She's human, but she's not like any human I've ever operated on. Kraft hardly lost any blood."

"But she was covered in it!"

"That's not hers." Payton looked to Kraft's cut-off clothing, so saturated with blood it buckled stiff in the corner. "Judging by how she looks like she swam in it, she must have killed at least twenty men."

"There's a hole in her belly big enough to stand in."

"I know." Payton shook her head. "By all I know as a doctor, Kraft should have died shortly after getting shot. However, she managed to crawl to you and tried to drag you onto *Mutiny*."

"With that wound?"

Payton nodded. "Even though she was dying, she seemed bound and determined to save you." Payton looked at Jace. "I find Kraft vulgar at times, and I don't understand half of what shapes her, but she's—" Payton searched for the word "—honest." Payton shrugged. "Her behavior has not been marked by subterfuge. She is not what you thought, but she has not violated the code that made her show mercy to us. Everyone on this ship knows that in the derelict Basic Kraft could have easily killed us all, taken the goods and our ship. But she didn't."

"No, she didn't."

"Have you ever asked yourself why?"

"Because she is an honorable thief." Jace looked down at Kraft's face. Blood and sweat still smudged her cheeks even after Payton and Charissa's efforts to clean her up. Her hair, twined with black linen, lay in a lifeless clump under her neck. Like her clothes, it was thick and stiff with blood. Saturated by those she had killed to protect those she loved.

"Drugged or not, Kraft is nothing if not honest. If you had asked her directly to tell you the whole of her past, she would have done so without hesitation. Kraft would never have volunteered the information, because she wanted to be judged on her actions, not her past, on who she is, not who she was. But she would have told anyone of us had we asked."

"We just didn't ask the right questions."

"There is that, but more so, she gave us no reason to doubt her. She's never acted IWOG. Her code is her own, and more and more, I find her code is like mine. She said something to Charissa, shortly after she came aboard that has stuck with me."

"What?"

"I give as good as I get."

"You think it means what?"

"Treat her with honor and respect, she'll do likewise."

"Will she walk again?"

"I don't know." Payton shook her head. "Her regaining consciousness at all is nothing short of a miracle." Payton checked Kraft's heartbeat and noted it on her chart. "She wants to live, Jace. Kraft has a will to live like nothing I've ever witnessed. Don't chain her up if she succeeds."

Jace sat quietly at Kraft's side, held her hand and waited. When his eyelids drooped, Payton let him sleep on one of the tables, drawn up to Kraft's. He fell asleep holding her hand.

Jace awoke to find Kraft standing over him. "Am I dreaming?"

"If I look worse than I feel, you probably are." Kraft leaned close with a grin.

Jace sat up. She looked like she'd been dipped in maroon mud. "You look wonderful."

She shook her head. "Guess you're awake and I'm alive, then."

"You're standing."

"Yeah." Kraft gave him a curious tilt of her head. "You want me to lie back down?" She shot him a lopsided grin. "I'm all for a friendly tumble with you, Captain Lawless, but I think we should wait until I get all these tubes and wires off me." Kraft wavered ever so slightly and gripped the edge of the table. "On second thought, horizontal is seeming a lot easier to maintain then vertical."

Jace rocketed to his feet. With a cup of his hands here and there, he helped her back to the table.

"What are you doing up?"

"I was going to go make dinner or lunch or whatever meal it is." Kraft laughed. "To tell you the truth, I don't even know what day it is. All I know is I'm glad to be alive and I'm so hungry I'm almost sick with it."

"You're in no condition to cook." Jace glared at her. "Kraft, you are in no condition to even stand."

"Yeah, I'm starting to get that." She sighed. "But if I don't eat something I'm not going to get better. My engine won't run without fuel."

After checking with Payton that it was okay for her to eat, Jace opened the com to the bridge. "Bailey?"

"Garrett here, Captain."

"Where's Bailey and Charissa?"

"Asleep."

"Wake them up and tell them to report to the galley."

"Yes sir."

"What are you doing?" Kraft asked.

"You are about to have your first cooking show."

Kraft pondered it. "Oh, good idea."

"I'm not just another pretty face." He winked.

"No, you are so much more than pretty."

He felt her smile all the way down to his toes.

"Captain?" Charissa asked over the com. "I'm in the kitchen with Bailey. What do you want us to do?"

"Kraft is going to walk you through a meal. Okay?"

"Okay," Charissa said slowly. She obviously thought this was some kind of cruel joke.

"Don't worry, you'll do fine," Kraft said. "You're going to make the easiest dish in the world. Spaghetti."

"What do we do first?"

Jace could just imagine Bailey and Charissa contemplating the vast array of pots and pans.

"Take a deep breath," Kraft said.

"Okay. Now what?"

"Bailey, in that big pull-down bin in the pantry you'll find a bunch of onions. Grab three of the yellow ones."

Patiently, Kraft walked them through preparing the meal. No question was too silly or strange, she answered them all with a clear and soft voice. She gave them lots of encouragement.

"Well, it's ready," Bailey said.

"It smells good too," Garrett said.

"Wonderful. Garrett? Please fix two plates and bring them down to the infirmary."

"On my way."

Meanwhile, Jace stacked pillows and blankets behind Kraft's back so she could sit up.

"You are not feeding me when he gets down here, so don't even think about it." Kraft settled back.

"You're injured, not incompetent. Trust me enough to tell the difference."

"Just so we're clear."

"You really are a control freak, aren't you?" Jace rolled his eyes. "Even with two broken arms you'd want to feed yourself."

"As you can see," Kraft said, flexing her arms, "my arms are in perfect working order." She considered. "However, if they weren't, you're probably right."

Jace leaned over, very close, and breathed in her ear, "I know it's like to be impossible for you, Kraft, but try real hard to let us help you."

"I'll try," Kraft whispered. "Just don't smother me with it."

Jace pulled back. "At this moment I'm apt to smother you with a pillow."

"Yeah? Get in line," Kraft said with a grin.

"Twa plates of especial spaghetti," Garrett said with a terrible French accent as he entered the infirmary. "Vith a side of garlic toast." He set the plates down and bowed. "Vill madam and mauser be requiring candle light zis evening?" His horribly mangled accent made him spit all over the place.

"Say it, don't spray it." Kraft jokingly wiped her face off.

"Pardon my French," Garrett said. He snorted at his own joke. "Should I open zee vine or—"

"If you find an actual accent, hop on! You're vacillating between French and German, but I must say, dinner with a show is a rare treat."

"You're welcome, little lady," Garrett said, with his normal voice and a slightly more forced western twang. "We aim to please at the Mutiny Saloon."

"Surreal Saloon is what I'd dub it. Tell you what, I'm starting to wonder if I'm really awake." She took a bite of the spaghetti. "Oh, now I know I'm awake. Bailey? Charissa? This is wonderful!"

Jace nodded to Garrett. "Before you fill your belly, take a plate to Heller."

"Will do."

Garrett left and Jace sat down to eat. Kraft wasn't being kind; the meal was incredible. After the gaily colored glop Charissa had made, Jace doubted her ability to boil water so this was doubly amazing.

"I tell you what, I'm not ever standing over that stove again. I'm just going to lie back and tell them what to do."

"You planning on sticking around for a while, then?"

"Unless you've got some sudden urge to toss me out an airlock."

"Not at the moment." Jace shrugged. "Long as you stay in bed and mind your manners."

"Where's Heller?"

"He's not going to bother you."

"Nice dodge. Where is he?" Kraft dropped her fork. "He made it, didn't he?"

"Relax, he's alive and kicking. Right now he's probably sucking down about four plates of this, so if you want your fair share you best eat."

Chapter Twenty-seven

Heller was indeed alive and kicking. He was kicking the door of his prison cell with all his might. "Let me out!"

"Back off, Heller, I'm trying to open the door," Garrett said over the com.

Heller backed off and Garrett entered with a plate of food. Heller took a deep sniff. "The bitch lives."

"If you mean Kraft, yes, she does, but she didn't make this. Bailey and Charissa did."

"In a pig's eye!" Heller grunted. "You working with her to get rid of me?"

"Yes, Heller, we're all out to get you." Garrett set the plate on the table.

"I knew you had itchy pants for her—how many times did she spread for you?"

Garrett felt an overwhelming urge to punch Heller in the face as hard as he could. By years of exercising an iron will, Garrett only glared. "Kraft nailed you dead-on, Heller—ugly fits you like a tailored suit." Garrett strode from the room and closed the door. Heller threw himself against it.

"How the hell am I supposed to eat with my hands bound behind my back?!"

"Use your snout, you pig." Garrett shook his head and returned to the infirmary.

Kraft and Jace were just finishing up.

"Captain? A word?"

Jace followed Garrett into the hall.

"Heller hasn't calmed down. If anything, the burr up his butt has only grown in a right fertile ground."

"He's itching for a fight."

"Something fierce. I didn't dare uncuff him to eat. But I'm not sure if I was honestly protecting his hide or mine. He said something damn foul to me."

Jace sighed. "Will you stay here while I go and see if I can talk him down a notch?"

Garrett looked at Kraft, who sat silently watching them from her bed. Kraft resembled a horror-show extra. Fore to aft, port to starboard, her body looked dipped in gore despite all efforts to gently clean her. Her shirt hung in stiff, blood-thick tatters against a blanket that covered most of the spotless bandage on her belly. He'd helped Payton cut away the worst of it, but they were reluctant to lift her to remove her shirt entirely. "I think I can keep her in check, Captain, whilst you tend to our resident mad man."

Jace grinned as he looked over his shoulder at her. "Don't ever mistake her easy. She's feisty as a live wire but she's rational." Jace touched Garrett's shoulder. "Oh, and good news? She can walk."

Garrett brightened, pleased the question of a spinal injury was now moot.

"Counterpoint? Don't let her."

"Easier said than done," Garrett said. "But I'm delighted at the challenge all the same."

Jace made the short trip down the hall to where Heller was being kept. He opened the com.

"Heller? I want to talk to you."

"Captain?"

"I'm coming in, Heller." Before he slapped the button to open the door, he withdrew his pistol, flicked off the safety, but kept it pointed to the floor.

Heller backed off when he saw it.

"At the moment, I've got no call to use this and I hope to God you don't give me one."

"I won't, Jace."

"Fine. Sit down at the table."

Heller did. Jace closed the door, holstered his gun and unlocked the cuffs. "Go ahead and eat."

"Kraft made it."

"No she didn't. Bailey and Charissa did."

"Not much dif, they want me dead too."

"No they don't. You're letting paranoia run you, Heller, and I can't say I blame you, being held here for three days."

"Because of her."

"Because of you."

"Jace—"

"We are cutting to the bone right now, Heller." Jace laid his palms flat to the table. "You are in here because you tried to wrest control of *Mutiny* from Garrett when I was down. Garrett is second in command and you know that. *Mutiny* may be her name, but it's not an invitation."

"He wanted to save Kraft and not you."

"Garrett wanted to save everyone."

"Her first." Heller crossed his arms.

"You might have seen it that way," Jace allowed. "But that's not the way it really was. Honestly, Heller," Jace sighed and said, "I'm not sure if loyalty to me drove you or your absolute and unending hate for Kraft did."

"I got all kinds of reasons for hating her and—"

"I know it, Heller. Stop preaching to the choir. She's ex-IWOG. I know. But even before that you did nothing short of despise her."

"I knew she had a secret—"

"You and I both know why you hate her, because you and I both tussled with it." Jace looked right into Heller's eyes. "Kraft bested us."

"No she didn't!"

"Yes she did. More than once. And it chafes our pride. Because we're men. By nature we expect to be better than women. When we're not, it's difficult to accept."

A touched confused, Heller nodded.

"But it's not impossible to accept. Because if you really think about it, Heller, everybody has their bests and worsts. Even you and me."

"But she's good at things she shouldn't be," Heller said.

"Like what?"

"Fighting."

"You're good at that too," Jace said.

"Not as good as she is."

"So?"

"So? That ain't normal, Jace!"

"Is it normal that she knows how to cook?"

"Well, yeah."

"Is it normal for her to know the real thing rather than that IWOG gunk?"

"No, but that's still okay. It's a girl thing to cook."

"And a boy thing to fight."

"Right."

"Wrong."

"That's the way it should be!" Heller bellowed.

"In your mind, yes, but that isn't the way it is in real life, Heller. I'm trying to get you to see the difference."

"So now I'm supposed to be her best bud?"

"No. But you leave her alone. Everyone else too. Including Bailey. Stop baiting everyone."

"I don't—"

"Yes you do. You spout vulgarity like a geyser and then glare at everybody you soak."

"Garrett asked for that."

"I don't know what you said to him, but you're damn lucky he didn't bust your lights out." Jace shook his head. "You know better than to mess with Garrett. I figured one time of him busting your chops would be enough."

"Well, Bailey had no right to—"

"You refused to follow Garrett's direct order. In the chain of command, Bailey came next."

"No, I did—"

"Until you went against Garrett."

"So where does Kraft stand?"

"Did she issue an order after I went down?"

"No."

"Then the question is moot."

"But I was the only one trying to protect you—"

"Enough." Jace stood. "I'm going to say this once, Heller, so listen up. From this day forward, if I'm out of commission, Garrett is in charge. If he goes down, Kraft is. If she goes down, you are. If you're smart you'll get down on your knees and pray you never get the chance to find yourself captain of *Mutiny*."

"So now that IWOG bitch is above me?"

Jace slapped the table hard. The plate of spaghetti jumped and Heller flinched. "Do not call her anything but Kraft."

"I've been here longer than that—I've been here a lot longer than her and I don't think it's fair—"

"You don't? You don't think it's fair the way I want to run my ship? You think time in gives you some right to dictate how things are going to run around here?"

"No, but—"

"Grasp hard and fast, Heller. I'm in charge of *Mutiny*. What I say goes. If you don't like it, I'll gladly show you the door."

"Kraft ain't normal."

"Only to your mind, Heller." Jace sighed. "She's a hell of a fighter, isn't she?"

Heller glared, considered, in the end he nodded reluctantly.

"Rather than hate her for it, why don't you just accept it."

"'Cause it ain't right."

"Has it ever crossed your mind that you could learn something from her? That if you just asked she would teach you some of her tricks?"

"That freak-show—"

Jace smacked his hand to the table and Heller flinched.

"She ain't gonna share her tricks with me."

"You ever ask her to?"

"No."

"Before you condemn her, you best try to get along. Because I got news for you, Heller. I'm going to do everything in my power to keep her on my ship."

"Don't tell me you actually love that—her."

"What if I do, Heller? Is that my business or yours?"

Jace touched the com and opened the door. He closed it and locked it down from the outside. "Bailey?"

"Yes?"

"Keep the door to Heller's room locked. Keep the com channel open as send only. If he gets an urge to chat, let me know. I'll be in the infirmary."

Jace could hear Kraft's laughter long before he entered the infirmary.

"You have to stop telling me limericks or I'll bust my seams." Kraft was flat on her back with her eyes closed.

"These are the mild ones, darling," Garrett winked at

Payton as she filled a basin. He was sitting on the counter next to the sink, one knee drawn casually up to his chest by his linked arms.

"Tell her something that won't make her laugh so much," Payton begged as her giggle sloshed water down the sink.

"There's a saying from Earth about laughter being the best medicine," Kraft said. "But I think I've had enough." She crossed her hands over her chest.

Payton dropped a sponge into the basin and Jace grasped she was about to give Kraft another clean up. He stepped forward, lifted his finger to his lips, shook his head, and took the basin over to Kraft. He waved bye-bye to Payton and Garrett. They left with grins that almost swallowed their faces.

Jace wrung the sponge out and dabbed it to Kraft's face.

"You two get bored playing slap and tickle over there? Or do I look so bad you're trying to clean me up before Captain Lawless gets back?" Kraft opened her eyes and looked right into his. She didn't miss a beat. "Well hello, sailor." She smiled slow and lazy and sexy. "Come here often?"

"Only when there's a crazy lady in need."

"Crazy? I thought I was impossible."

"Both?" he asked.

"Crazy impossible?"

"Impossibly crazy."

"Either way it doesn't sound good." Kraft flinched. "What are you doing to my face?"

"Hold still, I'm trying to clean it."

"By kissing it with a sponge?" Kraft sat up, grabbed the sponge, and swabbed her face quickly. "Is that better?"

"I aimed for gentle, not quick."

Kraft wrung the sponge out and gasped when the water turned a dull, muddy maroon. "I thought I got hit in the belly."

"You did, but the blood spattered up."

"That's not just my blood, that's—" Kraft closed her eyes and carefully inspected herself. Her fingertips touched lightly but she flinched each time she made contact. "I'm soaked in—"

Jace grabbed her face, pulled it close. "Listen to me."

"No, no." Kraft clenched her eyes shut, shook her head then started ripping off the remains of her blood-drenched shirt.

"Listen to me," Jace demanded.

Kraft's eyes went wide with horror. Then narrowed with anger.

"You did what you had to do to protect the crew."

"I killed clueless—"

"You killed those who would have thoughtlessly killed you and yours. You did what you had to do, Kraft. You did exactly what you had to do in order to dance another day. There's no shame in that."

"You—dare—hold me accountable for atrocities then forgive me for them when it benefits you?"

"That's not what this is about."

"I killed fifty people so seven could live." Kraft winced. "Who am I kidding? I would have killed them all just so *I* could live."

"Would you have killed me to live?"

"That's not the point."

"No? Would you?"

"Have killed you?" Her eyes were wild, confused.

"They were gunning for you, gunning for me and everyone on this ship. They would have killed us all without a pause, and you know it."

"So that justifies—"

"You give as good as you get, don't you?"

Her jaw dropped. "Forgive me, Captain Lawless, but I need a reality check because for the life of me I don't know why you're standing here defending me to my own face."

"Because you're too quick to condemn yourself behind your own back."

She sighed. "I can't grasp this right now." She moved to stand.

Jace held her back. "Where do you think you're going?"

"I have to wash this off."

"I don't think Payton would appreciate water in the stitches."

"Then help me cover it with plastic because I'm going to take a shower. You don't know what it's like to feel this now, suddenly, this blood on me. It's, it's—"

"Horrific." Jace nodded. "I have an idea."

"What?"

"How opposed are you to me seeing you stark again?"

"You want to shower with me?" Her eyebrows drew high.

"Now really isn't the best time for a round of slap and tickle!"

"If you lie on your back, in the tub, holding a plastic sheet over your wound, I can wash you."

"Like a piece of dirty meat?"

He recoiled. "That is the most horrible analogy I've ever heard."

"Mighty apt, don't you think?"

"Take it or leave it, Kraft. If I don't do it then you pick someone else to."

"Me. Alone. I can wash myself off just fine without any help."

"I don't think so. It's either me or Payton."

"No."

"Then you'll have to suffer with it."

"I'm capable of—"

"Decide."

"Fine. You. No hanky-panky. No googly eyes."

"I won't if you won't."

Jace helped her into the bathroom. "Let's do your hair first, okay?" He tried to untie the linen around her hair. He had to cut it free to start unwinding it. It crackled. Little maroon flakes of dried blood covered her back and the floor.

Kraft groaned low in her chest.

"Try not to think about it."

"Easy for you to say."

"Think about something else."

"What?"

"Tell me a recipe." It was all he could manage off the cuff. As she did, he sat her down, her back to the tub, tilted her head back, pulled down the handle and washed her hair. It was a good thing her face was to the ceiling because she would have howled at the muddy red mess that came off her hair. It took almost five minutes for the water to run clear. He used half a bottle of lilac shampoo to soap the long black strands. He wondered how she could wash its length herself. When he was finished, she wrapped it up.

"Here, sit down and let me get your boots off." He pulled them off and winced. The blood inside was still slick and they slid right off. The smell was unbelievably rancid. Payton told him she'd debated removing them. In light of a potential spinal injury, she'd elected to leave them be until they were certain tugging on them wouldn't damage Kraft further. "Keep your eyes closed and tell me another recipe, a dessert, something really sweet."

As she did, he stood her up and helped her take off what remained of her clothes. Passion did not fill him. Her body was streaked in crimson and maroon. He helped her into the tub, onto her back.

"Hold this towel over the bandage."

He washed her carefully, then stood her up to wash off her back. When he was finished, he wrapped her in a towel and she just stood there shivering. He pulled her to his chest. "You okay?"

She nodded. Suddenly she laughed. "I'm right back where I started."

"Where you started?"

"On your ship, Captain Lawless." Kraft looked up. "And I don't have any clothes."

"You can wear mine. And I don't think Bailey would mind lending you his boots again."

"I guess the Void will keep inflicting this on me until I learn."

"Learn what?"

"That I can't do it all myself."

Jace tucked her into bed in the passenger room next to her old room.

"Why is the door to my old pris—bedroom locked?"

"It's a long story."

"Then tell me a bedtime story or I'm apt to get up and go look."

"Don't open that door, Kraft."

"Shades of Bluebeard."

"What?"

"A tale from Earth. Bluebeard took wives unto his home, bid them entrance to all but a locked room. When they opened it, they found the bodies of his other too-curious wives." Kraft grinned. "I'm all for wondering at a mystery and, as they say, curiosity killed the cat, but you best tell me why I shouldn't open the door to my old room."

"Heller's in there."

"You're keeping Heller prisoner now?"

"When I was down, Heller tried to take control of the ship from Garrett."

Kraft tried to grasp but couldn't. "He's more loyal to you than a puppy, Captain Lawless. I can't fathom him going against the chain of command."

"Well, in his mind, he had a compelling reason. It doesn't excuse what he did, though."

"But why—"

"Enough." Jace shook his head. "I'm exhausted, Kraft. Let me tell you the rest in the morning."

"Okay."

He leaned over, kissed her forehead, then murmured, "I'm glad you're okay."

"Me too." She smiled. "I'm glad you're okay too."

Jace cupped her face and left the room before he gave into the urge to climb into her bed.

"You're doing fine, Garrett. Now, take the chopped potatoes and put them in the water."

"Are you sure? This isn't what mashed potatoes look like."

"You have to cook them before you mash them," Kraft said.

"What are you doing?" Jace asked, entering the kitchen.

Kraft was sitting on the kitchen counter, dangling her bare feet as she watched Garrett. She wore Jace's old shirt and trousers and had twined her hair with a white strip off an old sheet. Kraft tilted her head at him. "Is this a trick question?"

"Hell, Jace, she's forcing me to cook—save me before I kill us all!" Garrett exclaimed.

"Looks like you're doing fine," Jace said, "but she shouldn't be out of bed."

"One more day of looking at the ceiling would have driven me insane."

"Short trip," Garrett said, winking at her.

"Would be with you driving," she returned with a grin.

Payton entered and Jace cornered her. "Should she be up and around?"

"If she thinks she's ready." Payton shrugged.

"So now she's a doctor too?"

"I've never witnessed a recovery so swift. If Kraft thinks she's ready, then she is." Payton lowered her voice. "I understand you want to protect her, Jace, and that's admirable, but Kraft isn't exactly the delicate little flower you seem to think she is."

"I don't think that."

"Then stop treating her that way. Look at her." Payton lifted her chin. "Kraft is in full command of her faculties. It also looks like she's able to laugh again without pain. Perhaps you should take a page from her book."

"I just don't want her to push herself too hard."

"I think you're afraid."

"Of what?"

"If Kraft can walk, she might walk away."

Jace considered the remark as he watched Kraft. Payton voiced his greatest fear. It frustrated him that he couldn't hold Kraft, couldn't keep her. She would only stay long enough to recover and then she'd be gone. Most like, as soon as they landed on Corona, city of Borealis, Jace would be saying goodbye to Kraft for good.

"She's like an exotic bird, Jace, it would be cruel to keep her in a cage." Payton touched his arm. "However, there's nothing that precludes you from giving her a compelling reason to make your cage hers."

"What do I have to offer her?"

"She said, very clearly, that she loves you."

"When she was barely lucid."

"You think she lied?"

"I don't know."

"If you honestly want to know, ask her." Payton considered. "But then, you'd have to admit the truth."

"What truth?"

"That whether or not she loves you, you most assuredly love her." Payton walked over to the stove. "What are you making?"

"A mess!" Overwhelmed by timing the flipping of seven steaks, Garrett stabbed his fork in the air.

"Steady." Kraft touched Garrett's back with a gesture that

conveyed strength. "He's doing an admirable job of making chicken-fried steak and mashed potatoes with country gravy."

"You should have started with something simple, like soup," Payton said.

"Hell, I love this, but didn't realize how hard it is to make."

"You're doing fine," Kraft assured him. "All you have to do now is mash the potatoes and make the gravy." Kraft carefully walked him through it and clapped her hands. "There you go. Start serving up plates."

Beaming with pride, Garrett served everyone then himself. "Do I have to eat in the kitchen since I cooked?"

"I think we're going to start a new tradition. Everyone, including the cook, eats at the table," Jace said.

Everyone sat down. Kraft sat beside him on the little bench at the head of the table. In the midst of taking a bite and finding it wonderful, everyone cast their eyes at the empty place where Heller usually sat.

"I'll take him a plate," Kraft offered.

"I'm not having my hard work end up thrown against the wall," Garrett said.

"I'm not having my stitches ripped out," Payton insisted.

"Let Jace do it," Garrett said.

"Why would he throw it against the wall or my stitches—"

Jace sighed. "Fill her in, Garrett, while I go attend to our resident bad boy." Jace filled a plate and left.

He tapped the com on the outside of Heller's prison. "Heller? I have dinner if you're interested."

"Did that—did Kraft make it?"

"No, Garrett did." Jace opened the door. Heller stood well back with his hands up. "Sit down at the table."

Heller did and Jace closed the door behind him. He plunked the plate to the table and nodded to it.

"You can eat it or not, Heller, I don't really care. I'm here to ask you one question. Will you follow my orders or not?"

Ready with his fork in his fist, Heller threw it aside and glared reproachfully at Jace. "Ain't fair if it changes every day."

"No, but if it does, will you follow my orders or not?"

Heller kicked back from the table. He flexed his arms and his legs, showing off the power of his young body. In his prime at twenty-two, seven feet and three hundred pounds, Heller embodied fierce male pride. "I won't sit back and let a woman lead."

Jace flexed his body. Older, slower, even more so with the wound. He realized the absurdity of competing, on a physical level, with Heller. "Even if she can take you from garbage cans to credit vaults?"

"She turned on her own, for that IWOG transport job, and that attack ship. She's no better than an alley cat."

"Kraft saved you."

"No—"

"Who knew how they'd attack?"

Heller remained silent.

"Kraft knew."

"Because she's IWOG scum!"

"Because she was once IWOG. She turned on those who crafted her. She made it so we could live, Heller." Jace slapped the table. "Look at me. We are alive, right now, debating this because of her. I will not argue another fact with you until you grasp that one."

"She turned on her own."

"So did you."

"Because I wanted—"

"And that makes what you did okay? Tell me, Heller, when is committing mutiny okay? When Kraft did it or when you did?"

"Ain't a fair question."

"Because you've got no answer. It's not so black and white, is it, Heller? Right and wrong takes on all kinds of shades of gray. Kraft may have gone against the IWOG, gone against her roots, but in the whole of the time we've known her, she has not crossed us once, has she?" When Heller crossed his arms and folded into himself, Jace slapped the table hard. "Has she? Don't you shy away now, Heller. You answer up."

"No, she's not crossed us."

"No. Kraft hasn't. What seems a lifetime ago, on a derelict Basic, Kraft could have hacked my head off."

"I could have killed her first—"

"If you had pulled the trigger do you honestly think we'd be alive debating this right now?"

"Jace, that ain't a fair question—"

"Why not? Seems damn fair to me, Heller. Know it then or know it now, that was the biggest haul we've ever taken. Ever, Heller. And we can thank—" that crazy wonderful and strange woman, "—Kraft. You grasp that now or I'll kick you free."

Heller locked his arms around himself, clutched himself hard. "Why, Jace? IWOG gives no favors."

"Then you acknowledge Kraft gave us a favor."

"She wants *Mutiny*."

"Really? Why would she wait until now?" He shook his head and realized he used the same argument Kraft had given him. "You took her money belt to my bunk. You looked in it, didn't you?"

"She said she had 500K and I—"

"Wanted to make sure she wasn't lying. You looked, you counted it. Kraft did indeed have over 500K in that money belt, didn't she?"

"So what if she did?"

"She had that money ready to go buy her own ship. She doesn't want my ship, she wants her own."

"Kraft read that table at the Den of Ishtar. And at the Double Whammy. She's a reader, Jace. She cheats at cards and everything else."

"Did she cheat when she took you to your knees?"

Heller hissed out breath between tight lips. "She tricked me."

"How? My understanding is she told you she would take you down with two fingers. Did she lie?"

"No."

"Tell me one lie Kraft has ever told you."

Heller thought about it long and hard. "Kraft didn't lie, but she never told the truth neither."

"And now you can ask her every question in your mind and she'll answer it."

"'Cause you told her too?"

"Because that's the way she is. Ask her. She'll tell you. Ask her to show you how to drop an opponent with two fingers. One will get you ten that Kraft will."

"Why would she show her enemy—"

"That's it right there, Heller. You are not her enemy. You are part of her crew. And Kraft would die defending you. She

261

damn near died trying to save us all. She had no idea that you wanted to leave her to die on the floor like a stuck pig."

"She lived, didn't she?"

"Not with your help."

"I wanted you to live."

"At her expense." Jace slapped the table hard. "You thought you had to choose when you didn't."

"Kraft isn't—"

"What?" Jace stood away from the table. "Tell me, Heller. Blast her hard and fast, because that woman made it so my crew lived. Kraft made the wind turn to me against fifty hardcore fighters. We fought off an IWOG attack ship because of her. If you look to blast her, you best have something spectacular."

"You make me compete against—"

"You make yourself compete against her, not me. Kraft has proven herself, again and again, and I can't fault you for not seeing it when I've had such a difficult time."

"You love her."

"And if I do, what does that mean for you?"

"Jace, you're asking me to give up—"

"What?"

"I would have killed them if not for her—"

"Fifty IWOG? How good do you think you are? Kraft took out, by her blade, over twenty, and you and I and Garrett and Payton took out twenty with automatic weapons. She got up close and personal, not us. Who wiped the ship, Heller? Who wiped that fucking ship?"

"You're swearing, Jace, you don't do that—"

"I do now. I'll swear up one side and down the other if that's what it takes to make you see the light. Kraft saved us, Heller. I don't care how you carve it, we are alive because of her. You accept it or I'll kick you free."

"So she's staying."

"I don't know, but for the time she's here you are going to get along with her, and everyone else too. Now, do you want to stay locked in here or eat with the rest of us?"

"As long as she doesn't think she can boss me—"

Jace shook his head. "What's the chain of command?"

"You, then Garrett, then—Kraft—then me."

"Grab your plate and let's go."

They went back to the kitchen and everyone made a point of greeting Heller warmly, even Kraft.

"This is really good, Garrett," Heller said.

"Thank you, Heller," Garrett said, "Kraft helped me."

"That's a good idea, you teaching everyone how to cook something." Heller barely managed to make eye contact with Kraft before his gaze darted back to his plate.

"I'd be happy to teach you to make your favorite, if you want." Kraft took another bite.

A long pause spun out.

"I like that chicken thing, the spicy one." Heller glanced up at her then away.

"Kung Pao Chicken." Kraft nodded, licking gravy off her lips. "That's a good one."

"And beer."

"Okay. I'd be happy to show you how."

"This is so sweet I think I've got a mouthful of cavities," Garrett said, rolling his eyes and clapping his hands to his chest. "It warms the cockles of my heart." He wiped an imaginary tear from his cheek.

"What are cockles, anyway?" Bailey asked Payton.

Payton searched her memory. "It's not a medical term."

"I think it's a clam from Earth," Kraft said.

"Then why would you have them in your heart?" Jace asked.

"I don't know. Maybe Garrett's just a clammy guy."

The conversation degenerated into a discussion of weird idioms from Earth and everyone tossed out their favorite, then the conversation became a discussion of oxymorons. What could have been a terribly awkward moment wasn't because everyone tried very hard to get along. Jace could see it took tremendous control for Heller to refrain from making his usual nasty comments and Jace was proud of him. When he offered to do the dishes, you could have knocked the rest of the crew down with a feather. But Jace knew Heller was trying desperately to atone for what he'd done.

"I'll help," Kraft offered.

Heller gritted his teeth, but said, "Thanks."

Everyone left, but Jace, still not trusting Heller to be alone with Kraft, eavesdropped from the bridge.

"They told you what I did," Heller said.

"I grasp it, Heller."

"Gonna get back at me?"

"No."

Jace couldn't hear what they were doing but he imagined they passed dishes. "What you did is between you and Jace. I was just the catalyst."

Heller grunted. "I don't know what that word means."

"A catalyst starts a chemical—actually, it's not the best word." Kraft sighed. "I'm not holding a grudge against you, Heller. I don't want to fight with you. I think it's unlikely we'll ever be friends in the full sense of the word, but if we both try, I think we can get along. I'm willing if you are."

"That's what Jace wants."

"Well, Captain Lawless has a good reason for it. It's hard to run a crew when two of them are fighting. It's harder still when one of them has a death wish on the other."

"Yeah. Does that mean you're planning on sticking around?"

Jace's heart seemed to stop beating for a moment then thundered in his ears as he waited for what she would say. He heard a loud crash.

"Shit howdy!"

"I got it," Kraft said.

Heller continued to swear.

"Don't worry about it. Soapy water is going to do this floor a world of good. You finish up the dishes and I'll swab the deck."

They worked silently for a while.

"If, uh, you're gonna show me how to make beer and that chicken thing, could you also show me that finger thing?"

"Finger thing?"

"Yeah, that thing you did to my hand."

"Sure. I'll also show you how to get out of it."

"There's a way out of it?"

"For every trick, there's a treat."

Jace didn't have to see her face to know she'd just made that slow, lazy and sexy smile.

Chapter Twenty-eight

"We're about a day off from Borealis," Jace said, entering the kitchen where Kraft sat drinking a foamy beer and playing solitaire. "Should you be drinking that in your condition?"

Kraft sighed. "It's one beer, Captain Lawless. Why don't you grab one and see if it can improve your sullen disposition?"

"No, thanks." He dropped her money belt on the table.

Kraft flinched back and stared at it. 500K in script. Enough to buy a ship, a crew, a whole new life. But she knew she'd never touch it again. Heller, filled with hate grasping it when he took it to Jace's room. Jace too had touched it when he'd been filled with loathing for her. They tarnished it in a way that couldn't be undone.

"Don't you want it?"

Kraft looked up and realization came. Jace didn't want her on his ship anymore. He couldn't forgive her for being an IWOG assassin. He expected her to get off at Borealis and make her own way in the Void. "Sure I do. I'm just in the middle of a game here." It took all her control not to burst into tears and run. Instead, she laughed. "Besides, it's not going anywhere." She kicked out a chair. "Why don't you sit down a play a few hands of poker with me?"

"So you can keep your skills up for Borealis? What's the name of the hell there?"

"Robber's Roost. I've never been there, but I hear it's got a high-roller table. Which means no scans on the door."

"You've never been on Corona?"

"Nope. That's why it's a safe place for all of us to go."

"Safe?"

"You realize—" Kraft stopped herself. He didn't know what she had done and she should probably tell the whole crew when they were together. "Is everyone still up?"

"I think so."

"Could you call them in here?"

"What's this about, Kraft?"

"Your new lives."

Jace called the crew into the kitchen and everyone sat down with an expectant air.

"Well, there's no easy way to say this so I'll just get right to the point. You're all dead."

Everyone exchanged puzzled glances.

"While I was on that IWOG attack ship, I used their Tasher link to make some history. I entered that they easily overtook *Mutiny* and killed everyone on board. And then, a freak accident destroyed both ships. In order for it to stay true, I had to create new bonafides for all of you, and a new commission for your ship, Captain Lawless. Or should I say Captain Baxter of *Prospect*."

"We all have new names?" Garrett asked.

"New names linked to your old fingerprints. These are bonafides that will get you onto any IWOG planet. You'll be able to go legitimate."

"You mean *Prospect* is a registered transport ship?" Jace asked.

"Yes. I had enough time to create a rather short but easily verified resume. You'll find several opportunities on Corona."

"What about our new names?" Charissa asked.

"Well, what I did was give you new last names and new birthplaces, but your first names stay the same."

"Isn't that a little dangerous?" Garrett asked.

"You all have fairly common first names. It's not going to raise any eyebrows or red flags as long as when you deal with folks you make a point of using your last names. But one caveat: you can't ever go back to any world where you're known. Not ever. It's too risky. Folks like Trickster would turn on you in a flash."

"Hell, I won't miss dealing with that fetch," Garrett said.

She gave them all their new names. "One last thing I managed to do for you. Under the commission *Prospect*, sits a credit account with 150K in it as a bond."

"We're bonded?" Garrett's eyebrows rose so high they almost rolled off the back of his head.

"Yes. That way you can get high script jobs with minimal risk."

"Handing it all to me on a silver platter," Jace said. No one but Kraft noticed how cutting his voice was.

"With a very nice bow too," Garrett said.

"I aim to please. Any questions?"

"What's your new name?" Bailey asked.

Kraft stared down at the table and sighed.

"She didn't bother to make herself one," Jace said. "Even if she did, she wouldn't tell us."

"I couldn't."

"You didn't expect to survive, did you?"

"It ain't that."

"Then what is it?"

"My fingerprints are always gonna be hot. Even though I'm listed as dead, the IWOG will keep them on file. Just in case. I'll never be free of them."

"I do believe that is the first bold-faced lie you've ever told," Jace said.

"You don't know how the IWOG works."

"No, but you do. You want me to believe that you crafted six new bonafides, with fingerprints and all, but couldn't manage to wipe yourself from their computer? Did I wake up with idiot printed across my forehead today?"

"I did the best I could in the time I had." Every word out of her mouth sounded more defensive than the last, even to her own ears.

"That I believe. You did your best to save everybody else, but managed to find a way to keep punishing yourself."

"Hell, Jace, what is your problem?" Garrett asked.

"My problem is I'm sick of this!" He slapped the table hard and stood. "Let me guess, Kraft. As soon as we land you're gonna go out, deck yourself in black, get a ship, then find yourself the most dangerous jobs you can."

"What does her fashion sense—"

"It's mourning, Garrett. And I'm wondering if she's ever going to come out of it."

"I'm not mourning anything." Kraft looked out the window in the ceiling. It was easier to concentrate on the vast nothingness than see the disappointment and the crushing reproach in Jace's eyes.

"You treat life like it's a damn punishment!" His voice rose in concert with his fury. "And how great this must be for you. You can punish yourself for being an IWOG assassin, you can punish yourself for the loss of your crew and now, now you can add the death of fifty IWOG to your mighty burden. You know what I think? You're more afraid to live, but you won't die either because then your punishment of yourself would stop, wouldn't it?"

"I am not punishing myself." Kraft stood. "And I'm not going to sit here and let you yell at me like I'm a wayward child."

"The moment your life gets anywhere near happy you find a way to destroy it." Jace stood as well and faced her. Not once in her life had any man called her out so directly, not even Fairing.

"Happy? When has my life gotten anywhere near—" Kraft cut herself off when the one time she'd been truly happy flashed in her mind. Those three incredible days with Jace. She had been happy then. So happy. And she'd gotten sucked into what might be. But she hadn't been the one to destroy it. "You think what you want, Captain Lawless. You either take what I gave you or not, it doesn't matter to me. Go back and deal with Trickster or Kobra again. I don't care." Oh, but she did care, way too much, and that was the problem.

"Right. Because you'll be on your way soon enough." Jace picked up the money belt and threw it at her. "Don't forget your ticket to a new start at bigger and better punishments. I guess you really are a masochist. You seem unsurprised that I won't be your sadist."

The money belt flumped to the floor at her feet like a dead snake. Kraft did not want to touch it with her bare hands so she kicked it into the hall and picked it up using the cuff of her shirt, Jace's shirt, to block her fingertips from making direct contact. When she got to her room, she dropped the mass of money on the table and left it there.

Kraft threw herself on the bed, winced when her belly protested, then pondered what Jace had said. It wasn't true. When her life had been happy, he was the one who messed it up, not her. And she didn't wear black because she was in mourning—she wore it because it didn't show dirt. At least, that's what she'd always told herself.

She'd started wearing black eight years ago when she'd taken Parkhill to Kali. After giving him most of the money from the sale of the ship, she sold her IWOG uniform to a woman hucking clothes off her doorstep. Kraft found crisp black clothes that fit her perfectly and a private place to dress. She emerged to the street from the cold, bare room.

"Riven's," the woman said, nodding. "Had 'em made for her love's funeral, but she never made it that far."

"Riven died before she could attend her lover's funeral."

The woman nodded resolutely, obviously pained that she would likely lose the sale for her honesty.

Kraft considered what she wore. The fabric was impossibly new, clear of any emotional impression. She'd felt nothing when she'd pulled the clothing on. Considering the exhausted woman before her, Kraft said, "You made it for her."

"I did."

"Black for a funeral." Kraft looked down at herself again. Black was oft a color for mourning and, even though she had much to celebrate, Kraft had much to mourn. "Do you have anything else Riven or her love wore?"

The woman's eyes did not light with dollar signs. Instead they burned with understanding. She fished about the racks of clothing and handed Kraft an almost impossibly worn soft leather duster and also a pair of thick black boots.

"Beck wore these, almost the whole of his life."

"How'd you get them?"

"They forced her to cremate him. I found them in the trash behind."

Kraft nodded. She knew well the drill. It was cheaper to burn them than to bury them. When Riven protested, they shot her. The IWOG officers striped them both then tossed the clothes and burned the bodies. "What do you want for them?" Kraft had still not touched the boots or the leather duster.

"In trade for an official IWOG officer uniform? I'd call it even."

Kraft nodded. "So would I."

To Kraft, it was a journey. A penance. Almost as if a

crusade. She didn't look to glorify any god, but only to find out who and what she really was. And she did it in cast off clothing...

She bolted upright on the bed. It *had* started as mourning. And she'd just gotten comfortable with it. Jace was a better reader than he knew. But he made it clear he didn't want her on his ship. And if she was very honest with herself, she knew she'd fixed it so she couldn't stay.

There was a tentative knock on her door. "Can I come in?"

"It's your ship, isn't it?"

Jace opened the door, his expression guarded. "It's time for another round of let's cut the crap and I still think it's ladies first. You lied, didn't you? You very literally killed yourself."

"Yes." The single word hung there for a moment, shocking her with how final it sounded. "There is no Julie, no Kraft. My fingerprints won't trace back to anyone, anywhere. I'm a non-entity. And you have no choice but to put me off your ship." Unable to look him in the eye, she turned her attention to smoothing her bedding. "You can now go legitimate. And with that you can't have an unknown on board."

"You really fixed it well, didn't you?" She expected him to sound bitter or angry, but instead, he sounded sadly disappointed.

"I gave you back your life, as close as I could."

"By killing yourself."

His accusation grated because it was far too close to the truth. "It's not like that."

"Explain it to me. I'm too pretty to understand."

She flashed him a brief smile that vanished when she saw the hard cast of his jaw. "I'm not like you. I'd never make it in the legitimate world because those old warrants of me are going to be floating around for at least another ten years. I've got no choice but to keep living in the very darkest reaches of the Void."

"Just the way you like it."

"You think I like being a hunted woman?" She practically snarled the question as she dug her fingers into the bedcover.

"You must. Because it didn't have to shake out that way." Arms tight at his sides, he refused to look away.

"Lord on high, you've got some kind of inflated notion of

what I'm capable of doing. I can't use the power of my brain and destroy all those old warrants. I can't wipe my face from every IWOG ditto-head's brain."

"That warrant is eight years old, Kraft. And you don't much look like that photo anymore." He shook his head, clearly dissatisfied with her excuse. "I've not noticed one IWOG officer raise so much as a curious brow your way when you walk past."

"I'm not going to argue this with you anymore." Pushing herself up from the bed, she strode toward the bathroom.

"Because you know I'm right."

She stopped mid-stride but didn't turn around. "Because it isn't your choice."

"You're right. It's entirely up to you if you want to live like a cockroach."

Slowly she turned and faced him. "Nice analogy."

"It's true enough, isn't it?" Jace asked, arching his brows, challenging her with his gaze.

"What do you care?" she asked, challenging him right back. "In twenty-four hours I'll be off your ship, out of your hair, and out of your life forever. You got my word on it."

"Because I sure as hell don't have a choice in the matter, do I?" He crossed his arms over his chest as if holding back the true force of his fury.

"Just for fun, let's pretend that you do have a choice in the matter, what would you choose? Are you willing to toss the safety of your crew aside just so you can diddle me?"

Jace shook his head and looked at her dumbfounded. "That's honestly what you think this is about? That I just haven't scratched my itch enough?" He groaned and scowled. "If that's what you think of me why did you tell me that you love me?"

Kraft felt the moment spin out like salt water taffy in the sun. She made the decision to end everything permanently by making it easy for him. "I lied."

Jace stood there for a moment, just looking at her.

"Don't get me wrong, it was fun and all, but nothing I'd be willing to give my life up for." She studied her short nails, checked her non-existent watch. "If I told you that I loved you, you'd be more inclined to save me, just like you did."

"Then why did you do all of that? Make up the bonafides, the bonded commission?"

"I felt sorry for you." She laughed, deliberately low and mean. "You folks are so clueless! I can't believe you've survived seven years in the Void running salvage. You're better off going legitimate. Leave the tougher stuff to those who can actually handle it."

"Like you."

"Yeah. Cockroaches like me."

"You are determined to leave this on a bad note."

"No, an honest one. Like you said, I don't pull any punches. You'd never survive the world I live in. You barely made it through seven years. If I hadn't pulled your butt out of the flames, you'd be dead. Twice, no, three times over by my reckoning."

"You seem to forget we pulled your butt out too." Jace didn't sound defensive, only determined to remind her of the truth. If nothing else, he wasn't going to let her belittle his accomplishments.

"No, I'm not forgetting that. I give credit where credit is due. I owe you for saving my life. Twice over, I think. Means I'm one up on you."

"Tit for tat."

"An interesting turn of phrase."

"What do I owe you?"

Caught off guard, Kraft asked, "For what?"

"The IWOG attack ship, the bonafides."

"A hundred and fifty."

"K?"

"No. Flat. That's a tenth of what you paid Trickster for me, right?"

Jace counted it out, tossing fives and tens to the battered table in her new bedroom. "I guess this squares us."

"I guess it does."

"I'd appreciate it if, before you left, you'd keep your word to Heller."

Jace just confirmed he'd been eavesdropping on her conversation with Heller. "I will."

"Good night then, Kraft."

"Good night, Captain Lawless."

He walked away with his head held high and she had to admire his spirit. She'd kicked him, hard, again and again, but he just wouldn't stay down.

"He's stronger now than he was before, and he's better off without me." Kraft pondered that for a moment. "Then why do I feel like crap?"

She stood, slapped the com to close her door and considered the money on the table. A money belt with over 500K and a measly, scattered pile of one hundred and fifty flat.

One was so tainted she didn't dare touch it with her bare fingertips. The other? Well, both were tainted but the smaller pile less so. She slipped the one fifty flat into her pocket before she felt the full impression from it. Even in the quick flash, pain filled her. Jace had shelled it out willingly enough but he gave it to her, reluctantly, for he didn't agree with her assessment of their affair.

The word turned over in her mind.

Affair?

Why did that strike her with such curiosity?

So what if he called it an affair? What would she call it? Courting? Kraft rolled her eyes. A minor interlude. A dance that went fast and slow but ultimately ended.

"And so I set the tune for a new dance."

She checked her possessions. She wore Jace's shirt, his trousers, Bailey's boots, her own blades. One fifty flat barely made a lump in her pocket.

"Got everything I need."

She looked around the room again. A mirror image of the room next door, her bedroom turned prison, where Heller had been kept.

"For mutiny or for turning on me?"

She wondered. It didn't really matter why. Heller did what he did and it all turned out for the best.

"I'm still alive."

Kraft laughed.

"Barely. But still."

She looked at the money belt again and sighed. She really should leave some kind of note. Take a stab at explaining.

"And just what would I say? Here's a bunch of script. Take it and buy yourselves whatever kind of life you want, because

I'm happy that I still have feet." She wiggled her toes in Bailey's old boots. They were a shade too tight but she hadn't stressed her toe leather too much.

She'd done what she said she would. Call it delusions of grandeur but she didn't lie about her abilities. "The IWOG crafted me into an incredible weapon. Thanks to them that's all I'll ever be." She looked at the money belt again.

"Script opens wide the doors to the hell on any port city."

If she flashed the money belt around, she'd be whisked to the big table so fast her head would damn near fall off, no matter what she wore or even if her picture hung behind the bar riddled with darts. Lots of script made everyone sit up and play nice.

But that would be too easy.

Kraft would take the one fifty flat and go from there. Let Jace and his crew take the other. They would need that kind of script to upgrade the ship. If she did nothing else, she should at least tell them what they should get to upgrade *Mutiny*.

"*Prospect.*" She corrected. She'd thought it odd anyone would name a ship *Mutiny* and when she'd been under pressure to craft a new name, she'd plucked *Prospect* out of the air. It was far better than *Mutiny*. More so in that mutiny had been committed aboard *Mutiny*. "*Prospect* is at least more hopeful."

So what would she name her new ship?

"*Dismal.*"

For that's how she felt. She'd lied when she told Jace she didn't love him when she did. Told him she was dead in the Void when she wasn't. She'd not been willing to tell him or his crew the truth because she was safer if she didn't. He couldn't ever be in the position to rat her out if he didn't know, nor could his crew. When Kraft had saved Parkhill, she'd made the same call.

It wasn't that she didn't trust Jace, it was just safer if she disappeared and started over yet again. A new name, a new ship, perhaps as a cook—

She shook her head as she made her way to the bridge of *Prospect*. She'd enjoyed being a cook again while on Jace's ship. And too, she'd enjoyed passing along her recipes. Maybe she'd take her one fifty, wager it up and start an underground cooking school.

She laughed. Given her druthers, she'd rather teach every

soul in the Void to cook rather than teach even one more soul to fight. Still laughing to herself, she entered the bridge.

"Having a good time?" Jace sat in the pilot chair. He didn't turn to look at her.

"I thought Bailey was on duty."

"I gave him the night off for good behavior." Jace turned and faced her as she stood in the doorway. "Let me guess." He put his fingertips to his forehead, closed his eyes and hummed. "You are here, to..." He shook his head as if reading the vapors. "You are here to tell me how to live high off the hog in the IWOG world."

Kraft clapped slowly but precisely. "Very good."

Jace bowed while sitting.

"Do you do kids' parties?" As soon as she said it she realized how cutting those words were.

"Not since my three were killed." Jace yanked the chair around and faced the console. "Spit it out, Kraft, whatever it is." His back, cold and unconcerned, cut her in a way she was not prepared for.

"Upgrade your ship. Your console, including your sensors, fore and aft, need a good twenty year upgrade. So does your engine. Put in more responsive engine controls for your pilot. It's ridiculous to expect Garrett or Heller to fill in for what Bailey should be able to access from the bridge." Even though she'd installed a small Tasher unit, she suggested putting in a full Tasher drive.

"Excellent idea." Jace nodded. "I'll do that as soon as we hit Borealis."

"Good. That's what I wanted to tell Bailey."

"I'm sure he'll pass it along to his next captain."

"What?"

"He's not staying with me. He knows he can do bigger and better elsewhere." Jace swiveled the chair so that he faced her. "He wants to make a play for your ship." Jace laughed. "Bailey, Bailey."

"You think I aim to steal him from you?"

"No, I think Bailey is one step from having his heart stomped. Lucky me, I get to watch you do it." Jace glared at her. "Bailey doesn't suspect a thing."

Kraft stiffened. "I'm not after your crew. If Bailey has some grand plan to follow me, he'll be disappointed."

"I know that, and you know that, but Bailey doesn't. We know that he'll be disappointed as hell, because as soon as we hit port, you'll disappear."

Kraft laughed. "Any reason I should stick around?" Jace didn't react. "I didn't think so."

"Try real hard not to crush him."

"Bailey?"

"Poor boy."

"No, he's not. He won't follow me, Heller will. And perhaps you."

"No, not me. I don't care anymore, Kraft." Jace turned his back on her. "Go kill yourself. That's your goal, isn't it?"

"Fuck you."

"Such vulgar language for a lady." Jace laughed while eyeing her reflection in the bridge window. "Besides, by my recollection, you've already done that."

The next morning, Kraft taught Payton how to make omelets. Payton was easy to teach and did everything with neat, quick, medical precision. "You're a natural."

"I learned a bit of cooking, back on Gilgamesh."

Kraft nodded. "Before you ran from your abusive IWOG husband."

Payton almost dropped the spatula. "Jace told you."

"No."

"Then how?"

"I'm a reader, Payton."

"I thought that was just a myth."

"Readers are real. When I first came on board, I knew then. I know what you've been running from, what you've protected Charissa from."

"Jace has protected us both." Payton said as she worked at the stove. "He's a good man who would—"

"You don't have to worry anymore." Kraft did not want to talk about how good Jace was as both a captain and a friend. "Your husband won't look for you anymore, Payton. You're safer now than you've ever been. So is Charissa."

"Thank—"

"Please don't thank me for giving you a life in the dark. I don't think I can bear it right now." Kraft turned away and buttered toast. "I really don't know if I've done any of you any favors by doing what I've done."

"Regardless, you want no thanks for it." Payton's voice was surprisingly calm.

"No. I don't."

"Because you might have to thank us too."

"I do thank you, Payton. You saved my life, and for that I am truly grateful."

"But I can't be grateful in turn."

"Like I said, I don't know if I've really done you any favors."

Jace came in, took one look at her and left.

"Well, that was odd." Payton flipped one of the omelets. "He must have forgotten something."

"His memory works fine. I do believe he'll be avoiding me on this last day."

Payton considered her then the empty doorway. "Will you be teaching him how to cook something?"

"Oh, I think I've taught him quite enough."

Payton called everyone to breakfast, and Kraft was relieved she didn't have to sit next to Jace. As if reading her mind, he came in and sat, as close as he could, on the little bench. Mashing into her side, Jace let loose a deep breath that tickled her neck.

"Isn't this cozy?" he whispered.

Kraft flushed with pleasure, but shook it off by intently slathering jelly on her toast.

"It's wonderful, Payton," Garrett said.

"Thank you. And thank you for teaching me, Kraft." Payton was all ripe pride in cooking for the object of her affection and the crew.

"You're welcome," Kraft offered.

"You're teaching me that chicken thing for lunch?" Heller asked.

"Yes. And beer."

"And what will you be teaching me?" Jace asked.

Her brain felt frozen, like it'd just been hit with a blast of liquid nitrogen. She took a bite of her toast to stall.

"One of us ought to learn how to make bread. That's

simple, right?" Charissa asked.

Kraft nodded.

"And a dessert," Garrett said. "Someone should know how to make something loaded with sugar."

"I think Kraft can teach me that, don't you?" Jace asked, turning his head so he breathed the question right in her ear.

If she said no, it would just raise a bunch of awkward questions. But she still couldn't find her voice. She nodded as she continued to chew on her bite of toast.

Chapter Twenty-nine

Heller shocked her by learning quickly. Kraft only had to walk him through making beer once and he had it down.

"You seem sorta surprised." Heller scratched his head.

"It's just that it's complicated and most people don't grasp it that fast."

"I guess when you wanna learn, it helps you remember."

He learned the hand trick and Kung Pao Chicken just as easily, and Kraft found she had a good time. She pushed the thought of leaving to the back of her brain.

"Can I talk to you, Bailey?"

"Sure." He set the cards down and made room for her on the couch in the rec room. Expectation on his face fell to hurt when she sat down on the far end.

"Jace said you were planning to leave the ship."

"Yeah, well, I was thinking you'd be in need of a pilot." His pale blue eyes were bright with excitement.

"You can't come with me, Bailey. I'm not like a circus you can run away to."

He frowned at the archaic expression.

"It's from Earth. When children fought with their parents, they would threaten to run away and join the circus."

"I'm not a child!" His voice was shrill.

"No, you're not," Kraft said, keeping her voice calm. "But you still can't come with me."

"Is your ship going to be all women again?"

"I don't know. But you belong here, Bailey."

"Where I'm treated like a child."

"Jace doesn't treat you that way. And even though *Prospect* is going legitimate, he'll still need a kick-ass pilot."

"But I really like you." Bailey tried to meet her gaze, but ended up looking at the floor.

"I know you do. I like you too. But not that way, Bailey."

"Not the way you do Jace." Bailey crossed his arms.

"No, not that way."

Bailey crumpled up like a used tissue.

"You are sweet and funny and so talented it astounds me. I'm not sure what you do better, Bailey, fly this ship or play your guitar."

He perked up a bit.

"I care about you a lot, an awful lot, but not in the way you want me to. I'm way too old for you. You deserve someone a lot less jaded than I am."

"You can't stop me from leaving." He lifted his chin but kept his gaze on the floor.

"I know that. I can't make you do anything. But I also know you're smart enough to see the truth in what I'm saying. And even though you don't like it, you know following me is only going to get you hurt." Kraft sighed. "Or killed."

Bailey stood. "Jace had it right, didn't he? You're trying to find a way to punish yourself and get yourself killed." Bailey shook his head. "Why do you hate yourself so much when everyone on this ship likes you? Can all of us be wrong?"

Much to her dismay, Bailey forced her to reconsider her reasons for leaving.

"Maybe I should have let Heller let you die. By the way you're acting, it would have made you happy." Bailey shoved the cards away and stood.

"Bailey, wait—"

"I don't want to talk to you anymore! Go get yourself killed. Go live a long and miserable life since that seems to be what you want." Bailey stomped out of the rec room.

Kraft sat on the ratty couch and sighed. This was not going well at all. Her last hours aboard *Prospect* were going to be nothing short of pure misery, and yet everyone seemed to think that was the way she wanted it. Given her druthers, she'd like to shadow right now and slip quietly off when they hit Corona.

Just a few more hours, she reminded herself, as she made her way to the kitchen. A few more hours and then it'd all be over and she could start again. The last hours were going to be the hardest, though, since she had to spend them in the kitchen right next to Jace.

"Lord on high, help me get through this."

Jace waited for her in the kitchen, wearing that green shirt that drove her nuts. That green shirt that matched his exotic-sunset green eyes. That simple shirt that she wanted to rip off him with her teeth.

"You ready?" he asked.

Her vision of him under her gnashing mouth caused her to utter, "Yeah. Okay. First thing we'll start with is the bread."

That went simple enough. Jace learned fast, but he also took notes.

"Just in case," he said with a grin. "I'm so pretty it might just slip my mind."

Kraft wouldn't bite. He gave her opportunity after opportunity to flirt, and even though the words came automatically to mind, she swallowed them down. Determined, she kept her voice and posture entirely professional. She showed him how to make Apple Brown Betty and also a simple potato and corn chowder the crew dubbed Wowder Chowder.

Jace asked her every question he could, and she knew he was deliberately dragging things out since Jace had a mind like a durosteel trap.

"You've got it all written down. You'll be fine. Why don't you call everyone up for dinner?"

Dinner did not go well. Bailey refused to even look at her and Jace kept rubbing his leg against hers. He did it as if he was utterly unaware, but she knew he wasn't. It was the most horrible torture she'd ever suffered. Kraft couldn't wait to get off the ship, yet wanted to stay.

"We'll be docking in an hour," Bailey said, standing. "Then you can get on with the whole killing yourself thing." He stomped off to the bridge.

"You must have told him he couldn't come with you," Jace said, watching Bailey exit the galley. "I take it your chat with him didn't go well."

"Not very." Kraft sighed. "But he's got no illusions about me anymore. He knows exactly what kind of a bitch I really am."

"Hell, girl, wish you'd reconsider," Garrett said. "We could really use you here."

"I appreciate it, Garrett, but—"

"She's got that punishing herself thing to tend to and we'd only get in her way." Jace stood.

Kraft gritted her teeth. Jace behaved as badly as Bailey. Perhaps worse, since Jace should have been capable of at least *acting* like an adult.

"I don't think there is any call to get nasty here," Payton offered. "Kraft has every right to leave the ship, Jace."

"Right. Lord knows there's nothing that could make her stay." Jace tossed his napkin onto his now bare plastiware plate.

A small voice, somewhere very deep in her heart, called out that there was one thing she'd stay for. Kraft bit it off and stood. "I think I'll make myself scarce."

"Shouldn't you give a big good-bye speech? You know, something about all the good times and all that?" Jace asked.

"And you say I bait everyone?" Heller grunted.

Everyone turned surprised eyes on him.

"You've done nothing but bait her for two days, Jace. Why don't you two just shake hands and be done with it?"

"And lo, the voice of reason comes from—Heller?" Garrett shook his head.

Kraft offered her hand. It hung in the air for a long time while Jace just looked at it. In the end, she withdrew it. "Fine. I hope you all have many happy trails. I hope you all find what you're looking for."

"Well, I hope you don't."

His tone and his words stung.

"Hell, Jace, what is up your butt?" Garrett hissed.

"You want her to get what she wants? She wants to punish herself or die trying. I don't want her to get that. I hope she finds the opposite. I hope every nice and wonderful thing that could ever happen to you does." With that, Jace thrust out his hand.

Kraft took it. "I hope the same for you." She made a point of not letting her voice sound like a curse.

Dark of night saturated the port of Borealis. Kraft shadowed her way off *Prospect* and a good distance into the streets. She ducked into an alley and made sure no one followed her. There was a touch of disappointment when she realized there was no way they could have.

Finding her way to Robber's Roost was easy. She just followed the main street to the biggest, most out of place building. Sure enough, amid the rubble and new buildings, she found one that looked like an oversized saloon from Earth.

She'd never pondered why, but the IWOG liked their hells to look like something out of the books they banned, as if they thumbed their noses at themselves.

"Waste of time trying to figure out the mind of the IWOG," Kraft said to herself as she pushed open the door. A familiar smell of high-dollar hooch and cologne couldn't mask the smell of desperate sweat. A piquant stench that no amount of after-shave or even the best air exchanger could ever rid the hells of. She hated the reading of failure, stung pride, and decimated lives that emanated from the very buildings. If she could, she'd wear gloves to protect herself from the onslaught, but then she wouldn't be able to read the tables either. She never hankered for a bath as much as she did after working one of the hells.

Kraft strode to the bar, ordered the best whiskey straight up and knocked it back like a pro. No one questioned whether or not she belonged because she looked, walked and acted like she owned the damn place. Eyeing the various tables, she saw one, in the back, that would suit her. Four IWOG officers, dressed in strange civilian clothes, played a lively game of poker. They bet fortunes. Those who lost did so with laughter and gruff back-slapping. It would take some finagling, but she knew how to get into the game.

"Men are men, no matter where they're from," she whispered to herself. She sauntered over to the empty chair. "Mind if I join?"

They eyed her and she could tell they were all well into their cups. Perfect. Reading drunks was like reading a comic book.

"I wouldn't mind a pretty lady joining us, but I don't think you've got the scratch to play with the big boys."

Kraft wanted to groan at his horrible western affect. He'd probably read a banned book or two and thought himself an expert. She tailored her face to look a bit more wide-eyed and simple.

"I only have a hundred, but couldn't you play one lesser hand for me?" She batted her eyelashes and pouted. "None of the other tables will let me play."

They sucked up her sugar-sweet act like thirsty sponges.

She won the first hand and the next. Carefully, she lost half of it in the third hand, but won it right back in the fourth. Dancing, twirling them along, buying them drinks, she worked her paltry script up. When they drank, or slapped each other, she would hide part of her winnings in her boot. They had no idea how much she'd already won from them.

"You seem to be doing right well for a lady," the big man said. His funny shirt with the strange buttons drew tight across his huge belly.

"Must be beginner's luck." She smiled and blushed. "If you want, I can give it back—" she offered, knowing they'd never take it but offering always shamed them into letting her walk away unscathed.

"No, of course I don't want it back! That ain't nothing but petty cash, little girl. You take it an' buy yourself something right pretty."

It took all her will not to roll her eyes. "Well, thank you all so much." She tucked the money to her pocket and made her way through the crowded tables. A sudden rush of regret washed through her and she grabbed the back of a chair. Her eyes closed, she gritted her teeth and swallowed hard. Determined, she strode to the bar.

"I need a room for the night."

Giving her a dubious once over, the barman drawled, "3K, lady."

"Fine." She plucked a wad of script from her boot and shelled the money out. "And a bottle of your best sipping whiskey."

"Three flat."

"Fine." She shelled out more. Looking up, she added, "A hundred for you if you give me the quietest room you've got."

He smiled and handed her a key. "Four eleven. All the way on the top in the back. You won't hear a peep."

Kraft took the key, the bottle, and made her way up the

stairs.

Jace, slumped down at a corner table, watched her go. For a lady who was on her way back to her preferred lifestyle, she sure didn't look happy. He gave her ten minutes then followed her up.

A heavy carpet lined the hallway and muted his steps. He found her room and stood there with his hand raised to knock.

"What in the Void am I going to say?"

His argument with Heller filled his head. Heller, of all people, telling him he was a clunk-head if he let Kraft go.

Jace touched the door and to his amazement it opened. He couldn't hear anything, so he pushed it then peered around the edge.

Fancy room, he thought. Lots of thick fabric, all in browns and blacks, very western, lot of hide and leather deco crap strewn about. Sitting in the middle of the room was the biggest bed he'd ever seen. It had to be fifteen by fifteen feet. It was bigger than the bed at Michael "Overlord" Parker's place. No doubt it was made for IWOG officers who had more than one bed partner.

Water splashed and he realized she was in the tub. He slipped into the room, carefully closed and locked the door. Chucking his boots off, he made his way to the partially open bathroom door.

Peering around the edge, he found Kraft up to her ears in water, her twined hair dangled off the back of the massive, red claw-foot tub. A whiskey bottle sat untouched on a marble side-table.

Kraft sighed. Not one of contentment, but one of resigned acceptance. More and more Jace became convinced she was as miserable as he was. If not more so. He leaned casually against the doorframe and toed the door open.

"That was quite an act."

Kraft shot out of the tub. Water splashed all over the white marble floor as she groped frantically for a towel. "What the hell do you think you're doing! This isn't your ship. You have no right to bust in here, invading my privacy and—"

"I didn't bust in. I walked in. The door was open." He tossed her a cherry red towel.

"I'll make sure to lock it after you leave." Kraft wrapped the towel around her.

Jace relaxed against the doorframe.

She took a deep breath and blew it out through pursed lips. "Well?"

"What?"

"Leave."

He considered. "No."

"Tell you what, you better be on your way. You're not captain here, and I don't owe you a damn thing."

"Oh, I think you do at that." Jace unbuttoned his shirt.

"What the hell do you think—"

He pulled her money belt off. "You owe me an explanation."

She looked at it as if he held a gun on her. "You need it more than I do."

He tossed it on the table by the whiskey bottle. "You know, for a lady who doesn't love me, you sure seem to go out of your way to make sure I'm well taken care of."

"Maybe I just forgot it."

"Maybe you really are in love with me."

"Maybe this conversation is over." Kraft stepped from the tub and grimaced at the sopping floor. She threw a few towels on the mess then strode past him. Her trembling hand yanked at the door and she started swearing when she discovered he'd locked it. Furiously, she scrabbled at the lock.

Jace took her hand and she flinched back.

"Get out of my room."

"Not until we sort this out."

"I could easily pitch you right out of here."

"You won't."

"And just what is stopping me?"

"For one, you don't want to attract a lot of unwanted attention to yourself. I'm sure they've got a Breaker Squad on reserve here." Jace stepped forward and caressed her face. "For another, I really don't think you could hurt me."

"Are you doubting my skills as a fighter?" Kraft put her hands on her hips.

"I'm doubting your ability to hurt the man you love."

"I told you I lied!" Exasperated, Kraft threw up her hands. Her towel pooled around her feet. Her face turned almost as red as the towel as she yanked it back up. In her frustration, she wasn't able to cover herself. "Just, just," she stammered, her lip quivering. "Just leave me alone."

"So you can make your way all alone and lonely?" Jace noticed but deliberately ignored her nakedness.

"I'm not lonely."

"Yes, you are." Jace caught her gaze, focused on her eyes despite everything else he could see. "You know, I finally unpacked it, Kraft. Why your eyes have haunted me since the day I first laid eyes on you. You have hungry eyes, Kraft. You have the hungriest eyes I've ever seen. And I finally figured out what it is you're so damn hungry for."

He pulled her into his arms and kissed her. She struggled, briefly, then gave herself up to his embrace.

"If all you want is one more night in my bed—"

"Nice try." Jace laughed softly into her ear as he held her tight. "But it isn't sex, it isn't scratching an itch, for me or you. You want love, Kraft. You want to be loved so desperately that when you found it, it scared the hell out of you because you seem to think you don't deserve it. You tried to destroy it. When you realized you couldn't, you ran."

"I told you I lied." Her voice was so soft even she didn't buy what she was saying.

"Well, I don't believe you," Jace said. "And that's not what you're running from. You know I love you. You've known it for quite a while and that's what you're running from. Because it's exactly what you've been looking for your whole life. You think now that you've found it, somehow, your life is over."

"That's crazy!"

"Sure is. But it's also the truth." He pulled back a bit so he could look into her eyes. "I love you. And that humble truth shakes you in your boots. I can best you, and you know it."

"Let go of me."

"Even if I physically let go, I'll never really let go." He nuzzled her ear. "I'm in your head, I'm in your heart. Just like you are with me."

"Yeah, well, I'll get over it."

"No, you won't. I won't either. We'll drift through the Void, thinking about each other. There might come a time when one of us is lucky enough to find someone else. But it will always have a hole in it because you and I never even gave this a chance." Jace kissed her, almost a whisper to her lips. "Come back to *Prospect* with me, Kraft. I love you. And God help me because I need you too."

"A ship can't have two—"

"Captains. I know that's what they say. Just as they say there is no honor among thieves." He looked into her eyes. "We proved that wrong, didn't we? And how do we know about two captains unless we try?"

"We already tried it and it was a disaster. I hurt you and everyone else on your ship. And now you have a real chance to start over, Jace. A real chance at a real life where you don't have to wake up and wonder if this will be the last day you suck down a breath. I worked my ass off to give you that chance and now you want me to take it away."

"No. I want you to take that chance with me. A real life, Kraft. Where you don't have to work salvage. Where you don't have to deal with men like Trickster or Kobra. Where you don't have to put on an act to win money from worthless scum in tacky hells." Jace sighed. "I've been watching you all night, Kraft. You're not happy trying to go back to this life."

"I don't know how to live any other way."

"Then let me teach you."

"And if it doesn't work?"

"Why wouldn't it work?"

"I like being captain."

"So do I."

"See? There it is." Kraft extracted herself from his embrace and tried again to cover up with the towel. "I like being in charge. Just like you said, I'm a control freak. I don't know any other way to be except for the one running the show."

Jace considered. "Okay."

"Okay what?"

"You can be captain of *Prospect.*"

Her jaw damn near hit the floor.

"If it means that much to you, if that's the only reason holding you back from being with me, then it's yours."

"You can't be serious."

"I am. I wouldn't even have a ship if not for you. I wouldn't even be standing here right now, if not for you. I'm telling you, none of it means a damn thing to me unless you're there to share it with me."

"You're crazy!"

Jace laughed. "Once upon a time, didn't you tell Charissa that love makes folks do all kinds of strange things?"

"Tell you what, I didn't think you'd ever give up your ship."

"Then I guess we both know how far I'm willing to go."

"What about your crew? You can't expect them to follow this."

"They can choose. If they don't want to follow your lead, then they're free to go." Jace shook his head. "Finding new crew members will take some time, but we have that because we have money."

"But—" Kraft shook her head.

"What?" Jace asked. "Keep throwing up blocks and I'll keep knocking them down."

"I don't want your ship!"

"Fine. We'll sell it and buy another one."

"Doesn't that ship mean anything to you?"

"It's a thing, Kraft. It's replaceable. You're not."

"What about Bailey? Charissa and Payton? Garrett—holy, hell, Heller! You can't just kick them out!"

"Didn't say I would. They could decide. I think they'd stay. Everyone would have to learn, dance as you say, but I think we dance together rather well, friction and all. If I deemed you Captain, put you in charge, everyone would at least try to get along. Maybe, in the end, they wouldn't, but they'd at least try. Can you at least try?"

Kraft gave a short gasp and shook her head, frustrated that she'd run out of roadblocks.

"You're either certifiably crazy or you must really—" She searched for the words.

"Love you." Jace nodded. "I do. If you took it into your head that you wanted to live here, I'd stay with you."

"Jace, I—" Kraft fell against him and buried her face in his chest.

He held her and murmured, "I have been afraid for so long, Kraft. Afraid to fall in love, afraid to lose everything I have, then you came along and suddenly, I'm only afraid when I try to picture my life without you. You see, none of it means a damn thing without you."

"I've been running for so long. Running from my past, running from myself. I tried running from you, but I just can't seem to make things work the way they once did." She sighed. "I'm exhausted."

"Then stop running."

"I lied, you know. About loving you."

"I know." He smoothed her shoulders.

"How did you know?"

"You were willing to give up what you swore you wanted all along."

She pulled back and regarded him with a curious frown.

"All you said you wanted was to be back on your own ship, but you left behind the money that would have done that for you because you thought I needed it more."

"Well, that's not quite true. I was afraid to touch it, to feel what Heller had felt when he touched it, what you felt when you did."

Jace chuckled. "You may have told yourself that but deep down, you were willing to sacrifice as much, if not more, than I am."

"You're not serious about giving up your ship."

Jace tilted her face up. "Yes, I am."

"I can't let you do that."

"Then don't, *annyae*."

That Jace used that endearment stripped her of any resistance. "You are so much more than pretty."

He smiled. "So are you. I'll make you a deal. We'll be co-captains. I'll run the ship, you run the jobs. What have you got to lose?"

She considered. "Nothing. I've lost all of my secrets, lost and regained my honor, lost my heart to you, gained yours in exchange."

"Is it a deal?"

"Deal."

Kraft stuck out her hand, Jace shook it, then pulled her close and kissed her. The kiss deepened and her towel slipped. She tried to pull it back up, then groaned and let it fall.

"You know, it's been a long time since I've been in a tub," he said.

"You know, the room's paid for."

"From your ill-gotten booty."

"After all they've put us through, I think they owe us a night in an expensive, albeit tawdry, hotel."

Jace couldn't get out of his clothes fast enough. They settled themselves in the tub.

"What about Bailey?"

"He wants you on the ship. He's been kicking himself for all kinds of a fool for leaving things with you in a bad way. He'd be happy for a chance to put them right."

"And Heller?"

"He's the one who told me I'd be a fool to let you go."

"Heller?" Kraft's jaw almost fell off her face. "Are we talking about the same big lurch of a guy who—"

"You changed something in him when you forgave him for what he'd done. It surprised him, that you had no intention of seeking revenge. When you showed him your hand trick, that's when you made a friend for life. He not only likes you, Kraft, he respects you, and not many can lay claim to that. Me, Garrett, and now you. I do believe you are the first and only woman Heller has ever held as an equal."

"It's been one hell of a complicated dance, hasn't it?"

"It's a dance that's way too good to end, Kraft."

"And I can run the jobs?"

"Always worried about that power aspect, my little control freak, aren't you?" Jace kissed her quick. "Yes, Kraft. You run the jobs. Because you know how. I'll run the crew, because I know how. Together? We'll make a daring team."

"We could become famous."

"Let's shoot for anonymously rich."

Epilogue

A year later, Jace and Kraft were in the kitchen on the now fully upgraded *Prospect*. The jobs had been not only easy, but they paid well. Life had settled into a comfy pattern. Except for the difficulty with Heller's girlfriend. Mouthy, bossy, but Heller seemed to love Jocinda in spite of the fact that most of the rest of the crew couldn't stand her. Luckily, Jocinda spent most of her time in their bunk listening to what she called music.

"Discordant garbage," Bailey dubbed it but laughed. "If it moves her, so be it."

Bailey had matured a lot in a year. He and Charissa were courting, and it was sweet. Garrett had finally gotten off his duff and married Payton. They were spending their honeymoon on Corona.

"Just found out some funny news over the Tasher, wonder if you know anything about it." Jace plunked down on the kitchen counter.

"What news?" Kraft kneaded bread dough with quick, sure movements.

"Trickster was found dead in the middle of his office in a pool of blood with both of his legs hacked off at the knee." Jace reeled the information off deadpan.

"Ouch. Bet that hurt."

"You don't know anything about it?"

"*Moi*? How would I know?"

"Don't play the wide-eyed innocent with me, sugar-britches." Jace laughed, winked. "I'm not buying it. You took a week off when we were a hop, skip, and a jump from Byzantine. You never did tell me what you were up to."

"Do you really want to know?" Kraft asked, her gaze riveted

to that oddly misplaced kitchen window.

Jace laughed. "I already do. Did you make him beg for his life?"

"No point in making a man beg for something I had no intention of leaving him with." Kraft smoothed the bread dough and plunked it in a bowl to rise.

"Remind me never, ever, to get on your bad side."

"You couldn't, even if you tried. And Trickster was convinced I was still alive. He had men looking for us, Jace. There was no way I was letting that fetch cut in on my dance with you again."

"Speaking of dancing, I've got a job offer for you."

"Really?" Kraft tumbled the last of the dough into a bowl then set it in the oven to rise.

"Got lousy pay, terrible working conditions, but I hear the fringe benefits are good."

"Sounds awful. What is it?"

"Wife."

Kraft didn't miss a beat. "That is a lousy job. It's not much better than captain slash cook."

"Well, you'd still have to do that."

Kraft smiled slow and lazy and sexy. "The fringe benefits would have to be damn good."

"You tell me."

"Could I still fight?" Kraft asked.

"With me?"

"Captain—"

"Jace," he reminded her.

"Jace. You know what I mean."

He nodded. "As part of the crew, I'd expect you to defend the ship, if we're ever in need. Haven't really needed to lately, have you noticed that?"

"We certainly made *Prospect* one very bad ship to mess with."

Jace grinned. "So, you want the job?"

"I do, I do."

About the Author

Anitra Lynn McLeod has been writing since she was twelve. Creating unique worlds is her forte, combining unlikely genres such as historical, fantasy, futuristic and erotic into a steampunky—and steamy—brew. Reading, writing, and whitewater rafting are the three things she enjoys the most.

You can visit her at www.AnitraMcLeod.com;

Write to her at alm@AnitraMcLeod.com;

Or fan her at: http://facebook.com/pages/Anitra-Lynn-McLeod/323123001356.

You can also follow her on Twitter @AnitraMcLeod.

Or if all else fails, you can also snail mail her:

Anitra Lynn McLeod
PO Box 16631
SLC, UT 84116-0631

Send a SASE for a free bookmark.

His beast will have her beauty...but only on his terms.

Prince of Dragons
© 2010 Cathryn Cade
Orion, Book 3

Sirena Blaze has left a string of smiling males across the galaxy—but she's not smiling now. After two attempts to sabotage her ship, it's time to call for backup. Her warriors deserve the best, and that means recruiting a member of the elite Serpentian guard as co-commander.

One look at Slyde Stone, and Sirena's smile returns. She sets out to indulge in the sensual delights for which his people are legendary.

Slyde would like nothing more than to bed the famous beauty, but a secret binds the hands that burn to take her. He is a half-dragon shifter, a race thought to be nothing more than a myth. He's real, and so is the code he must live by—he can mate only once.

Sirena's fury at Slyde's refusal knows no bounds—until saboteurs loose a pair of deadly serpents on board the *Orion.* And the infuriating man has the gall to make a wager. If she finds them first, she can have him. But if he wins, she must agree to be his alone—for life.

Warning: Space cougar on the prowl, a handsome virgin in her sights. Hot love scenes, and even hotter dragon shape-shifting.

Available now in ebook and print from Samhain Publishing.

CPSIA information can be obtained at www.ICGtesting.com
Printed in the USA
LVOW041801061112

306136LV00001B/51/P

9 781609 282950